Books by Alyssa Maxwell

Gilded Newport Mysteries
MURDER AT THE BREAKERS
MURDER AT MARBLE HOUSE
MURDER AT BEECHWOOD
MURDER AT ROUGH POINT
MURDER AT CHATEAU SUR MER
MURDER AT OCHRE COURT
MURDER AT CROSSWAYS
MURDER AT KINGSCOTE
MURDER AT WAKEHURST

Lady and Lady's Maid Mysteries
MURDER MOST MALICIOUS
A PINCH OF POISON
A DEVIOUS DEATH
A MURDEROUS MARRIAGE
A SILENT STABBING
A SINISTER SERVICE

Published by Kensington Publishing Corp.

MURDER AT KINGSCOTE

ALYSSA MAXWELL

KENSINGTON
PUBLISHING CORP.

www.kensingtonbooks.com

To Lisa Stuart and the members of the Point Association of Newport, RI, for their passion and dedication to preserving the history and well-being of this unique American treasure that is the Easton's Point neighborhood.

Lisa, thank you for adding magic to our yearly trips to Newport! Your friendship means the world to us!

Acknowledgments

Once again, I must thank the Preservation Society of Newport County, not only for the invaluable work of preserving Newport's legacy, but for providing a wealth of information to all who seek it. Special thanks go to tour guide Carla Francis, who not only led us on a very enjoyable tour through Kingscote, but helped me straighten out a few of my details. If I have made mistakes, they are mine and not hers.

Heartfelt thanks also go to John Scognamiglio and the entire Kensington team for their continued support of this series, and to Evan Marshall for his encouragement and assistance every step of the way.

MURDER AT KINGSCOTE

Chapter 1

❦

Newport, Rhode Island, July 1899

Bellevue Avenue teemed with color, fragrance, and a wide-eyed wonderment at the country's newest technology. It was the summer of 1899, and something extraordinary had arrived on the shores of Aquidneck Island—something that promised to change our world forever.

Overhead, a deep cerulean sky embraced a vista of gleaming, sun-golden clouds, while the deepest greens of the European beech trees swept the avenue's front lawns and gently grazed the borders of perfectly geometric flowerbeds. But, oh, the spectators who had gathered today. A sea of people had turned out in their very best summer attire, wealthy vacationers and workaday Newporters alike having dug deep into their wardrobes, trunks, and cupboards. Seersucker and linen and fine flannel suits for the men. And for the women, silks, cottons and muslins, moirés and taffetas, all in vivid florals and stripes, each outfit topped by a hat sporting blossoms and ribbons and feathers and even whole birds, dyed impossible hues to match the wearer's attire . . .

"Good gracious, Miss Cross, have you ever *seen* such frippery?" The speaker hovered at my shoulder, his notepad and pencil at the ready. Ethan Merriman held the position of society journalist for a small local newspaper, the Newport *Messenger*, and I, Emma Cross, had the unlikely distinction, as a woman, of being his editor-in-chief. "Why, I keep thinking some of these chapeaux are going to take wing and fly right off the wearers' heads."

I replied with a laugh and said, "In New York, such hats have been all the rage for some time now."

"Poor birds," he cried heartily and scribbled some notes.

I returned my attention to the crowd. It seemed all of Newport lined Bellevue Avenue from Bath Road, past the Casino shops and along the fence lines of the city's most costly properties, all the way to Ledge Road at the very southern tip of Aquidneck Island. Adults stood a good half-dozen deep along the sidewalks on either side, and children perched in threes and fours on gateposts and perimeter walls, or straddled the lower boughs of trees.

"Is anything wrong, Miss Cross?" Ethan had stopped scribbling, his pencil held aloft over the page while he studied my expression.

Had I forgotten to school my features? It seemed, at least to me, that only one individual in this happy multitude was experiencing twinges of apprehension and finding it necessary to admonish herself time and again not to show it. Experience in recent years had left me cynical of such crowds; hard lessons had taught me at best to suspect the antics of our wealthy summer cottagers, and at worst, to dread them.

"It's nothing, Ethan. Just something I . . . need to do when I return to the office."

"You should enjoy yourself, Miss Cross. Parades like this don't come about every day, you know. And there's that fat envelope you'll receive at the end."

"You're absolutely right." The envelope he spoke of would contain a portion of the entrance fee from the participants in the parade. Today's event wasn't merely for the entertainment of Newport's citizens, but would raise funds for several charities, including one near to my heart, St. Nicholas Orphanage in Providence. Ethan was right, and I put on a cheerful face for the children's sake. This seemed to appease him, for he returned to jotting down his observations.

Perhaps I worried for nothing and I'd be proven wrong. Perhaps it was nothing more than that, unlike the colorful multitude, I wore my typical workaday outfit: a dark blue pinstriped skirt and a starched shirtwaist that boasted a mere smidgeon of lace at the collar and a bit of ribbon piping at the cuffs. My plain straw boater sat straight and smart on my head, my hair pulled back into a tidy French knot. I hardly presented an aspect one would consider festive.

But as a working woman, I had learned not to compete with the ladies of the Four Hundred, that elite number of guests who fit comfortably into Caroline Astor's New York ballroom, and which had come to define the parameters of society's most prominent members. My wearing anything approaching finery today would have been an affront to their sensibilities, an impertinent suggestion that I might be as good as they. Never mind that I was a cousin of the Vanderbilt family; that I was the great-great-granddaughter of the first Cornelius.

Unfortunately for me, or perhaps fortunately, depending on one's point of view, I traced my lineage through one of the "Commodore's" daughters, and that formidable old curmudgeon hadn't believed in leaving much of anything to women. My lack of fortune combined with the benevolence of a great aunt who had left me with a house and a small annuity had led me to what I considered my vocation and a measure of independence most women never dreamed of.

Speaking of my vocation, I very nearly opened my velvet handbag—rather threadbare at the edges, to be sure—to dig out my own writing tablet and nub of a pencil. It had become a professional habit during the past several years. But as editor-in-chief of the *Messenger*, a position I'd come into last summer, I was no longer required to take meticulous notes on every frock that entered my field of vision, or the height and shape of every boot heel, or which young lady held the arm of which eligible gentleman. That responsibility belonged to Ethan, and I knew I could trust him to make a fine job of it.

"I should move through the crowd now," he said, and I waved him on. His dark hair slick with Macassar oil, he weaved his tall figure along the sidewalk, his pencil flying across his notepad. From time to time he stopped to speak with this or that spectator and jotted down his or her reply. He possessed an unerring sense of which of our summer denizens sold the most papers to our readers. And yet it was with a twinge of envy, one I couldn't entirely explain, that I watched him go.

I threaded my own way through the milling spectators, stopping periodically to chat with friends and acquaintances. For a penny I purchased a small bundle of roasted peanuts from a vendor cart. In vain I searched the faces around me for Nanny, my housekeeper, and Katie, my maid-of-all-work, who had ridden to town in my carriage with me earlier. I couldn't find them but never mind, we had an agreed-upon place where we would meet later.

The crowd stirred with a tremor of excitement, like an electrical current that shivered through the air. Once again, a vague foreboding rose up inside me, and I found myself bracing for . . . I didn't know what, only that it would not be anything good. Then, a woman with dark curly hair piled high beneath a hat sporting a bird as large as a cormorant, approached one of the objects of Newport's present fascination.

I could not have said what color the Duryea Runabout automobile might have been. Giant bunches of blue and pink hydrangeas bedecked every outer inch of the vehicle, along with an artificial tree sprouting American Beauty roses growing behind the leather seat. My relative Alva Belmont primly mounted the running board and climbed unassisted into the vehicle, where she stood on the floorboards facing out over the line of similarly decorated vehicles stretched out behind her toward Bath Road. In many respects, these motorcars didn't appear much different from ordinary carriages, except for the engines mounted beneath the chassis or behind the seats. Aunt Alva had organized today's event, and now at her signal, the other participants began clambering into their flower-strewn automobiles and readying themselves for Newport's first-ever auto parade.

Among them I recognized, of course, Vanderbilts and Drexels, Oelrichses and Goelets, Taylors and DeForests and a gaggle more who were brave enough to display their fledgling skills at the steering tiller. I noticed Harry Lehr helping a now aging Caroline Astor into his automobile, and Winthrop Rutherfurd, who had once been my cousin Consuelo's sweetheart, handing Miss Fifi Potter onto the rich, brocade seat of a Riker Electric Triumph sporting green and white clematis and tiny Japanese lanterns. This was, after all, a competition, and prizes would be awarded to the most gaily decorated autos as well as the most proficient motorists.

Farther down Bellevue Avenue, directly in the path of the vehicles, wooden figures littered the roadway, forming an obstacle course to challenge the drivers' skills. For more than a week now, our summer cottagers had been practicing in fields and on their own driveways, resulting in several mishaps, or so my friend Hannah, a nurse at Newport Hospital, had confided to me. Injuries had been minor, thank goodness, and I hoped today would see no further accidents. Aunt Alva caught my eye, waved, and grinned as she pointed toward a Hartley Steam Four-seater with bright yellow wheel spokes, idling not far from me. Brilliant blue cornflowers enveloped the vehicle, with an umbrella of the same blossoms shading the front and back bench seats. Three individuals stood beside the auto, their heads together in some inaudible but fierce debate. I grinned back at Aunt Alva, understanding.

I couldn't resist moving closer to the Hartley. The engine puttered and tufts of steam panted from its exhaust pipe, while the chassis shivered on its wheels as if with pent-up excitement. I knew each of the individuals continuing their deliberations beside it. They were Newporters, albeit far above my own social and economic standing. The one closest to my own age of twenty-five saw me and offered me an encouraging smile. I approached the group.

"Miss Cross, do lend your efforts to our own in persuading our mother to ride in the parade." Miss Gwendolen King, only two years my junior, raised an eyebrow and winked with amusement. She wore her golden-brown hair upswept into a bun beneath a tilted straw hat crowned with a burst of flowers that matched those on the automobile. Her carriage suit, too, was of a brilliant blue, and the parasol she carried in her gloved hand promised an equally dazzling display once opened. "Mother is being most stubborn and not at all sporting."

"I hadn't been aware your family had purchased a motorcar," I replied with a laugh. As a former society reporter, I still kept track of such happenings. But Gwendolen King knew very well I'd never venture to persuade her mother of anything; it wouldn't have been my place.

"We certainly have not," Mrs. Ella King said forcefully and with a pointed glare at the third member of their party, her son, Philip. For a middle-aged woman, Mrs. King, a widow these five years past, had retained a slim figure well suited to the elongating lines of her summer frock, of a paler blue than her daughter's but which nonetheless complemented the vividness of the cornflowers. Her hair, too, was a lighter blond than Gwendolen's, partly due to strands of encroaching gray, and framed her face with a middle part. She wore a hat with a large bow and a feather that curled cunningly along the line of her cheek.

Mrs. King's expression and tone lightened when she spoke again to me. "Nor do I plan to own one, Miss Cross, and you may quote me on that. Give me a sound horse any day. I'd far rather canter across the countryside than motor down an avenue. Really, what *is* all the fuss about? I don't believe these contraptions will last as long as the paint covering them. And all the work simply to start them! Fill this tank with water, that tank with gasoline, open this valve, light the pilot—my head positively spins. We didn't dare turn it off when we arrived. It's all well and good to dress up a motorcar as we've done today for a bit of entertainment, but I hardly believe them dependable when it comes to daily life. What do you think, Miss Cross?"

"I think time will tell, ma'am," I replied tactfully. In truth, I envied the parade entrants and wished I'd secured an invitation to ride along. I'd ridden in an automobile while in New York City and had found the experience exhilarating, if a bit unnerving. "But I can't see automobiles ever completely replacing horses."

Mrs. King gave a little sniff and tugged a lace glove more firmly onto her hand. "I should think not, indeed."

"Mother gave me no choice but to borrow for the occasion, though I'm eager to exchange my cabriolet for one of these beauties just as soon as can be. An electric one, though, if I have my way." Twenty-one-year-old Philip patted the automobile's rear panel as if stroking a prized horse. And he might have been, for it was obvious he coveted not only a vehicle of his own, but the status that went along with owning one. His boastful intentions reminded me of my younger cousin Reggie Vanderbilt, a young man with too much time on his hands and too few responsibilities to keep him occupied. And as with Reggie, I detected in Philip's blue eyes the gleam of craving but no spark of ambition.

Apparently, his mother thought so too, for she said, "If you want an automobile, son, you must choose a profession, work hard, and earn one. But your horse and cabriolet will prove far more trustworthy, mark me on that."

Philip rolled his eyes and emitted a long-suffering sigh. "Really, Mother, you're positively archaic. And of course Miss Cross believes motorcars are the wave of the future, as do I and most other people. She's simply too polite to say it."

Oh dear. I didn't like being thrust into the middle of a family dispute. With the siblings being of one mind contrary to their mother's opinion, I decided Ella King needed an ally. "What I do know is that Mrs. King is one of Newport's most accomplished equestriennes, rides some of our finest horses, and is peerless in the art of dressage."

"Why, thank you, Miss Cross." Mrs. King beamed with satisfaction. She was so delighted by my pronouncement that she placed her hand in her son's and allowed him to help her up into the front passenger seat of the Hartley. She smoothed her skirts and leaned down to address me again. "Will you be following along on foot?"

"I will, Mrs. King. I shan't miss a moment of the fun." The parade would proceed from our present location, on the avenue between the granite walls of Stone Villa and the shingle-style architecture of the Newport Casino, all the way south to Ledge Road at the end of Bellevue Avenue.

Mrs. King nodded in satisfaction, but fidgeted with her

purse strings and repeatedly compressed her lips. I turned to her son and murmured, "I trust you are knowledgeable when it comes to operating a motor vehicle?" As always, I felt protective of my fellow Newporters. I would loathe to see Mrs. King, a generous philanthropist, come to any harm. He replied with a laugh that did nothing to fortify my confidence in him, his breath being laden with a sharp scent of spirits. While he turned away to assist his sister into the Hartley's rear seat, my stomach sank. Was Philip simply enjoying the day? I wished to believe it, but I knew better. I'd worked the society pages too long not to have heard the gossip about him.

"It would be awfully sporting of you to let your mother take the tiller," I suggested, hoping I sounded lighthearted rather than worried.

"As if she would. I think not, Miss Cross."

"Your sister, then. She wouldn't be the only woman driver. My aunt Alva intends to operate *her* vehicle."

As if I'd suggested something so outlandish as to not warrant the least consideration, he grinned and shook his head at me. Then he circled the Hartley and swung himself up onto the seat beside his mother. With a salute he dismissed me, or so I thought. "I'll own one of these yet, Miss Cross, mark my words."

Perhaps, but his mother's expression told a different story.

Applause and cheers went up, and I shaded my eyes as I glanced along the avenue to see Aunt Alva's Duryea Runabout begin creeping forward. Beside her, her husband, Oliver, shouted instructions, which I'm quite sure she ignored. The grind of gears, the hiss of steam, the whine of electric motors, and several backfires filled the air as, one by one, the entrants in line prepared for the trek. I prepared for my own trek on foot, but before I could take the first step a woman's voice carried shrilly above the commotion.

"Enjoy your privileges now, Mrs. King. They shan't last much longer, I promise you that."

Startled by the threatening nature of those words, I turned back to the Kings' automobile. A woman in dusky violet wearing an ostrich-plumed hat stood gripping the top edge of the side panel as if to hold the motorcar in place. She set one booted foot on a lower spoke of the front wheel.

"How dare you." Philip's profile hardened and the knuckles of his right hand whitened around the steering tiller. "Release this vehicle at once or I'll accelerate and let you be dragged along."

As I took in this shocking exchange, Philip's mother put a hand on his forearm to quiet him and peered down at the defiant woman. "Mrs. Ross, haven't you done enough damage? Your demands are irrational and unjustified. Please, go away and let us be."

The name *Ross* struck an awareness inside me. I had heard it before, and knew this woman, Eugenia Webster Ross, had been an unwelcome fixture in the King family's lives for more years than they would have liked to count.

Mrs. Ross emitted a harsh laugh, her sallow complexion darkening with anger. "Be assured, I shall never go away, nor will it do you a lick of good to wish me gone. Kingscote and everything in it rightly belongs to me, and I'll not rest until I see you out of the place and myself in my proper position." Her accent told me she didn't hail from New England, nor any state in the north of the country.

"Don't listen to her, Mama." Gwendolen slid along the back seat, putting more space between her and the woman. She even tipped her hat brim lower to block Mrs. Ross from her view. "She's obviously unbalanced."

The vehicle in front of the Hartley, a two-seater electric Rambler decked out in roses and a fortune's worth of vibrant, multihued dahlias, rolled forward. It was the Kings' turn to move. Philip released the brake and with clenched teeth repeated his earlier threat. "You'd do best to release your hold now or you *will* find yourself dragged along the road."

Mrs. Ross lowered her foot and let go of the seat with a flick of her fingers as if to dislodge an unsavory substance from her glove. But then she raised a fist in the air and shouted threats as the motorcar rolled away. She captured the attention of the spectators on either side of the roadway, though only momentarily. The spectacle of so many automobiles proved too tantalizing to allow a common feud to dampen their excitement. Eugenia Ross was left to vent her anger on deaf ears.

That was, until she whirled about and encountered me.

"You're Emmaline Cross, aren't you?"

Her bluntness took me aback. I blinked, rendered briefly mute. She might have learned my name in relation to my position at the *Messenger*, but she and I had never met. I wondered how she recognized me by sight, but didn't give her the satisfaction of expressing my surprise. "I am."

"Are you a friend of the Kings?" Her Southern accent asserted itself more insistently.

"As much as someone in my position can be a friend of the Kings, yes," I replied without irony, but rather a simple statement of fact.

"More fool, you. Do you know who I am?" She spoke the words as if challenging me to a contest of wits.

"I didn't at first, until Mrs. King mentioned your name. Then I realized you are the woman who has been attempting for years now to undermine the Kings' rightful inheritance from their uncle William."

"William Henry King was *my* relative and owed the King family nothing. They took advantage of his bearing the same name and invented their ties to him."

"That hardly makes sense." I started to chuckle at the ridiculous claim. Motorcars rumbled past us, their tires crunching on the hard-packed dirt of the avenue at a pace not much faster than most people walked. Mrs. Ross took issue with my lightness of mood.

"You find me funny, do you?" She stepped closer, the pointed toes of her high-heeled boots nearly touching mine. Her dark eyes on a level with my own, she attempted to stare me down. Her shoulders squared, and her chin jutted at me with menace. I suddenly felt threatened and darted glances around me, hoping someone would notice my discomfort and come to my aid. No one did. No one returned my glance, too enthralled as they were with the passing automobiles festooned in their floral displays. "Is it also funny, Miss Cross, that they shut him away in an asylum and took control of his money?"

"Mrs. Ross," I said with feigned calm, albeit my heart pounded in alarm, "is there something you wished of me? Can I be of assistance in some way?" I hoped not, for I wanted only to be away from this woman, but it was all I could think of to defuse the situation.

My words did seem to placate her. Her threatening posture relaxed and she opened the space between us by several inches. I breathed more freely, then nearly choked on a gasp when she said, "Take up my cause."

"I beg your pardon?"

"Write an article telling my side of the story. I've been vilified for years by the press. Let people know my cause is just."

"Is it?" That was more than I knew. "Will you explain the exact nature of your supposed relation to William Henry King?"

"Supposed? Why you . . ." She moved closer again, prompting me to pull back. Though she was approximately my size, the fury flickering in her nearly black eyes made me once again fear for my immediate well-being. I might have called out to the nearest spectator, except that at that moment, someone called my name. A moment later, a firm, warm hand came down on my shoulder.

"Emma, is there a problem here?"

I recognized the voice immediately and craned my neck to look up at Derrick Andrews, standing slightly behind me. He smiled, his face shaded by the brim of his boater, the grosgrain band of which matched the rich amber brown of his suit coat. His hand dropped to his side, but its warmth and reassurance lingered. Ignoring Mrs. Ross for the moment, I turned to face him, hardly able to contain the flurry of emotions set loose by his sudden appearance. Happiness, exhilaration . . . apprehension. I took a steadying breath and schooled my features to reveal none of it—not here, on a bustling parade route. "I didn't know you were in Newport."

"Only just arrived. With my mother," he added with a quirk of his eyebrow only I would have noticed. Yes, the source of my apprehension—Derrick's mother, Lavinia Andrews. "I'd hoped to surprise you. I see I have."

A gleam in his eye mirrored my own delight. He looked perfectly wonderful—fit and robust, and slightly tanned from his summer pursuits of golf and tennis and riding. "She wished to see the parade. In fact, she's riding in an auto, several back." He gestured over his shoulder with his thumb. "She's staying on a couple more days to attend the Jones's charity cotillion."

"Oh, is Edith in Newport, too?"

Before my excitement could take hold at the prospect of reuniting with the budding author, Edith Jones Wharton,

Derrick shook his head. "No, I'm afraid not. She's still in Europe."

I let my sense of letdown pass. "It's good to see you."

He leaned closer, bowing his head to deliver his murmur to my ears alone. "And it's wonderful to see you, Emma. Wonderful to see you smiling back at me. I feared my time away might have . . ." His face hovered barely a kiss away from mine, though our lips never touched. His smile turned wistful. "Well . . . it seems something or other always sends us in separate directions." He raised his hand and gestured with his chin. "Are you going to introduce me to your friend?"

I whirled about. I'd completely forgotten about Mrs. Ross, still standing near me and staring daggers now at both Derrick and me.

"We are not friends, sir." Eugenia Ross fingered the strand of golden pearls hanging over the front of her bodice. "I approached Miss Cross in hopes of persuading her to do a bit of unbiased reporting on my behalf, but it seems she is too heavily influenced by those she considers her superiors."

Both Derrick and I opened our mouths to reply. What he might have said, I couldn't say, but I intended to relieve this woman of her misconceptions, there and then, by assuring her the *Messenger* reported only verifiable facts, and thus far she had verified nothing about her outlandish claim. Before either of us could speak, however, Mrs. Ross set off toward Bath Road.

"She'll miss the parade," Derrick said as he watched her strut away. "What did she mean by unbiased bit of reporting?"

"She's Eugenia Ross. Does the name mean anything to you?"

"Indeed it does. There was that big to-do at the McLean Asylum in Massachusetts a few years back. She tried to have Willie King released and actually managed to do it on one attempt. The courts ordered him placed back into custody the very same day, and then he was moved to the Butler Hospital in Providence. She's tried multiple times again, but to no avail." He glanced again toward Bath Road, but the woman in question had disappeared from sight. "Good grief, is that really the same Eugenia Ross?"

"The very same." I told him what had occurred between her and the Kings before Philip had driven away down the avenue. The vehicle's bright yellow spokes and brilliant blue cornflowers stood out against the dusty road, and I could see that the Hartley had reached the edge of the Kings' own property, Kingscote. The automobiles had picked up speed as they proceeded, though none seemed to be moving at the heady fifteen miles-per-hour they were capable of. The Kings would reach the obstacle course a few dozen yards farther along. I worried again about Philip's ability to handle the vehicle, and turned back to Derrick. "I'd like to walk. Will you accompany me, or do you need to rejoin your mother?"

He had secured my hand in the crook of his elbow before I'd finished asking the question. Dare I say my fingertips felt utterly at home there, against the strong muscle covered by sturdy serge? "Mother will be just fine. In fact, why don't we hurry along before she catches up to us?" He set us in motion with a brisk step, while deftly steering us through the milling spectators.

"I take it your mother's opinion of me hasn't changed."

He said nothing, his jawline going tight.

"It's all right. I'm used to it by now."

"I'm not," he said tersely, then sighed. "If not for my father's health and my need to be in Providence making sure the *Sun* continues to thrive . . ."

He spoke of his family's primary newspaper, though they

were invested in numerous others throughout New England. I shook my head when he continued to speak. "You needn't explain, Derrick. I understand."

"I don't want you to think it's all merely an excuse to keep me away."

"I don't. Your faith in my abilities to run the *Messenger* says all I need to know." Indeed, Derrick had bought the small local newspaper less than two years ago, had taken it from little more than a failing broadsheet, and in mere months had built up its influence and its subscriber list. Last summer, when family duties had called him back to Providence, he asked me to take over the running of the *Messenger* as its editor-in-chief. We had known each other several years by then, had shared both harrowing and meaningful experiences on multiple occasions, and yet had always seemed at cross purposes when it came to the affections we each harbored for the other. He had once proposed, early on, long before I had been ready to consider such a thing. And then, as he had said, something or other had consistently sent us in separate directions.

Our moods lightened after that. We continued down Bellevue Avenue, caught in the general flow of spectators, chatting and catching up since we'd seen each other several months ago. We passed Kingscote with its Gothic peaks and gingerbread trim, but I refused to let Eugenia Ross invade my thoughts. I had been apprehensive at the outset of the parade, and, in a way, Mrs. Ross had given substance to my misgivings. For now, at least, she was gone, leaving me to enjoy a festive, beautiful summer day on the arm of a man I esteemed and cared for very much, and who shared those feelings for me.

Under a thick canopy of shade trees, we passed Bowery Street. Berkeley Avenue came into view, and just beyond, the obstacle course with its wood and canvas figures representing pedestrians, delivery carts, trolleys, and more. The first few automobiles weaved their way around the barriers, the laughter of the occupants audible above the puttering engines. I saw Aunt Alva's Runabout swerve perilously close to an object that, in the distance, appeared to be a mule pulling a plow.

"Slow down, Aunt Alva," I couldn't help uttering under my breath, eliciting a laugh from Derrick. I wondered if her husband, Oliver, clutched the edges of his seat in trepidation for his very life.

My cousin Willie Vanderbilt—Aunt Alva's son—waved to me as he drove past with his new wife, Virginia. Their automobile had been transformed into the shape of a locomotive decorated with immense gilded bows interwoven with white tulle, and at each corner of the vehicle hung a golden cage of canaries amid trailing vines and poppies. It was all truly fantastical, and anyone suddenly transported to the scene would have believed themselves to be dreaming or to have taken leave of their senses.

The bright sunny spokes and blue blossoms of Philip King's Hartley Steamer brought my attention back to the family as they, too, entered the course. My worries for them eased, as Philip seemed to be guiding the automobile well enough. He wobbled a bit along the course, but certainly no more than Aunt Alva had. Perhaps the whiskey I'd detected on his breath had been the result of but one drink.

Derrick and I fell to discussing newspaper business. The *Messenger*'s profits had been steadily rising in the past year, especially now that the summer people were back in town. We discussed our newest investors—or his, really. I couldn't claim even the smallest share in the business, for I couldn't afford to buy in and was, essentially, merely an employee. But if one's heart and hopes mattered, I was as heavily invested as anyone else.

One topic I avoided was that of my former office manager, Jimmy Hawkins. Once employed by the *Sun*, Jimmy had come down from Providence to work with Derrick when he'd first purchased the *Messenger*. Jimmy had stayed on to work with me when Derrick returned to Providence, but things hadn't proceeded as one might have hoped. I'd had to let Jimmy go, and when Derrick first asked me why, I had answered vaguely that Jimmy and I simply hadn't worked well together and he had decided to return to the *Sun*. Apparently, Jimmy had given Derrick a similar explanation.

I doubted Derrick believed either of us. The next time I'd seen him, last winter, he'd made the same inquiry, and I'd given him the same answer, resulting in a look of disappointment that made me wish I'd told him the truth.

Almost. But doing so would have meant explaining how Jimmy had betrayed both Derrick's and my trust, and would reveal the role Derrick's father had played in the deception. That, more than anything else, stilled my tongue, for I didn't wish to come between father and son.

Would he bring it up again? We reached Bellevue Court, walking on the opposite side of the avenue from the building site of The Elms, one of Newport's newest and largest homes to date. An actual house had taken shape, although there was still much work to be done. Last year, the site had been a giant rectangular opening in the ground while the engineers and electricians had prepared Newport's first all-electrical system, with no gas power as backup. The plans hadn't been without controversy, as workers from our local gasworks, the Newport Illuminating Company, had marched to the site to protest what they saw as the eventual loss of their jobs. So far that hadn't happened, and now I mentioned this to Derrick, as much to discuss the prospect as to forestall any questions he might have been planning to ask about Jimmy.

"There are several all-electric mansions going up in Providence now, and New York, too, although The Elms will beat them to completion." He smirked. "I think that's important to Ed Berwind," he added, speaking of the home's owner and president of the Berwind-White Coal Mining Company.

I started to answer, when the sound of skidding tires gave way to a crash, a crunch, and the splintering of wood.

Chapter 2

Derrick and I exchanged startled looks. A collective cry went up among the spectators, and the leisurely stroll along the avenue became a rush to see what had happened.

We hurried along with the rest. The line of cars had come to a halt beside us, which could only mean there had indeed been an accident up ahead. Just beyond the south corner of The Elms property, a crowd had formed across the road, their backs to us. Glimpses of blue and yellow peeked through the milling press of bodies.

"I think it's the Kings," I said, and moved forward more urgently.

With Derrick shouldering the way through, I found myself at the forefront of the shocked spectators to see the Hartley Steamer at a perpendicular angle to the road, as if it had spun a quarter turn. Its front end abutted a pile of broken wood and canvas. Philip had climbed down from the driver's seat, while the two King women remained in their seats with their palms pressed to their bosoms.

"What happened?" Derrick demanded of the nearest individual, a townsman in a battered derby and ill-fitting flannels.

"Don't exactly know. One minute they were going around that trolley over there"—he pointed at a painted, miniature version of the electric trolleys that ran through town—"and the next they'd plowed right into a nanny pushing a pram."

"Good heavens," exclaimed a woman who had just come up beside me, "are they terribly hurt?"

"They don't look hurt," I assured her, judging each member of the King family to be a bit shaken, but not injured.

"But that poor baby," the woman persisted. "The pram is lying on its side, half under the motorcar. Someone must do something. We must summon an ambulance."

I quickly took in her silver hair, crepey skin, and frail, diminutive stature. It was Mrs. Jenson, a friend of my housekeeper's, who had once run a bakery in town along with her husband. I placed my hand gently on her forearm. "It's quite all right, Mrs. Jenson. The pram and the nanny aren't real. They were part of the obstacle course meant to challenge the drivers."

"Oh, I see." Her rheumy gaze wandered back to the scene of the mishap. "Well, it seems the challenge proved too much, didn't it?"

Indeed it had, especially for a young man in his cups.

"Let's go make sure they're all right." Derrick reclaimed my arm. When we reached the Hartley, several men were working to clear the wooden victims away, not an easy task as the front wheel had rolled over part of the "nanny's" body. The task was made more difficult by Philip snapping orders and getting in the way. Derrick and I stopped beside the motorcar. He set a hand on the seat back and leaned in. "Are either of you hurt?"

Mrs. King, intent on watching the activity at the front of the car, gave a startled cry at Derrick's question. Her hand found its way back to her bosom and she exhaled with relief. "Derrick Andrews. You gave me a fright."

"Sorry about that. Are you and Miss King all right?"

"I believe I'm fine. Just rather astonished at this turn of events." Mrs. King twisted around to view her daughter. "Gwendolen?"

"As I've already said, Mother, I'm quite all right. But I've no intention of continuing this ride. Hello, Mr. Andrews. Would you help me down, please?" She extended a gloved hand to Derrick, and he assisted her to the ground. As I watched the elegant Miss King, a thought dashed through my mind that Gwendolen King would make a far more suitable wife for him than I ever could. His family would welcome her with open arms, and she would surely be a favorite among Providence society.

Yet, once on the ground, Miss King issued a polite thank-you and proceeded to study the efforts of the men attempting to clear away the rubble. Derrick's attention lingered not a second longer than necessary before he turned back to her mother. "Mrs. King?"

"Yes, me too, please." Once on solid ground, Mrs. King raised her skirts and sauntered to the front of the Hartley. "Gwendolen and I have had quite enough, Philip. If you continue, you continue alone."

"Oh, don't be that way, Mother. You and Gwennie did the decorations. Don't you want to be there when they hand out the awards? The car is fine, by the way. Barely a scratch on her." He stared down at the crumpled nanny and pram. "Which is more than I can say for them, but luckily no one will miss them."

"What happened?" I asked Gwendolen while her mother took her son to task. "The brakes didn't fail, did they?"

"No. I suppose he thought it might be fun to swerve a bit. He made some joke about it being like steering a boat, and then he lost control and couldn't straighten us out before hitting the obstacle." Miss King shook her head in obvious disgust.

Anger burst to life inside me. Here was Philip King joking, when his mother and sister could have been seriously hurt. Had he been traveling at a greater speed, one or both of them might have been thrown from their seats. Or he might have struck another vehicle, or even one or several spectators. Philip had been nothing short of irresponsible and inconsiderate in his behavior today, and to see him chuckling about it raised my gorge. So typical of many young men of the Four Hundred. I found myself grumbling under my breath, until a light touch on my arm from Derrick snapped me out of my broodings and reminded that there were just as many honorable, generous men among the wealthy set.

Shaking her head, Mrs. King turned away from her son and rejoined us. She offered Derrick her hand as if this were a chance encounter and the past several minutes hadn't happened. "It's lovely to see you. How are you? Is your mother in Newport with you?"

"It's good to see you as well, Mrs. King, and yes, my mother is here."

"Oh, good. You must both come to dinner tonight. I'm giving a small party, a quiet affair, nothing fancy."

"I'm afraid my mother already has an engagement tonight."

"Oh, that's a pity. But you must come anyway." Her gaze swerved to me. "And you as well, Miss Cross. The Wetmores will be there, and I know you're quite well-acquainted with them."

The invitation surprised me—startled me, really—and the first thought that popped into my head was, What would I wear? It wasn't often I dined with members of the Four Hundred, not even the Wetmores, although I had done them a good turn two summers ago and they had been more than cordial to me ever since.

But invitations to dinner? I tended to receive those only from my Vanderbilt relatives, and they didn't seem to mind that I didn't wear the latest fashions from Paris. In fact, on formal occasions I typically donned castoffs from my cousin Gertrude, after they were hemmed and tailored to fit me. But Gertrude was married now and traveling much of the year. I didn't see her often, and her hand-me-downs reached me less and less frequently.

"Please say you'll come, both of you." Mrs. King's tone offered no debate on the matter, and Derrick and I accepted her invitation to dine at Kingscote later that evening.

The parade resumed soon after, but neither Philip nor Mrs. King received any awards at its conclusion. Mrs. Hermann Oelrichs, the former Theresa Fair, won first place for the best-decorated vehicle, her prize being a large sterling-silver box of bonbons, which evidently delighted her. I was certain her inclusion of doves among the hydrangeas, wisteria, and cascading satin ribbons decorating her automobile had much to do with her victory. And I, I'm happy to say, was equally delighted with the donation handed to me for St. Nicholas Orphanage in Providence.

"Mrs. King said nothing fancy, but you know what that means," I said later to my housekeeper, former nanny, and the closest thing I'd had to a grandmother in many years. Mary O'Neal had cared for me as a child, and when my great aunt Sadie, my mother's aunt, left her property to me several years ago, dearest Nanny, a widow by then, had eagerly agreed to move in with me. Ostensibly, she held the position of housekeeper, but I wouldn't see her aged hands at any labors harder than rubbing a roasting hen with herbs, or rolling out a ball of dough for one of her delectable pies.

Nanny perched on the edge of my bed, the mattress depressed under her rounded bulk, and watched as I rummaged through the armoire. I'd worn all of my dresses several times over, and even though Nanny's deft needle made frequent alterations—new pin tucks here, fresh lace there—there was no hiding the staleness of my mostly second-hand wardrobe.

"Are you fussing over the opinions of the Kings and the Wetmores," she asked in that ever-so-soft way of hers, "or over what Derrick will think of you?"

My hands went still and dropped to my sides as I turned to face her. I drew in a breath and let it out heavily. "You're quite right, of course. As you usually are."

"Usually?" Her eyes gleamed knowingly at me from behind her half-moon spectacles.

"It's been so long since we've been together, I just want to . . ."

"He won't care a whit about what you're wearing, I promise you that."

I swept across the small space between us and sat beside her. With my arms around her, I gave her a hearty squeeze. "Darling Nanny. Yes, you're right again—I hope." We both chuckled as I returned to the armoire, this time barely hesitating before whisking a jade silk gown by Raudnitz and Co. from its hanger. It had the tiniest of cap sleeves, a sweetly rounded neckline in front and back, and vines rendered in silver thread down the skirt. "It's at least four years out of date and I've worn it several times to the Casino and to Neily and Grace's house, and Derrick has seen me in it before, but . . ."

"I especially like that one on you, Emma." Nanny struggled to come to her feet; I hurried back to her to offer her a hand. "Wear that one. And stop being so nervous. It's only dinner."

I breathed another sigh. "I'll be fine once I have the dress on and you've done up my hair for me."

"Once you've donned your armor," she said with a shrewd look.

Yes, Nanny was right again. In my dark blues, I wore the armor of a journalist and felt enabled to tread anywhere, ask any questions, and demand my answers. Gowns like this one, on the other hand, allowed me to sit at the dining table of someone far above my social reach—who could not understand what it was to *have* to work, to count one's pennies, to go without—and converse and laugh and pretend I hadn't a care in the world. People often credited me with more courage than I possessed. What I had in abundance, what I'd cultivated through the years, was a great ability to pretend when I needed to, and to tell myself I'd take the time to be frightened later, after the fact, as soon as I'd completed whatever task needed doing. But perhaps that's all courage really was.

My armor served me well that night. Nanny had positioned a lovely pair of filigreed tortoise-shell combs in my hair and I wore Aunt Sadie's cameo brooch along with the tiny teardrop diamond earrings that had been a gift from my parents after my father had sold one of his paintings. A pair of elbow-length satin gloves, a bit yellowed with age, completed my attire.

Derrick arrived at Gull Manor, my home on a craggy headland along Ocean Avenue, sharply at eight thirty. Dinner parties among the Four Hundred rarely occurred earlier than nine o'clock. He kissed my cheek in greeting and told me I looked beautiful, and I was glad for the shadows that hid my blush of pleasure. The weather had stayed fair, and as we traveled eastward along Ocean Avenue in his two-seater gig, we caught glimpses of a calm sea awash in the deepening blues of dusk wherever the twisting, rocky coastline permitted. We passed Crossways, the grand Neo-Colonial mansion on its hill overlooking the water. Like one night nearly a year ago, electric light spilled from the windows and carriages choked the front drive. Despite my affection for the irrepressible Mrs. Mamie Fish, I was glad Crossways was not our destination that night. I'd had enough of crowds earlier that day at the parade. And after that dreadful night last summer, I'd had enough of Mamie Fish's parties to last a lifetime.

"You're quiet," Derrick observed as we traveled a short distance along Coggeshall Avenue before turning onto Bellevue. "I'm enjoying the ride." I didn't tell him a large part of that enjoyment stemmed from the sensation of his shoulder jostling against mine. We passed the gates of Rough Point and I wondered who had leased the house for the summer. My relatives Frederick and Louise Vanderbilt no longer cared for Newport and rarely visited here anymore, preferring the pastoral tranquility of Hyde Park instead. I imagined someday soon they'd sell the estate. I turned to Derrick, thankful of the deepening twilight as I couldn't help adding, "I'm enjoying being with you again."

There had been a time I would never have uttered such a thing—never have made myself so vulnerable. But Derrick and I had been through so very much together, had nearly died together—and apart—too many times to allow pretense and reticence to come between us now. That kind of armor, that of social niceties, I would not wear, not with him. Nor did I have to.

He held the reins in one hand and laid his other, clad in kidskin, over my satin-gloved one where it lay against my thigh. I breathed in the scents of the night—the freshness of the ocean, the sweetness of the gardens, the strength of the man beside me. For, yes, he smelled of confidence and authority—it was in his shaving soap, the starch of his collar, the superfine of his jet-black evening coat. But to balance the role he'd been born to, that of a master of business and profit, he possessed unending generosity and a keen sense of fair play. Otherwise, I would not have been sitting beside him in his carriage.

And I couldn't help but wonder . . .

"Does your mother know who you're spending the evening with?"

His hand tightened ever so slightly around mine. Before replying, he waited until several carriages filled with party-goers passed us on the avenue. Then, "She does." A tiny muscle moved in his cheek, the only sign my question had struck a nerve. "I'm not about to lie or hide anything from anyone."

I smiled. "She was angry."

"Does it matter?"

I studied his firm, patrician profile before turning to face straight ahead again. "It matters very much, to her. And to your father. And perhaps, someday, it will matter to you and me again."

"What do you mean?"

"I mean that right now, you are obligated to be in Providence, while I am tied to Newport. And because of that, your parents' objections won't change very much. But in time . . ."

"Their objections will change nothing, not now, not six months from now." He spoke harshly. "Not ever."

I didn't know why I was pressing the issue, why his parents' dislike of me—or rather, the idea of me—should intrude upon such a beautiful, temperate evening. When I was not with Derrick, which was most of the time, I hardly gave the matter a thought. Now, when we should be reveling in our time together, treasuring every second, I seemed bent on tossing a pall over the evening.

"Let it go," he whispered as if reading my mind, which at times I was most certain he could. He raised my hand and

pressed it to his lips in a lingering kiss that swept all thoughts
of his parents from my mind, leaving only him and me and
the intermittent moonlight falling through the leafy canopy
above Bellevue Avenue. And then we were turning on to
Bowery Street, and onto a driveway bordered by beech and
elm and Japanese maples. A sprawling, irregular house of
steeply pitched gables with towers on the east and west wings;
crenelated trim and diamond pane windows stood silhouetted
by the last traces of the sunset. We had arrived at Kingscote.

My first indication that Derrick's and my joint arrival surprised Mrs. King came as the butler ushered us in from the
vestibule, through the Gothic archway between a pair of
quatrefoil columns and into the Stair Hall. Elaborate woodwork surrounded us, from the painstaking design of the her-
ringbone floor, to the heavily paneled wainscoting and
ceiling. The only relief from all that wood came in the wall-
paper above the wainscoting, but its dark reds imitated
heavy brocade and maintained a somber aspect.

Mrs. King stepped out from a doorway to our right and
extended her hand. She paused suddenly, and her eyebrow
twitched, nothing more, but that was enough to express . . .
What? Curiosity? Surprise? Disapproval? It struck me that
she had fully expected us to arrive separately. True enough,
she had invited Derrick to dinner, and she had invited me as
well, but it now became glaringly apparent that she hadn't
dreamed we might make the journey here together. In her
mind, this implied something significant, something she hadn't
known before. Something, perhaps, about me, of which she had
no choice but to disapprove. Her breeding won out quickly
enough, however, and with an amiable smile she continued
toward us, first taking my hand, and then Derrick's, and offering a hearty welcome.

She led us into the adjoining drawing room, or double

drawing room, as two richly yet comfortably appointed rooms opened onto each other and occupied the entire east wing of the house. Here, the dark paneling and Gothic accents continued around doors and over windows, while wide, mossy-green stripes alternating with lighter jade ones in luxurious silk covered the walls, complementing green velvet draperies. Rose-colored upholsteries provided a lovely contrast, and a quick glance into the rear drawing room revealed a similar motif, except the colors of the walls and the Louis XVI furnishings had been reversed. Adding to the charm of the parlor we inhabited, the first floor of the north tower provided a polygonal bay with double casement windows looking out over the front garden. Along the room's east wall, floor-to-ceiling windows opened onto a covered piazza.

A pair of gentlemen stood as we entered the room. I recognized George Wetmore, the U.S. Senator representing Rhode Island, and, to my delight, my own cousin Neily—my uncle Cornelius Vanderbilt's eldest son, though no longer his heir. The reason for his disinheritance occupied the larger of the tufted settees; Neily's wife, Grace, came to her feet and hurried over to embrace me while Derrick greeted the others. She wore emerald-green silk, which brought out the green in her eyes and fire in her auburn hair. The waistline, I noticed, had been loosened and raised, with a cascade of black lace down the front to help conceal the swell of her belly.

"Emma, darling, this is a wonderful surprise." Grace turned a playfully accusing look on Mrs. King. "And you never said a word, you sly thing, you."

Mrs. King folded her hands at her waist and returned Grace's surprise with a mischievous grin. "It was Neily's idea to surprise you both. I see our little plan worked."

"It has indeed," I exclaimed. After greeting the others, I sat beside Grace, our hands entwined. "How long are you and Neily in town for?"

"I'm afraid it's a quick visit this time, and tomorrow we're heading back to New York, where I'll begin my confinement." Grace swept a hand over her tummy and then gave my hand an apologetic squeeze. "That's why running into you tonight is especially delightful. I'd fretted over not seeing you this trip."

"Are you feeling well?"

"Oh, I had the typical malaise in the beginning, but I've no complaints these days except for my poor ankles." She raised a satin-clad foot a few inches off the floor and flexed it this way and that.

"And little Corneil? How is he?"

Grace's laugh pealed with the clarity of a porcelain bell. "Growing like a weed and demanding daily when his brother or sister will be arriving."

"He's got his grandfather's persistent temperament," Neily said with a wry grin as he perched on the arm of the sofa. "It's wonderful to see you, Emmaline."

"And you, Neily." Of all my Vanderbilt cousins, I had been closest to Neily growing up. We had been playmates and confidants and, sometimes, partners in mischief. But our friendship had, of course, tempered once he married Grace, and we no longer shared our intimacy of old. That didn't mean I didn't worry about him, and sympathize with his being ostracized by the rest of the family because of his choice of wife.

The others present were Mrs. Wetmore, of course, and her younger daughter, Maude, about my own age. The Wetmores' elder daughter, named Edith after their mother, was apparently still away in Europe with an aunt. Gwendolen King was also present, looking dramatic in pale silk overlaid with black lace and appearing none the worse for this afternoon's mishap.

I resisted a slight urge to frown as I perceived the imbalance of the party, for there were two more women there than men. The Four Hundred were always precise in their social pairings—a man for every woman so that guests might proceed two by two into the dining room. Whose arms would Gwendolen and Maude take? I realized Philip was missing, and perhaps one of his friends as well?

Mrs. King did indeed seem to be waiting for something. My stomach had begun to growl and the butler had checked on us several times before our hostess finally let out a disappointed sigh and led us to the dining room.

I had been inside Kingscote before and found this room enchanting. Its most beautiful and fanciful element, undoubtedly, were the expansive windows made of opalescent glass tiles flanking the fireplace, each one a work of multicolored art by Louis Tiffany. Transoms above the windows carried similar designs. During the day, sunlight bathed the room in a fanciful array of jewel-tone colors.

Meanwhile, the wall opposite the windows and fireplace wasn't a wall at all, but an elaborate screen composed of delicate spindle work in black walnut with two leaves in the center that opened onto a wide hallway, lending an open and airy feeling to the room. The eye was further beguiled by a blend of designs from diverse times and places, from the built-in American Colonial sideboard, to the Japanese-inspired cork ceiling, to the Elizabethan coffered paneling, all enhanced by touches of Moorish and aesthetic design. Stepping into the dining room was like stepping into a world free of constraints, where art joyfully flourished in whatever manner it wished.

The question of who would escort Gwendolen and Maude to the table was solved by Neily offering an arm to both Grace and me, while Derrick accompanied the other two ladies. From the consommé through the last course of terrapin and lobster à la Newberg, the conversation never ceased as we discussed the latest developments in Newport, the newest homes being erected, and an upcoming excursion, on horse-back, across Aquidneck Island.

At this, Gwendolen turned an eager gaze upon Derrick, and then glanced across the table to me. "There will be a pre-arranged location for a picnic, and the servants will meet us there with lunch. Won't you join us, Mr. Andrews? And you, too, Miss Cross?"

While Derrick replied that he would enjoy it very much, I shook my head. "Thank you, Miss King, but I'm afraid I'm not a proficient enough rider. I'd only hold everyone back."

"Oh, nonsense. Surely you've been on horseback be-fore?"

"Yes, but not like the rest of you. I don't leap over rock walls or across streams. I very much doubt it would end well if I tried." I chuckled. "Neily can vouch for the truth of it."

"You could always ride out with the servants in one of the carriages," my cousin suggested. A grin tugged at his lips. "Or Philip could drive you in his automobile."

This earned a round of titters and a reminder from Mrs. King that the automobile didn't belong to Philip, and if she had her way, it never would. Two footmen entered the room with trays of dessert and proceeded to set plates of poached pears in pecan cream before each guest. The aromas of brown sugar, pecans, and bourbon drifted to my nose and informed my quite satis-fied stomach that it could yet squeeze in a bit of this delec-table trifle.

Mrs. King turned her attention to each of her guests in turn. "Does anyone desire anything else?"

"No one could desire another thing after such a meal, Ella." Senator Wetmore patted his slightly bulging stomach beneath his evening coat.

"Good heavens, you'll have to roll me home, George," his wife said with a happy groan. "Miss Cross, I wanted to thank you for your help with the St. Nicholas Orphanage fundraiser last month, and with today's donation from the parade."

"I'm always happy to help St. Nicholas, ma'am," I said. "In fact—"

I broke off at a loud voice coming from the front of the house, but advancing nearer with each second. The words of a ribald song echoed in the sitting room next to the dining room, prompting each of us at the table to exchange startled glances. I recognized the voice before its owner made his way into the dining room—or stumbled, I should say.

"Philip!" Mrs. King exclaimed. She started to rise, but quickly lowered herself back into her chair. "Where have you been?"

"Hello, Mother. Hello, everyone." Philip King looked surprised to see our faces staring up at him. He aimed a smirk at the carved angels on either side of the fireplace. "Sorry I'm late. It's thick as corn chowder out there. Rolled in off the harbor about half an hour ago."

With a giggle at nothing in particular, he took a wobbly step closer. The seats he and his friend might have occupied had been cleared away at Mrs. King's direction, and now the blond footman hurried back into the room to make a place at the table for Philip. This necessitated that Gwendolen and Derrick scoot a few inches over. Poor Mrs. King looked ready to melt into the carpet, despite Derrick and the other guests assuring her the sudden addition of her son presented no inconvenience whatsoever.

Gwendolen obviously thought differently, and gave her brother a good jab in the ribs as he hovered unsteadily over the chair the footman held out for him, then plopped down into it without the slightest decorum. His mother's eyes burned with embarrassment while the rest of us looked politely away, as if we hadn't noticed Philip's inebriation.

"How's everyone tonight, eh?" he asked without apparent

interest, his attention instead focused on the plate of pears *Adelia* the footman had placed in front of him. Philip leaned down and sniffed the aroma. "What's for supper?"

"You missed dinner," his mother said with a tight smile. "We're on dessert. What happened to Francis? He was supposed to be here with you."

"Crane? Oh, he had me drop him next door at Stone Villa. Bennett's having a gentlemen's cards night. Asked me too, but I said, no, no, my mother is expecting me and I cannot disappoint the old girl. And so here I am."

"You're being such a rotter," Gwendolen murmured, and stirred her pears around her plate. Apparently realizing she'd spoken aloud, albeit in a whisper, she blushed a furious shade of crimson.

"You're just put out that your sweetheart didn't show up."

"Shhh! He is not my sweetheart and you know it," she shot back in an angry hiss and blushed hotter still.

One of the footmen offered a tray of liqueurs, which made Mrs. King frown yet again. "Where is Baldwin? Why isn't he serving with you? Has something happened?"

The footmen exchanged puzzled glances, and the blond one spoke. "We're not quite sure, ma'am. He was in the kitchen after we served the fish course and said he'd be right back. But last we were in there, he hadn't. Come back, that is."

"How odd." Mrs. King didn't seem overly concerned, but, like her footmen, puzzled.

"Oh, you know how it is, Mother." Gwendolen gathered a small pile of pecans on her plate and transferred them to the hollow of one of her pears. "Something is always coming up that needs the butler's attention. Meanwhile, Martin and Clarence are taking good care of us." She indicated the footmen, who acknowledged her praise with bobs of their heads.

"Would you like us to send him in as soon as he's finished

doing whatever it is that's detained him, ma'am?" the darker-haired one offered.

"No, that's all right, thank you, Clarence." Mrs. King put down her dessert fork. "We'll take our coffee in the library, thank you." She came to her feet, the men doing likewise—all but Philip, who made swirls with his fork in the pecan cream on his plate. We ladies rose from our chairs, too, and we were all about to file out of the room, leaving Philip to his own devices, when urgent shouts made their way in through the open windows and sent us running to the front of the house.

Chapter 3

"Why, I think that's Donavan." Ella King pressed herself up against the window in the small reception room, which flanked the front entrance opposite the front drawing room. The shouting continued. I stood at Mrs. King's right shoulder—Gwendolen stood at her left—and the three of us pressed our faces close to the glass. With difficulty we peered out into the murky darkness interrupted by amber swirls of illumination beneath the gas lanterns on the drive. Philip had declared the night as thick as corn chowder, and he hadn't been far off. Fog stretched languidly across the property, blanketing everything in its path.

"What do you see?" demanded Mrs. Wetmore from behind us. Mr. Wetmore had led Neily and Derrick outside with an order that we women remain in the house. Now they surrounded the man Mrs. King referred to as Donavan.

"I can't see a thing. What are they doing?" Grace stood directly behind me, her hand braced on my shoulder. She practically pressed against my back as she craned her neck to look out. Maude's face hovered above Mrs. King's and Gwendolen's shoulders.

"Over there." I pointed to a gnarled shadow, hunched and twisted like a creature from the underworld. "By the beech tree."

"Goodness, Mother, open the window wider." Without waiting for her mother to comply, Gwendolen shoved the window higher. We all three stuck our heads out, and that was when I saw the fog-blurred lines of the rear panel of an automobile, stripped now of its colorful flowers, jutting out from beneath the European beech tree.

Mrs. King saw it, too, for she drew back with a strangled whisper. "Oh no. Philip . . ."

"What is it, Mother?" Gwendolen clutched her mother's hand, then appealed to her friend. "Maude, can you see anything? Miss Cross?"

But I had already headed for the front door, was descending the steps and turning onto the drive when Donavan, nearly in tears now, choked out, "It's him. It's Baldwin. I think he's dead."

The mist ran clammy fingertips across my face and down my arms, raising shivers. I ran to the beech tree, nearly tripping over a root hidden in the grass, as Derrick, Mr. Wetmore, and Neily disappeared beneath its canopy of branches. The man called Donavan hovered off to the side, watching warily as the leaves swished back into place around the rear of the Hartley Steamer. I heard footsteps behind me and turned to see Grace, indistinct and ghostly in the fog. Behind her, the other women approached at a much slower place, as if dreading what they were about to learn.

I ducked beneath the tree. The fog hadn't drifted through the dense sweep of the branches and although the lawn lanterns didn't penetrate either, visibility was better. The men were grouped around the front of the motorcar and something wedged against the trunk of the tree. My eyes soon adjusted to the darkness and I realized the object was a man in a formal dark suit—a butler's attire. His legs and lower torso were pinned against the trunk, his upper body draped facedown over the motorcar's vertical front panel.

Bile rose in my throat as the horror of death filled me. Yet in the same instant Derrick cried out, "He's still alive. We need an ambulance here. Immediately."

Could it be? Derrick was leaning over the body—no, leaning over the butler, Mr. Baldwin—with his fingertips pressed to the side of the man's neck. I went nearer, and perceived, barely, the slight rise and fall of his spine. I moved farther still, until I could see more of the man's form. His head dangled over the footboard. In this position he looked as though he might merely have been drunk and keeled over, except that a rattle, hollow and bleak-sounding, issued from his throat, and a dark bubble grew at the corner of his slack mouth. Blood.

Less than half an hour later, we were all back in the house—all but Mrs. King's butler. The ambulance and the police had arrived, the former bringing medical staff who dislodged Mr. Baldwin from between the vehicle and the tree, and the latter securing the scene. It appeared to have been an accident, but one caused by the reckless misbehavior of a certain young man. Before I'd gone inside, I had asked a brief question of the doctor in charge. Would the man live? He had shaken his head in doubt.

Mrs. King ordered coffee laced with cognac and insisted we all drink it. Each Wetmore—the senator, his wife, and their daughter—had taken the news with stoic calm. I believe Gwendolen might have become a good deal more distraught had it not been for the calming influence of Maude. Mrs. King flitted about, seeing to her guests' needs, which were few, really. But it kept her busy, kept her, perhaps, from fearing the worst. And the worst, for Mrs. King, centered not on her poor butler, though his likely fate clearly upset her, but on her son and whether or not he was responsible for what happened.

As for Neily and Grace . . . A few years ago, they had become involved in an investigation into the death of a member of the Four Hundred, one Virgil Monroe. As with tonight's incident, questions had arisen then as to whether Virgil Monroe's demise had been a mere accident, a result of some form of incompetence, or something more deliberate. As continually seemed to happen, I'd been drawn into those questions, and Neily and Grace with me. I believe at first Grace had found excitement in our search for the truth, but soon enough came to recognize the dangers.

Was she thinking of that time now? Was that the reason for the deep etches across her brow? Or was she simply attempting, as were we all, to puzzle out whether Philip, arriving late and tipsy and in the fog, could have run his automobile into Baldwin, and then strolled into the dining room as if he hadn't a care in the world.

Now, his coat unbuttoned and his vest rumpled, Philip sat slumped in a wing chair beside the fireplace, staring down at the flames reflected on the tips of his shoes and looking very much like a boy who'd been taken to task for his misdeeds. The police had questioned him briefly, and I could see by their expressions that his inebriated state raised their speculations as well as their disgust. His replies had been little more than two- or three-word sentences, surly and reluctant, but he had insisted he'd pulled the Hartley onto the drive without incident. Certainly without plowing into the butler. One of the officers had jotted down his claims. Then they left him to stew with the rest of us, and had gone back outside to rope off the area and make some preliminary observations. To that end, they'd ringed the area with Dietz canister lanterns, whose bull's-eye lenses intensified the beams of light.

From outside came the sound of a newly arrived voice, issuing commands. I set down my cup and saucer and quietly made my way back out to the lawn. Derrick followed me, as I knew he would. But the others remained in the library, sipping their coffee and cognac in tense silence.

"Jesse." I greeted the Newport Police Department's head detective succinctly, and he returned my greeting with a mere nod, as if my being there came as no surprise. Jesse Whyte was about a decade my senior, with auburn hair and a fair, freckled complexion that hinted at his Irish heritage. He and Derrick also acknowledged each other with brief nods. "What have your men told you so far?" I asked him.

"If you mean did they mention Philip King having driven this motorcar all day after crashing it at the parade, and arriving home drunk right before the butler was found—"

I held up my hand. "So they've told you mostly everything, but perhaps not this. When Philip came into the dining room he acted as if nothing was wrong. He seemed completely at ease."

"And drunk," Derrick put in.

"Yes, and drunk," I conceded. I couldn't have said why I felt a need to defend Philip King. He *had* arrived in the motorcar and he *had* been—make that still *was*—drunk. Despite the sobering effects of the incident, he still lacked steadiness and a clear head. "Do you mind if I watch?"

"Stay out of the way. Please." Jesse's tone softened at that last word, turning what had started as a command into a request. I had no desire to interfere with police business, but possessed an insatiable need to reach my own conclusions. It had been that way for several years now, and Jesse had learned to trust my observations.

Was this the scene of an attempted murder?

To prove to Jesse I'd keep my distance, instead of moving toward the Hartley, I walked in the opposite direction. The fog still hung thickly in the air, muffling sight and sound, but what I sought could just as easily be felt as seen. Mrs. King's guests, including Derrick and me, had parked their carriages on the east side of the circular drive, to the right of the house. The tree Philip's motorcar struck stood to the left of the house, on the stretch of drive that led out through the gates. I walked slowly along the gravel. Derrick joined me, and we went all the way to the road, guided by the gas lanterns.

"What are you looking for?" he asked me when I'd turned around to once more face the house.

"Ruts." I pointed to the gravel. "If Philip had come barreling from the road onto the drive, the gravel should have been much more disturbed than it is. There's nothing here to indicate his careening wildly out of control."

"Perhaps he didn't careen. Maybe he rolled onto the property, and kept on rolling until he'd pinned his butler to the tree."

"Quite possible." I studied the angle of the automobile. It wouldn't have been a completely straight path from the driveway to where Baldwin had been pinned to the trunk, but given Philip's inebriated state and the uneven ground, the vehicle easily could have listed off its course. Or had Philip veered off on purpose? Had he accelerated at the last minute? I leaned down to study the gravel more closely and wished it were daytime. Sunrise was still many hours away, and I'd learned from experience that the sooner evidence could be thoroughly examined, the better. As I straightened, I saw Jesse emerge from between the branches of the beech. "Let's go hear what he has to say."

"I'm told the butler's midsection is practically crushed."
Jesse turned to regard the rear end of the Hartley. "They're much heavier than carriages, these automobiles." He turned back to Derrick and me. "How long would you estimate between the time Philip arrived in the dining room and when you heard the coachman's shouts?"

Derrick held out a palm. "The coachman?"

"John Donavan," Jesse clarified. "It was he who alerted everyone, wasn't it?"

I peered up at Derrick. "It was about ten minutes, would you say?"

"About that, yes," he confirmed.

Frowning, Jesse asked, "Do you remember hearing him arrive? The engine. Screeching tires. A thunk?"

"The thunk of the Hartley hitting the tree?" Derrick shrugged. "I never heard a thing before Philip sang his way through the house. Emma?"

"No, nor me, either. But you know how this fog muffles every sound."

Jesse breathed in deeply, then let it out in a rush. "So it's altogether possible Philip drove onto the property, hit the butler, perhaps without even knowing it, considering he'd been drinking all day, and calmly went in to dinner."

"Might the vehicle have rolled on its own? Philip might have parked at an angle toward the tree and then neglected to set the brake," I suggested. If so, the butler's injuries would still have been Philip's fault, but somehow this possibility seemed preferable to his drunkenly slamming into another man. The former was merely an oversight; the latter, an act of criminal recklessness.

"Or is there a defect in the Hartley's brake lines?" Like me, Derrick sounded hopeful. "Perhaps that first mishap at the parade wasn't a coincidence, and none of this is Philip's fault."

Jesse acknowledged this with a tilt of his head. "We'll have a mechanic take a look at the vehicle tomorrow. In the meantime, why don't you both go home? Emma, do you need a ride?"

"No," Derrick answered for me. His voice took on a slightly defensive note, or was it possessiveness? "Emma came with me. I'll drive her back to Gull Manor."

I braced for the old rivalry between the two men. I'd known Jesse all my life and had thought of him as my father's friend, albeit a much younger one—until a few years ago, when he suddenly exhibited an interest in me that exceeded that of a family friend. I realized then that he was closer in age to me than to either of my parents, and I came to view him in a new, and shall I say, handsomer light. At the same time, I met Derrick Andrews, scion of a Providence publishing family, and he had also expressed a desire to be more than friends.

One man my social equal and a fellow Newporter; the other, a member of a society that would never accept me as good enough. His parents had certainly made that painfully clear. But Jesse and Derrick did more than pay casual court to me. At times they'd nearly come to blows, and had insisted I choose between them. Or no, to be fair, perhaps they didn't insist; perhaps the insistence had been my own. Either way, I'd found myself unable to choose, wanting each man for different reasons, until some part of me that understood the truth, somewhere deep inside, did the choosing for me. And that choice had been Derrick, the man who sparked my passions, who inspired me sometimes to the brink of recklessness, who made me feel exuberant and wholly alive.

And Jesse? He hadn't suffered long. Though he'd taken his time in telling me about her, he'd found a courageous, spirited young woman of whom I fully approved. I'd have been a fool not to, as she had once saved my life. But that's not the story I'm telling just now.

If I'd feared Jesse's reaction to Derrick's possessiveness, it soon became apparent I needn't have, for he grinned and nodded. "Good. See that she gets inside safely. Or you'll answer to me."

"There's something for you here, Miss Emma." Katie Dillon, my maid-of-all-work, strode briskly into the morning room carrying the usual stack of morning newspapers. Besides the *Messenger*, I also subscribed to the *Newport Daily News*, the *Newport Observer*, and the *Providence Sun*. I felt it important to stay abreast of what my competitors were printing.

The young Irishwoman set the stack on the table beside my elbow and propped an envelope against my coffee cup.

I raised it between two fingers. The inscription bore my name, but in no handwriting I recognized. "What's this?"

"I'm sure I don't know, Miss Emma. It was on top of the rest. I can't even tell you how it got there." Bright red tendrils escaped Katie's topknot to frame her curious face. Her cornflower-blue eyes practically begged me to open the missive. I did so at once.

And frowned in perplexity.

"What is it, Emma?" From across the table, Nanny lowered the book she'd been intent upon. "Not bad news, I hope. Or has it got to do with last night?"

Upon arriving home last night, I'd invited Derrick in for a cup of tea, and the two of us had told Nanny and Katie all about the happenings at Kingscote. They had joined us in hoping Baldwin would recover, and that the Hartley Steamer had been at fault, not Philip King. Now, as I read the note, I wondered if more malevolent forces had been at work.

"Listen to this. 'Despite what the Kings think, all is not well with their servants. Baldwin got what he deserved.'" I looked up. "There's no signature."

Nanny reached out a plump hand. "Let me see that." When I handed it across to her, she smoothed the folds out flat and bent her face close to it. "It's not a practiced hand, in my opinion. Not that of a formally-schooled person." She held the paper up toward me and pointed to a line of words. "The script is neither the Spencer style nor the newer Palmer method. There's very little uniformity in the shapes and slant of the letters, which to me suggests the writer didn't learn his or her penmanship in a classroom. Probably schooled at home. It could even be from one of the Kings' servants."

Katie had moved to look over Nanny's shoulder, and she nodded at Nanny's assessment. Nanny straightened and glanced up at her. "Have you heard anything about the goings-on at Kingscote?"

"Nothin', ma'am." Katie's brogue became more pronounced than usual. She had come to America from Ireland some six years ago and, at times, she sounded almost like the rest of us. Clearly Nanny's question caught her off guard and made her uncomfortable.

"Katie, if there's anything," I said, "it would be a good idea to tell us. Philip King is being held responsible for the butler's injuries, though the police believe it was a reckless accident. If you have any other information . . ."

"I don't. At least nothing definite." Katie pulled out a chair at the table and sank into it. She propped her chin on her hands. "You know the Kings release most of their servants every year when they leave Newport for the winter, and hire new each spring."

I nodded. The Kings' system wasn't typical of the Four Hundred. Most took their servants to their other estates when they left Newport, leaving a skeleton staff here to keep their summer cottages secure during the winter months. But the Kings had no other estates. When they left the island, it was to travel to Europe, where they rented lodgings in whatever country they inhabited. With Kingscote not being quite as large as some of the other cottages, Mrs. King hired a local caretaker to watch over the property in her absence, and her longtime groom stayed to care for the horses. The housekeeper, who had also been in her service many years, traveled with her.

"Well," Katie said, "there have been some whispers that the butler has a bit of a checkered past."

"What does that mean?" I asked her.

"That's just it. I don't know. But I *have* heard he has an eye for the ladies. The *young* ones, if you catch my meaning, Miss Emma."

I shook my head in disgust. "I do. And that could very well be what this note is getting at. But who wrote it? One of Kingscote's own servants, or someone who worked with Baldwin in the past?" I regarded Katie again. "Have you heard anything about where he worked before he came to Newport?"

"Somewhere in New York, is all I've heard." She shrugged. "Mrs. King should know, shouldn't she?"

"If Mr. Baldwin told the truth," I said. "References can be forged, which he might have done if he'd had troubles at his last post."

"I can probably find out." Nanny studied the note again. "I'll make inquiries."

Yes, Nanny had access to information denied the rest of us. Though I thought of her more as a grandmother and dear friend, society would have termed her a servant. No one knew more about the goings-on in the great houses than the servants who worked in them, and their connections to one another stretched from region to region, from New England to New York City, to Long Island, and beyond. Nanny had only to make a few telephone calls to set that informative network abuzz; she'd probably have answers by the end of the week.

After breakfast I drove my buggy into town, to the diminutive offices of the *Messenger.* Another thing I had done last night was telephone our news reporter, Jacob Stodges, and give him the details of the accident. When I'd first taken the position of editor-in-chief of the *Messenger*, we'd had tensions between us, Jacob and I. I had been largely to blame, though it had taken me some time to admit this. My tendency had been to run with a story rather than assign it to Jacob, and he had been justified in resenting me for it. I loved reporting; my goal had long been to become a hardnews reporter, and someday I would make that goal a reality. But I'd taken the position as editor-in-chief when Derrick offered it, and my first responsibility was to him, our readers, and to the smooth operation of the business.

When I arrived, I discovered Jacob had gone to Kingscote to learn if there had been any further developments, and to try to speak with Philip King. I doubted he'd meet with success in the latter case, but I'd give him credit for trying. In the meantime, I'd brought the anonymous note with me, intending to bring it to the police station at the first opportunity. Jesse's midmorning appearance in my front office made that unnecessary.

"I've just come from the mechanic," he said after he'd greeted me and I'd offered him a cup of our typically bitter coffee. "The motorcar is sound. There is nothing wrong with the brake system. Which means responsibility rests firmly on Philip King's shoulders."

"Perhaps not." I handed him the note. "This was waiting for me on top of our morning newspapers."

Jesse unfolded it and read the brief contents, then looked sharply up at me. "How did I know things wouldn't be simple?"

"Because they never are," I reminded him.

"This note could be someone's idea of a prank, a deplorable one. Or one of Philip's own friends attempting to exonerate him. Who was supposed to accompany him to Kingscote last night?"

"His mother spoke of a Francis." After finding Baldwin beneath the beech tree, I'd all but forgotten the exchange between Philip and Gwendolen concerning this Francis Crane. Philip seemed to believe his sister harbored romantic sentiments toward the young man, or was it the other way around? Difficult to tell, for Gwendolen's fierce denial could just as easily have stemmed from aversion to Francis Crane as from a desperate attempt to keep her attraction a secret from the rest of us seated around the table.

"Ah, yes. Crane. Francis Crane. Family's in coal. New money." Jesse's eyebrows rose speculatively. "Came down from Providence at the start of the summer, and he and Philip King are often seen together about town. Maybe he sent the note. A good friend would not want to see his chum in legal difficulties."

"Look at the handwriting. Nanny judged it to belong to someone who isn't well schooled, at least not as members of the Four Hundred are. If Francis Crane comes from money, new or otherwise, he would certainly have attended some of the best schools." Jesse gazed down at the paper again, nodding vaguely. "Besides," I went on, "even Katie has heard rumors about Isaiah Baldwin. Nanny's looking into where he worked before coming to Kingscote."

He shot me a look of comprehension. "I'll ask Mrs. King, of course, but yes, have Nanny make her inquiries." He stared down at the note again and rubbed his temple with the back of his hand. "Motive, shed directly onto Kingscote's servants."

"So then . . . possibly an attempted murder."

Chapter 4

Jesse left the *Messenger* and set out for Kingscote. Several minutes later, Jacob Stodges returned from that very same house. "Did you learn anything?" I asked him as soon as he'd walked through the door. "Were you able to speak with Philip King?"

"I was, actually." Before answering further, he dragged the rolling chair from the other desk—the one that had been vacant ever since I'd ordered Jimmy Hawkins to leave and never return—closer to my own. "Philip swears he didn't run into the butler last night. When I suggested he might have forgotten given the state he was in, he said drunk or not, he'd damned well know whether he rammed a person against a tree, and that only an idiot would make such a preposterous suggestion."

Jacob didn't apologize for swearing, nor did I require him to. I had entered a man's world in taking this position, and I certainly wasn't going to blanch at its occasional lack of refinement. I leaned back in my desk chair, swiveling it slightly side to side. "I suppose a person *would* have to be blind drunk not to realize they'd just driven into someone else. And Philip didn't strike me as quite that indisposed. So either he isn't responsible at all, or he did it, *knows* he did it, and is lying."

"I'm inclined to believe he's lying," Jacob said without hesitation. "You know how these cottagers are. Think they can get away with anything."

"That isn't always true." I ignored his cynical look. "Besides, I received a note this morning at home. I've given it to Detective Whyte, but it basically said Baldwin hadn't been a fair man to work under, and that he got what was coming to him."

Jacob whistled under his breath. "I wish you still had that note."

"Jesse's at Kingscote now with it, interviewing the servants. Did you talk to any of them?"

"Mrs. King gave orders not to let me in the house," Jacob began, and I cut him off.

"Then how did you manage to speak with Philip?"

"Found him outside, with a friend. Playing badminton, of all things."

At the thought of Philip King enjoying himself today I very nearly swore myself. I narrowed my eyes. "Was this friend Francis Crane, by any chance?"

"The same. Why?"

I shook my head. "He was supposed to accompany Philip to dinner last night, but made other plans. I suppose it's not important. What about the servants?"

"I spoke with two of them. There was a maid hanging up laundry. A pretty Irish girl, name of Olivia Riley." He pulled his notepad out of his pocket and appeared to check his information. With a nod, he went on. "This Miss Riley was hired in June and said so far she'd been content with the position. Said it was a fair place to work and the Kings treated everyone well enough. Feels awful about what happened to the butler. Said she hopes he's back at work soon."

"And she didn't indicate any problems with him? Not even in her tone or perhaps a stray frown?"

"No, and I would have noticed otherwise." He became rather defensive as he said this. I held up a hand.

"I believe you. But mightn't a woman who had just rolled an automobile onto her superior put on a cheerful face and pretend all had been well prior to the incident?"

"Fair point. Not to mention that in her line of work, she'd have the strength to do it."

"Undoubtedly. Did you speak with anyone else?"

"Yes, the coachman who first found Baldwin. That is, I did until a footman spotted us. He ordered Donavan back to the carriage house and me off the property. Before he did, though, I asked Donavan what he was doing at the front of the property last night. He said he was smoking a cigarette, that he often strolls the property at night."

I thought about that a moment. "If he was already outside, he might have heard something. Did you ask him that?"

He gave me a withering look. "Of course I asked him. That was when the footman broke up our little tête-à-tête."

"Then we can only hope Jesse gets an answer. Mrs. King can't have her footmen chase *him* off."

"Going back to Francis Crane for a moment. A time or two, I sensed he was about to say something, but held back. Possibly because whatever it was, he didn't wish to say it in front of Philip King."

This surprised me, and I wondered what Mr. Crane might have to say. An instinct of long habit rose up; I longed to question Francis Crane myself. But I'd given the story to Jacob. Going back on my word would erode much of the progress we had made as colleagues over the past several months. With an inner sigh, I said, "I wonder, Jacob, if you might track down Mr. Crane when he isn't with his friend and see if he won't talk to you."

"I believe I could manage that," he said with a grin that left no doubt in the matter.

By late that afternoon fatigue clutched at my shoulders. I prepared to leave the office and set out for home, but I would be delayed. Jesse returned to discuss his time at Kingscote earlier.

"Have you finished here for the day?" he asked upon entering the front office. When I said I had, he made himself comfortable in the extra desk chair. I removed my hat and gloves and resumed my own seat. "According to Mrs. King," he said, "Isaiah Baldwin last worked in a house just to the north of Cranston. The Hill family. Owned a jewelry factory—enamel, paste, that sort of thing—until about three years ago, when they sold off their inventory and equipment and shut down. According to the information Mrs. King has, they sold the house last winter and are now living in the South of France. Baldwin had accompanied the family to New York to help see them off, and then began applying for new positions."

"Convenient, isn't it, that his last employers are out of the country and for the most part, can't be contacted. No way to verify whether this reference is legitimate or not, at least not in a timely manner."

Jesse raised an eyebrow and nodded. "Which leaves it to Nanny to find out the truth, unless the man miraculously awakens and is able to speak to us."

"Is there much chance of that?"

"It doesn't sound good, from what the hospital shared with me this morning. He remains in grave condition. This could, at any moment, become a murder investigation." Jesse stared down at his hands a moment, then looked up. "In the meantime, I've talked to the Kingscote servants. From what each staff member had to say, one can only conclude they're the happiest group of servants that ever lived. All eight of them."

"All?" The claim made me incredulous. "That's so rare as to be impossible."

"I couldn't agree more. Either they're afraid complaining will lead to the loss of their jobs, or they're adhering to that ridiculous code of servants handling their problems among themselves, without outside help."

"Either way, can you blame them? Servants aren't typically afforded the benefit of the doubt," I reminded him. "You say there are eight of them altogether?"

"Besides Baldwin, yes. Two footmen, the coachman and groom, the housekeeper, housemaid, the cook and her assistant. The gardener is a local man who comes weekly. Any others the household might need are hired for specific occasions. There were no extras there last night."

"Eight servants," I pondered, thinking again about this morning's note. "And of those, are there any who can't account for their time last night? For instance, I'd find it difficult to believe either of the footmen could have found the time to commit murder."

"They're in the clear," Jesse confirmed. "The cook and her assistant as well, as they never left the kitchen, which the housekeeper verified, just as they verified that she was in her parlor all night going over the inventory books. They can see her there from the kitchen."

"And Donavan, the coachman?"

Jesse gave a thoughtful nod. "Yes, the individual who was conveniently outside at just the right moment last night, yet who didn't see what happened."

"He told Jacob he went out for a cigarette."

"He repeated the same to me. And the end of a cigarette was found in the grass near the beech tree, so it was probably Donavan's. But there's no one to corroborate that *all* he did was smoke a cigarette. Did he find the injured butler after the fact, or did he do it? And as for the housemaid, she was off for the night, but at the house, supposedly in her room. None of the others can verify her whereabouts. They were either in or near the kitchen, outside, or, in the groom's case, off the property visiting family in Middletown."

"Can you verify when he left and returned?"

"My men have talked to his parents, a brother, and several of their neighbors. He spent the night and returned to Kingscote in the morning, early."

That seemed to exonerate the groom. My thoughts drifted back to the scene beneath the beech tree. "I wish we knew why Baldwin went outside."

"We didn't find another cigarette stub, so that's unlikely. He might simply have gone out for a breath of air."

"During dinner? It seems so unlikely, not when he knew he'd be needed. Although, that cigarette could have been his and not Donavan's." My mind wandered back to the previous summer, and to another man who had been in the wrong place on the grounds of a mansion when he shouldn't have. It hadn't ended well for him, and it had taken much searching to discover his reason for being outside at the time . . .

"Are you having one of your hunches?" Jesse wanted to know.

"No, I was thinking about that night at Crossways last summer. But that was another matter and nothing to do with the present." My eyebrows went up as I tallied up the possible suspects for *this* crime. "If it wasn't Philip in the driver's seat, it looks to be either Donavan or this maid—Miss Riley?"

Jesse nodded at the name. "Yes, Olivia. But would a woman, a maid, have the knowledge to operate a motor vehicle? Starting those steamers isn't easy. It practically takes an engineer."

"The Hartley might simply have been pushed. All someone would need to do is release the brake and give a good shove." My features tightened as I tried to recall the details of the previous night. "Isn't there a downward slope from the driveway onto the lawn and to the tree?"

"Not much of one, but enough to aid in setting the vehicle rolling, I suppose."

"And don't forget how foggy it was. Someone might have stolen quietly to the car without Baldwin noticing until it was too late."

Jesse nodded his concurrence. "The thing is, anyone might have crept onto the grounds and done the deed. I can't only focus on the servants."

Jesse spoke the truth, but Baldwin hadn't been in Newport very long, only a few months. Not long enough to have made many enemies among the locals. Had someone followed him here from his last posting? Learning more about his background was essential to discovering who carried enough of a grudge to pin the man up against a tree.

"Where were most of the servants hired?" I asked.

"In New York, when Mrs. King returned from Europe. Everyone but the housekeeper and the groom. They've been with her for years now."

Which meant none of the rest of them had established any particular loyalty to Mrs. King or her family. Or to each other.

Early that next morning, I received a telephone call from Newport Hospital.

"Emma, it's Hannah." Hannah Hanson had grown up near me on Easton's Point. She worked as a nurse at the hospital, and what's more, my half brother, Brady, was sweet on her—a circumstance of which I thoroughly approved. At the grim sound of her voice, a chill traveled up my spine. "I'm sorry to have to tell you this, but he died. His spleen ruptured."

She didn't need to tell me to whom she referred. It came as no surprise, given Isaiah Baldwin's injuries, but hearing of someone's death, and understanding all it would mean to those involved, knocked some of the wind out of me. "I'm sorry to hear this, Hannah."

"Do you understand what it signifies?" Without waiting for me to respond, she elaborated. "To rupture his spleen like that, it means the vehicle didn't simply roll into him. It had to have been driven or pushed, forcefully."

I gripped the wire to the ear trumpet and leaned against the wall beside me. "Jesse was already braced for a possible murder investigation. He's got one now."

"There's more. There's trouble in town, and now that Mr. Baldwin has died, I'm afraid that trouble could become violent."

"What do you mean? What's happened?"

"Do you even have to ask?" I heard the faintest impatience over the wire. "A man is dead, a workingman. The townspeople are demanding to know why no one is being held accountable. Why Philip King hasn't been arrested."

"But we don't know for certain that Philip King is responsible."

"Perhaps not, but in the minds of most Newporters he is, and he's being let off because of his family's money."

Sudden indignation had me standing up straighter, away from the wall. "If Jesse determines that Philip is responsible, he will take the necessary steps to see him charged."

"You and I know he'll try, Emma, but we also know his superiors have the final say, and if they decide to let Philip King go, Jesse will have no choice."

I couldn't argue the point. I'd seen it time and time again.

The Four Hundred had the money to influence not only the local police, but policy makers from mayors to governors to the president of the United States.

But then I considered the present circumstances. Ella King didn't strike me as a woman who coddled her son or bowed to his whims. Then again, she had never before faced the prospect of her child being accused of murder. Even if she personally couldn't afford to sway legal opinions, she had connections to plenty of those who could.

"Tell me what's been happening," I said into the receiver.

"I passed by the police station on the way here to the hospital a little while ago. There was a group of men outside, shouting for justice for Isaiah Baldwin and chanting that Philip King should be behind bars."

"Has word spread yet of his death?"

"No, it happened right before I telephoned. The police have already been notified, though, so Jesse will know by now."

I felt a sudden fear for my friend. Would Jesse attempt to reason with the disgruntled crowd outside the police station? Would those men take out their frustrations on him, perhaps with violence? How badly might matters escalate, especially if there was no arrest?

"Emma, I have to go back to work. I just wanted to let you know what was happening."

"I appreciate it, Hannah, thank you. As soon as Brady gets into town, you're both invited here for supper." After we hung up, I made two more telephone calls. One was to the *Messenger*. Jacob Stodges didn't have a telephone at home, but I knew he'd be at work within the half hour. I left a message with Dan Carter, the newspaper's head press operator, who came in before dawn every day to prime the press for the morning's first run. I asked him to let Jacob know about Isaiah Baldwin's death and the unrest at the police station. Next, I telephoned Derrick.

"Can you meet me in town?"

I heard a faint yawn. "Of course. Has something happened?"

I related my conversation with Hannah. Then I said, "I'll leave my carriage at the livery and take the trolley over to the hospital. Can you meet me there?"

"Better still, I'll meet you on the trolley."

Derrick was as good as his word and hopped on the electric rail trolley at the Washington Square stop. We rode up Broadway and minutes later arrived at Friendship Street. Apparently, word of Isaiah Baldwin's death had gotten out, for the unrest had spread here from the police station. A small crowd of about a dozen men and women milled on the corner outside the hospital, a two-story cottage that had once been a private home. Their simple, durable attire identified them as local people, Islanders, and what they lacked in numbers they made up for in vehemence. Their shouts reached us before we stepped off the trolley, and the tensions they generated reached out to tie a knot in my stomach.

Derrick's hand came down on my forearm as I reached for the handrail to step down. "Maybe we shouldn't stop here."

"I wish to know if the doctors have discovered anything else about Baldwin's death, and also what these people want. I sent Jacob over to the police station. That leaves me to observe events here."

He nodded in resignation, as we both knew he would. Of course he'd had to try to dissuade me, even if only for appearance's sake. But he'd long ago accepted my driven nature—or stubbornness, as most people might call it.

We stepped down from the trolley and several words I wouldn't care to repeat reached my ears. Derrick and I exchanged startled looks, which turned to alarm as we each realized, simultaneously, that the crowd had formed a circle and was now closing in on some unfortunate individual who had become their target.

A few stragglers skirted the activity. They held notepads, I realized, and I recognized one of them. Ed Billings, the paunch-bellied, slouch-shouldered reporter for the *Newport Observer.* Until two years ago I had been the *Observer's* society columnist, and Ed and I had frequently butted heads. Somehow, he had rarely been on hand during most of Newport's more dangerous crises, yet he'd been all too happy to use my notes and attach his name to the resulting article. And all with our editor-in-chief's blessing. I tried to catch Ed's eye, and I believed he saw me but glanced quickly away.

Meanwhile, Derrick rushed forward, and I followed close behind. Through the circle of bodies I made out a pair of broad shoulders encased in tailored cream flannel. Whoever had been cornered was not one of these people, not a local. A disquieting thought struck me. Could it be Philip King? A thud sounded, and a grunt, followed by more. Derrick, at least half a head taller than most of the other men, forced his way through, and as a collective growl went through the crowd, I worried for him, too.

And not without cause.

"Leave this man alone." Derrick grabbed at a flailing fist, halting it in midair. The young man in question stood shielding his face with one arm, the other hand catching the blood that trickled from his nose. "You're behaving like a bunch of lunatics. If you don't disperse immediately, we'll send for the police."

"Good, send for them. Philip King needs to pay for his crime!"

"That's for the police to decide," Derrick countered in his baritone.

"Mind your business, you don't belong here." Several people intoned this, while others nodded vigorously.

"You're the problem," a man shouted. "You and him and all o' your kind."

"Get off our island." A fist shook in the air. "You're not welcome."

The scene reminded me of one last year, when a riot nearly broke out between gas and electrical workers at the construction site of The Elms. Now, seeing Derrick threatened, a ball of panic clogged my throat, and I thrust forward, my arms out, my voice loud. "Stop this. You're all acting like children. What's gotten into you?"

They were so riled up, I'll never understand how I caught their attention. But almost as one they turned to stare at me, their gazes swimming with hostility. I resisted the urge to gulp. Began to regret my interference. Then one of the women spoke.

"And who are you to—" Her anger flitted away. She looked uncertain, then embarrassed. "Oh. It's Emma Cross." She half turned to address the others. "Arthur and Beatrice Cross's daughter." She turned back to me. "I went to school with your mama. I'm Evelyn Chambers."

For an instant I thought to plunk my hands on my hips and remind her of the folly of revealing her name to a journalist, but realized that would not have helped matters. Instead, I tamped down my own anger and summoned civility. "Yes, I remember. It's nice to see you, Mrs. Chambers." It wasn't, not under these circumstances, but why point out the obvious? I ventured closer to the group, now much more subdued than previously. Somehow I'd managed to break the thrall that had held them, and they became downright docile.

"What's happening here?" I made my way through the loosening circle to discover, not Philip King at its center, but another young man I didn't recognize. Not a member of the Four Hundred who summered yearly in Newport.

But his identity wasn't imperative at the moment. His clothing was rumpled and blood oozed from his nose.

"We need to get him inside," Derrick said, and aimed a warning glare at the others. They looked away and began to disperse. Derrick addressed their victim. "Can you walk, or do you need my help?"

"I can walk," the youth said, for a youth he obviously was, now that I saw him clearly. He had light brown hair, tipped bronze by the summer sun, and nice, even features unmarred by wrinkles, though he was not classically handsome. Pleasant and friendly looking, would sum up his appearance, but for the dripping blood and his affronted scowl. He took a handkerchief from his inner coat pocket and held it to his nose.

The reporters, too, eased away from us, but I forced Ed Billings to stop and turn to me by calling out his name. I left the young man's side for a moment. "Did you not think to help him," I demanded of Ed in a fierce whisper. "You and the rest of your cronies here?"

His lips curled downward in a show of disdain. "A good reporter observes, Emma. He doesn't interfere."

A single word reverberated in my mind: *coward.* But I didn't say it. I merely shook my head, spun on my heel, and returned to Derrick and the young man.

"Why did they think you were Philip King?" I asked him as we made our way inside.

"I don't know that they did," he replied. "I think they'd have gone after anyone in a tailored suit of clothes." He flicked a glance at Derrick, who stood several inches taller. "Although not you, apparently. Nor you either, ma'am. I don't know what kind of power you hold around here, but I'm beholden to you both for coming to my rescue."

"You're very welcome. And we have no special power. I grew up in Newport, and this gentleman owns a local newspaper. In this town, everyone knows everyone. As soon as they recognized me it was like seeing a member of their own family and they became ashamed of their actions. I'm Emma Cross, by the way, and this is Derrick Andrews."

"Pleased to meet you both. I'm Francis Crane."

Chapter 5

"If you don't mind my asking, Mr. Crane, why did you come down here today?" I hoped he didn't find my question impertinent, but his presence at the hospital this morning piqued my curiosity.

He had been seen by a doctor, who had stemmed the bleeding from his nose and pronounced him in otherwise sound health. When asked if he wished to press charges, he'd waved the notion off. I'd thought it more than sporting of him. Now he, Derrick, and I occupied the tiny waiting room, once a receiving parlor on the cottage's first floor. We were waiting for Hannah to come and tell us any new information she had about Isaiah Baldwin's death.

Mr. Crane lifted a hand to touch his nose gingerly; slightly swollen, it must still have been throbbing. "I suppose for the same reason as you. To learn what I could about the butler."

"Were you acquainted with Isaiah Baldwin?" I persisted.

"No, but I'm well acquainted with Philip King." He spoke in a somber undertone and shook his head as if at a lost cause.

That much I had known, but my curiosity prompted me to interrupt him. "May I ask how you and Mr. King know each other?"

"We both attend Brown, both members of Delta Phi." He said this with an air of pride and not the usual nonchalance of wealthy young men whose fathers, brothers, and uncles had been fraternity members as well. That he'd been accepted obviously meant a great deal to him. It was information I tucked away, to be considered later.

"So you know each other quite well, then," I said.

"Yes, and I'm worried about Philip." He paused, glancing down at his feet. He gripped his hands together, the fingers interlaced. "I came to the hospital hoping for news that the butler would recover and be able to say what happened to him. But now . . . I'm afraid . . ." His gaze drifted downward again as he trailed off, and a sense of apprehension closed around me.

"Please, Mr. Crane, you can trust us."

"Can I?" He regarded each of us, his brow creasing warily. "You're reporters, aren't you?"

"But not like the ones who stood by while that crowd outside threatened violence against you," Derrick assured him. I nodded in agreement, and in encouragement for Mr. Crane to continue. Presently, he drew a decisive breath.

"I'm dreadfully afraid Philip is going to be blamed. And I don't mean as he's currently being blamed, for an accident." He pulled in another deep breath. "You see, I overheard an argument he had with Baldwin the day before the parade. It was over money."

Derrick and I exchanged a look of surprise. A servant and the son of his employer arguing over money?

"Did the Kings owe Baldwin back wages?" I guessed out loud. No wonder Jacob had gotten the sensation that Francis Crane had something to say yesterday, but didn't wish to mention it in front of his friend.

"No, it isn't that," he said. "Baldwin lent Philip a sum to cover a debt. It wasn't the first time, I understand."

"Philip borrowed from the butler?" I exchanged another incredulous look with Derrick. He frowned vaguely, his eyes narrowing slightly at Mr. Crane.

That young man chuckled and showed us a sad smile. "I've lent him money myself, a time or two."

"For what?" I couldn't help asking.

Francis Crane shrugged. "Purchases, gambling debts . . ."

"And did he pay you back?" Derrick bluntly asked.

"Some of it. From what I heard of the argument, he should have paid Baldwin back within a week of the loan, when his allowance came from the bank." He swallowed and gave a little wince that I believed hadn't been caused by pain—at least not of the physical sort.

"But he didn't, and they argued," I finished for him, and he nodded again, a corner of his mouth twisting with regret. "But where does a servant come up with the extra cash to lend anyone?"

"That I can't say. But their argument doesn't mean . . ."

"No, Mr. Crane, it doesn't mean Philip is guilty of anything more than defaulting on a loan," Derrick said firmly.

Francis Crane showed him a look of relief. "No, it doesn't, does it? But still, Mr. Andrews, now that Baldwin has died, things could go very badly for Philip, couldn't they? And I feel partly to blame."

"How is that?" I asked him.

"I should have gone to dinner at Kingscote that night. If I had been there, with Philip . . ." His features went taut. He finished in a murmur. "The butler might still be alive."

"Mr. Crane," I said, "you seem to believe your friend is responsible. Perhaps he had nothing to do with the butler's death."

"But Philip arrived at Kingscote in the same motorcar that killed Baldwin. Who else could have done it?"

"It's possible, isn't it, that someone pushed that motorcar once Philip had gone into the house?"

"I suppose." His expression turned hopeful.

"In which case, it wouldn't have made a difference if you *had* come to Kingscote." Once again, my curiosity prompted another question. "May I ask why you *didn't* come to dinner?"

He shrugged, released his hands, and wrapped them around the arms of the chair. "It sounded like a stuffy affair, and Philip and I . . . well, we'd made the round of several friends' homes and did a fair amount of drinking all evening."

Earlier than that, I thought, remembering the whiskey on Philip's breath as the parade began. "You went instead to Stone Villa to play cards with Mr. Bennett and his friends?"

Looking surprised that I knew this, Francis nodded. "Honestly, I didn't wish to hear Mrs. King chastise Philip for his drinking."

"Does she chastise her son often?" Derrick asked, making me think of his own mother who, while not having much to complain about in her son, always made her opinions perfectly clear to him nonetheless.

"Seems she has cause for one complaint or another on a daily basis," Francis replied sullenly.

"That must provoke Philip's resentment," Derrick said as if merely musing aloud. Then, more sharply, he asked, "Tell me, did Mrs. King know about this unpaid loan?"

"Certainly not." The very notion seemed to startle the younger man. "Although . . ."

"Yes?" Derrick prompted.

"Well, Baldwin came at Philip in a high temper the day they argued. He wanted his money, and he swore he wouldn't be making any further loans to Philip. And then he—" When he broke off, I opened my mouth to prod him to go on, but it proved unnecessary. "Baldwin said he'd go to Mrs. King if he didn't get his money by the end of the week."

* * *

Whether he had wished to or not, Francis Crane had provided a compelling motive for Philip to have murdered Isaiah Baldwin. He had owed the man money he hadn't been able to repay, and the butler had threatened to appeal to Philip's mother, a woman who, according to Francis, found one fault after another in her son. He had also revealed that Philip was dependent, financially, on his monthly allowance, which indicated that his mother kept him on a tight leash when it came to supplementing his income.

But these were the opinions of only one young man, and Francis Crane, despite his shows of remorse and reluctance, had been all too willing to confide in us—two individuals he had never met before. Why?

"Do you think we can trust his word?" I asked Derrick after we left the hospital. Mr. Crane offered us a ride in his carriage, but we thanked him and declined. The trolley stopped for us, and Derrick helped me on.

He compressed his lips and paid the fare for both of us. Once we had taken our seats side by side, he shook his head. "I don't know. Something felt . . . rather forced. As if he'd been eager all along to tell someone what he knew. But it could simply have been the effects of his nearly taking a beating out there on the street."

I nodded in agreement. By the time we arrived at the *Messenger*, we had devised a plan to learn more about what had been going on behind Kingscote's walls. Only one problem existed.

Jacob had returned from the police station, and we found him in our tiny press office tapping away at the typewriter. Ethan hunched over his own small desk, pen in hand. As Derrick and I entered the room, Jacob's fingers stilled and the machine fell silent.

"Good morning, Mr. Andrews." Jacob rolled back from the typewriter and hopped up from his chair.

Derrick waved him back into his seat. "No need for that. Tell us what happened at the police station."

"It's just as Miss Cross's friend told her. People are up in arms about Philip King getting away with murder, as they're saying. Never mind that no one has yet termed the butler's death a murder." He emitted a low whistle. "They're hungry for blood, these locals. But Police Chief Rogers came outside and assured them Philip King was being put under house arrest pending an investigation."

This development took me by surprise, although it had happened in Newport before, when another cottager had been accused of murder. "Did it appease them at all?"

"Barely. At most I'd say it relieved tensions for a time. But if nothing comes of this house arrest, if a real arrest doesn't follow quickly enough, I'm afraid of what might happen."

I nodded, understanding his meaning. Ethan had observed the exchange, his eyes large and his mouth a tight, thin line. Times of trouble and unrest didn't appeal to him. He much preferred reporting on society's triumphs, its aspirations and achievements. I sighed and prepared for what I had to do next.

"Mr. Andrews and I have a plan to try to find out how Baldwin's fellow servants felt about him, and whether one of them might have pushed the automobile into him." I glanced at Derrick, and he nodded his encouragement. "This is strictly voluntary, mind you. We would never force anyone to do something they didn't wish to do."

Jacob rolled his chair toward us several inches. An anticipatory gleam entered his eyes. "What are you proposing?"

"Well, first we'll have to take Mrs. King—and Detective Whyte—into our confidence. But we propose sending in a temporary butler to replace Baldwin. Someone who can talk to the servants and perhaps even interact with Philip King—"

"Like a spy." Jacob was grinning openly now.

"We prefer *investigative reporter*," Derrick corrected him with a lift of an eyebrow.

"Yes. This sort of thing has been done before, with good results." I didn't bother mentioning the woman who had inspired me in my own career, but my thoughts went to Nellie Bly entering the mental asylum on Blackwell's Island a dozen years ago to expose the horrific way patients were treated. This wouldn't be as dangerous, but it might not be without its risks either. I fidgeted with the cuff of my sleeve. "As I said, this is voluntary, and—"

"I'll do it." Jacob stood up. "Of course I'll do it. I could disguise myself so they—"

"No, Jacob, not you." I turned my gaze on Ethan, who colored to the roots of his slicked-back hair. "It would have to be you, Ethan. Jacob was at Kingscote only yesterday, and it's likely he'd be recognized. But you . . . You've only been on the job a year now, and the Kings have been away much of that time. Besides, their servants are all new and they won't have seen you before. Mrs. King will of course know who you are and why you're there. I think she'll agree to it. I think she'll see it as a chance to exonerate her son."

I left off as I noticed Ethan shaking his head in nervous little side-to-side twitches. "I can't, Miss Cross. I . . ."

"Ethan, at least think about it." I moved around his desk and perched on the edge beside his chair. "You can do this. I know you can."

Jacob, too, was shaking his head. "This should be my job. I'm the news reporter. He won't know what to look for, what questions to ask."

"I know it should be you," I told him, not without sympathy. I understood his longing to take up this challenge, to stretch his journalist skills. "But you were just there. The risk of someone recognizing you is too great." I turned back to Ethan and looked into his frightened eyes. "Will you do it?"

His lips parted and he moistened them with the tip of his tongue. "Do I have a choice?"

I leaned down lower, bringing my face level with his. "Yes."

He exhaled. "All right. But what do I know about being a butler?"

"Enough, I'm sure," I said. "Think about it. You've been reporting on the cottages and their elaborate affairs for over a year now. You know how these houses are run."

"I suppose I do . . ."

"What's more, we'll arrange for Mrs. King to give you a complete list of tasks every day. But remember, your job, for the most part, will be to make sure everyone else does their job. Now . . ." I assessed his appearance, running my gaze over him from head to toe. "Less hair oil, and part your hair on the side, rather than combing it straight back. Do you have a morning coat?" When he shook his head, I appealed with a look to Derrick.

"We'll get him properly suited up. He'll need another name, too. People might not know what Ethan Merriman looks like, but they'll recognize his name from his columns."

"You're right. Good, then." I slid off the desk. "You two work on that, and I'll speak to Mrs. King on my way home from town later." I headed for the corridor, but stopped short and turned around. Jacob had moved to his own desk and stood leaning one hip against it. "Jacob, I'm sorry. I know you wanted this, but you've still got the story, and I expect you to follow it daily."

He nodded morosely, then met my gaze and offered me a resigned smile. "I'll be on it."

❊   ❊   ❊

I returned to Kingscote later that afternoon, after taking care of the day's business at the *Messenger*. After a short wait, Mrs. King met me in the library, a pleasant room papered in a soft blue-and-gray willow pattern, with a large bay window overlooking the west lawn. She wore deep plum today with a high, tight collar buttoned beneath her chin, and leg-o'-mutton sleeves of delicate silk crepe that fluttered as she moved. Her hair had been piled on her head and secured with numerous pins that winked when they caught the light. She looked imperious, but I realized it was no more than an illusion, a deliberate attempt to conceal her very real fears for her son's future.

"What may I do for you, Miss Cross? The detective was here earlier, and I doubt very much I can tell you anything I haven't already told him."

She bade me sit in one of several chairs placed near the Gothic paneled fireplace on the wall opposite the bay window. She offered me refreshment, but I politely declined. Once we'd both settled, I explained the plan to install Ethan at Kingscote as temporary butler. Before I left town, I had also telephoned Jesse, who had given the plan his tentative blessing on the condition that Ethan did nothing more than use his eyes and ears. I assured him the last thing Ethan would do was confront a murder suspect.

"Do you really believe someone besides my son might be responsible for my butler's death, and that the note you received wasn't merely a prank?" Her expression held a mother's desperate hope.

"I don't think it was a prank," I replied truthfully. "But whether or not it relates directly to Baldwin's death is something I'm hoping my reporter will be able to find out. The servants don't seem willing to confide in Detective Whyte about the nature of their relations with Mr. Baldwin, but they might talk more openly in front of one of their own. Secrecy is key, ma'am. Even your son and daughter must not know who Ethan Merriman is, or they might inadvertently give away his identity. He'll go by Edward Merrin."

"Yes, all right. You say he'll start tomorrow?"

We discussed the particulars of what Ethan could expect upon reporting to work in the morning. Mrs. King agreed to make sure his list of duties would be straightforward and easily carried out. Then I mentioned Francis Crane.

"I understand he was supposed to be at dinner the other night, ma'am."

"That's right. Don't you remember Philip saying his friend had decided not to come? Francis had gone to Stone Villa instead."

"He was at the hospital this morning, checking on Baldwin's condition, and was put upon by some townspeople."

She gasped. "But why would they do such a thing? And why would Francis be at the hospital? He barely knew Baldwin."

"Apparently he's worried Philip will be blamed, especially now that Baldwin has died. Unfortunately for Mr. Crane, he walked straight into a crowd of working people who feel your son should be arrested for the crime."

"Crime? Good heavens. Even if Philip did hit Baldwin with the automobile, he certainly didn't mean to. It was an accident—*if* he did it. But again, why should they harass Francis?"

"They'd have harassed any well-dressed man. They're angry about the injustice of a wealthy young man being treated with care when one of their own would be languishing in a jail cell."

Would she balk? I realized my comment might elicit a vehement response, but Mrs. King both surprised and impressed me by calmly nodding. "One can understand their argument, I suppose. It's simply hard, as a mother, to agree with them." She frowned. "But I still don't understand why Francis was there. What had he hoped to accomplish?"

"He said he felt guilty for not accompanying Philip to dinner that night, that if he had stayed with your son, Baldwin might be alive."

She took this in with very little reaction, except for a gradual tightening of her brow, and took several moments to contemplate what I'd told her. Then, quietly, "He seems frightfully certain Philip is to blame, doesn't he? That makes me wonder about his motives, Miss Cross."

"Motives? What do you mean, ma'am?" I schooled my features not to reveal my eagerness to hear her answer.

"I'm going to tell you something in the strictest confidence, Miss Cross. Francis has shown a keen interest in my daughter this season and wishes Philip to pave the way for an engagement between them."

She hadn't completely surprised me with this news, as I remembered how Philip had teased his sister about her "sweetheart" not showing up for dinner. "Is your son in favor of the match?"

"No. Unfortunately for Francis, Philip laughed away his request and told him such a thing would be impossible."

"Why impossible, ma'am?"

"Because of Francis's background. Philip told his friend he simply wasn't good enough for Gwendolen. You see, the Cranes were simple merchants not long ago. Francis's own father grew up learning the mercantile trade, but soon branched out into delivery services. Once he diversified into coal deliveries, his fortunes burgeoned. So you see, Francis comes from very new money and rather common origins."

I nodded my comprehension, but made no comment. Such views were the norm, of course, among the Four Hundred. It mattered not a bit that I didn't happen to agree. My own Vanderbilt relatives had until recently been shunned by society for the same reason, albeit they were now in their fourth generation of hardworking, innovative men. I very nearly pointed out that Francis Crane's family had sought to better themselves, while Philip, so far, showed no aptitude for adding to his family's wealth. I held my tongue, and in the next instant I was glad I had.

"For my own part, I'd have no complaint with my daughter marrying into a self-made family. But I didn't take issue with Philip's objections in this case because I fear Francis is of an undisciplined nature, not unlike Philip himself. It is so common, Miss Cross, among well-to-do families. Where fathers work themselves to illness and early death in order to achieve success, the sons are all too happy to embrace leisure and extravagant living." She sighed heavily. Her own husband had died suddenly five years prior, due to an inflammation of the abdomen. Although he had hailed from a prominent family, he had made a fortune of his own by joining his uncles in the China import trade. His son showed little inclination to follow suit.

"Has your daughter expressed an opinion on the matter?" I asked as delicately as I could, so as not to imply that Gwendolen King had anything to do with Isaiah Baldwin's fate. But a small part of me wondered—had she? Perhaps a way of getting back at her brother?

Mrs. King gave a little shrug. "Gwendolen doesn't seem to have strong sentiments either way when it comes to Francis. But you know how young men are. They are not to be put off by a girl's reticence. In fact, reserve and caution in a young lady is considered a sign of good breeding. Highly desirable in a wife. I believe Francis is still hopeful."

I took several moments to ponder what she had revealed, and the conclusion I reached unsettled me. "Do you believe Mr. Crane is intentionally trying to incriminate Philip? Would he go to such an extreme out of resentment?"

Some of the conviction left her features, leaving them slack and revealing her age. "It does sound rather outlandish when it's said out loud, not to mention highly vindictive. I'm not implying Francis wants my son to be convicted of murder. No, I don't believe he could be as cruel as that. But having Philip conveniently out of the way for a time might suit Francis's purposes when it comes to wooing my daughter. He may simply be taking advantage of an opportunity."

Perhaps. But suddenly both Francis Crane and Philip King appeared to have had motives for attacking Isaiah Baldwin. Had Philip pinned him to the tree trunk because of an overdue debt and the desire to prevent his mother from finding out? Or did Francis roll the car into the butler, believing Philip would be blamed and arrested? And if the latter case proved true, what might Gwendolen King have known about it?

Chapter 6

Afternoon was swiftly becoming evening when I left King-scote. After the long day I'd had, I yearned to turn my buggy south to Ocean Avenue, toward home and a hot cup of tea with Nanny and Katie. A niggling thought sent me in the opposite direction and I backtracked a short distance up Bellevue Avenue.

There were already three carriages parked on the short front drive of Stone Villa, a granite-trimmed Greek Revival mansion that stood across the street from the Newport Casino. This meant that the owner, James Gordon Bennett, had company, and I considered calling on him another time. He wouldn't be particularly happy to see me at any rate. I had worked for Mr. Bennett's *New York Herald* for a year, until my disappointment in my duties there had prompted me to resign my position. My decision had shocked him, and I'm quite sure he considered me an ungrateful, impertinent young woman.

But only he could verify whether Francis Cole had been at Stone Villa the night of Baldwin's death. Mrs. King had inad-

vertently put a thought in my mind, and there was no dislodging it until I'd asked some questions. If Mr. Cole indeed
bore Philip King ill will, how far *would* he be willing to go
to destroy his friend?

Mr. Bennett's butler had me wait in the sparsely fur-
nished receiving parlor on the first floor, while he climbed
the stairs, probably to the comfortable study where I'd spoken to Mr. Bennett the last time I'd entered this house. I
didn't expect to be invited up again. I heard men's voices
upon being admitted to the foyer, so even if James Bennett
hadn't been peeved with me, it wouldn't be at all proper for
me to enter into their society even for a few minutes.

The gentleman kept me waiting longer than was polite,
but this hardly surprised me. Did he think I'd grow frustrated and leave? No, he knew me better than that, and when
he finally entered the room, it was with a look of resignation.

"Miss Cross, what can I do for you?" With short-cropped
hair, a prominent nose shadowing his long mustaches, and
piercing eyes that seemed to accuse even at his most cordial
of moments, Mr. Bennett's countenance informed me my
time here was limited.

I came right to the point. "Was Francis Crane here two
nights ago, playing cards?"

"What if he was?"

"This is important. Surely you heard about the Kings'
butler."

"Are you suggesting Francis Crane had something to do
with it?"

"I'm merely trying to get a clear picture of the facts.
Mr. Crane was to accompany Philip King to Kingcote for
dinner that evening, but he didn't. Mr. King said he came
here instead."

"Have you joined the police force now, Miss Cross?"

It seemed he was determined to respond to my inquiries

with irrelevant questions. "No, Mr. Bennett," I replied calmly, "I have not. I am a journalist, as I have always been."

"You are sticking your nose where it doesn't belong, as you have always done." Despite the harshness of this pronouncement, he spoke with a chuckle in his voice, and those hard eyes of his warmed fractionally. He was teasing me, putting me to task for having spurned what he had seen as a generous offer of employment. He didn't realize, however, that I'd found being a society columnist in New York no more satisfying than being one in Newport, as I had been when I worked for the *Newport Observer.*

I tried again. "Mr. Bennett—"

"I suppose I won't be rid of you until I answer your question." Again, I recognized the teasing nature of his words. "Yes, Francis Crane was here until well into the night. Does that satisfy you?"

"And he never left your sight?"

He ran his fingers over one side of his mustache. "*Never* satisfied," he said more to himself than to me. "Miss Cross, there were nearly a dozen men in my drawing room that night, and it's impossible to keep that many individuals in one's sights at all times. All I can tell you is that Francis Crane was here, and that he left sometime after midnight. Now, are we quite finished?"

"One more question, Mr. Bennett, if you would. Did Philip King by any chance owe you money?"

He laughed, a short bark of a sound. "Who doesn't Philip King owe money to? Yes, Miss Cross, he enjoys his cards and horses and tennis tournaments as much as any man, and yes, money changes hands during those activities. Unfortunately, more of it leaves our dear Mr. King's grasp than otherwise. Now, if you'll excuse me, I really must get back to my guests. Good day."

On his way out of the room, he called for his butler to show me to the door.

I arrived home with my mind churning over Mrs. King's assertion that Francis Crane had reason to resent Philip King. I believed Mr. Bennett's claim that Francis had been at Stone Villa that night, but that still didn't mean Francis hadn't lied when he spoke of Philip's debt to Isaiah Baldwin. James Bennett had lent credence to this notion, however; it seemed it was Philip's habit to run up debts everywhere.

Nanny had a fish stew simmering on the stove, its savory aromas filling the house and greeting me in the front foyer like a favorite friend. It had another hour to cook, so she brewed a pot of tea, and she, Katie, and I sat around the kitchen table discussing the day's news. It didn't take long for us to settle on the topic on everyone's minds, that of Isaiah Baldwin's death.

Katie could hardly contain her excitement. "So it really looks like murder, Miss Emma?"

"The doctor saw evidence in the types of injuries he received, so yes. It's unlikely he died as a result of an accident."

"I don't know about Philip King, but I hate to think of that nice Mrs. King having to suffer seeing her only son hanged for murder." Nanny, like many of Newport's servants, knew Mrs. King by reputation as well as by sight due to her ongoing philanthropy here in town. She was among the more well-liked cottagers. "I hope someone else did it."

"Any word on where Mr. Baldwin worked before coming to Kingscote?" I asked her.

"Not yet, but give it time. I'll find your answer." Nanny sipped her tea, then set the cup on its saucer and stared into the curls of steam. "What about this Mrs. Ross?"

"Eugenia Ross?" I'd been about to drink from my own cup, but set it down, too. "What about her?"

"Well, she claims she's the rightful heir to Kingscote and the family fortune, so she has reason to wish ill on the Kings, doesn't she? And she was at the parade. She saw Philip driving the motorcar and probably heard about how he crashed it at the obstacle course. What better opportunity to harm the family than to push the motorcar into Mr. Baldwin and let Philip take the blame."

Katie gasped, her bright blue eyes becoming animated. "I'll wager she did it, Miss Emma."

I shook my head. "She'd have to have been following Philip around all evening to know when he arrived home."

"Maybe not," Katie said, clearly excited by the idea. "All she had to do was skulk about Kingscote and wait for him."

"But how would she have known the butler or anyone else would come outside at the right moment?" I reached for the teapot to refill Nanny's cup and my own.

Katie skewed her lips as she pondered that question. "Perhaps she didn't have an exact plan. Or perhaps she planned to damage the vehicle somehow, so that when Mr. King returned it to his friend, he'd have to pay for the damage. Mr. King was awfully rude to her at the parade, not that she didn't deserve it from what you said, Miss Emma. But then when Mr. Baldwin came outside, she quickly devised a new plan."

Nanny's eyebrows rose. "You know, Emma, that's not too farfetched."

I didn't agree. It *was* farfetched, yet nonetheless a possibility. The woman had spared no contempt toward the Kings at the parade. She had gone to great, almost impossible lengths to associate herself with William Henry King and had even managed to have him temporarily released from an asylum. To me, that implied a woman who possessed unending stores of bitterness, determination, and patience.

Another, more devious thought occurred to me. "Perhaps

her intended victim wasn't the butler. Perhaps she thought it was Philip who had come back outside."

"You mean she meant to murder Mr. King, Miss Emma?"

"The fog had settled thickly that night, Katie, so yes, she might have mistaken Baldwin for Mr. King." I drummed my fingers on the tabletop as I thought. "Or, perhaps Eugenia Ross came there to meet with Baldwin."

Nanny regarded me above her half-moon spectacles. "Why would she do that?"

"She's been trying to prove her claim to William King's fortune. Perhaps she had enlisted Baldwin's help in some way. She might truly believe she is the heir. A self-delusion, no doubt, but real to her. In that case, she may have paid Baldwin to search the house for any records that would prove her case."

"And her claims being false," said Nanny slowly as she puzzled it through in her mind, "Baldwin wouldn't have been able to find anything."

I nodded. "Which might have infuriated her to the point that she took revenge right then and there."

"Not only revenge, Miss Emma." Katie's excitement returned. Her complexion turned pink and her gaze darted back and forth between Nanny and me. "She would have wanted to silence him, wouldn't she, so he couldn't have warned Mrs. King about Mrs. Ross's latest plans."

"She might have at that, Katie." I traced the curving handle of my teacup. "Of course, this is all speculation. Eugenia Ross wanted me to write an article about her so-called right to William King's fortune, to tell her side of the story. I think I'll do just that. What better opportunity for me to ask the woman some pointed questions?"

"If any of these things are true, we're talking about an extremely unbalanced woman." Nanny rose and went to the stove to stir the pot of stew. The spicy aromas flooded the kitchen as she lifted the cover. "Will it do any good to tell you to be careful?"

"Nanny, when am I ever not careful?"

She snorted and covered the pot with a clank.

In deference to Nanny's concerns and in the interest of common sense, I contacted Jesse about my desire to question Eugenia Ross. He came to Gull Manor in the morning, and he and I discussed matters while strolling the perimeter of my property, a headland whose rocky borders teased the Atlantic Ocean.

"Why now?" he asked me after I'd explained my suspicions concerning the woman. He walked with his hands clasped behind his back, his derby angled low over his brow to shield his eyes from the morning sun. "She's been fighting the Kings in the courts for years now. And William King died two years ago. Why wait until now to take specific action against the family?"

"Haven't you heard?" Behind us, my aging roan carriage horse gave a snort. I glanced at him over my shoulder as he once again lowered his head to nibble on tufts of sedge and bluestem grasses, ripping the roots from the ground in loud tears. Barney no longer pulled my buggy; Derrick had gifted me with a handsome bay Standardbred named Maestro, young, sure-footed, and dependable. But I refused to part with loyal Barney, who had conveyed first my great aunt Sadie, and then me, to nearly every corner of Newport through the years.

A gust of wind slapped at my skirts and threatened to steal my hat and undo my coif. I raised my hands to protect both. Turning back to Jesse, I said, "Mrs. King is in the process of purchasing Kingscote outright from all of William's heirs. No one else seems to want it, except Eugenia Ross. She must somehow have gotten word of it."

"And she's angry." Jesse stooped to pick up a flat stone, and with a flick of his wrist sent it skipping over the waves. "Maybe angry enough to frame Philip for murder."

"Or to murder Philip," I said. "Visibility was low that night. She might have thought it was Philip who'd come outside."

I heard the slam of the kitchen door, and moments later my dog, a brown-and-white spaniel mix named Patch, came bounding across the headland toward us. He pranced around my skirts and then made friendly jumps at Jesse. Jesse accommodated Patch's enthusiastic greeting by crouching and administering a vigorous petting around his ears and neck and down his back. Patch's tongue lolled from one side of his mouth, and his tail, curled into a feathery crescent, wagged madly. In the distance, laundry basket in hand, Katie waved to us. I waved back to indicate that she needn't come and bring Patch back to the house.

Jesse shook his head and laughed as he straightened. "I wish everyone could be as happy as this little fellow."

We continued our stroll, Patch running ahead through the stunted, windswept vegetation before circling back in joyful leaps, only to set out ahead of us again.

"If not Mrs. Ross," Jesse said with a note of resignation, "we have Philip himself, John Donavan, or . . ."

"Francis Crane, who may or may not have been at Stone Villa all night," I finished for him. "And who seems to have a reason to wish ill on Philip."

"There is also Olivia Riley," he added, and reminded me, "she doesn't have a defined motive—yet—but she also doesn't have an alibi."

"Either John Donavan or Olivia Riley might have had enough of Mr. Baldwin's high-handedness. Perhaps he threatened to fire one or the other. I hope Ethan will be able to find out more. Derrick is preparing him for his first day as

Kingscote's butler. He's even supplying the letter of reference, for appearance's sake."

"That's good of him." Did I detect a twinge of sarcasm in Jesse's voice?

I hid a smile. "I take it you'll be looking into Philip's debts?"

"Of course. I'll be speaking to some of his friends."

"What of my plan to interview Mrs. Ross on the pretense of writing an article about her claims?"

Jesse drew a breath and let it out slowly. "She's taken rooms in a house on Rhode Island Avenue, not far from the hospital."

"Then I'll have to pay her a call, won't I?"

I stopped first at the *Messenger*, where I found a communication from Derrick. Ethan had arrived at Kingscote without incident and with very few questions so far from the staff. Having Mrs. King in on our deceit had been the right decision. I longed to hear the results of his infiltration into the household, but realized it could take days for him to learn anything significant. I only hoped he didn't lose his nerve and quit the position.

There was more from Derrick. He'd wired his personal secretary in Providence to do some checking on Mrs. Eugenia Webster Ross, and had discovered something interesting. The King fortune had not been her only goal through the years.

After seeing to the morning's business, I caught the Spring Street trolley, changing at Washington Square to continue up Broadway. Newport's Colonial saltbox architecture, so prominent in the center of town and on the Point, gave way to much newer and, for the most part, larger homes, many graced with front porches, gable rooflines, and even the occasional turret.

At Rhode Island Avenue I alighted and walked until I reached the address Jesse had given me. The house was a charming green clapboard trimmed in white gingerbread, with a hexagonal turret to one side, and a covered, semicircular front porch. Armed with the information Derrick had provided me with, I climbed the porch steps and pulled the bell.

An elderly lady opened the door, her blue-gray curls tucked beneath a lace cap whose floral design matched a lace shawl thrown loosely around her shoulders. I handed her my card, and she bade me wait in the center hallway while she climbed the staircase to the second floor. There she disappeared along a hallway, though I could hear the creaking progress of her footsteps toward the back of the house. Minutes passed, and then she reappeared and gestured for me to make the climb myself. We met in the middle as she made her way down, and she said she would send her girl up with tea.

Mrs. Eugenia Webster Ross met me at the door to her rooms, which comprised a small parlor and, through a wide doorway whose curtains had been drawn back and tied to either side, a bedroom. The rooms were bright and well-appointed with attractive furnishings and paintings whose scenes I recognized as local places of interest on Aquidneck Island. My impression of these lodgings, of the house itself and its elderly owner, was one of respectability and propriety.

Mrs. Ross wore a simple, three-quarter-sleeved tea gown of peach muslin and had pulled her dark hair neatly back from her face while allowing the rest, thick and wavy, to fall between her shoulder blades. She might have been any well-bred woman enjoying a quiet morning at home, except that her midnight eyes held a calculating look as she scrutinized me. Though not unattractive and her hair had not yet gone to gray, she was not young, was my senior by some twenty years, by my estimate.

For several seconds we stood silently taking each other's measure. Then she burst into a grin and extended her hand to me. "I am delighted to see you, Miss Cross." Her accent once again revealed her Southern origins. "Please, make yourself comfortable. You're going to be here a good while, I should think."

Chapter 7

"I was born in Port Gibson, Mississippi, to James and Mary Calhoun, and lived an unremarkable life while growing up. My father was in the cotton trade—not a plantation owner, mind you, but a merchant—and made a moderately good living at it, even after the war."

"Where did you attend school?"

My interruption seemed to disconcert her for a moment, and then her expression cleared. "My mother taught me my letters and figures, and I attended Miss Davis's School for Girls for a couple of years beginning when I was twelve. But getting back to what I was saying, it was because of my father's connections in commerce that I met my husband, Isaac Ross, who captained a steamboat on the river."

"When were you married, Mrs. Ross?" I held my pencil on the page of my notepad, ready to jot down her answer. But I'd already learned some much more important information: Mrs. Ross had received only a basic education. A knock sounded at the door. Mrs. Ross rose to admit the young maid, who brought in a tray of tea and cakes.

Mrs. Ross resumed her seat and reached for the teapot. "Where were we? Oh yes. My marriage. That was in 1876. But he died a mere two years later."

"I'm very sorry to hear that. What did you do then?" I set my pad and pencil on the small cherrywood table beside my chair and accepted a cup and saucer from her outstretched hand.

She offered me the sugar bowl and tiny silver tongs as she spoke. "My husband left me his modest savings and a small home. Cream?" At my nod, she handed me a pretty porcelain creamer in a colorful floral pattern. "And there was his boat, which I sold, of course. He'd owed money on it, unfortunately, and after paying off the debts I was left with enough, all in all, to live unpretentiously. Frugally." Her genteel façade fractured slightly, and she raised her teacup, in my opinion, to hide her expression.

I had learned only hours ago that she had done more than arrange to live off the monies her husband had left her, but I was content to keep that knowledge to myself for now.

She passed me a small plate holding a generous slice of pound cake. I broke off a piece with my fingers and brought it to my mouth. The sweet, buttery flavor melted on my tongue, nearly as delicious as Nanny's, though not quite. "When did you first seize upon the notion that William Henry King was your relative?"

"Seize upon?" Her eyebrows rising, she assessed me with an imperious look. "I seized upon nothing, Miss Cross. My relation to William King is simply a fact."

"All right, then. When did you first realize this?"

"I've always known it. My father used to speak of William all the time."

"And they were . . . ?"

She hesitated before replying, once again scrutinizing me,

searching for whatever trap I might be laying for her. "Let's just say they were cousins, of a sort."

"Of a sort," I repeated, hoping to prompt more.

"Indeed." Her lips curled in a catlike grin. "As you and the Vanderbilts are cousins of a sort."

"I can trace my lineage to the Commodore through his daughter, Phebe, who married James Cross. From there it's a very straight line to my father and then me." My challenge implied, I held her gaze. Could she offer up a similar pedigree for the King family?

Her mouth again took on a cunning slant. "Perhaps I cannot trace the line as directly as you can to the Commodore, but I assure you, my relation to William is undeniable. Whereas, Ella King, her husband, their children, and all the rest of this family who were so eager to lock William away and steal his money, are no relation at all."

My mouth fell open, my shock at her statement unfeigned. "You deny the relations of the entire family?"

"Oh, I don't deny they might be related to *a* William King." She paused to sip her tea, to nibble at her cake, while I waited in suspense. Then she continued, "But not to *my* William King."

"You're claiming there are two men of the same name, which I suppose is entirely possible. But the King family's history in Newport stretches back generations." Indeed, three generations ago, David King, a prominent physician here in town, had administered the first smallpox vaccines given in Rhode Island. His son, George, became a representative to the Rhode Island Assembly. George's sons, Edward and William, established an import company in China and amassed a great fortune. It was this William King whose identity was now in question, along with that of his relations.

"That is so," she agreed. "But these people who have invaded Kingscote, who have taken it over as though they have a right to it, are no relation to the man who bought the property from its original owner. As for the fortune, it rightfully belongs to me, not them."

"But, Mrs. Ross, how could so many people have conspired to wrongfully claim ties to a man if no relation existed? Especially when the family has such an illustrious history here in Newport and abroad? William King had brothers, and those brothers had children, who are adults now. They should know who their uncle was."

She dismissed this with a flick of her hand. "They should, shouldn't they? But you see, while there has been a King family in Newport for several generations, as you say, the William King to whom I am related, and who bought Kingscote, hailed from the South, as did the man who originally had Kingscote built, George Noble Jones. Mr. Jones left the North during the war, and afterward sold the house to my relative, William King. These Kings—these Newport Kings—then decided to take advantage of the similarity in names and have William King declared insane and locked away, to help themselves to his possessions and fortune."

Ah, there it was, her accusation against the Kings clearly laid out. But she had yet to define her relationship to William King. "You claim there might have been two men named William King. What happened to the other one, then? Where is he?"

"How should I know? That doesn't concern me." No, I didn't think it would; nor did I believe in this second, phantom William King she had invented. "What does concern me is that my cousin—"

"Of sorts," I couldn't help putting in.

She gave me a nod that seemed to say *touché*. "Of sorts, was deprived of his freedom and now these unscrupulous people are attempting to deprive his rightful heirs of their inheritance."

"Are there other heirs besides yourself? I hadn't realized."

At this she pinched her lips together, then lifted her teacup to them and sipped. She eyed me over the cup's rim, and I knew I would not receive an answer to that particular question. I decided to try a new angle.

"I've heard it said you searched for William King, your cousin, for many years before you found him. Is that true?"

"For a number of years, yes. I even followed him to Europe. We kept missing each other. William had possessed a bit of wanderlust in his soul. I'd no sooner arrive in his last known destination, when I'd discover he'd already moved on. It was this, along with his love of collecting beautiful artwork and personal items, that first prompted these Newport Kings to lay claim to him and have him declared insane. They wanted his fortune, and they wanted it before he had a chance to spend much more of it. It's a terrible thing, Miss Cross, to deny a man the right to spend his money as he sees fit. Wouldn't you agree?"

That the King family believed William's lifestyle to be a result of his mental incapacitation, I understood to be true. They considered him to have had no self-control, no powers of discernment when it came to how to spend his money. Apparently, they also feared for his safety, not only due to his reckless lifestyle, but to his inability to judge whether others intended him harm or wished to take advantage of him.

As I believed this woman had wished to do. Or was she so deluded as to believe her own story? I decided it was time to use the information Derrick's secretary had discovered.

"Mrs. Ross, I understand this isn't the first time you've attempted to secure funds for yourself where your rights to that money have come under question."

She took on a wary look, her black eyes flashing a caution. Was that caution aimed at herself, or me? "I'm sure I don't know what you mean."

"Didn't you sue your own father for money years ago?"

She gave a contemptuous laugh. "You've been listening to malicious rumors, Miss Cross."

"Perhaps. But it seems you do have cause to scorn the King family. Especially Mrs. King."

"Indeed I do. They've been unkind at best. They are thieves at worst."

Once again, I met her gaze, those eyes as black as a stormy ocean. "Do you scorn them enough to take revenge against them?"

She stiffened. "What do you mean by that?"

"Where were you the night an automobile struck Mrs. King's butler?"

"I have no experience driving motorcars, Miss Cross. Besides, why would I harm a butler?" Her laugh seemed to rise out of genuine amusement.

I answered her steadily and calmly. "So Philip would be blamed, as he has been. And the guilty party needn't have been driving the car. Sending it rolling with a good push would have sufficed."

Her amusement didn't abate. "Not a bad scheme, Miss Cross. I almost wish I had thought of it. But as it is, I didn't need to, because young Philip King is a drunk and he *did* drive his automobile into his butler."

"And you were where at the time?" I persisted.

She placed her teacup on the tray and came to her feet. "It's time you left, Miss Cross. I believed you came here in good faith to hear my side of a perplexing dilemma. Instead, you're practically accusing me of murder." She crossed briskly to the door and swung it open.

With no choice, I gathered my pencil, notepad, and hand-

bag and followed her to the door. Just as I was about to cross
the threshold, she said, "As it happens, I was at the Opera
House that night. Wait here." She retreated to the bedroom
and returned holding a strip of green paper. She held it up,
and I saw it was a ticket to the Opera House, torn in half.
"For a seat on the mezzanine. Satisfied?"

"Were you accompanied?"

"No. I went alone. But there were plenty of people who
saw me, I'm sure."

Perhaps, but would anyone remember a lone woman in a
crowd of hundreds? She might have arrived, taken her seat,
and later slipped out. How could I possibly track down
whoever sat near her? When she flashed the ticket briefly in
front of my nose, I happened to glimpse the seat number: E22.
Nodding my acknowledgment of her rather flimsy alibi, I
took my leave of her, far from satisfied. Which brought me to
my next stop.

The three-story brick building on the south side of Washington Square stood directly in my path on my way back to
the *Messenger*; thus it gave me the perfect opportunity to try
to verify Mrs. Ross's claims of having been there following
the auto parade. I alighted from the trolley and crossed the
square via the green with its benches, fountain, and statue of
Oliver Hazard Perry gazing down onto Long Wharf. The
Opera House would not be in operation this time of day, but
as I gazed up at its rows of arched windows beneath a steeply
curved mansard roof, I hoped for an unlocked door and a
ticket collector or usher who might remember Mrs. Ross.

The door yielded to my entreaty. I entered the long, wide
lobby, the plush velvet carpet cushioning my feet. To my left
ran a counter and the dark recesses of the cloakroom behind
it; to my right, between two wide round columns, nestled
the concession stands for refreshments. A deeply paneled and

gilded ceiling arched above me; two crystal chandeliers hung suspended from medallions. Neither was lit, but enough light poured through the glass doors and windows behind me.

"Hello, is anyone here?"

Receiving no answer, I continued through the arched entrance into the theater proper. Gas sconces burned dimly, giving off just enough light to see. Another pair of doorways led down into the aisles between the rows of seats. To my left, a staircase wound upward to the balcony. I peeked first at the orchestra seats, the rows pitched downward as one proceeded toward the stage. More gilding, elaborately carved, embraced the soaring opening around the stage and the box seats along the side walls. The stage was empty of set decorations. Mrs. Ross said she had sat on the mezzanine, so, failing to come upon anyone here, I retraced my steps and climbed the staircase. A firm hand on the banister guided me as the shadows thickened. At the top, however, I once again found sconces set at their lowest level, which provided enough light to see what I needed to see.

The mezzanine curved in a wide semicircle from wall to wall, and comprised two sections, one lower and one upper. I stood and studied the configuration, then walked through the rows, bending low to make out the seat numbers until I found the one indicated on Mrs. Ross's ticket, about halfway along the row. From that location, had Mrs. Ross attempted to leave at any time during the performance, she would have disturbed everyone around her. It might be possible to track down theatergoers who would remember such an annoyance, but it would not be easy. If Mrs. Ross had left during the intermission, no one would have noticed her absence at all.

Admitting the futility of my visit, I descended to the first floor, intending to make my way to the lobby and outside. Then I heard voices coming from the stage.

Suddenly, electric lighting burst over the orchestra section, startling me and drawing a gasp from my lips. I blinked in the glare. "Hello? Is anyone here?"

An odd squeaking came from somewhere backstage, and a moment later two young workmen entered the stage from one side, wheeling a long, open cart between them stacked with boxes. A third man entered after them and began issuing instructions and pointing. He was older than the other two, better dressed. I recognized him and walked down the aisle toward the stage.

"Mr. Manuel, hello."

He squinted to see past the stage lights. "Who's that? The theater is closed, you know. The box office doesn't open for a couple of hours yet."

"Mr. Manuel, it's Emma Cross. Are you moving in set pieces for the next performance?"

Elton Manuel, and his brother, Edwin, owned a local moving company, the Manuel Brothers. They had begun small, just the two of them, but now employed several workers and drivers, and moved many members of the Four Hundred in and out of their cottages each summer. It appeared they also serviced the Opera House, as Mr. Manuel nodded unnecessarily to my question.

"A new performance opens in two days. We're moving everything in today so the carpenters and set designers can get to work." He crouched at the edge of the stage and hopped down beside me. "Nice to see you, Emma. How is your family?"

"Very well, sir, thank you." At least, the ones I could account for were well. I'd had a telegram from my parents about a month ago. They were in Marseille with a group of other artists. My father had developed a passion for painting seascapes. But I didn't go into these details for Mr. Manuel.

He seemed more curious about me than my scattered family. "What brings you here at this odd hour of day?"

I debated whether to take him into my confidence, then decided I had no reason not to. "You've heard about the butler who died after being struck by an automobile?"

He nodded. "Terrible accident. They say Mrs. King's son probably did it."

"He might have, but there are some developments that point in other directions. Possibly even murder." He absorbed this with a surprised lift of his eyebrows. "I came here to see if a person could gracefully steal out and back in again during a performance."

"Who?"

"I can't tell you that. It's only a hunch I have."

"And how is it you're always involved whenever something like this happens in Newport? A slip of a girl like you."

I took no offense at the comment. Mr. Manuel was some twenty years my senior, and he had known me all my life. I had no doubt he still saw me as a little girl in short skirts chasing after my older brother, Brady. "I seem to have a knack for it. It's a skill that comes from working in the newspaper business. Besides, you know how the bureaucracy works. There are sometimes avenues I can explore that the police can't."

He nodded sagely. "I do understand. But tell me, what makes you think this person came and left, and then came back?"

"I assumed—" I hesitated, having almost said *she.* "I assumed the individual would have to cover his tracks."

"Mightn't he have waited till the intermission to arrive, instead of coming in before the start of the performance?"

"I hadn't thought of that. I saw a ripped admission ticket and assumed it meant the person attended from the beginning. But I suppose there would be someone checking tickets at the intermission, too. The shows typically start at nine o'clock." I thought a moment. "Which means the intermission would have been anywhere from ten to ten thirty." Which meant Eugenia Ross could have been at Kingscote earlier in the evening, pushed the Hartley Steamer into Baldwin, and had plenty of time to enter the Opera House during the intermission.

Later that day, I found myself beside Derrick in his carriage, a pair of horses conveying us north into Middletown. He had encountered James Bennett the night before, and had gotten more answers out of him about Philip King than I had, or more specific ones, I should say.

"Philip's got a passion for gambling on boxing," I mused aloud. "Is that a typical interest for wealthy young men? I've never heard Neily talk about it, nor his brothers, either."

"It's not a sport gentlemen discuss in front of ladies." Derrick turned his rig off the main thoroughfare that traveled the west side of the island and sent us winding along a series of lanes and country roads. We passed fields dotted with horses, cows, and sheep, the occasional farmhouse and barn, and a windmill whose sails flashed like gulls' wings in the sunlight. "It's considered too brutish and violent for a lady's sensibilities. I don't know why I allowed you to talk me into taking you along on this errand. Nanny, not to mention Jesse, will have my head."

We were traveling to a farm whose traditional use had long ago been abandoned in favor of the much more lucrative sport of boxing. The isolation kept the authorities away. While there were no laws against boxing in Rhode Island, all forms of gambling had been outlawed three years ago, and apparently the two went hand in hand.

I studied Derrick's profile while I considered his last statement. He knew better than to treat me as though I were delicate, and after a moment I saw his attempt to hide a grin. And yet, for the most part he spoke the truth. Men seldom talked in mixed company about anything they believed might upset a woman's equilibrium. "So it's a well-kept guilty secret."

"In the kind of polite society we're used to, yes. But not for the rest of the population. I wouldn't be surprised if a number of women attended the fights where we're going. Accompanied, mind you, but I've heard some members of your sex enjoy a good bout."

I scrutinized him again. He never turned to meet my gaze, which prompted me to draw a conclusion. "You've been to the ring, haven't you?"

His smile reappeared. "A time or two, yes."

"I hope only as a spectator."

"These days, yes. But I boxed a bit while at university, informally. I was on the rowing team, and boxing was considered a good way to keep up one's arm strength during the winter months."

"I see. Did you enjoy it?"

He thought for a moment, his jaw squaring. "At first, I suppose. There's something essential in such a sport, one might even say primal, that appeals to a man's more primitive instincts."

I interrupted him with a laugh I could not contain.

This time he turned to face me full on. "What's funny about that?"

"The idea of you as a primitive." Even as I spoke, I took in his broad forehead and patrician features, his tailored suit of clothes, his long-fingered hands. "I'm sorry, but it's a rather humorous notion, don't you think?"

"Then you consider me something of a dandy?" He sounded

flabbergasted, slighted. Uncertain. I hid a smile of my own and quickly sought to reassure him.

"No, not a dandy. Not at all." My amusement left me as I seriously considered the source of my regard for the man beside me. "You're far too intelligent to ever be considered a primitive. Too even minded, too self-assured, too willing to use your authority when it's needed and step back when it isn't, and you've the wisdom to know the difference."

He was silent a moment, his chest rising and falling on a deep inhalation. Then he turned back to me. "Flatterer."

I laughed again and wrapped my hands around his forearm, going so far as to lean against the warmth of his side. There was no one to see us on this country road, no tongues to wag about it later. He angled his head toward me, as far as our hats would allow, and whispered a thank-you.

Not long after, we turned onto a dirt drive, all rocks and ruts and dry dust that swirled in protest around the carriage wheels. At the end of the drive stood a barn, its red paint peeling to reveal the weathered boards beneath, its main doors spread wide as if beckoning us in. I was surprised to see several wagons, buggies, and a few saddled horses tied to a rail.

I felt a twinge of apprehension. "I didn't think there would be this much activity at this time of day."

"Probably the fighters are here practicing, sparring to ready themselves for the evening's matches." Derrick brought the carriage to a halt and set the brake. He stepped down and hesitated, looking up at me. "Are you sure you want to come in? You could wait here."

In reply I reached for his hand, and he helped me down beside him. "For whom are we looking again?"

"The man who manages the place is Tyson Dooley."

"Tyson Dooley." I nodded, squared my shoulders, and drew a breath. "Well then, let's go inside and find Mr. Dooley."

Derrick waggled an eyebrow and offered me his arm. As we stepped into the barn's interior, the dimness rendered me momentarily blind, and where I expected an onslaught of the scents of hay and hide and manure, I was instead enveloped by the odor of male sweat.

My vision soon adjusted. There were gas lanterns, large ones, illuminating a fighting ring—a raised platform surrounded by ropes—and rows of benches arranged on all four sides of the ring. Men were scattered along the benches, their attention on two men inside the ropes, each stripped to his long drawers, and shirtless, who appeared to be prancing in circles while facing each other. They held their hands, encased in leather, aloft before them.

I found myself momentarily entranced by the spectacle. Would they truly hit each other? On an intellectual level I knew they would; it was the whole point of the sport. But on some other level, an essentially female one, I supposed, the prospect of the fight—of pain and blood and injury—filled me with horror. With revulsion. And yet . . . I watched, unable to look away.

One man pulled back a gloved fist and thrust it at the other, who bounded a step backward and evaded the blow. He then leaped forward and swung, but while his opponent anticipated a strike to the head and blocked with his hands, the first man came at him from the side and delivered a blow to his ribs. Suddenly, both were swinging madly, their gloves thudding against bone and muscle, bodies shuddering from the impact, feet moving in a rhythm that would confuse the most accomplished debutant in a ballroom. Around the pair, the men on the benches surged to their feet, yelling out advice, groaning, swearing, and tossing punches in the air at invisible foes.

"We can leave," Derrick leaned to murmur in my ear. The prospect tempted me. Though I didn't shock easily, this display of brutality coupled with such a gleeful disregard for either fighter's physical wellbeing filled me with dismay and urged me to make a hasty retreat to our carriage. But we'd come for a reason, to discover more about Philip King's gambling habits.

Before I could answer, a voice sounded in my other ear. "What in damnation are you doing here?"

Chapter 8

❧

The voice startled me, to be sure, but I was not about to be put off. I turned to a man of later middle years, stocky, not much taller than I, with a fringe of silver hair showing below his battered, shallow-crowned derby. An unlit stub of a cigar protruded from the corner of his mouth, its aroma sharp and stale. He stared back without apology in expectation of our reply.

"Are you Mr. Dooley?" I asked him in as blunt a tone as he had used to address us.

"Who wants to know?"

In the ring, the fight, which had momentarily paused when this man barked his question at us, continued as if there'd been no interruption. The men watching soon lost their interest in Derrick and me as well.

I began to identify myself when Derrick stepped half in front of me and extended his hand. "Derrick Andrews of the *Newport Messenger*. This is my associate, Miss Cross."

Mr. Dooley sized us both up, looking none too impressed. He didn't shake Derrick's offered hand. "Well, get out."

"But, sir—"

Once again, Derrick spoke over me. "We're not here in an official capacity. We only want to ask you a couple of questions."

"There are two things we don't need around here, Mr. Andrews." Tyson Dooley snatched the cigar from his mouth. "Reporters and coppers. In my experience, all any of them want to do is kick up trouble for folks. Not that we're doing anything wrong here, mind you. Boxing's not illegal in the state of Rhode Island, last time I checked."

"Believe me, Mr. Dooley," I said, speaking this time before Derrick could, "we aren't here to scrutinize your activities or start any kind of trouble. Our questions have to do with a certain young man who we believe frequents your establishment on a fairly regular basis."

The man compressed his lips, his eyes narrowing. Then he opened his mouth with a pop. "And why would I want to infringe on the privacy of one of my patrons? You going to go telling tales to his wife?"

"He's not married," I informed him.

"Doesn't matter." Tyson Dooley gave a dismissive flick of his hand, the one holding the cigar. The bitter scent wafted beneath my nose. I resisted the urge to cough. "I'm sure you've got your reasons for asking your questions, but you see, I have no good reason to answer them. Excuse me, I have a business to run."

"Mr. Dooley." Derrick stepped in the man's path. Mr. Dooley's face reddened with ire, and I half expected him to either swing at Derrick or call for one of his fighters to intervene. He did neither. Instead, he smiled, but without a hint of humor.

"You want to ask me questions? All right, my dear sir. First you have to prove your worth."

An unpleasant feeling crept over me. "What do you mean?"

"I mean, if you want answers, you"—he pointed at Derrick with the end of his cigar—"will have to fight for them. You game?"

"Certainly not," I said with an indignant huff.

"Sure," Derrick replied at the very same time. I whirled to confront him.

"Don't be ridiculous. You cannot—"

"Does the lady always make your decisions for you, Mr. Andrews?"

To my complete dismay, Derrick unbuttoned his coat and shrugged his arms from the sleeves. His vest and necktie came next. Then he pushed his braces off his shoulders and removed his shirt, pulling the braces back over his sleeveless linen small shirt. Rendered mute with shock by this turn of events, I avoided gazing directly at him as he handed me each article of clothing, creating a small pile in my arms, topped by his homburg hat.

I stole a peek at him, and a burning tide of fascination heated my face. A dark fuzz of hair, not terribly thick, but there nonetheless, covered sinuous forearms and peeked from the neckline of his small shirt. His upper arms were smooth yet sculpted as sharply as stones. I wondered how a man who did no hard labor developed arms such as those, but he had already answered that question: rowing and boxing. I thought of those too-rare occasions when he had held me and I'd felt the strength and safety of his embrace. How I'd wrestled with what was proper and what, in my heart of hearts, I most wanted.

Finally, I pulled my gaze away from the objects that captivated me—astounded me—and found my tongue. "Derrick, please don't . . ."

"I'll understand if you don't wish to watch and would rather wait outside." He turned to Mr. Dooley. "Who will I spar with?"

"Let's see who wants to take you on." The man went over to the ring and made a general inquiry. The others debated who would take the "swell" on, and finally a burly, barrel-chested fellow stood up from one of the benches. A good head taller than Derrick, he wore the rough cotton and denim of a workman, the bulges in his biceps testing the soundness of his sleeves. After a steely look at Derrick, he began removing his shirt.

Derrick nodded, a small smile playing about his lips. "Good enough."

"Why, you're looking forward to this." A wave of incredulity, and with it anger, wiped away the last of my fanciful thoughts. Derrick was about to do something that could result in serious injury, and the foolish man acted as though it were a mere tennis match at the Casino.

I searched the space around me until I spotted an oblong wooden table along a side wall. I marched over to it and dropped Derrick's clothing onto its surface. When I turned back around I discovered he had followed me. I stiffened and glared up at him. "It appears I was wrong. You *are* something of a primitive. I've a good mind to not only walk out of this barn, but to take the carriage and leave you stranded here."

I expected my outburst to astonish him, but he came closer and spoke quietly, calmly. "Good, I'd rather you waited outside. Or if you wish to take the carriage, I'll find another way back. But please don't worry, I'm a fairly good boxer. I believe I'll come out all right."

"All right?" I gestured at the giant of a man waiting to enter the ring with him. "Do you see him? His size? He's obviously a man who uses his muscles to make his daily living."

"It's going to be all right, and once it's over Mr. Dooley will answer our questions." After bestowing a placating pat on my shoulder that very nearly had me spewing flames, he left me. He approached the ring and shook his opponent's hand. Tyson Dooley helped him into a pair of leather gloves, more like mitts, and then both men climbed between the ropes into the ring. On the benches, a murmur rose. I heard dollar amounts, odds, speculation.

Did I take the carriage and leave Derrick stranded? No, I did not. I did not even go outside. I stood rooted to the spot, my lips clamped shut, my trembling hands clenched together, my eyes wide.

Yet as the two men danced around each other and jabbed and ducked and swung, I gradually felt my fears abate and my fascination grow. I saw, not two men brutally attempting to injure each other, but a science, a strategy, an . . . art. My amazement grew as I realized Derrick, though not well-matched physically with his opponent, more than equaled the other man in skill. And in patience, too, for he rarely advanced on his rival but that his gloved fist made contact. Yes, there were moments when I turned briskly away, when the thudding of blows prompted me to cover my eyes, when I sucked in breaths of dismay. But there were many more moments when I looked on in admiration, reluctant at first to be sure, and then with a kind of odd elation that brimmed inside me.

"That's enough." Tyson Dooley went to the platform and pulled himself up between the ropes. I once again held my breath as he appeared to walk directly into the fray, holding up his hands. He spoke loudly and with authority. "That's enough, you two. I don't need Glenn here incapacitated for tonight's match, nor the swell leaving with a broken jaw."

Heaving and panting, Derrick and the man named Glenn each landed one final blow—by tapping each other's gloves—and stepped apart. Some ten minutes later Derrick had wiped away the perspiration with a borrowed rag and donned his shirt and vest. As I helped him on with his coat, I detected no bruising on his face, although I knew sometimes such discolorations took their time in appearing.

"You see?" he said. "I'm fine."

I pursed my lips and refused to let him see the depth of my relief. I even ducked away to prevent him from seeing the sudden tears that pricked my eyes. "Lucky for you."

Tyson Dooley sauntered over to speak with Derrick. "You handled yourself well, young man."

"Thanks."

"Wouldn't have thought you had it in you. But you never can tell with you swells. Boxed at school, did you?"

"A little, yes."

"I'd say more than little." Mr. Dooley chuckled and cuffed Derrick on the shoulder. "All right, what is it you want to know?"

Derrick buttoned his coat. "Maybe you heard about a death the other day. One Isaiah Baldwin."

The humor drained from Mr. Dooley's face. "Baldwin? Dead? No . . . I hadn't heard. Don't go in much for the newspapers. Don't go into town much, either. Neither do most of them." He jerked his chin toward the ring.

"You knew him," I said, rather than asked. Mr. Dooley nodded.

"He comes to watch . . . *used* to come to watch the fights," he said, his voice filled with questions.

"Baldwin was a boxing fan?" Derrick seemed taken aback, as I certainly was. "Did he wager?"

"Surely. Had a good instinct for picking winners, too. Often made himself tidy sums. But when he didn't, he took his losses like a man."

This certainly explained how a butler was able to extend

loans to his employer's son. Derrick and I exchanged glances, and I nodded to him. He said to Mr. Dooley, "What about a youth named Philip King? Do you know him?"

"King? Sure. He comes here, too. Pretty loose fisted."

"He boxes?" The notion couldn't have surprised me more.

"That wet-nosed pup?" Mr. Dooley shook his head. "'Course not. I meant with his cash."

"So he did a fair amount of betting." Derrick darted another glance at me. "Did he tend to lose much?"

"Much? Ha! Mostly all." His sympathy for Baldwin apparently forgotten, Mr. Dooley appeared highly amused by the turn the conversation had taken.

"Does he pay his debts?" Derrick asked.

"Eventually. Usually."

"Had he ever had a run-in with Isaiah Baldwin?" I asked.

"Not that I ever saw. Wait . . . there was one time, a couple of weeks ago. King asked Baldwin to front him the cash for a wager."

My pulse sped up at this bit of information. Derrick asked, "Did Baldwin accommodate him?"

"Don't think so. King was put out, sulked like a baby."

We understood the reason for Baldwin's disinclination to accommodate young Philip. The youth had already owed him money.

"Did Mr. Baldwin ever have a problem with anyone else here?" I asked, wishing to learn if the butler might have made other enemies.

"Baldwin? Not that I ever saw. Didn't mix much, though." He hooked his thumbs into his vest pockets. "Any more questions?"

"Yes, one," I said. "What about a young man named Francis Crane? He's a friend and a schoolmate of Philip King's. Does he come here with him?"

"Crane . . ." Mr. Dooley rubbed a hand along the back of his neck. "Don't know the name. But King does come in with his friends. This Crane could be one of them."

"Light brown hair, greenish eyes," I said, hoping a description might jog his memory.

He only laughed. "A body could have purple eyes, and I'd never notice." His face took on a more sober look. "There was one fellow, now that I think about it, who came in with King once. He didn't look too happy to be here, though. Not a boxing fan. King seemed disappointed about it, tried working up some enthusiasm, but it didn't seem to have any effect. Haven't seen him back."

"Could you describe him at all?" Derrick asked.

"Well dressed, clean, looked down his nose a lot. Beyond that, I couldn't say." Mr. Dooley shrugged. "As long as gents behave, I've got no reason to keep track of them. Now, if that's all, I've got things to do before tonight's bouts."

On the way back to Newport, we discussed what we had learned, avoiding the subject of Derrick's fight with the giant, Glenn. My anger had dissipated, but I thought perhaps it was better he didn't know that. I didn't wish to encourage him in any more acts of recklessness.

I studied the open, rolling fields we passed, bordered by tracts of forest. "Do you suppose the friend Mr. Dooley referred to was Francis Crane?"

"Hard to know without a description. We could ask Francis, but I don't see how it makes much difference. Sounds like Philip dragged him along hoping to have a fellow boxing enthusiast who perhaps might lend him wagering money when he needed it. It doesn't sound as though Francis Crane, or whomever Dooley referred to, was willing to play Philip's game."

"No, it doesn't. But we certainly have another link between Philip and Isaiah Baldwin, don't we? And not one that helps set Philip in an innocent light."

"If anything, it seems their squabble over money had become a continuing theme between them. I've seen it before, where a youngster whose parents slow his income to a trickle appeals to an upper servant for loans. The servant is afraid to anger the youth because in any argument, the parents are likely to side with their offspring, while the servant, even one as high up as a butler, is dismissed."

"Yes," I agreed. "Even considering his mother's disapproval of Philip's actions, Mrs. King would be more likely to defuse a situation by letting the butler go. She certainly can't dismiss her son." I held on to the seat as the carriage jostled its way along the dusty, weather-pocked lane. "And as for Francis Crane, his claim that Philip and Mr. Baldwin argued right before the incident is in keeping with what Mr. Dooley told us. Mrs. King suggested Francis was inventing stories out of revenge for Philip not furthering his friend's interest in Gwendolen. That seems unlikely now."

This drew Derrick's interest, and he angled his face toward me. "Francis Crane wishes to court Gwendolen?"

I nodded. "Don't you remember Philip teasing Gwendolen about her sweetheart not coming to dinner that night? Seems Francis wanted Philip to intervene on his behalf with Gwendolen, but Philip refused. He said Francis wasn't good enough." I further explained Mrs. King's theory of Francis wishing to have Philip out of the way for a time so he could press his suit with Gwendolen.

"Some friend," Derrick murmured as he faced the road again.

"Which one do you mean?"

"Neither of them score highly in that category. Not if what

you're saying is true. Still, one does feel sorry for Crane, basically being told he's tolerated by people like Philip, but will never be one of them. Never considered good enough."

Yes. I leaned my head back against the carriage seat. One could sympathize with Francis Crane, especially when one was in a similar position. As I was. Nothing could change my standing as far as Derrick's parents were concerned. Even in the unlikely circumstance that they came to accept me as part of their son's life, they would always look down on me, always consider me less than he deserved. There would always be a struggle between us, no matter how subtle.

And I wondered, would Derrick come to feel sorry for me, too?

"Is something wrong?" He took his right hand off the reins and touched the back of mine. "You look troubled."

I found a smile for him, and forced genuine sentiment into it. "I'm only thinking about what we've learned, and reconciling myself to the possibility that we might never have any good news for Mrs. King."

"Indeed, and that will be a pity. She deserves better."

She did. And so did I. But I saw no clear path to having what I wished *and* what I deserved: Derrick and a contented family life. It was a choice I had no desire to make.

The following morning, I again went in to work early. Derrick and I had informed Jesse of Philip's and Baldwin's ties to the boxing club, as well as my less-than-cordial conversation with Eugenia Ross and the alibi she offered. She had said she'd been at the opera the night Baldwin was hit by the motorcar, and she had showed me a ripped ticket. Now it was up to Jesse and his men to find witnesses to corroborate her story and prove she hadn't simply paid her fee and left. Perhaps she didn't murder Isaiah Baldwin, but this woman was no innocent, and certainly not someone whose word could be trusted.

The morning passed peacefully, or as peacefully as could be expected at a newspaper office. The presses rumbled smoothly at the back of the building, and our newsboys filed in on time to collect their bundles, some to be delivered to subscribers, the rest to be hawked on Newport's street corners. Just as I thought to dash out to the market several doors down to purchase something for my lunch, the street door opened and in walked a breathless Ethan Merriman.

I blinked at him in surprise. "Why aren't you at Kingscote?"

"I was, and I'm on my way back there now. But there's something you should know." He paused to catch his breath, and I motioned him to the vacant desk chair across the room from mine. He rolled it closer and sat. "Once breakfast has been served and cleared away, I have free time each day until luncheon. So does Olivia, the housemaid. I followed her into town."

"You followed her? I hope you had a good reason."

"I believed so, and I was right. She received mail yesterday and was awfully cagey about who sent it. You know how it is, Miss Cross. Letters always interest the whole household. Where did it come from? Is there anything important happening in the world? Any fearsome weather that might be headed this way? It doesn't matter that a letter contains personal messages, everyone wants the general news, and most people who get a letter are happy to oblige."

"So perhaps Olivia is a particularly private individual. Or there's an emergency at home." I rolled my fingers to signal Ethan to get on with what he had to tell me.

"She didn't act like there was an emergency. She went about her duties as cool as you please. But both the cook and her assistant were puzzled. They said Olivia is typically generous in sharing her letters from home. And, she gets them often. That's a bit unusual, don't you think?"

I shrugged. "Not necessarily. Is there more?"

"There is. This morning she was like a whirlwind, getting all her work done. And then she asked Mrs. Peake—that's the housekeeper—"

"Yes, I know."

"—for time to go into town this morning," he ran on as though I hadn't spoken. "Said she wanted to buy a few personal necessities."

"That's not odd."

He spoke faster, more urgently. "No, except that she rode the trolley all the way to Washington Square and headed straight to the Western Union office. Luckily she never noticed me hop onto the trolley after she did. She rode in front, I stayed at the back. At Washington Square I stood by the Western Union window and peeked in. She was sending a wire, and by the length of time she was inside, I'd say she sent money. And then she ran back up the square to catch the trolley back across town."

"Ethan, there's still nothing unusual in any of this. Perhaps she simply didn't want the others to know her business. Many servants wire money to their families. It's often the reason they take a position, to help the family."

"Then why lie about it? She didn't shop as she said she planned to do . . . I say she's hiding something . . ."

His enthusiasm nearly had me laughing. Was this the same individual who only a couple of days ago trembled at the thought of posing as a butler? Perhaps my society columnist had missed his true calling of becoming a police detective.

I didn't laugh, however. I didn't even smile. Ethan had embraced his role, and if I thought he was going about it with a bit too much zeal, I couldn't simply dismiss his suspicions out of hand, especially since the note I'd received indicated that one or all of Kingscote's servants had borne a grudge against the butler. "Ethan, there isn't enough evidence to alert the police about Miss Riley, but continue to watch her. Watch the others as well. And talk to them. Be a lenient and agreeable superior to invite their confidence." I frowned at a thought. "I hope Miss Riley didn't see you following her."

"I don't think so. I was careful to stay well behind her, and at the Western Union office she never turned around to look out the window. If she did see me, it's easily explained by my having business of my own in town."

I sent him on his way with a reminder that he not attempt to confront a suspect, but merely observe. Before today I wouldn't have thought the caution necessary, but apparently we had awakened in Ethan an investigative spirit that raised my concerns for his welfare. Suddenly I understood every scowl and shake of the head Jesse had turned my way these past few years. Perhaps I owed him an apology. Or a basket of Nanny's luscious baked goods.

Speaking of Nanny, when I arrived home that evening, she had news for me.

"About Baldwin?" I eagerly removed my hat and gloves and laid them on the hall table.

Her cunning smile supplied my answer. "Come into the kitchen. Jane Meeker is here."

"Jane Meeker?"

"She's the new housekeeper at Rough Point." Nanny filled me in as she led the way through the house. "She used to be head housemaid for the Morgans at Beacon Rock. She recently talked to their cook, who told her about the new footman, Gregory, who worked for a short time for a family called the Hendersons in Bristol . . ."

"Nanny, please."

"Patience, my lamb." She affected a wounded air and sniffed as we entered the kitchen. Sitting at the large round table was a slim woman whose dark hair, streaked with silver, was pulled into a neat bun at the nape of her neck. She wore a housekeeper's typical black broadcloth and sensible, low-heeled boots.

"You must be Emma." She rose from her seat and extended a fine-boned hand to shake mine. Her fingers were long and slender, more the hand of a musician than someone who had come up through the household ranks. "I'm Mrs. Meeker, but please, call me Jane. Mary has told me so much about you." She referred, of course, to Nanny, whose full name was Mary Reeve O'Neal.

"It's lovely to meet you, Jane. Nanny tells me you have news involving a footman over at Beacon Rock?"

"Not so much about him, as the goings-on at the Henderson home in Bristol. Mary explained all about your quest to learn where Mr. Baldwin worked before Kingscote. According to Gregory, the Hendersons employed a butler by that name until about two years ago. Do you think it is the very same man who lost his life the other day?"

"Isaiah Baldwin isn't the *most* common name, is it?" I felt a thrill of excitement at our first lead about where the butler had worked prior to coming to Newport. His references had indicated he'd worked for the Hill family in Cranston. A lie, apparently. "Did this Gregory know Isaiah Baldwin personally?"

"I'm afraid not. He started at the house right after Baldwin left, but he heard tales from the other servants. One of those tales included a kitchen maid who was let go—without a reference, mind you—after becoming in the family way. Everyone at the house believed Baldwin was the father. And then *he* was let go, although the Hendersons supplied him with a reference and told the rest of the staff he'd resigned to pursue other opportunities."

"Assuming this *is* the same man, he told Mrs. King something very different and presented her with forged references," I said. "He obviously didn't want the Hendersons ever to be contacted, nor anyone else from that house."

"No, because he had a lot to hide, from the sounds of it," Nanny agreed. The kettle began spurting jets of steam. She brewed a pot of strong tea and brought over a platter of oatmeal-raisin scones, her own grandmother's recipe.

I mulled over Jane's information as I savored a bite and washed it down with a draft of tea. "This kitchen maid. Did Gregory know where she went?"

"No idea." Jane Meeker raised her eyebrows and blinked several times, as if at an unpleasant sight. "Where do such girls go?"

"We know the answer to that question all too well, don't we, Nanny?" I stirred a bit more cream into my tea. Through the years, first under my great aunt Sadie's patronage, and then mine when I inherited this house, Gull Manor had provided a temporary haven to young women who found themselves in trouble and abandoned. I wished this poor child from the Hendersons' household had found her way to my front door. More likely she had gone to Providence in hopes of working in a factory, only to have been dismissed yet again once her condition became apparent. After that . . . I shuddered and pushed the thought away.

At the same time, I wondered . . . "Nanny, do you think it's this kitchen maid who sent me the note? She might have found a way to keep track of Baldwin."

"Note, what note?" Jane took on a look of keen interest.

Nanny ignored Jane's question and met my gaze. "More to the point, could she be responsible for what happened to him?"

Good heavens, first Ethan and now Nanny, talking like seasoned, cynical police detectives. But she had echoed my own thoughts, although I silently took the notion a step further. Could the kitchen maid and Olivia Riley be one and the same?

Chapter 9

Later that same evening, I heard from Ethan again, this time on the telephone. "She was here, Miss Cross, that woman who claims to be William King's heir."

I propped one hand on the wooden telephone box and leaned closer to the mouthpiece. "Eugenia Ross?"

"Yes. She knocked at the front door just as bold as you please." Ethan spoke in an undertone. He was no doubt using the telephone in the butler's pantry. Even with the door closed, he would wish to take precautions against eavesdroppers. "You can't imagine my astonishment when I opened the door to her."

"Did you allow her in?"

"I didn't know what else to do, so yes, I bade her enter the foyer and hurried to find Mrs. King. What a brave woman she is, Miss Cross. She went right down the stairs and stood face-to-face with that Mrs. Ross, though she did not invite her into the parlor to sit."

"No, I would imagine not. What did they speak about?" I didn't bother asking *if* Ethan knew what they discussed; I knew very well he had lingered within earshot.

"Mrs. Ross mentioned another court date set to determine William King's true heirs. It'll be in September. Mrs. King didn't sound at all surprised, not until Mrs. Ross said there'd be a doctor from the Butler Hospital in Providence who would come and attest to Mrs. Ross's rightful claim on the King estate." He left off a moment, and I could hear him catching his breath. "Do you think there's any truth to it?"

"That this doctor will prove her claims? No, Ethan, I don't, but it's possible Mrs. Ross believes it, and that's nearly as troublesome as if it were true. Did you hear this supposed doctor's name?"

"She never said it, and neither did Mrs. King ask."

No, Mrs. King would not have shown any interest in such a matter, for then Mrs. Ross would know she had unsettled her foe. "It does sound as though Eugenia Ross has a new trick up her sleeve. It's merely a bluff, I'm sure, but perplexing all the same. When will the woman cease her nonsense?"

"You don't suppose"—Ethan paused for the length of a breath—"that there's anything to her claims, do you?"

"Absolutely not." I neither hesitated nor wavered in my certainty. Yet, I sympathized with Ethan's doubt, however fleeting it might be. Confronted by someone who simply refuses to give up often leaves one wondering about what's true and what isn't. But in this case, Eugenia Ross's claims were beyond absurd. "There are simply too many members of the King family who were part of William King's life for decades. They can't all be lying. Have you learned anything else?"

"No, not since I saw you this afternoon. But I'll keep watch, don't you worry."

"I've no doubt about that, Ethan. Thank you, and do remember to be careful."

After disconnecting I remained in the alcove beneath my staircase to make a couple of necessary calls. The first was to Derrick, who agreed to the impromptu plan I relayed to him. Then I asked the operator to connect me with the police station.

"Goodness, is everything all right out there by you, Emma?" Concern poured over the wire to me from Gayla, Newport's main daytime operator. "You're so isolated from town, I worry about you."

"You may set your mind at ease, Gayla. Everything is fine out here. This is more of a personal call."

"I see. Looking for Jesse, are you?" Like me, Gayla had lived all her life in Newport and knew just about every other soul who had grown up here as well. Added to that, Gayla was something of a busybody and loved to hear all the town gossip. Not that she possessed a mean-spirited bone in her body. I liked Gayla very much, if she often taxed my patience by asking a host of questions each time I wished to make a telephone call.

I decided, however, to satisfy her curiosity this time. "Yes, I am. There's been a development in the death of the butler—surely you heard about that."

"Of course I did. I read about it in the *Messenger*. So shocking, a man being mowed down by a horseless carriage. I'm all for progress, but not when it poses a danger to ordinary folks going about their daily lives."

"Indeed, Gayla. Now, the police station, if you would . . ."

Jesse wasn't in, but I left a message for him. I went to bed soon after, and rose extra early in the morning. Once again I raised the ear trumpet and cranked the telephone to rouse the operator, a different woman at that time of the day. Once connected to the *Messenger*, I let Dan Carter know I wouldn't be in until much later and that I couldn't be reached until then. He assured me all was well with the presses. Nonetheless, a wisp of guilt tugged at my conscience that I would be missing nearly an entire day's work.

After stabling my horse and carriage in town, I met Derrick at Long Wharf, where we caught the first ferry leaving the island. In Newport's shipbuilding past more than a hundred years ago, those ferries would have been large and piled high with goods intended for the seafaring coastlines of Rhode Island, Massachusetts, Connecticut, and destinations farther flung. Now, that type of merchandise, along with ships themselves, were manufactured on the mainland, while most of what Newport produced remained here for local use.

The craft Derrick and I boarded was small in comparison to those long-ago freighters, although quite a number of other travelers squeezed in around us. This particular route took us around Jamestown and on to the mainland, where we disembarked and secured transportation, in the form of a public coach, to the train depot in North Kingstown. We purchased two tickets to Providence. Determined to find out more about Mrs. Ross's connection to William King, we settled in for the ride.

The hired carriage conveyed us north past the city proper to a wooded area along the Providence River. I began to worry the driver had taken a wrong turn, when we came upon a wrought-iron fence that bordered the road, leading to a set of wide gates. They stood open, and we passed through them. A long, sweeping drive, lined with large potted trees—palms, of all things—stretched before us, leading to a brick edifice whose soaring four-story main section was flanked by two shorter sprawling wings. Gothic arches above the front door and around the bay windows, along with several gabled peaks, lent the building an austere, decidedly grim aspect.

But no, I had seen such details on residences without the chill that raced down my arms now. My impression of the place—dark, lonely, inscrutable—had less to do with its architecture than my knowledge of who and what the Butler

Hospital for the Insane harbored within its walls. At least I detected no iron bars across the windows.

"Ready?" Derrick turned to me with an uncertain smile that told me he shared my qualms. At my nod, he opened the carriage door and stepped down, then offered his hand.

"Wait here for us," he said to the driver, and we went to the main door.

We were stopped immediately upon entering the foyer by a formidable desk that stood directly in our path, manned by an equally formidable-looking secretary. With craggy shoulders straining his coat sleeves and a high, bony forehead that reminded me of a ram's curving horns, this man left little doubt as to his ability to keep out unwanted intruders while preventing patients from leaving.

"Welcome to the Butler Hospital." Despite his appearance, his tone issued a cordial welcome. "Have you come to visit one of our patients?"

"No, sir." Derrick and I stepped up to the desk. Derrick explained, "We'd like to speak with a doctor—"

"Ah," the man interrupted. "Which one?"

"We don't exactly know." My admission earned me a frown. I hastened to add, "A doctor who was here while William Henry King was a patient. Mr. King is deceased now, so you wouldn't be betraying patient confidentiality."

"King, you say?" He studied us carefully. Apparently finding something trustworthy in our appearance, he nodded. "Wait here." Rising, he called into an adjoining office, whereupon another man, thinner, younger, but with a confident air, came and took the seat behind the desk. The balding secretary nodded to him, to us, and disappeared down a hallway.

He reappeared some minutes later followed by an older gentleman in a frock coat, his extensive beard and muttonchops obscuring the front of a stiff, stand-up collar and simple black necktie. He held his pocket watch in his hand, a signal that our time with him would be limited.

He came around the desk to greet us. "I'm Dr. Winston. How may I help you?"

"Thank you for seeing us, Doctor." I stepped closer to him and held out my hand. "I'm Emmaline Cross, and this is Derrick Andrews."

Dr. Winston stared at me as though I'd sprouted horns, taking me aback. He shook my hand weakly, offered me a tepid smile, and turned his attention to Derrick. "I'm quite familiar with your name, Mr. Andrews. Are you here on behalf of your family's newspaper?"

"No, nothing like that." Derrick reached out to shake the doctor's hand. "We have a few questions about William King and a woman named Eugenia Ross, if we might have a few minutes of your time."

"Are you relatives of Mr. King?"

"No," I said. "But we're both well acquainted with his relatives in Newport, especially Mrs. Ella King. We are here on her behalf." A slight stretch of the truth, perhaps, but I didn't wish to be turned away before learning what we could about William King's last days and, more importantly, his relationship to Mrs. Ross.

"I see." Once again, the doctor scrutinized me as the beginnings of a disapproving scowl crept across his aging features. "Let's walk outside. I've had a long morning and could use the air. Miss Cross, perhaps you'd care to wait here in the lobby, where you'll be out of the sun and more comfortable. Perhaps a cup of tea?"

He rendered me momentarily speechless. Then I found my tongue, though I tempered the words I wished to speak. "I don't require tea, thank you, Doctor, and I'm quite happy to walk in the sun."

Dr. Winston shrugged. Derrick offered me his arm and we all three stepped outside. The doctor led us along a path that ran parallel to the front of the building where well-kept shrubs and flowerbeds brought a sense of cheer to the grounds.

"Did you know William King well, Doctor?" Derrick asked.

"I did indeed, Mr. Andrews. An interesting case. The man often seemed as sane as you or I."

"Then why was he here?" I knew the answer, yet I wished to hear it in this man's words.

"He was here because he needed to be." Dr. Winston gave a distinctly condescending chuckle. "My dear Miss Cross, the human mind is a complex thing. Too complex, certainly, for a lay person to understand."

"Try us," I couldn't help challenging him.

He chuckled again. "Suffice it to say the insane can be frightfully clever. They are often able to fool others by appearing completely rational and under control."

"But perhaps such people are sane, Doctor." I knew I was antagonizing him but was unable to help myself. "Perhaps they merely suffer from the occasional bout of melancholia."

"William King suffered from much more than that, I can assure you, my dear Miss Cross."

I felt a slight warning pressure from Derrick's hand where it lay over mine, before he said, "Had he ever posed a danger? To himself or anyone else?"

"Not exactly a danger, not physically at least."

"Then how?" I persisted.

The doctor sighed at my tenacity. "His inclinations bordered on recklessness. Do you realize that before he was committed, he disappeared into Europe where no one could find him? Simply disappeared without a word and was gone for months."

"Is that insanity," I asked, "or merely a wish not to be found?"

Dr. Winston appealed to Derrick with a frustrated glance, which Derrick, bless him, thoroughly ignored. "During that time"—the doctor sighed and went on—"he went through untold thousands of dollars. Had he not returned to America where his family could intercede on his behalf, he might have spent his entire fortune."

"But isn't that a man's prerogative?" I struggled to control my own frustration. "He earned his fortune in the China trade through his own efforts. Why must he answer to anyone else for how he spent it?" A terrible realization stole over me. While Mrs. Ross might not have had William King's best interests at heart, his family might not have acted selflessly either. Had they merely sought to conserve their relative's fortune for themselves? I thought of elegant Mrs. King, her daughter Gwendolen, and the charitable work they did each year in Newport. I couldn't imagine either of them so greedy as to deny a sane man his freedom. But what about the rest of the family?

They had all along denied Eugenia Ross's claims and called her an opportunist. And that was probably true. But, had she perhaps forged an arrangement with William King— a generous reward in exchange for helping him regain his freedom?

"Miss Cross, I'm afraid I don't have the time to explain the exact nature of Mr. King's dementia. You'll simply have to trust me when I say he needed to be here."

We reached a corner of the building, where the path turned to bring us toward the rear of the property. Here, patients and attendants were walking on the lawn, and beneath the branches of a towering elm tree, several patients sat together on benches.

"Now then, Mr. Andrews," the doctor said, "I believe you have some specific questions you'd like to ask?"

He spoke as if my queries were of no importance. My ire grew by the moment, sending the hackles rising at my nape. He also raised my fears. Not for myself, but for the female patients under his care, for he obviously felt little or no regard toward members of my gender. If he didn't find me competent enough to engage in a simple conversation, how might he judge a woman brought here by her family as a means of disposing of her? It happened more frequently than anyone would care to believe. Husbands wishing to be rid of their wives, fathers frustrated by their daughters' headstrong ways, brothers unwilling to share inheritances with their sisters, found an easy solution by convincing a doctor to declare her insane. Here, I suspected, was one doctor who wouldn't need much persuading to consider any woman incompetent.

However, for the sake of our errand, I decided to hold my tongue for the rest of the visit and let Derrick do the talking.

"I understand," he was saying, "that William King was brought here from the McLean Asylum in Somerville, Massachusetts."

"That's correct," said the doctor. "He didn't spend much time here. Not quite three years, I believe."

"And was the reason for his transfer his near escape from the McLean Asylum, aided by Eugenia Webster Ross?"

The doctor linked his hands behind him as he strolled. "That is also correct, Mr. Andrews. It was determined, by Mr. King's family as well as by the authorities, that the McLean Asylum had become lax in their security. The staff there claimed they were faced with a court order produced by Mrs. Ross and an associate of hers appointed by the court as a representative for Mr. King, but they should never have allowed the patient out of their sight. As a matter of fact, an emergency court order, initiated by the family, had him returned within hours."

To have achieved freedom, only to lose it so quickly and without an opportunity to prove he deserved to be at liberty . . . how crushing, how despairing that must have been for him, whether he had been truly insane or not. William King had spent decades incarcerated, however gently, for it was said he filled his rooms with luxurious furnishings and ordered the best food for his meals. Still, to languish behind walls while the spirit withered away year to year . . . I couldn't imagine it.

"And what can you tell us about the woman herself?" Derrick's question snapped me out of my musings. I waited while the doctor pondered his answer.

At length, he said, "Not an unintelligent creature. Certainly persistent."

"Yes," Derrick agreed, "we'd already figured that out for ourselves, simply judging by her actions through the years. But did she disrupt the hospital with her visits? Did she unsettle the patient? Was she argumentative?"

"Ah, I see what you're getting at. For the most part, no. There were no outbursts, no threats or demands made of the staff. She gave us no reason to bring her own sanity under question, although to tell you truly, I did often wonder."

"How so?" I asked, disregarding my own aversion to the man.

"Isn't it obvious? Her claims were outlandish. Only a diseased mind could have conceived of such a scheme and stuck to it for so many years. Yet, without a family member or legal authority registering a complaint against her, we had no cause to hold her here under observation."

I found myself, oddly, cheering for Mrs. Ross. "Then you are not intending to testify at an upcoming hearing on behalf of Mrs. Ross's claims."

The man sniffed. "Certainly not."

Derrick's gaze wandered to a large, well-muscled man in a shabby dressing gown and an equally muscular attendant who exited the building through a nearby door. They strolled together across the grass. Rather, the attendant strolled slowly while the patient picked his way along, his arms held out to his sides as if he feared he might stumble. "Did she visit him often?" Derrick asked.

"Quite a lot in the beginning. Less as time went on, though

she never entirely abandoned him." The doctor pushed out a grim chuckle. "Rather, she never abandoned her hopes of taking possession of him, and thereby his money."

The man in the dressing gown, his thinning dark hair gone wispy from the breeze, had begun walking in circles, taking short staccato steps in a pattern that seemed vaguely familiar. He kept up a steady stream of mumbling, as well. His attendant stood aside and watched with a bored air, indicating this was something that happened regularly. Perplexed, I studied the man's movements as the doctor's and Derrick's words faded from my ears.

"I'm afraid that's all I can tell you," Dr. Winston was saying when I pulled my attention back to him. "Is Eugenia Ross sane? Probably not, not completely. Is she dangerous? She had never shown any sign of it here, but she is singularly intent on a specific goal. In my experience, such an individual, when faced with untold obstacles, can be all too willing to go to great lengths to achieve the desired end."

"Thank you, Doctor." Derrick held out his hand, and the other man shook it.

"I must be getting back to my patients. You can see yourself back to your carriage, yes?"

He didn't wait for a reply. Extracting a set of keys from his coat pocket, he walked away and let himself into the building through one of several rear-facing doors.

"Well, I don't believe that was worth the trip up here." Derrick let out a disappointed sigh. "We haven't learned much we didn't already know. We didn't even learn whether Mrs. Ross might be capable of violence. Emma?"

I was barely listening, my attention focused once again on the man in the dressing gown. Derrick stepped closer to me and murmured, "What is it? Do you know him?"

I shook my head. "Look at the way he's moving . . ."

Frowning, Derrick joined me in studying the patient's odd dance.

Dance. "I know what it reminds me of." I set out across the lawn until I reached the man in the dressing gown and his attendant. Pasting on a bright smile, I said, "Hello. How are you today?"

Up close, I saw he was not a young man, his face scored by the lines of middle age and something more. Sadness. Tragedy. His dancing steps didn't cease as he regarded me. "Getting ready for the big fight tonight."

I allowed my smile to widen, though I knew there could be no truth behind the man's words. Not now, not in this place. But I said, "Are you? That's wonderful."

"Must be ready." He held up his hands and curled them into fists.

"Where is the match?" I asked to keep him talking as long as his attendant allowed it. At any other time this patient would have earned my sympathy, to be sure, but I very much doubted I would have been drawn to him in this way. But now, having been to the boxing club in Middletown only yesterday, I found it an extraordinary coincidence, one I could not ignore. Footsteps thudded through the grass behind me. Derrick appeared at my side, his brow furrowed.

Without warning, the patient lunged at him. Instinct sent me backing out of the way, while Derrick held his ground. Before the man could take another step, his attendant moved swiftly in front of him and seized his forearms. "Steady there. That's not your opponent, Harry. That's just a visitor."

"Visitor?"

"That's right, champ. Just came over to say hello." The attendant gradually loosened his hold on his charge, and finally released him. "Steady now, Harry?"

The man nodded. "Steady now."

"Harry . . . champ . . ." Derrick murmured. His eyes narrowed and his lips moved silently before compressing. Then, "Dear God, is that Harry Ainsley?"

I moved back to his side. "You know this man?"

"Heaven help him." Derrick swallowed. "I know *of* him."

Chapter 10

"Yes, he's Harry Ainsley," the attendant confirmed. "Been here nearly ten years."

"I don't understand." I appealed to both Derrick and the attendant. "Who is he?" Then, realizing we were talking about the man as if he couldn't hear us, or as if he weren't there, I gazed back at him. "Who are you?"

"Harry," he said with a grin. He formed his hands into fists, holding them up but making no move to use them. "The Hawk."

"The Hawk," I repeated, and he smiled broadly, nodding. My heart dropped as I realized his was the mind of a child.

Derrick's hand touched my sleeve. "Harry Ainsley was a fighter, a good one, well on his way to becoming an East Coast champion. Fought mostly in Providence and Boston, although if I remember correctly, he was on his way to Madison Square Garden to fight the greats. Never made it, though."

"What happened?"

Harry Ainsley had resumed his dance, striking the air

with his fists in short, sharp jabs. The attendant positioned himself between his charge and Derrick and me. He said, "He was put in a coma during a fight, and when he woke, he was like this."

"Good heavens. What happened to the other fighter?"

Derrick shook his head. "He was fine apparently. He disappeared. You see, this wasn't an official fight. This was at one of the backstreet clubs where amateurs could challenge each other to make a little money. A lot of it was bare-knuckled street fighting. But not this fight. They used gloves, which were just beginning to be used at the time."

I didn't understand what he was getting at. "Don't gloves make boxing safer?"

"Not at first. If anything, they made matters worse," he explained.

I shook my head. "How so?"

The attendant held up his fists. "The gloves not only protect the hands, they dull a man's sense of how hard he's hitting. Because he doesn't feel the pain in his knuckles, you see." He gestured toward Harry Ainsley. "Nowadays there are rules about where and how many times a man can be punched in the same place before the referee steps in. In *that* fight, Harry was knocked senseless and then some."

I shook my head, still mystified. Derrick said, "Harry suffered a barrage of punches to the head before the referee could stop the fight. His opponent practically had to be pried off. Harry had lost consciousness well before he hit the floor. They didn't think he'd live."

"From what I've been told, it was a miracle he did," said the attendant. In the next moment, he shrugged. "On the other hand, not such a miracle. Not what anyone would wish for. But back then, no one realized what kind of difference gloves would make, and they were late in changing the rules." He glanced back at the patient. "Too late for Harry."

My throat tightened as I contemplated this poor man's loss. "Did no one hold the other fighter accountable?"

Both the attendant and Derrick shook their heads. Derrick said, "He entered under a kind of stage name, the Bald Eagle, if I remember correctly from the articles my father ran in the *Sun*. But nowhere had his true name been recorded. Those amateur clubs were like that."

"Besides, the other fighter really didn't do anything wrong," the attendant pointed out. "Not legally, anyway. It was the rules that were wrong."

With mounting sadness, I regarded Harry as he resumed sparring with the air. "Have you worked with him long?"

"Only these past two years. I came here from another hospital. Because of my size, I was given the responsibility of taking Harry out for his daily exercise."

Derrick studied Harry's movements. "Does he often become combative?"

"Not usually. But sometimes when he encounters another man he doesn't recognize—not one of the doctors or orderlies—a man like yourself," he said to Derrick, "he goes off a bit. Nothing I can't handle. You saw how fast I calmed him."

"What a terrible fate," I murmured.

"He's not alone," the attendant surprised me by saying. "It happens more than most people realize. Maybe not this severely, but when a man gets knocked senseless over and over again, it takes its toll. I've seen it before."

My opinion of the sport of boxing, already low, plummeted farther still. Several words sprang to mind: *ridiculous*, *foolhardy*, *childish*, to name a few. I kept them to myself, for while my ranting might allow my anger some release, it wouldn't change Harry Ainsley's condition.

"We should be going," I said quietly. "Thank you for speaking with us—" I broke off as one more question occurred to me. "This is a private institution. Who pays for his room and board?"

"Family, I would imagine," Derrick said, but I doubted that very much.

"Do the sons of wealthy families become boxers?" I observed, rather than asked. The attendant shook his head.

"Back in the day, Harry had several wealthy patrons who took pity on him. Set up a fund to pay for his needs. Good thing, too, because he doesn't have any family."

A hollow sensation formed in the pit of my stomach. "No one?"

"If he does, they don't come to visit."

How tragic. How deplorable to be locked away and forgotten. It at least gladdened me that this attendant seemed to care about his patient, and his ability to calm Harry Ainsley indicated that they had established a kind of rapport. I gazed at the manicured grounds, and then up at the brick building with its Gothic architectural features and lack of barred windows. I thought about the report Nellie Bly had written about the asylum on Blackwell's Island. Harry's life, I believed, could have been worse. Much, much worse.

Derrick and I arrived at the *Messenger* by late afternoon. At first, his desire to accompany me there surprised me, and I began to explain that my work would keep me occupied a good while, until I remembered the newspaper belonged to him and he had every reason to be there.

As it turned out, we didn't settle in for long. I had no sooner opened the sales ledger to view the morning's revenues when the telephone on the wall summoned me with a sharp jangle. Upon raising the ear trumpet and letting the caller know he or she had reached the *Messenger*, a breathless and familiar voice came over the wire. "Miss Cross, this is Gwendolen King."

My surprise could not have been greater. Although I spoke fairly regularly to my Vanderbilt relatives on the contraption—one of which my uncle Cornelius had installed at my home—members of the Four Hundred typically did not make telephone calls. Rather, they adhered to the tradition of sending calling cards to the homes of their friends, letting them know they could expect a visit during "morning calls," which actually occurred after lunch.

"What may I do for you, Miss King?"

"Can you come out to Kingscote?"

"I . . . suppose so, yes. When might be a convenient time?"

"Is now too soon?"

Good heavens. "Has something happened? Has your brother . . ."

"Philip is still locked in his room. No, this has nothing to do with him. But I don't wish to speak of it on the telephone. Please, will you come?"

"Of course. I must do one or two things here and then I'll be on my way."

We disconnected and I hurried through the offices searching for Derrick. I found him in the typeset room, watching as an afternoon extra was prepared for the press. Drawing him aside, I quickly explained my cryptic call from Gwendolen King. Minutes later we exited the building on Spring Street and walked toward the harbor, to Stevenson's Livery on Thames Street to retrieve my horse and carriage.

Afternoon traffic clogged the roads coming into town and slowed our progress, but since Kingscote sat near the Newport Casino, we didn't keep Miss King waiting long. Another carriage sat on the circular drive not far from the front door, a gleaming, lacquered two-seater with plush leather seats, its top down, harnessed to a beautifully proportioned bay horse who dozed where he stood.

"Someone is here," I said unnecessarily. "I wonder if this visitor has anything to do with Miss King's call."

"We'll find out momentarily."

As we stepped down, the front door opened upon my society columnist, Ethan Merriman, in his formal butler's attire. At the same time, a man in brown tweeds and a shallow derby came striding around the house and asked whether Maestro needed tending. He spoke to Derrick, and seemed nonplussed to discover the horse and carriage were instead mine.

"He's fine where he is," I said. "Thank you."

The man, sinuous and not much taller than I, his mutton-chop sideburns grizzled a deep iron hue, tipped his hat. "Very good, miss."

He started to walk away, but I stopped him with a question. "Are you Mrs. King's full-time groom?"

He turned back and removed his derby as he addressed me. "I'm her *only* groom, miss."

"And you were not here when Mr. Baldwin's accident occurred. Is that right?" I could feel Derrick's puzzled gaze on me. Jesse had already verified the man's alibi for the night, yet I had my reason for asking again. Ethan, too, waited at the front door with a perplexed expression, probably wondering how long I would require him to hold the door open for us.

"That's right, miss. I was visiting my family."

"Oh. And where do they live?"

"Up Broadway, miss, just past the Middletown line."

Which meant most of his business would have been conducted in Newport. I got to the point. "I've lived in New-port all my life, and you aren't familiar to me, sir. Not very much, at any rate." Perhaps I had seen him in town a time or two. Surely we had never before spoken.

His eyes registered surprise at my use of the term *sir*. It was simply my habit to treat others respectfully, regardless of their occupation.

"I'm from Tiverton originally, but I came with the Kings up from Washington when they took over the house a few years back. My family moved here to the island when they inherited a house from a great uncle of mine."

"That would explain it, then." Or at least well enough, I supposed. Jesse had said not only the family, but some of the neighbors had vouched for the man's whereabouts the night of Baldwin's attack. Seeing his unfamiliar face had made me leery nonetheless. I held out my gloved hand to him. "I'm Emma Cross. I run the *Newport Messenger.*"

If I had taken him aback by addressing him as sir, I'd dumbfounded him by introducing myself and offering to shake his hand. He fumbled a moment before briskly wiping his hand on his trousers. "Brian Farrell, miss."

I let him get back to his domain in the stables at the rear of the property. As Derrick and I walked up the path to the door, where Ethan continued to wait for us, I murmured, "What do you think? Is he telling the truth?"

"Don't you trust Jesse's instincts?"

"Jesse didn't interview him. One of his uniformed officers did. As soon as I saw him I knew he couldn't be a local New-porter."

"Do you know every single soul who lives within these borders?"

"If they were born and raised here, yes." While Derrick chuckled at that, I turned my attention to Ethan. "Sorry to keep you waiting."

"I questioned the groom, too, as a matter of fact." Ethan closed the door as we stepped inside. He took Derrick's hat. "I could have told you his family was new to the area. There are his parents, an unmarried sister, and an elderly aunt. Farrell's mother's sister, I believe."

"Good work," I said. "Is Mrs. King at home?"

We spoke in whispers. Apparently neither Miss King nor anyone else in the household were aware yet that Derrick and I had arrived, and I wished to put these few minutes to good use.

"No," Ethan replied, "she's attending a luncheon this afternoon."

Which perhaps explained Gwendolen King's insistence that I come immediately. Whatever she wished to discuss with me, she must not want her mother knowing about. "Has something happened here today?"

Ethan looked puzzled. "Nothing that I know of. Why?"

"This isn't a social call," Derrick told him. "Miss King telephoned the *Messenger* and asked Miss Cross to come right over."

Ethan glanced up at the staircase. Seeming satisfied there was no one to overhear, he said in a rush, "I don't know anything about that, but Miss King has been acting awfully strange. She's always following me about. I've even caught her peeking around doors more than once. Her and her friend, Miss Wetmore."

"Maude?" I said.

Ethan nodded.

"Is that Maude Wetmore's carriage on the drive?" Derrick gestured in the general direction.

"No, that belongs to Francis Crane."

My eyebrows went up. "How long has he been here?"

"About an hour. Been here nearly every day since the whole to-do happened."

"Sounds like our Mr. Crane is taking advantage of a situation," Derrick said, referring to the young man's desire to court Miss King. "While Philip is locked away, Francis will play."

"Philip *has* remained locked in his room, hasn't he?" I asked.

"He even has his meals there." At a thud from upstairs, Ethan glanced up at the stairwell again and hurried on. "His mother isn't taking any chances."

Derrick frowned. "That he tries to make his escape?"

"No," said Ethan. "That he doesn't do anything stupid that will incriminate him further."

I changed the subject to one I deemed more urgent. "Have you been able to learn anything significant about the servants? Most especially John Donavan and Olivia Riley?"

Ethan raised an eyebrow and nodded. "The rest all seem very straightforward, except for those two. John Donavan disappears into his quarters above the carriage house for hours at a time. When I tried engaging him in conversation a couple of times, he made excuses and hurried away."

Derrick made a dismissive gesture. "Not everyone has the desire to make idle conversation."

"No," Ethan agreed, "but it's more than that. Just this morning the groom was searching for him to ready Mrs. King's carriage for her travels through town today. Farrell went to the carriage house, and I could hear him pounding on Donavan's door for some minutes before he got a response."

I pondered that before concluding aloud, "Do you think Donavan was in there drinking?"

"Heaven help him if he's driving Mrs. King around town while intoxicated." Derrick formed a fist and tapped it at the air.

Ethan shook his head. "That's what I assumed, but when

he came down, he appeared perfectly lucid and steady. It's very odd."

"And Olivia Riley?" I asked, once again changing the subject, knowing our time was limited.

"I find the number of letters and wires she receives highly unusual."

"Telegrams, too?" This *was* unusual. Telegrams were expensive and generally reserved for emergencies. How would the family of a housemaid be able to afford such communications frequently? More importantly, what was so urgent it couldn't wait for a letter to be sent through the mail? "Have you asked her about this?"

Before he could reply, a woman called down from the top of the stairs. "Merrin, do I hear voices? Has company arrived?" A ruffled hem bordered with lace appeared at the turn in the staircase. By the time Gwendolen King had finished speaking, she had descended the steps fully into our view. "Good, you're here, Miss Cross. And I see you've brought Mr. Andrews."

This seemed not to perturb her in the least. Derrick bobbed his head to her. "Good day, Miss King. I hope I'm not intruding."

"No indeed, Mr. Andrews." She descended the rest of the way to the Stair Hall and extended her hand first to him, and then to me. "Thank you both for coming." Her cordial expression cooled with annoyance. "Merrin, I hope you haven't detained my guests longer than necessary. Why didn't you let me know immediately that they were here?"

"We've only just arrived," I said hastily.

"Yes, well." Her mouth tightened in disapproval. "Merrin, please go up and ask Miss Wetmore to join us in the north drawing room. And then have tea brought in. After that I wish you to attend to the inventory of the picnic silverware. Mother hopes to have her outing as soon as matters are resolved, and if anything has gone missing she'll need to know now."

Ethan did his best to hide his dismay at the prospect of counting untold pieces of cutlery. "Yes, miss."

Miss King issued him a final, silent rebuke as she gathered Derrick and myself on either side of her and walked us through the first drawing room and into the second. "Along with my friend Miss Wetmore, Mr. Crane is here as well." I detected a note of impatience at this second pronouncement.

"Will he be joining us for tea?" I asked, wondering if whatever Miss King wished to tell me involved that young man.

"No, I shouldn't think so. He's just gone to my brother's room. Our housekeeper, Mrs. Peake, will let him into Philip's room and stand guard until he leaves. Then she'll lock the door again."

I searched for signs of distress as Miss King divulged this information to us. Was she distraught over her brother's confinement? She showed no sign of it. Rather, she almost spoke with relief, and I couldn't help wondering if it was because with Philip locked in his room, he could come to none of his usual mischief. Drinking, gambling money he didn't have . . . these activities must have sorely taxed his mother's and sister's patience.

We made ourselves comfortable while Gwendolen King passed several minutes remarking on the weather and the number of people who had descended on Newport for the summer Season. The floor-to-ceiling windows had been slid open to admit a temperate, slightly salt-laden breeze. Miss King seemed in no particular hurry to get to the point, and I had the distinct impression we were waiting . . .

With brisk steps, Maude Wetmore crossed the adjoining room as though driven by a sense of purpose. I found her to favor both of her parents equally, possessing her mother's genteel refinement and her father's forthright determination. From both George and Edith Wetmore, she had inherited a keen intelligence and a disinclination to suffer fools. She and I had butted horns subtly several years ago, and I had come away with a healthy respect for the woman, one year my senior. And I, it seemed, had earned her regard as well.

As Maude greeted us and took her seat, the footman named Clarence entered from another doorway that led through the back of the house to the kitchen. As soon as he'd set a tray of tea and refreshments on a side table, Miss King dismissed him, then waited another moment. Once she could no longer hear his footsteps, she peered into the other drawing room.

"Please, help yourselves." She motioned to the tea tray. Her gaze pierced my own as she spoke in a hurried whisper. "Miss Cross, Mr. Andrews, my friend and I have reason to believe our new butler, Merrin, is not who he says he is."

"Oh . . ." This announcement took me utterly by surprise. I darted a glance at Derrick, who had schooled his features not to reveal his thoughts. I hoped my own attempts proved as successful. "What made you reach such a conclusion, Miss King?"

It was Maude Wetmore who replied. "He doesn't know the first thing about a butler's duties. He's all thumbs and he's constantly referring to any number of cue cards he carries in his pockets. He's a fraud, and that's the truth."

Miss King nodded at her friend's assessment. "I fear he might even have had something to do with Baldwin's death." Her eyes opened wider. "A scheme to take over the position, perhaps."

"Miss King, do you really believe a man would commit murder for a butler's position?" Derrick rose from his seat and went to the side table. He began pouring tea and handing cups to each of us, followed by the sugar bowl and creamer. "That's rather extreme, wouldn't you say?"

"Who am I to judge what lengths to which someone will go?" She accepted the teacup from his outstretched hand and selected a lump of sugar from the bowl. "The position is a coveted one among those in service, isn't it? No one is higher up than the butler, except possibly the housekeeper."

Her mention of housekeepers gave me an idea. "Have you consulted Mrs. Peake about this? Perhaps she has an opinion as to Merrin's qualifications." I wondered if Ella King had taken her housekeeper into her confidence concerning Ethan's identity and his reason for being here. Although Mrs. King had promised to keep our secret, I understood her house-keeper to have been with her many years, and whenever Mrs. King traveled, Mrs. Peake accompanied her. Obviously a deep trust had grown between them. "Perhaps Merrin hadn't served as a butler very long before coming here. Which could explain his lack of expertise. He is quite young, after all."

"With that taken into account," Derrick said before either of the two young women could reply, "is he really doing all that badly?"

"Yes," the two friends said simultaneously.

Derrick passed me the platter of sponge cake. I selected a small slice. "And have you spoken to your mother about this, Miss King?"

Maude spoke up first. "*I* urged Gwendolen to call the de-tective. What is his name?"

"Detective Whyte," Miss King supplied. She turned an anxious look on her friend. "That won't do, Maude. And no, I have not consulted my mother. I don't want her hearing of this. Not yet. Not until we know more. It would alarm her overmuch. That's why I telephoned you, Miss Cross, and why I'm glad you came along as well, Mr. Andrews. With your newspaper experience, you are both well versed in the art of investigation."

"I'm not sure what we can do to help you," I began slowly. "We could perhaps speak with Mr. Merrin, but beyond that . . ."

"You could search into his background, couldn't you?" Miss King shook her head to Derrick's offer of cake. "He could be a criminal for all we know. And Baldwin's killer. I tried asking Mother where she found him, but her answer was so thoroughly convoluted I could not attempt to repeat it to you. Something about Mrs. Astor's lady's maid's daughter's brother-in-law who works for the Berwinds, who knew Merrin's uncle . . . and so on."

I bit back an urge to laugh, and across from me, Derrick ducked his head in a similar attempt. So often, when Nanny tracked down details through her connections to Newport's servants and beyond, the path the information took sounded much like Miss King's description of Ethan's references. With a hand over my mouth, I pretended to cough. Once I'd brought my mirth under control, I said, "Truly, Miss King, I'm sure this young man is harmless and merely new to the responsibilities of a butler."

"What if that's not so? What if he's dangerous?" Miss King clutched her hands in her lap. "What if he murdered Baldwin?"

A doubt rose up to shadow my original resolve of keeping Ethan's identity a secret. I had reasoned the fewer people at Kingscote who knew the truth, the better our plan would work. Not that Miss King couldn't be trusted, generally speaking, to keep a secret. But I knew how easily a revealing word could slip out, however unintentionally. Still, I saw how this was distressing Miss King and sending her imagination on a riotous course.

With a sigh, I appealed silently to Derrick, who gave the slightest of nods. "Miss King, there's something you should know. You see—"

Heavy footsteps pounded above our heads. There came a deep shout of, "You will not, by God," followed by a woman's shrill threat to call the police.

Chapter 11

Gwendolen King turned white. After setting aside her teacup with a slosh, she jumped up from her seat. "What on earth?"

She scrambled from the room, the rest of us quick to follow. The argument upstairs continued, and though less threatening than the initial outburst, three voices—two men, one woman— carried an intensity that sent us charging up the staircase. The landing opened onto a large square gallery. Derrick made his way to the front of our little group and proceeded toward the sounds of the scuffle.

Philip King, Francis Crane, and Louise Peake, the house-keeper, stood outside a bedroom at the far side of the gallery. Although their shouting had ceased, the two men had each other by the fronts of their attire—Philip's shirt and vest, Mr. Crane's coat lapels. Each held bunches of fabric in his fists as they played a strange tug of war. Mrs. Peake was attempting to separate them by use of both vocal commands and shoves at their shoulders, but they weren't cooperating. In fact, I doubt they noticed her. They were both red faced and practically snorting like bulls. Derrick strode to them and added his efforts to the housekeeper's.

"Gentlemen, and I use the term lightly, what is going on here?" His tone demanded an immediate answer. Gripping each man firmly by the shoulder, he forced the pair apart. "That is quite enough."

The command proved unnecessary, for as they stumbled backward, they involuntarily released each other. Derrick moved between them and held up the flats of his hands, one at either man. "What the deuce prompted you two to behave so swinishly in a house where ladies reside?"

Mrs. Peake, a woman about Mrs. King's age, sighed with obvious relief and backed away to stand near Gwendolen and Miss Wetmore. Her agitation hadn't fully abated, and her bosom rose and fell with each labored breath. Clearly their behavior had left her shaken. Philip King noticed the rest of us hovering beyond Derrick and raised a hand to point.

"It's because of her—Gwennie—that I'd like to wring his neck." Philip started toward Francis again but Derrick stopped him with thump to his chest.

"What do you mean, Philip?" Without hesitating an instant, Miss King went to stand before her brother and set her hands on her hips. "How can you possibly think I'd want you to threaten Mr. Crane, or any guest in our home?"

"He doesn't deserve to be in our home." Philip's chin went up in a show of defiance.

His sister fanned her hand back and forth in front of her face. "You've been drinking, Philip, haven't you? That's why you're not making any sense. Mr. Crane is your friend. You've no business treating him in such a deplorable manner."

"Don't you wish to know why he's here?" Philip countered.

"He came to visit you, you dunderhead." Her voice started to rise. She paused a moment to calm herself. "But I do have one question for him. Mr. Crane, did you bring my brother liquor?"

"I most certainly did not, Miss King. I wouldn't disrespect you or your mother that way. Isn't that true, Philip? Why don't you tell us where you got your brandy?"

The question drew our curious stares to the young Mr. King, who shuffled his feet and pressed his lips together.

His sister poked his upper arm. "Well? If it wasn't Mr. Crane, who? Was it one of the servants?"

"It was no servant under my supervision, I can tell you that." Mrs. Peake spoke with wounded dignity. "And if I find out someone has been sneaking alcohol up to this room, it will be the last thing they ever do in this house."

"No, I don't suppose any of the servants would take such a chance." Miss King's countenance fell as her bravado failed her. "He probably had it hidden somewhere in his room. Is that it, Philip?"

The young man shrugged and angled his glance away, but only for a moment. When his gaze returned to her, it was with a burning intensity. "Beware of him, Gwennie. Yes, I believed him to be my friend, but it's not *my* friendship he seeks. He's reaching above himself. Thinking he can—"

Miss King held up her hand. "Philip, please, don't say such things."

"He's not good enough for you, Gwennie."

"I think it's time you returned to your room," she snapped. She turned to the housekeeper. "Mrs. Peake, you have the key?"

"I do, Miss Gwendolen."

"Well then." Miss King turned away from her brother and returned to her friend's side. Miss Wetmore slid an arm around her waist, and Miss King did likewise. As one, the pair turned and retreated across the gallery. Mrs. Peake remained, but moved off to a respectful distance, her key at the ready. Francis Crane hesitated.

"I'm sorry, old man. Didn't mean to stir up trouble for

you. Just wanted to see how you were doing, try to cheer you up and all that."

Philip shook his head slowly, his eyes narrow slits. "Liar. You're here for Gwennie, but it won't work. She has no inkling you want her, and do you know why?"

Francis Crane only shook his head, prompting Philip to chuckle.

"It's because she couldn't conceive of tying herself to the likes of you. The idea would be so outlandish as to never cross her mind."

"We'll see if I'm good enough or not," Mr. Crane said softly, but not so softly that I didn't hear him. But even if those two simple words weren't enough to prove Philip's point, what Ella King had confided to me previously led me to believe Philip's claim and suspect Mr. Crane's motives for coming to Kingscote today.

Which was not to say I didn't feel a certain sympathy for Francis Crane. If his intentions toward Gwendolen were honorable, why shouldn't the pair be given a chance to discover whether or not they suited each other? I understood social barriers better than anyone, and I also believed that an intelligent woman like Gwendolen King could make such decisions for herself.

"Leave my sister alone, Francis." Philip pivoted on his heel without waiting for a response from his friend, reentered his room, and shut the door behind him with a bang. Mrs. Peake moved swiftly to relock it, then proceeded along the corridor, presumably to the servants' staircase. Francis Crane brushed past Derrick and me. We lingered a moment before following him downstairs.

Along the way I whispered, "I wish we had been able to speak privately with Philip, but I don't suppose he'd be in a mood to answer our questions."

"No, I don't suppose so. Besides, what might he tell us that he didn't already tell Jesse? He's claimed innocence and hasn't wavered. We know where he was that night. We know he drank heavily all day and drove the motorcar that hit Baldwin. And we also know that when he entered the dining room, he behaved as if he hadn't a care in the world."

"None of which proves his innocence." We reached the turn in the staircase, draped in shadows. Derrick stopped me.

I looked up at him in silent question. He dipped his head and brushed his lips across mine, then pressed deeper in a warm and sensual kiss that left me rather giddy. Bemused, I gave a little gasp, a quick inhalation to replace the breath he'd stolen from me. He eased away, smiling, and touched a spot of moisture on my bottom lip with the pad of his thumb. "Shall we?"

As simple as that we continued down to the Stair Hall, to be greeted by the others in the front drawing room.

"I'm terribly sorry about that, Miss King," Francis Crane was saying. "I want you to know what he said isn't true. I merely wish to support you and your mother during a difficult time."

I glanced at Derrick, who quirked his lips in doubt.

"Yes, Mr. Crane, and thank you." Gwendolen extended her hand to him, which he took in his own. "Philip's accusations are terribly embarrassing, for both of us. I'm sure it's the alcohol talking, and that if my brother were in charge of his faculties he'd never say such things. But it's not the first time, as you may be aware."

"Yes, I am. I'd always chalked it up to teasing, but now . . ." He sighed.

Derrick and I remained in the Stair Hall, where we could hear but not yet be noticed by the others. I could make out Miss King's face only in profile, but I had a full view of Miss Wetmore. Her expression had turned wary, her features rife

with speculation. If Miss King gave Francis Crane the benefit of the doubt, I fully believed Miss Wetmore did not.

I returned to Kingscote sooner than I could have imagined—the very next day—and it was another telephone call
from Ethan that brought me there. This time, however, I
went in through the servants' entrance rather than the front
door.

Mrs. Peake admitted me with a shrewd look that made me
wonder if she had learned of Ethan's and my roles in the investigation. However, she said nothing and brought me directly to the butler's pantry, where I discovered Ethan sitting
at his desk, peering at the housemaid, Olivia Riley, who
perched stiffly in a hard-backed wooden chair. Unlike my
own fiery-haired maid-of-all-work who also hailed from
Ireland, Miss Riley possessed wheat-blond hair, pulled severely back beneath her linen cap, green rather than blue
eyes, and not a freckle to be found anywhere on her fine-
boned face. Jacob had termed her pretty. This was the first
time I'd ever seen her, and for a brief moment I found myself
envying her porcelain beauty.

Ethan stood when I entered the room. Miss Riley glanced
up in surprise, but also in unhappiness at whatever situation
had brought her to Ethan's pantry. Ethan wasted no time in
getting to the point. Mrs. Peake had followed me inside and
closed the door, heavy oak with a large frosted glass window.

"I caught her rummaging through Baldwin's room," Ethan
announced without preamble. Resuming his seat behind his
desk, he explained for my benefit, "It hasn't been cleared out
yet, and I've been assigned a smaller room on the third
floor."

"What excuse did she give for being in Baldwin's room,
Mr. Merrin?" Louise Peake, dressed in somber black punc-
tuated by a stark white collar and cuffs, folded her arms

across her bosom. "I've a right to know. The women servants do fall under my jurisdiction."

Ethan waggled an eyebrow at her, as if to say she had shirked her responsibilities. She seemed to read his meaning, for her nostrils flared and she stood taller. "She said she was cleaning the room," he replied.

Mrs. Peake stared down at Miss Riley. "Now, we both know that's a lie, don't we, girl? I've given you no orders to clean that room."

The girl took her time in answering, obviously weighing her options. It was clear she didn't wish to respond, but she must also realize failing to do so could result in a prompt dismissal. She drew a breath and let it out slowly. "I was searching for something that belongs to me." She spoke with a sharper brogue than Katie's more melodic, West Ireland dialect. "Mr. Baldwin took it from me. Or stole, is more like it."

"And what was the item?" I asked her.

"Why are you here?" she demanded in return.

"You're in no position to be asking questions," Mrs. Peake reminded her sternly.

Olivia Riley raised her chin. "It's my business and no one else's."

"Perhaps Mrs. King should be asking these questions." Mrs. Peake smiled without mirth. "She's home this morning. Shall I ask her if she has a moment?"

Miss Riley's mouth flattened and she shook her head. "Don't disturb the missus, please. It'll just get me sacked. I was looking for a brooch. *My* brooch. Belonged to my grandmother. Even during the Great Hunger, she refused to sell it. Not that selling it would have done much good when there was no food to be bought."

I found a stool near Ethan's hulking rolltop desk and brought it closer to Miss Riley. Sitting, I asked, "Why wouldn't you want us to know that?"

"Because it's valuable. I didn't want anyone knowing I had it."

"Or because you stole it from the missus," Mrs. Peake charged, "or from your last employer."

"I never stole a thing," the maid insisted with quiet dignity.

"What does this brooch look like?" Mrs. Peake persisted.

Miss Riley's mouth curled wistfully and she tilted her head. "Oh, it's lovely. A cameo inside a ring of seed pearls. Mounted on gold, it is."

"Where would you come by something that dear?" Mrs. Peake's skepticism filled the room.

"I told you. Twas my grandmother's."

Mrs. Peake nodded, obviously contemplating Miss Riley's story. "All right, so *she* wouldn't sell it. What about your mother? Is your family so well off they didn't need the money a piece of jewelry like that could fetch? I find it hard to believe."

"Mrs. Peake, please," I said, but Miss Riley didn't appear daunted.

"We're not well-off or I wouldn't be working as a maid, would I? But I won't sell it, not even as a last resort. It means too much. It's a reminder we Rileys weren't always poor, and a promise that one day we'll be prosperous again."

Would Mrs. Peake balk at such defiance? She studied Miss Riley for a long moment before releasing a breath. She spoke more gently, almost apologetically. "I'll have to ask the missus if she's missing any jewelry."

"Good. You'll see nothing has been stolen. Just don't bring my name into it if you don't have to, or I know I'll get the sack. Employers don't like hearing their servants' names tangled in any unpleasantness. It's always easier to send us packing than sort things out."

Had she been dismissed previously? Rather than voice

that thought, I asked a different question. "How and when did Baldwin steal your brooch?"

"It happened four days before the . . . accident." Miss Riley gave a little shudder. "He came into my room one night and caught me looking at it. Snatched it right out of my hand. Said I probably stole it—just like you all accused me—and he'd be looking into where I came by it."

Even as this disclosure sent a shudder across my own shoulders, Mrs. Peake's mouth fell open. "He had no such right. No man should ever be in your room, I don't care who he is. You should have come to me then."

Based on what I had learned about Baldwin, if all he had stolen from Miss Riley was a piece of jewelry, she had been lucky.

"I was afraid to, Mrs. Peake. He said he'd get me sacked if I put up a fuss, and I can't afford to lose this job. I truly can't." Here her composure slipped. Her lips quivered, and she quickly compressed them. As different as she was from Katie, I recognized her fear, her sense of powerlessness, and her desperation, for Katie had suffered all of this when she came to me for help four years ago. My heart went out to Miss Riley . . .

At the same time I acknowledged that here, perhaps, were motives for murder. "Miss Riley, did Baldwin make advances toward you?" My voice dropped in volume. "Did he violate you?"

After darting a glance at Ethan, she met my gaze without blinking. "No, ma'am. He might have shown a bit of interest, but I never gave him the chance. I know how to keep a man at arm's distance."

"Then why did he come to your room that evening?" This came from Mrs. Peake, once more allowing her skepticism full rein.

Again, Olivia Riley shrugged. "Whatever he wanted, he seemed more than satisfied taking my brooch instead."

She sounded adamant in her denials, yet I wondered whether or not a brooch existed. As Mrs. Peake had implied, a woman in Miss Riley's position owning such an article seemed highly unlikely. She might have entered Baldwin's room searching for an entirely different kind of item, such as evidence that somehow linked her to his death. Or had Baldwin given her a brooch, only to take it back once he'd tired of her? Guilt singed me at such thoughts, but I couldn't ignore them with so much at stake.

"Where did you work before this?" I asked her, remembering what Nanny had discovered about Baldwin getting a kitchen maid in the family way. I had wondered then if that maid and this one could be one and the same.

After a slight hesitation, she replied, "For a family in New York."

"Oh? Who would that be?" I asked. "I'm familiar with many of New York's fine families."

"The name was Jenson." Her throat bobbed as she swallowed. "Not a Four Hundred family."

Convenient, I thought. "I see. And what position did you hold there?"

"Housemaid, like here. But they were closing up the house for the summer. That's why Mrs. King hired me before she came up to Newport."

I indicated that I had no further questions for her.

"Well then." Ethan came to his feet. "We'll have to keep searching for this brooch. Did you check the floorboards, behind any pictures hanging in the room, those kinds of places?"

"No, sir." Miss Riley's voice sank to a murmur. "I checked the clothespress and the nightstand, and under the mattress, but you caught me before I could keep looking."

Ethan appealed to Mrs. Peake. "Do you have any more questions for her?"

"No, not at present."

"And is it your opinion that she should continue her duties here? If so, I concur." It pleased me to hear Ethan speak with calm authority. Perhaps taking on this position had built a new confidence in him.

"It is, sir," the housekeeper said. "For now." She aimed her next comment at Miss Riley. "But be aware that we will be watching you closely."

Miss Riley nodded and reached up to tuck some stray blond strands under her linen cap. She stood. "May I go, then?"

Mrs. Peake nodded. "You may."

Still, the maid hesitated, once again compressing her lips. The overhead light caught a glitter of tears in her eyes. "And if my brooch is found, will it be returned to me?"

Ethan and Mrs. Peake consulted one another silently, and nodded. "It will," the housekeeper said, "so long as we don't determine that it belongs to someone else."

"It doesn't." Miss Riley went to the door and let herself out.

Once she had left, Mrs. Peake turned to Ethan and me, her hands clasped at her waist and her eyebrows raised like a schoolmarm who had caught her pupils cheating. "I'll have you know this was highly irregular, having Miss Cross here while we questioned Olivia. Were it not for Mrs. King taking me into her confidence about who you are and why you are here, I would not have stood for an outsider—other than the police—interfering with a member of the household staff. As it is . . . Well."

"Thank you, Mrs. Peake," Ethan and I said at the same time.

"I hope you can clear Mr. Philip's name," she said more humbly. "For Mrs. King's sake if nothing else." The housekeeper excused herself, leaving me alone with Ethan. I took the chair Olivia Riley had vacated, while Ethan, with a sigh, sat back down at the desk.

"What do you think?" I asked him. "About Olivia," I added, lest he believe I meant Mrs. Peake.

He seemed slightly taken aback. "You want my opinion?"

"Of course I do. You've been among these people day and night. Do you think the maid is telling the truth?"

His brow wrinkled. "I don't like to think she's lying."

"How did she act when you caught her in Baldwin's room?"

The lines in his forehead deepened as he considered. "Disappointed."

The answer surprised me. "Not frightened or dismayed or . . ." I paused and hit upon the appropriate word. "Guilty?"

"Those things came after. At first, she only seemed disappointed not to be able to continue rummaging through the room. Do you think that means she's telling the truth?"

"I don't know, Ethan. Yet. But since she didn't take anything from the room, no crime has been committed."

"That we know of."

I changed the subject. "Tell me, have you interacted with Miss King today?" Before leaving Kingscote after the incident between Philip King and Francis Crane yesterday, I'd managed to warn Ethan about Miss King's suspicions.

"Not yet, but last night she took me to task for having coffee served in the wrong china. I should have listened to Martin. He'd tried to tell me which was the correct set, but I didn't think it was important."

"Oh, Ethan, those kinds of details matter very much to these sorts of people. Especially if she already suspects you. Did Mrs. King intervene?"

"She did. I give that lady a lot of credit for her cool ability to tell a white lie. She said she asked me to use the green Wileman china rather than the blue Meissen because the green put her in mind of the upcoming horseback excursion she's planning through the countryside."

"Ah, the reason Miss King asked you to inventory the picnic cutlery."

"Commanded, but yes."

"Any news about John Donavan? Is he still holing up in his quarters?"

"If Mrs. King doesn't require his services, yes. He's rarely seen except when he drives the carriage around to the front door to pick up the missus."

"See if you can discover what he does on his own time, then."

He promised he would, and I left him to get on with his work.

Chapter 12

"Several people are either acting suspiciously, can't account for their time the night Baldwin was struck by the motorcar, or both."

That evening saw me pacing my parlor while Nanny watched me from the sofa. Through the open windows came the sounds of the waves breaking on the rocky headland that bordered the rear of my property, the ocean as restless tonight as I was. The floorboards creaked beneath my feet, muffled each time I reached the threadbare area rug.

"Mrs. Ross attended the opera that night, but could have entered the theater during the intermission," Nanny repeated from the details we had just gone over yet again.

I nodded as I turned to pace back in her direction. "Which could place her at Kingscote at the correct time. But I have nothing to prove it. Then there's Francis Crane, who joined Mr. Bennett and his friends for cards at Stone Villa, but who has reason to resent Philip because of Gwendolen."

"Stone Villa is awfully close to Kingscote." Nanny picked up the shirtwaist stretched across her lap and continued sewing satin piping along the collar and cuffs. A little pile of buttons, pearly gray to match the piping, sat on the end table beside her. Thanks to her handiwork, I was able to stretch my wardrobe for years without appearing dismally out of date. "But would his resentment against Philip King be enough to prompt him to kill another man?"

"It might, if Mr. Crane wants Gwendolen badly enough." I came to a halt and crossed my arms. "Then again, the Crane family is wealthy, whereas Gwendolen's inheritance won't be nearly as spectacular as those of other young ladies of the Four Hundred."

"In other words, Francis Crane could do better?" Nanny nudged her half-moon spectacles higher on her nose and pushed her needle through the layers of fabric.

"In terms of character, no. I don't believe so. But financially? Most assuredly." I turned away and went to the front window, inhaling the salty night air. "I wish I knew what sent Baldwin outside that night. It's exceedingly odd, considering he had guests to serve and footmen to supervise. John Donavan claimed to be outside smoking a cigarette. Mr. Baldwin might have hurried outside to do the same, but no extra stub was found."

"Perhaps he went to meet someone," Nanny said from behind me.

I pivoted on my heel. "That's what I keep pondering. But who would he agree to meet during one of Mrs. King's dinner parties? I don't believe it would have been planned—" My hand went to my lips. I stood silent, thinking.

"What?" Nanny's needle stilled again. "Don't keep me in suspense."

I crossed back to the sofa and sat beside her. "If someone arranged to visit Baldwin that night, they had to have contacted him beforehand. No one at Kingscote mentioned having delivered a message to him, but perhaps someone telephoned him and asked—or demanded—he meet that individual outside. And if so . . ."

Nanny and I locked gazes. As one, we said, "Gayla might know."

I nodded vigorously. Gayla Prescott served as Newport's main switchboard operator and what was more, she and I had grown up together on the Point. She and another woman shared the switchboard, Gayla during daytime hours and Mrs. Graham, a widow, at night. But Gayla often worked late. Had she still been there when and if Baldwin received a telephone call that evening? I crossed my fingers that she had. Or, if Mrs. Graham had connected the call, perhaps Gayla could find out for me. I made Newport's switchboard office my first stop the next morning.

Gayla seemed delighted to see me, especially when I set an item on her counter and unwrapped the linen around it. She and I were about the same age, and today, dressed similarly in starched, high-collared shirtwaists and, in her case, a dark gray skirt with rows of black ribbon near the hem. Her hair had been coiled into a thick topknot from which a pencil protruded on one side, and a pair of gold-rimmed spectacles sat halfway down her nose. I'd always admired Gayla's lovely golden-brown eyes and olive complexion that spoke of her African great-great-grandmother.

Careful of her topknot, she whisked off her headset and leaned low to sniff the fresh, straight-out-of-the-oven freshness. "Mm. Is that Mrs. O'Neal's apple ginger cake?"

"It is," I assured her with a grin. I had remembered it was one of Gayla's favorites, and Nanny had been all too happy to oblige this morning, especially since she made one for us as well.

Gayla broke a tiny piece off a corner and popped it into her mouth. "To what do I owe the pleasure?"

"We haven't seen each other in months," I replied rather disingenuously.

"No, but we talk nearly every day, don't we?"

We did, whenever I placed a telephone call somewhere in town. For the most part, Gayla knew my work schedule and my social habits. "That's true," I conceded. "I was wondering if you might have connected a call to Kingscote the evening their butler was struck by that automobile."

Anyone else but Gayla might have taken issue with my ulterior motive for visiting her and bringing her cake. But not Gayla Prescott. Quite the contrary, she motioned for me to bring another chair closer and leaned in toward me. "You're on another case, aren't you? Is this for the *Messenger*, or for Jesse?"

"Both, actually. Do you remember a woman in particular telephoning the house that evening? Were you here, or would Mrs. Graham have taken over by then?" I held my breath, hoping for the former. Mrs. Graham, an older woman, was far more likely than Gayla to adhere to the American Bell Telephone Company's privacy guidelines.

"Let me think back . . ." She broke off another bit of cake, larger than the first, and appeared to consider as she chewed. "I've been working later than usual now that summer is here. Poor Mrs. Graham becomes rather frazzled if more than a pair of lines buzz at the same time. Once nighttime truly sets in there are fewer calls and then she's fine. Honestly, she isn't suited to the job, but I'd never say a word to anyone about it. She needs the money, don't you know."

"Gayla, are you remembering anything? Anything at all?"

"Oh, right. Let me see . . ." She picked up the cake and held it out to me in offer. I shook my head, and she set it back down. "Kingscote has so few calls. Mrs. King isn't one for the telephone. I'm frankly surprised she had one installed. And of course being so close to town it's not as though she really needs one . . ."

"Gayla," I prompted, dredging up every last bit of patience I possessed.

"Yes, now that I think about it, I do remember putting through a call in the evening. It's certainly a night that stands out in one's mind, what with the auto parade that day and then, why, someone actually being struck by an automobile that very evening."

"Do you know who called over to Kingscote?"

"Well, that I couldn't say, I'm afraid. It's not as though I listen in once the parties have been connected."

I happened to know better, but I didn't comment. Gayla's occasional transgressions could be forgiven when one considered she spent her days cooped up in this tiny space with nothing more than one small window overlooking a side street. It must be terribly boring. Until, that is, the telephone lines buzzed with some new scandal or controversy happening here in town among people she had known all her life.

I held out a hope. "Do you remember if the caller was a man or a woman?"

"Well . . . early in the day I connected a few calls about deliveries for that night's dinner." She suddenly became defensive. "I only know that because the callers each said hello to me personally."

"I understand. You know everyone in town."

"That's right." She relaxed, but then frowned. "But I do seem to remember it being a woman asking to be put through later in the evening. I couldn't tell you her name, though."

"Do you know who answered the call?"

"Hmm . . . now let me see." She consumed another broken corner of cake. "A woman answered, and then the butler came on the line. He sounded impatient, but at that point, I stopped listening, so I really can't tell you more." Again, the defensiveness. She rewrapped the cake and placed both hands around it, as if I might take it back for not having received satisfactory answers.

But I wondered. Had Eugenia Ross been the female caller? If so, how could I ever hope to prove it? The woman would never admit to having telephoned a man who died soon after. Could the caller have been someone else? Obviously, I needed to return to Kingscote and speak with whoever had originally answered the telephone that night.

I worked late at the *Messenger* that evening, making up for lost time. After the last of the staff had left the premises for the night, I double-checked that the back entrance and windows were secured before returning to my desk to complete paperwork that had gone unfinished due to my spending so much time attempting to clear Philip King's name of manslaughter. Not that I felt a great deal of compassion for yet another wealthy young scion who had fallen into dissolute ways. Yes, at times he reminded me of my half brother, Brady, who had since mended his life, or my young cousin Reggie Vanderbilt, who had not, but it wasn't Philip's similarity to either of them that spurred me on.

I simply didn't believe Philip could be guilty in these particular circumstances. I could not see how any human being, however debauched or drunk, could drive an automobile into another individual, leave him to die, sing his way to the dinner table, and look his own mother in the eye. Only a monster could behave in such a way, and however misguided Philip King might be, I didn't believe him to be a monster.

For now, I forced myself to thrust these thoughts aside and focus on the work in front of me. With stacks of receipts, subscriptions, and orders spread out on my desk, I filled in columns in my ledger book, added and subtracted, and checked my figures twice over. I became so absorbed in the ebb and flow of the numbers that when the telephone on the wall summoned me with a jarring ring, I flinched so violently I sent a flurry of paper cascading to the floor.

A few unladylike words might have slipped through my lips as I stumbled my way over the mess I'd created and snatched the ear trumpet off its cradle. "You've reached the *Messenger*."

"Emma, it's Jesse. Ethan's been hurt. Can you come to Kingscote?"

"Hurt how? Will he be all right?"

"He's been in a scuffle and he's very upset. Can you come?"

"I'll be there in a few minutes."

Having planned in advance to work late, I had already brought Maestro and my carriage up from the livery where I normally kept them during the day, and had parked them on Spring Street outside the *Messenger*'s front door. Quickly I shuffled the fallen papers into a neater pile, straightened a few more things on my desk, and hurried outside.

I reached Kingscote in a matter of minutes and stopped my carriage beside Jesse's on the service driveway. Brian Farrell, the groom, met me and helped me down. Although twilight had set in, I could detect a shadow of a bruise on his cheek. I pointed to it. Had he and Ethan fallen to fisticuffs? "What happened there?"

"We had a bit of a to-do here a little while ago."

"Yes, that's why I'm here." I spoke sharply, my anger rearing although I'd yet to learn the facts. "Was this *to-do* as you call it between you and Eth—um—Mr. Merrin?"

"Good heavens, no, miss. Between us and Donavan."

"Donavan? But what—?"

"You'd best come along, miss. The police are in the carriage house."

Partway across the rear lawn, I began to hear voices raised in urgency. "That would be Donavan again," Mr. Farrell said. "He's right schnockered, miss."

"Is he? Did he hurt Mr. Merrin very much? Or you? You have quite a welt blossoming on your cheek."

"I'll be fine. It's nothing that hasn't happened before, but I don't think Mr. Merrin has been in many fights in his life, miss."

"No, I don't suppose so."

"If you don't mind my saying so, I can't see why the detective asked you to come. Men get drunk, miss. They fight. There's not much of a story there and Donavan'll be back to his usual self in the morning."

"Does Donavan get drunk often? Does Mrs. King know?"

"Oh, now, miss, there's really no reason to go bothering the missus. Like I said, men get drunk. Sometimes they get downright soused and say things, and even do things, they don't mean. It'll all be all right."

Perhaps, but as we approached the wide sliding door of the carriage house, those voices, until now a confused hullabaloo, formed themselves into coherent words. And what I heard shocked me.

"I killed her. I killed her. God help me, I was to blame."

I shoved open the door wider and went inside. There were two carriages in the large wood-paneled space, kept cleaner than many people's kitchens. A worktable occupied a corner beneath one of the peaked windows, and there I saw Jesse and another policeman I knew, Scotty Binsford. They were standing over John Donavan, who sat hunched in his shirtsleeves on a stool. Ethan perched on another, holding a cloth-covered bundle of what I presumed to be ice to his jaw.

Jesse and Scotty acknowledged me with nods. At the sight of me, John Donavan moved to vacate his stool, though whether to offer it to me—unlikely—or to attack me, I'll never know, for Scotty seized the coachman by the shoulders and forced him back down.

"Don't you move. Not if you know what's good for you," Scotty warned him. A tall, broad fellow with abundant, apple-round cheeks and an easy smile, he was often underestimated, but I had seen him take down a troublemaker or two with ease. "Now, tell us who you believe you killed, and how?"

The coachman began to mumble again, something about driving through the rain late at night. Had there been a coaching accident? He slurred and stuttered over the words, leaving their precise meaning in doubt.

A shivery sound from Ethan drew my attention. Leaving John Donavan to Scotty and Jesse, I went to Ethan and crouched in front of him. "What happened?"

He shook his head in bemusement. "I hardly know. I was in the butler's pantry. Dessert had just been served. There's no company tonight other than Miss Wetmore," he added in an aside. "And I heard shouting."

"Mr. Donavan?" When Ethan nodded, I asked, "Who was he shouting at? The groom?" I glanced over my shoulder to where Brian Farrell hovered, watching, near the sliding outer door.

"No. I don't know where Farrell was. Probably in his quarters above the stable." He pointed to the far wall, which separated the building into carriage house and stable. "Donavan was outside alone. Alone and shouting. I came running out to see what was happening, and he charged at me, fists swinging. That's when Farrell showed up."

"Have you seen Donavan drunk before?"

Ethan shook his head. "Which isn't to say he hasn't been, but if so, he's kept to his rooms." He glanced upward, indicating the building's second story. Another shudder passed through him. "Miss Cross, I don't think I'm cut out for this kind of work."

I placed my hand over his where it lay on his thigh. "Let me look at you." Gently I moved his other hand, the one clutching the ice to his face, and lowered it. A nasty swelling was growing along his jawline on his left side, and I saw now that the seam where his sleeve met the shoulder of his coat had been torn. "Does it hurt very much to move your mouth?"

"Now that the ice isn't on it, yes."

I raised his hand and the cloth filled with ice back into place. "What about your shoulder, or is it your arm? It looks as though he grabbed you rather roughly." I ran my fingertips over the tear.

Ethan rotated his shoulder without dislodging the ice from his face. "Hurts a bit."

"I have my carriage here. We can give Dr. Kennison a call and then I'll bring you over to see him."

"No, I'll be all right." His voice shook.

"You don't sound all right, Ethan."

"He said he'd go to the missus." This came from John Donavan, who moaned as he spoke. He sent a sideways glance at Ethan.

Jesse leaned his face close to the other man's to recapture his attention. "Who said he'd go to the missus? Baldwin? Did he know about this incident?"

Donavan frowned as if confused by the question. His head sagged. "Yes, the accident . . ."

Jesse nudged him until he raised his face. "You'd better tell us what happened. And when."

"My last post," Donavan replied miserably. He looked up, the gas lamp on the wall illuminating a track of moisture on his cheek. "The daughter. She was so . . . so pretty. A nice young lady." He balled his hands into fists and pounded at his knees. "Didn't deserve. I shouldn't have . . ."

"Shouldn't have what?" Jesse pressed. "You said it was a rainy night. Were you drinking then, too? Is that why the accident occurred? And the young lady, your employer's daughter, did she die as a result?"

"Thrown from the carriage. Her neck . . . was broken." Donavan opened his fists and let his head fall into his hands. He wept loudly.

Jesse's eyes narrowed in a way he had when he was about to act on a hunch. My guess proved correct. "And Baldwin knew, and threatened to tell Mrs. King, didn't he? How did he know? Did the two of you work together in New York? Is that where this happened?"

"No, no." Donavan shook his head repeatedly.

"But Baldwin knew," Jesse insisted. "He knew and threatened to go to Mrs. King."

"He promised he wouldn't. Not if I . . ."

"If you what? Paid him?" Jesse, leaning low these past minutes, slowly straightened, but his gaze never left John Donavan. "Did you murder Isaiah Baldwin? Did you push the motorcar into him and pin him to the tree trunk?"

The coachman uttered a litany of denials, his hands tugging at his hair. Jesse and Scotty traded glances and nodded. Scotty unhooked the pair of hinged, ratcheted handcuffs from his belt and moved to secure Donavan's hands in front of him. Donavan didn't resist, but sat limply on the stool, moaning and shaking his head.

I left Ethan's side and went to Jesse. "Do you really think he murdered Baldwin?"

"I don't know, but if you ask me, he attacked Ethan because he believed him to be Baldwin."

"He mistook one butler for another." I nodded at my own conclusion.

"Considering his condition, we'll take him in for the night at least and question him more in the morning, when he's coherent."

"And hungover," I pointed out.

Jesse had the good grace to look chagrined. "The promise of a tall cup of water works wonders in loosening a man's tongue."

"As long as his tongue speaks true, and not what he believes you wish to hear." I treated him to an admonishing stare.

"We won't coerce him. You have my word on it." He lowered his voice. "But I would think you'd be glad to see Philip King exonerated."

"Only if you've found the guilty party."

"In the meantime, what of Ethan?" Jesse gestured at my erstwhile society reporter with his chin.

"I'll take care of him. He's having second thoughts about continuing his role here."

"Can't say I blame him." Jesse stole a glance at Brian Farrell, who still lingered by the carriages. "He may already have been found out."

"Mr. Farrell has been with Mrs. King a long time, and she trusts him. I suppose we can, too."

Jesse nodded and motioned for Scotty to walk the coachman outside. Ethan rose shakily from his stool and handed his bundle of ice to me. "Wait," he said, and disappeared through a door. I heard footsteps on stairs. A few minutes later he returned holding a tweed coat and a necktie. "He might want these, especially if he has to appear at the courthouse in the morning."

Donavan raised his cuffed hands together and pointed at Ethan's face. "Sorry I did that to you."

"You're not yourself tonight," Ethan replied. He held out the coat, and Jesse reached for it. Without an instant's hesitation, he checked the pockets. His search yielded nothing, but I noticed something that induced me to grasp the garment by its collar and peer at the clothing tag sewn into the lining near the pocket. "Take him out," Jesse said to Scotty. "I'll meet you at the buggy in a minute."

As soon as Scotty and the coachman left the carriage house, Jesse turned back to me. "What is it? What did you see?"

I handed the coat back to him. "The tag. It's from a shop in Bristol."

"So?"

"Where did Donavan say he was from?"

Understanding dawned on Jesse's face. "New York."

"I believe he might have been hired in New York, but this"—I pointed at the coat—indicates he's from Rhode Island, but perhaps didn't want anyone to know. Which makes sense if something terrible happened at his last place of employment, such as a girl dying in a carriage accident. Do you know who else was from Bristol?" I didn't wait for him to answer. "Isaiah Baldwin. He worked for a family named the Hendersons. At least according to Nanny's friend, Jane Meeker."

"And I'd put my money on Mrs. O'Neal and her friend any day of the week." He let out a breath. "Philip King might find himself freed from his luxurious imprisonment by tomorrow. Good night, Emma. I'll let you know if he confesses."

As Jesse left, Brian Farrell approached Ethan and me. He looked Ethan up and down. "Ethan and not Edward, huh? So, who exactly are you, then?"

Ethan sank back onto his stool, the bundle of ice once more pressed to his face. I answered the question for him. "Ethan works for me at the *Messenger*." Before I could explain more, Mr. Farrell's features lit up.

"Ethan Merriman?"

Ethan nodded, none too happily.

"I read your columns every week. And I know for a fact the missus and her daughter always look forward to them. But what are you doing posing as a butler?" His expression clouded. "I don't think kindly of anyone putting something over on the missus."

"He's not," I interrupted. "Mrs. King knows all about who Ethan is and why he's here. It's not for a news story. He's here to find out if one of the servants had a reason to murder Mr. Baldwin."

"Ohhh." Mr. Farrell's eyes opened wide. "And now you think Donavan . . ."

"That's for Detective Whyte to decide," I said firmly. "And this doesn't yet exonerate Mrs. King's son."

"I hope it does soon, for the missus's sake." He echoed what seemed to be a popular sentiment among the servants. Whatever they might think of Philip, they all seemed united in their esteem for his mother. Mr. Farrell chuckled down at Ethan. "You sure had us all fooled. Not that you're much good as a butler. You're not and that's the honest truth. But I doubt any of us could have guessed you're here as a spy."

"And so I am." Ethan surprised me by grinning up at the other man. "Will you keep our secret?"

"If this helps the missus, I surely will. You can depend on it."

"And will you stay on?" I challenged rather than asked Ethan. "At least until we know whether or not Donavan is our killer?"

His forehead puckered and for an instant I thought he'd balk, but he slid the ice away from his face, stood up, and squared his shoulders. "You can count on me, Miss Cross."

Chapter 13

I accompanied Ethan to the main house and into the kitchen. When the other servants glimpsed the swelling bruise on his face, they immediately gathered around and fired questions at him. He winced as the cook examined his tender jaw with her fingertips. Olivia Riley touched his torn coat sleeve.

"I can fix this for you, Mr. Merrin."

"Thank you, Olivia. Thank you all for your concern."

"But why did he attack you, sir?" the dark-haired footman asked.

A faint frown crossed Ethan's face. "I don't think he meant to, Clarence. He's drunk, and I simply got in his way. My mistake," he added with a wry grin that made him wince.

His answer impressed me, for it showed his ability to think on his feet. Before we'd left the carriage house, I'd told him of Jesse's theory that, in his drunken state, Donavan had mistaken him for Baldwin. Though Ethan hadn't voiced his fears, he must have considered that if Donavan had wanted Baldwin dead, believing him to be alive might have prompted a much more vicious attack. He might have come at Ethan with a knife or a pistol. Ethan had been lucky.

He passed the now dripping cloth of melting ice to the cook's assistant. "Now then, have Mrs. King and the young ladies finished dinner?"

"They have, sir," the blond footman told him. "We covered for you, sir. The missus has no idea anything was wrong. Although, when you didn't return to the dining room to ask where she wanted coffee served, she went all white, like she thought you'd met with the same fate as Baldwin."

"She didn't hear Donavan's ranting?" Ethan expressed my own thoughts. How could Mrs. King and her daughter not have heard Donavan's shouting? Thank goodness the carriage house was set back from the main house.

Clarence grinned. "The ladies did hear something, sir. But Martin and I"—he pointed at the blond footman—"we looked out the hall windows and saw Mr. Farrell and you dragging Donavan into the carriage house. We told the missus a drunk had wandered onto the property, but not to worry, Mr. Farrell was taking care of it. Mrs. King surmised the intruder had come from one of Mr. Bennett's parties at Stone Villa." This earned him a chuckle from the others.

"Thank you, Clarence, Martin. That was quick thinking on your part." Ethan shrugged out of his coat at Olivia Riley's insistence and handed it to her. "But we'll have to tell Mrs. King something in the morning. Donavan was taken to the police station."

"Well, back to work, everyone," the cook said, and Ethan's well-wishers dispersed. He and I sought the privacy of his pantry.

"I suppose we'll have to tell Mrs. King everything in the morning," I said as I perched on the edge of his desk, "no matter what happens tonight with Donavan."

"She's sure to notice this bruise. It'll be all manner of colors in the morning." He touched his fingertips to his jaw and winced again. "Maybe Donavan will confess to Detective

Whyte, and that will be the end of this whole deplorable matter."

I studied him. "If you want out of this arrangement, you can go. No one will hold it against you. I certainly won't."

"No, I said I'd do it." He sat at his desk and studied the items inhabiting the blotter. He ran his fingertip along the blade of a brass letter opener. "I heard what the detective said, that Baldwin knew something about Donavan, and that Donavan had to pay him to keep quiet."

"Blackmail is only a theory at this point. A guess on Detective Whyte's part."

"If what Donavan said is true, that this carriage accident took place on a rainy night, it might not have been his fault, unless of course he'd been drinking. But if Baldwin threatened to tell people about it, to tell Mrs. King unless Donavan paid him, that made Baldwin a bad person, didn't it?"

"There have been other insinuations that suggest Baldwin was a bad man, yes."

Ethan closed his fingers around the handle of the letter opener and tapped its point on the desktop. "Do you think bad people deserve to die, Miss Cross?"

He sounded vulnerable, reminding me that he was indeed young and not very experienced in the world. In working with him these many months, I had learned that Ethan loved beauty in whatever forms it took, whether natural or man-made. Beauty fed his soul and fueled an optimism that helped him overcome a timorous nature. Involving himself in murder had to be taking its toll on his spirit, on his faith in his fellow man. With a sad smile, I touched his shoulder. "That depends, doesn't it? But I don't think murdering a bad person is ever justified. A society mustn't allow it."

"Even if it means evil people can go on doing evil?"

"We have to believe the law will catch up to them." But even as I said those words, I remembered that when a man forced himself on a woman, as Mrs. Meeker indicated happened at Baldwin's last place of employment, it was the woman who lost her position, bore the brunt of an illegitimate pregnancy, and suffered the poverty and desperation that typically followed. The man, meanwhile, remained free to repeat his treachery.

The door stood open, yet the cook's assistant knocked just the same. She brought in a teacup and set it on the desk. "Thought you could use this, sir." She leaned a bit lower. "Splashed in a wee dram of whiskey, too." She turned to me. "I didn't realize you were still here, miss. Would you like a cup?"

I thanked her but told her no.

A pounding on the exterior service door startled us all. Ethan turned pale, as if the sound heralded ill tidings. When he made no move to answer it, I slid my feet to the floor.

"The footmen are probably clearing the dining room. Shall I get it?"

He quickly shook his head. "No. I'll . . . I'll go." Standing, he righted his vest with a tug and left the room. We heard his and another voice from down the corridor. When he returned, he held a missive. He turned to the cook's assistant, who lingered with eyes filled with curiosity.

"Trudy, will you find Olivia, please? She has a telegram."

With a nod, young Trudy scurried from the room.

"What do you suppose it's about?" I asked, wishing to break the seal on the envelope.

Ethan shook his head as he resumed his seat. He placed the telegram on the desk and lifted his teacup, cradling it in two hands. "One can only assume it's something urgent. Something that couldn't wait for a letter."

"So urgent the Western Union office deemed it prudent to deliver it tonight, rather than waiting till morning?"

He merely shrugged. Moments later, Olivia Riley came through the doorway alone. She had apparently been readying herself for bed, as she wore a house robe buttoned up to her chin, and her bright golden hair fell in a tidy braid down her back. Trudy had apparently returned to the kitchen, no doubt summoned back to work by the cook. There would be the dinner dishes and pots and pans to scrub. I was certain the girl must be sorely disappointed not to be able to discover the reason for Miss Riley's telegram.

"Trudy says there's a message for me, sir?" She cast her glance at Ethan, and then lower, to the small envelope with the Western Union globe insignia on the desk in front of him. Her lower lip slipped between her teeth. "I haven't finished with your coat yet, but it should be good as new, sir."

"Thank you, Olivia."

She hesitated again, this time with a question in her gaze.

Ethan swallowed another draft of tea and came to his feet. He held out the telegram to her. "We'll give you some privacy."

He and I left the room and closed the door behind us, but for a gap of an inch or two. We heard a gasp, and then Miss Riley opened the door and stepped out. She bore a feverish glow to her cheeks, and her eyes shone brightly. The telegram had been reduced to a crumpled ball in her fist. "Thank you, sir. Mrs. Peake is still up, isn't she?"

"I don't believe she's turned in yet," Ethan replied. "Not bad news, I hope?"

She didn't answer the question. "If you'll excuse me, sir." She spared a glance in my direction as she bobbed a wobbly curtsey. "Miss."

She hurried along the corridor, stopping to glance into the room I remembered to be the housekeeper's parlor. Apparently finding it empty, she turned into the kitchen. Ethan and I hovered outside his pantry, but at the sound of voices in the kitchen I slipped several paces in that direction and paused to listen.

I heard Mrs. Peake's voice, and then Olivia's. "Please, ma'am, may I speak with you. It's . . . er . . . a private matter."

Their approaching footsteps sent me rushing back toward Ethan. I made it to him, and the two of us dashed into his pantry just as Miss Riley and Mrs. Peake crossed the corridor into her parlor. I moved to tiptoe in their direction once again, but Ethan stopped me with a hand on my forearm. He removed it just as quickly.

"Forgive me, Miss Cross. But there's no need to eavesdrop. Remember, Mrs. Peake knows who I am and my purpose for being here. I'll simply ask her what Olivia wants."

"Do you suppose she'll be willing to tell you? She might not consider the matter as having anything to do with Baldwin's murder."

"But she knows I'm here to scrutinize the servants. An urgent telegram at night certainly falls into the category of something that needs to be scrutinized."

True to his word, Ethan telephoned me first thing in the morning. "Mrs. Peake was all too eager to accommodate my request," he said over a crackling connection. From where I stood in the alcove beneath the staircase, I could not see outside, but an earlier peek out my bedroom window at the calm sea had assured me the day would be a temperate one. "She says there's something about Olivia that doesn't sit quite well with her. At any rate, Olivia asked for a few hours off today, as soon as she's completed her morning chores. She was up extra early to start them."

Because of our tenuous connection, likely to be severed by the next gust of wind, I spoke loudly and clearly into the telephone's ebony mouthpiece. "Did she give a reason why she needed the time off?"

"An ill family member. Which explains her frequent communications, both the wires and the letters."

"Who is this family member?" I wished to know.

"She told Mrs. Peake an elderly aunt. Olivia must be supporting her with a portion of her wages."

That made sense, but why the secrecy? Olivia might be very close to this aunt. Indeed, the aunt might be a surrogate mother to Olivia, even as Nanny was a surrogate grandmother to me. Should any harm or illness ever befall Nanny, I would be beside myself. But why didn't this aunt live closer to Olivia? The need for a telegram suggested she lived somewhere off island, as did the fact that Olivia didn't go to her last night. Surely there were houses in need of maids, or even factories in need of female workers, closer to where the aunt resided. Or the aunt might have relocated to Newport or Middletown. And why did Olivia neglect to answer Ethan's question of whether she had received bad news, and tell Mrs. Peake she had a private matter to discuss?

I made a decision and spoke into the receiver. "Ethan, I'm going to follow her and see where she goes today."

"Miss Cross, she might see you."

"I'll have to take that chance. Or I could confront her. If she wishes to get where she's going, she might simply have to tell the truth about it. Olivia is hiding something and we need to find out what it is. Is she still working?"

"She is, and then she'll have to change her clothes before she leaves."

"Good. Has she arranged transportation anywhere?"

"Not that I know of. She hasn't asked to use my telephone."

"That means she'll probably be taking the trolley into

town, and from there . . ." I thought a moment and came up with the likely answer. "The train depot or the ferry." I explained my reasons for believing Olivia planned to leave the island. "Either way, she'll have to pass through Long Wharf."

We made our plan. Then I hung up and cranked the telephone again. As I expected, Gayla came back on the line. I asked her to put me through to Derrick's apartment on the Point. She made a little whistle, which I ignored. Gayla might think what she liked about Derrick and me, and she might not be far wrong.

Derrick answered the call sounding alert and eager to start his day. He sounded even more lively when he recognized my voice. I couldn't help chuckling at the contrast between telephoning him and telephoning my brother. At this hour of the morning, Brady was typically groggy and grumpy. I explained my plan, and he agreed to wait for me at Long Wharf.

I made one more call to the *Messenger*. Unlike Derrick, Jacob answered in a tetchy manner, which became more barbed when I explained I wouldn't be coming in until much later in the day, if at all. I couldn't give him an exact time because I had no idea where I might be going.

"Is this about the Baldwin story?" he demanded rather than asked.

"It might be, or it might be a wild-goose chase," I told him frankly.

"I thought the story was supposed to be mine. Instead, you've got Ethan at Kingscote—"

"You had already gone to Kingscote and interviewed some of the servants. We couldn't place you there as temporary butler."

"And now you're chasing after a suspect," he continued, apparently not mollified. "And I'm here, twiddling my thumbs."

An apology formed on my tongue, but I held it in check. It wouldn't have helped. If Jacob Stodges wished to delve into this story, or any story, I had no intention of holding him back. In fact, an idea came to me.

"Meet Mr. Andrews and me at Long Wharf. There is a nine o'clock train, and a nine-fifteen ferry today. I'm fairly certain we want either of those." Jacob began to question me, but I cut him off. "I can't tell you exactly, but be at the wharf before nine and wait with Mr. Andrews near the trolley stop. But not *at* the trolley stop. Wear your hat low and don't bring attention to yourself. Oh, and Jacob?" I waited for him to respond with a questioning grunt. "Let everyone at the *Messenger* know they're on their own today, and that Dan Carter is in charge."

A quarter hour later, I drove my buggy past Kingscote, Katie sitting at my side. We both wore wide-brimmed hats tilted low over one side of our faces. Mine had a wide ribbon that tied beneath my chin and did a good job of obscuring my cheeks and chin. Under the summer sun, I would be hot in such a hat, but in the interest of not being recognized I would have to endure it.

As we drove past the house, we saw Ethan standing on the side piazza that faced Bellevue Avenue. This, too, had been prearranged. When he spotted us, he waved a square of green fabric as if shaking the dust out of it. It meant Olivia Riley hadn't left the house yet. Good. Hoping I was right, Katie and I continued to the corner of Bellevue Avenue and Bath Road, where I alighted from the carriage. Katie turned onto Bath Road and headed west to Thames Street, where she would double back around to Bellevue, but farther south, past Kingscote. She would drive the vehicle home alone.

I, meanwhile, slipped into one of the shops lining the façade of the Newport Casino. This one sold fine ladies hats, gloves, scarves, and handbags. I pretended to browse, but I stayed close to the window where I could monitor those walking down the street. I hadn't long to wait, as within minutes a young woman with blond hair tucked up beneath a slouching felt hat proceeded along the walkway with a determined stride. A minute or two after that, the trolley clanged along on its rails and came to a stop at the corner.

"May I help you, miss?" The shop girl who approached me looked dubious, but inquired in a polite tone.

I shook my head. "Thank you, no. Perhaps I'll return later." With that, I hurried out the door and blended into the small crowd of people both disembarking and stepping up into the trolley. Olivia Riley found a seat near the front. I stood holding on to a pole at the back. She didn't see me, but to be sure I faced backward and only peered at her over my shoulder when the trolley made its stops along the route to Long Wharf.

But I wondered, might she alight at Washington Square and instead catch the trolley that traveled up Broadway? If so, I'd have to remain where I was, and Derrick and Jacob would wait for me—and Miss Riley—in vain.

My instincts proved correct. Miss Riley alighted at Long Wharf and from there boarded the northbound train. Derrick, Jacob, and I held back until we saw her select a seat in the third class car through the train windows. Then, separately, we boarded. Derrick went in through the first class car, though he planned to enter the third class car later. It was likely she had never seen him before. With my hat pulled low I found a seat several rows behind Miss Riley. Jacob disappeared into yet another car. He would keep watch out the windows at every stop, ready to jump off should Miss Riley disembark.

I didn't think she would—at least, not until we'd left Aquidneck Island. We traveled along the water's edge through Middletown and the farmland of Portsmouth, before the tracks curved hard to the east at the upper tip of the island and then down a few miles along the eastern coast. The train slowed for one last stop in Portsmouth. I tensed, watching Miss Riley's back from beneath my hat brim. She didn't move, other than to turn her head to peer out the window. I relaxed momentarily.

The train lurched into motion and slowly chugged out of the station, never quite resuming its former speed as it again turned, this time onto the bridge that spanned the Sakonnet River. White sails flashed in the sun to either side of the train. Barges, conveyed by much smaller tugboats, fanned their wide, shallow wake out behind them as they meandered along the channels. Out my window I studied the new rail bridge being constructed, with its skeletal arm that would swing open to the side to allow for the easy passage of boats. The very notion of such an engineering feat fascinated me, and I pledged to return once the bridge opened to watch its mechanical precision. Miss Riley, too, appeared arrested by the sight of all those crisscrossing steel beams taking shape over the water.

We reached the opposite shore within minutes and entered the town of Tiverton, Rhode Island. A seaside hamlet greeted us: clapboard homes and businesses, stone walls, a tall-steepled church. Miss Riley made no move to leave the train at the first stop, but remained settled in as the train resumed its coastal trek, this time along the western shore of the mainland. How far north would she go? She had asked for only a few hours off from her duties. She could not be going much farther.

Once again, my hunch proved correct. With each mile, houses grew smaller and closer together, and shared their narrow streets with shops and, farther along still, industry. The air inside the train grew thick with the odor of menhaden oil, the product of a fish by the same name, used for many purposes, women's cosmetics among them. The sidewalks and front steps here were crowded with children running and playing, and with housewives bringing their babies out for air and trading gossip with one another. Young newsies selling papers and men and women of all ages cried out, hawking everything from flowers to fruit to fish fresh off the piers.

Tiny white particles, like snowy gnats, sprinkled against my window. We had reached the textile district of North Tiverton, with its cotton mills that spilled over into neighboring Fall River. Again, Miss Riley made no move as the train reached its next stop.

Finally, she gathered up her belongings: her drawstring handbag, shawl, and a basket covered with a faded, checkered piece of fabric. Holding on to the back of the seat, she rose unsteadily as the train waddled up beside the next platform. We had crossed over into Massachusetts. Were Jacob and Derrick ready to disembark? I peeked over my shoulder, surprised to see Derrick seated in the very last row. I hadn't been aware of him entering the car. He winked at me but made no move to stand. Of Jacob I saw no sign. The train jolted to a stop, and a moment later a conductor opened the door from the outside.

"Fall River," he called out.

Now began the tricky part of our plan: following Miss Riley without being spotted. I doubted a housemaid would hire a coach to continue her journey. She could, however, hop on a trolley. Our plan was for Derrick and me to follow her together. Jacob would trail on his own.

We hadn't planned for Miss Riley's ability to slip so quickly into the crowded streets and virtually disappear.

However much she claimed to have worked previously in New York, her knowledge of Fall River proved formidable. She had to have lived here for a significant amount of time, for all she had been hired by Mrs. King in New York. I searched the milling faces for Jacob and once again came up empty. Had he been able to follow our quarry?

"Do you think she's on to us?"

I jumped at the deep tones of Derrick's voice in my ear. But he was right; Miss Riley must have sensed something amiss, perhaps sensed my eyes on her back, though I doubted she knew who had followed her. "I don't see Jacob anywhere. I'm hoping he was able to keep up with her."

"We'll have to wait here for him to return, although we need to be somewhere discreet in case Miss Riley shows up before he does." He scanned our surroundings with a wry look. "Not exactly the best part of town."

"No, but it's daytime and these people are merely going about their business." Still, I tightened my grip on my handbag, not wishing to be an easy target for pickpockets. "I'm famished. The ambience might not be what you're used to, but I'm wagering we'll find some excellent chowder and stuffed quahogs hereabouts."

"Ambience be damned." With his lopsided grin, Derrick offered me his arm. We hadn't far to go, and chose a small establishment whose front window overlooked the street in front of the train depot. If Jacob or Miss Riley returned, we'd see them.

The pub boasted no luxuries. Wooden floors, wooden benches at scarred tables, a few grimy paintings on the walls, and a large pot-bellied stove in the center of the room to provide heat in the winter.

Our meal came quickly, and Derrick rolled his eyes with delight as he forked a heaping mound of spicy breaded quahog right from its hand-sized shell for his first-ever taste. He moaned in appreciation. "Why have I never had this before?"

"I don't know. Perhaps because quahogs are best left to the peasants?" He laughed good-naturedly at my teasing and kept right on eating. I tasted a bite of my own, nodded in approval, and then turned my attention to my steaming crock of thick, creamy chowder. "Oh my. Nearly as good as Nanny's. I told you we'd find a good lunch here."

"We hardly deserve it," he said between forkfuls of quahog, "after the way we lost sight of Miss Riley. And we call ourselves journalists. We'll never live this down."

"Thank goodness for Jacob. Let's hope he stayed hot on her trail."

After that we kept our conversation light and avoided speculating on where Olivia Riley went. A sense of irony struck me about being in this place with Derrick, how a familiar and ordinary experience for me was for him quite novel; how our worlds differed so drastically. Our dissimilarities had the power to enhance our time together as we each introduced the other to unique circumstances, yet as I glanced around the admittedly dingy interior of the pub, I wondered if my world might gradually lose its appeal for him. If at some point he might recognize the often threadbare quality of ordinary life and turn away from it.

Many would happily advise me to let Derrick raise me up rather than insist he meet me part way. But all my life I'd tread with one foot among Newport's common people, and the other among the Four Hundred. I'd seen enough of both worlds to understand the advantages and disadvantages of both. The cost. The sacrifices. And my conclusion had been that I wished to belong to neither world and both at once. In short, to live in a world of my own making where I was free to make my own decisions. And if that included living in a shabby old house with shutters that creaked in the ocean winds, or eating simple but extraordinarily good food in less than genteel surroundings, so be it.

Could Derrick accept that—*really* accept it? On face value, I believed he could. But in day-to-day living, would the novelty of ordinary life, of my life and of *me*, eventually wear off? Could either of us change enough to make the other happy?

I simply didn't know.

And yet, the deep tones of his voice as we spoke of Newport and the *Messenger* lulled me into a sense of calm that made my misgivings seem absurd and had me questioning why I allowed them to intrude on the day. It had been the same, slightly rumbling baritone a year ago that had worked its way into my very being and made something perfectly clear to me. If I eventually shared my life with any man, it would be the one sitting opposite me now.

All too soon, we finished our meal and Derrick settled up with the proprietor. As he did, I spied Jacob approaching the train depot. He stopped and glanced up and down the street, then moved to a corner of the building and leaned with a shoulder against the brick wall. He angled his hat low on his brow.

Derrick and I hurried across to him, careful not to trip over the trolley rails that bisected the street. He looked relieved to see us and came out of the shadows to meet us. "I know where she is. We should hurry, I don't know how long she'll be there."

Jacob led us on foot away from the depot, heading inland through a maze of streets. We reached a corner where a drugstore sat opposite a dilapidated three-story hotel, and he stopped us. "Halfway down. That building there, with the faded green door."

"Do you know who lives there?" Apartment buildings stood interspersed with peaked-roof houses so close together neighbors could have reached out their side windows and held hands. I studied the building he'd pointed to. It reminded me of some of the smaller tenement buildings on the Lower East Side of New York City.

He shook his head. "She opened the door and went right in. I'm guessing there are several apartments inside. I didn't dare follow. I watched a while, and then I went back for you two."

We watched the front of the building, ready to slip around the corner if necessary. Meanwhile, I considered what to do. Her errand here could indeed be of a personal nature and have nothing to do with Isaiah Baldwin's death. We knew only that her actions in recent days were contrary to a typical housemaid's, and that made us suspicious of her. But if we made our presence known to Miss Riley, we would have no further advantage over her, and most likely would learn little more about her.

Suddenly, the front door opened and the subject of our curiosity stepped out. With an adjustment to her hat, she paused on the stoop and glanced about, not with any misgivings that I could perceive, but simply in preparation for her walk back to the depot. Derrick, Jacob, and I quickly went around the corner and down the street several yards. From there we saw her reach the same corner, cross the street, and continue down the next block toward the depot.

"Let's go after her." Jacob started forward, but I checked him with a word.

"No." Both he and Derrick turned to me in puzzlement. "Let her go. We know where she was. In a few minutes, once we're certain she won't turn back for any reason, I'm going to go knock on doors in that building." I frowned. "I just hope there aren't more than a few apartments."

"And what if no one answers?" Derrick didn't sound as though he challenged my strategy, but was merely curious.

"Someone is bound to. If not the individual she visited, then a neighbor who might know something."

"Well, you're not going by yourself."

"Derrick—"

His jaw hardened and his gaze turned steely, and I knew I'd not be going alone.

Chapter 14

"Jacob, wait outside, please. Miss Riley spoke of an elderly aunt. All of us showing up together might frighten the poor woman." Jacob sulked but moved a few feet away to wait on the sidewalk. I appealed to Derrick. "Really, even the two of us—"

"I'm coming, and that's final."

We walked up the front steps and entered the building, the door being unlocked. Derrick removed his derby and held it at his side. The mingled aromas of cooking—fish, cabbage, potatoes—perspiration, and a dank, moldy scent, assaulted our senses. A staircase rose to one side of a center hall. Beneath it, the front wheel of a bicycle and the canopy of a baby carriage peeked out. There was a door to either side of us, and one straight back. I squinted in the dim interior, lit only by a window at the half landing above, to make out if there were names on any of the doors. There weren't, only apartment numbers. We both pricked our ears, listening for telltale signs of people at home. A strange quiet pervaded.

"Well." I exchanged a resolved look with Derrick and knocked on the first door to our right. No answer. I tried the one on the opposite wall. Again, nothing. I gazed down the hallway to the rear apartment, but some instinct sent me up the stairs instead. Derrick followed at my heels.

I knocked at the first door I came to opposite the landing. This apartment would face out over the back of the building. To my surprise, the door opened almost immediately.

"Did you forget—oh. What is it?" The woman who squinted out at us spoke with a sharp brogue, much like Olivia's. A kerchief surrounded a mane of gray curls that straggled down her back. I judged her age to be anywhere between fifty and sixty, her skin creased and pitted with both advancing years and past illness. But it was not *her* face that took me aback, but another one that turned up to meet mine.

A sweet, cherubic face surrounded by a cloud of wispy blond curls. The child, no more than a year and a half, two at the most, had her mother's green eyes, the same slope of her nose.

She had lifted her head off the woman's shoulder to peer at me. Now she lay her head back down, her lips puckering to a pout. But in the instant we gazed at each other, I saw the feverish light in her eyes, the blush that suffused her cheeks. She twined her bare arms around the old woman's neck as she straddled the woman's hip.

"What is it," the woman repeated. She frowned at us and started to close the door. "I've a sick child on my hands. I've no time for fools."

"Is she all right?"

"Are you deaf? I said she's not well."

A lump of worry formed in my stomach. I knew how rapidly a mild illness in a small child could become deadly. "Has she seen a doctor? Can you take her to one?"

The woman nodded tersely. "Her mother brought..." She caught herself and changed course. "A doctor's been sent for."

Her mother brought . . . money for the doctor, I surmised. That Miss Riley had visited this woman—her elderly aunt?—and this child, I had no doubt. The little girl looked too much like her for it to be a coincidence. Wiring the money would have required a trip to the local telegraph office, not easy for a woman caring for a sick child.

She started to close the door. I made a quick decision. "We're looking for a former employee of ours," I lied. I snatched the first name that came into my head. "Katie Dillon. Does she live in this building?"

I could feel Derrick's gaze on me along with his puzzlement. We hadn't discussed using a false excuse, but I realized that, should we tell this woman we sought Olivia Riley, she would find a way to alert Miss Riley soon after we left. Far better we retain the advantage of secrecy, for now.

"You lookin' to rehire her?"

"Yes, that's it exactly." I crossed my fingers behind my back. I didn't relish lying, yet neither was I above the act if I deemed it necessary. "She was very good at her job and we'd like her to come back."

"Dillon, you say? There's a family by that name a couple of buildings over." The woman jostled the child higher on her hip. "Don't know that they have a Katie, though."

"Thank you. So sorry to have bothered you." Before she could back away and close the door, I reached out and traced my fingertip along the little girl's satiny soft arm. She had those little creases at her wrists that most babies have, and dimples at her elbows. I was glad to see it. Though perhaps slightly small for her age, she appeared well fed. But her skin radiated heat into my fingertip. She tugged at her ear. "An ear infection?"

The woman nodded.

I smiled at the child. "And what's your name, little one?"

I sensed the woman growing wary, pulling back. The child smiled weakly. "Fiona Wose."

"Fiona Rose?" I looked to the woman for consensus, and she gave a reluctant nod. "That's a beautiful name, for a very beautiful girl." I tickled her beneath her chin, bringing on a soft, half-hearted giggle. She turned her face away and pressed it into the woman's shoulder in a bout of shyness, only to whisk back toward me with a flounce of her curls. She grinned. Was she suddenly feeling better? She pointed to a tooth at the front of her mouth.

"Oh, is that new?" I received a proud nod. "Very impressive."

"I've work to do, and she needs to lie down again." The woman backed decisively away and closed the door, not with a slam, but with a firm message of finality. From the other side I heard a whimper of protest from Fiona that unexpectedly tugged my heartstrings. For several moments I didn't move, until Derrick placed his hand at the small of my back and gently nudged me.

"Are you all right?"

I blinked. "Fine. Let's go."

We made our way back outside to reunite with Jacob. He fired questions at us, and I let Derrick provide him with answers. I didn't feel much like talking. Only once we were back on the train, headed for Newport, did Derrick ask me what was wrong.

"The child. She could be Isaiah Baldwin's. The timing, according to what Mrs. Meeker said, is about right."

"She certainly could be," Jacob readily agreed. "I'll wager the bounder stood by while Miss Riley was fired, and then he abandoned them both. A motivation for murder if ever I heard of one."

All that was true. But it wasn't what weighed so heavily on me. "What we're doing could destroy Fiona's life."

"Surely you're not suggesting anyone should get away with murder?" Facing us, Jacob bounced against the back of his seat as the train pulled out of the depot.

"No," Derrick replied when I hesitated. "But if Miss Riley killed Isaiah Baldwin, it was one more tragedy in a series of tragic incidents, beginning with a man taking advantage of a woman under his supervision. She'd have believed she had little choice in the face of his advances and gone along with his demands in order to keep her position. Now, if she's guilty and convicted, her daughter faces an uncertain future, perhaps a disastrous one."

My throat had gone tight, achy, as I pictured that halo of flaxen curls and the sweet smile that rewarded me when I'd complimented the child. I nodded in response to Derrick's summation of the circumstances and swallowed back gathering tears.

He placed his hand over mine, unapologetic even when Jacob's eyes widened. "Don't worry. We know where she lives. I won't let her starve. That's a promise."

After we parted with Jacob in Washington Square, Derrick and I walked over to Marlborough Street to see Jesse at the police station. A knot of men—about a dozen of them—hovering outside made me glad I hadn't ventured there alone. Although not quite as irate or out of control as the crowd at the hospital after Baldwin had been brought there, these individuals held signs and shouted for attention.

FREE THE COACHMAN NOW, one sign read, while the individual holding it shook a fist and shouted at the front of the station, "Philip King is guilty! Arrest Philip King!"

Another cardboard placard proclaimed in bold black paint, NO JUSTICE FOR WORKING MEN, and still another asserted, THE RICH GET AWAY WITH MURDER.

Two uniformed policemen stood on the steps of the station, watching, their arms folded across their chests. They didn't answer the shouting, but remained unmoving and on the alert. Their presence brought some measure of reassurance, although if violence broke out among this many men gathered on the sidewalk, more than two officers would be needed.

Derrick brought us to a halt at the corner. "Perhaps we should come back another time."

"We need to tell Jesse our news now, and besides, I'm not afraid of them." I squared my shoulders, letting him know I would not be diverted. After all, I silently assured myself, I had shamed the last throng of malcontents we'd encountered into submission. These were local Newporters, and I was one of them. I searched for familiar faces; there were several I recognized.

I didn't blame them for their anger, nor their need to vocalize it in such a public way. Why should John Donavan languish in a cell while Philip King enjoyed the comforts of his bedroom? As long as they remained peaceful, theirs was a justified cause. But would they let us pass, or would Derrick and I fall prey to a frustrated mob's need for action? Would the two officers come to our aid before any real harm befell us?

My worries proved unfounded. As we neared the police station steps, the men parted to give us room to walk. They eyed Derrick with both suspicion and resentment, but then a few of them shifted their sights to me, and I heard my name dance across several pairs of lips. I nodded greetings, maintaining a somber expression to let them know I understood and sympathized. Still, Derrick took possession of my upper arm, a fierce sense of protectiveness communicating itself to me through the tension in his fingers. One of the policemen opened the police station door for us, and we proceeded inside.

We had to wait for Jesse, as he had gone back to the cells to talk to John Donavan again. When he returned to the main part of the station, he invited Derrick and me to sit at his desk. Between officers typing up reports, the ringing of telephones, and people coming and going, we needn't worry about being overheard.

He looked like a cat who all but had the mouse between his paws, but first he asked, "Did you meet with any trouble outside?"

"No," I replied. "They're angry, but not violent. But I can see you have something to tell us. What is it?"

Jesse tried to hide a grin but couldn't quite accomplish the feat. "He's admitted it. Donavan admits he and Baldwin worked together in Bristol, and that Baldwin had been blackmailing him in exchange for keeping quiet about the accident that killed the girl."

"How is it they both ended up working for Mrs. King?" Derrick brought a second chair closer for himself after I took the one already facing Jesse's desk. "Or was that Baldwin's doing as well?"

"That's right." Jesse shuffled some papers. "Baldwin kept tabs on Donavan these past couple of years. Made constant demands on him but kept his secret. When Baldwin's last job ended early last spring, he contacted Donavan, discovered he'd been hired by the Kings, and insisted Donavan pave the way for the butler position."

"I don't understand," I said. "If the family's daughter died as the result of an accident and it wasn't Donavan's fault, how could Baldwin have blackmailed him?"

Jesse stopped shuffling and met my gaze. "The fact remains, the girl died. How many people do you think would be willing to hire a coachman who had a passenger die on his watch?"

"I see your point." I fidgeted with the strings on my handbag. "I assume you asked Donavan if he murdered Baldwin?"

Jesse nodded. "He still denies it. As of course he would."

"What do your instincts tell you?" Derrick asked him. "Is he telling the truth?"

"Hard to say. One thing is certain. He'd been drinking—quite a lot. And now he's having a very hard time of it here, being deprived."

"That would explain what Ethan said about Donavan frequently disappearing to his rooms above the carriage house," I said, and shook my head. "Imagine drinking like that in his circumstances. One would think that after one carriage accident, he'd make sure he never had another one."

"I suppose when he knew he'd be driving Mrs. King, he abstained." Derrick leaned closer to the desk. "We discovered something today, too. And it might mean Donavan's telling the truth. We followed Olivia Riley to Fall River earlier. Just got back, actually." He sat back and deferred to me with a nod.

I said, "She has a daughter, Jesse. A baby girl about a year and a half old. She's being looked after by an older woman. At Kingscote, Miss Riley mentioned an elderly aunt."

"But she has never mentioned this child, at least not to me." Jesse's eyebrows went up in speculation without my having to confirm his hunch. "She didn't want anyone knowing."

"No," I replied. "Housemaids with children are not only looked down upon, they're rarely hired. Potential employers assume such a young woman possesses low morals and will only bring trouble. So no, she would not want anyone at Kingscote to know."

"Especially if Baldwin was the father," Derrick added.

At Jesse's surprised reaction to that, I said, "You remember my telling you about Nanny's friend, Mrs. Meeker, and her story of Baldwin getting a former housemaid with child."

"I do indeed." Jesse appeared deep in thought for several moments. The activity around us continued, the bustle of a busy police station. While Newport remained a small city, the influx of summer residents, constant shipments to the island, and the whirlwind of social activities meant issues were constantly arising that required police attention. Theft, drunkenness, and brawling were always at the top of the list, at least in the summer months. "They could both be guilty," Jesse said at length. "It's too much of a coincidence that they all three worked at Kingscote together. Do you still have Ethan in place there as butler?"

"He's still there," I assured him. "Despite his being attacked by Donavan."

"Have him ask the servants if Baldwin and Miss Riley seemed more familiar with each other than the rest of them. Remind him to be discreet. We don't want to give Miss Riley a reason to run."

"She already might think there's a reason," Derrick said. "We gave her aunt a false excuse for showing up at her door, but I've no doubt that as soon as she has a chance, she'll alert her niece to the two strangers who appeared only minutes after she left the apartment."

"I suppose that's true," I agreed, "but what other choice did we have? We needed to find out what she was hiding in Fall River. Besides, now that the truth is known, perhaps she should be confronted with it." I didn't need to point out that the child, if Baldwin's, gave Miss Riley a strong motive for murder. I turned back to Jesse. "Are you thinking Donavan and Olivia Riley acted together in Baldwin's murder?"

"Exactly that," he said. "As I said, it's too much of a coincidence that all three worked for the Kings. It sounds like they coordinated, doesn't it? Emma, see if you can't find out from Mrs. King exactly when each was hired. Was it all at once, or did one recommend another?"

Derrick shifted his long legs in front of him. "You do realize we might be wrong about Miss Riley. For certain she's been hiding a child, but the little girl might not be Baldwin's."

"Another coincidence," I said. "Like Jesse, I don't believe in them, not generally speaking. I've found that whenever a link appears to exist, there is one. But perhaps someone should persuade Miss Riley to acknowledge her secret in Fall River and see whether she has more to confess." Even as I spoke, guilt stabbed sharply. Fiona's beautiful features would haunt me, would steal into my dreams at night, should she be deprived of her mother due to my interference in the case. But what else to do? Ignore evidence and allow a murderer to walk free?

"Then again, there are still Eugenia Ross and Francis Crane, both of whom might have had reasons to commit murder. Both certainly have reasons to begrudge the Kings," I reminded Jesse.

"I haven't forgotten. But these two—Donavan and Olivia Riley—have a more direct link to Baldwin. Or so it appears."

I sighed. "In what's left of the afternoon, I should spend some time at the *Messenger*, or I could find myself out of a job."

"Never." Derrick started to reach across the space between our chairs to grasp my hand, but with a glance at Jesse, he let his own drop. Jesse angled his own gaze away with an ironic smile hovering over his lips, one that reminded me he had a secret of his own.

Her name, he had confided to me last fall, was Nora Taylor, and she worked as a maid at Ochre Court. She and Jesse had met a year ago during a police investigation. Their courtship had progressed slowly, and I wondered when they might openly acknowledge their affections for each other. But then, who was I to judge—I who couldn't make up my mind from one moment to the next if I even wished to be courted?

The late afternoon proved more productive at the *Messenger* than I had anticipated. I edited several articles that came over the wires for the next morning's edition, and I'd been pleased to discover several new businesses on the island inquiring about advertising space. All this left me with a deep sense of satisfaction on my way home that evening. Nanny had a sumptuous meal of pot roast and root vegetables waiting for me, plus a surprise, one not only she had kept, but Derrick as well. He greeted me in the front hall and helped me remove my carriage jacket and hat.

"I hope you don't mind. There was a message waiting for me when I arrived home earlier, an invitation from Mrs. O'Neal. I should have telephoned you at the *Messenger* to let you know . . ."

"There she goes again, playing matchmaker. I hope *you* don't mind."

He grinned, bent over me, and pressed a kiss to my lips. "That answer your question?"

He left me light-headed and a little breathless. Shuffling footsteps coming from the kitchen prompted me to give him a playful swat and step out from under his hovering, smiling features. "Nanny, this is a surprise," I exclaimed when she appeared in the corridor. "And everything smells delightful."

"My lamb has had a long day." She embraced me and stepped back. "That employer of yours works you too hard."

Derrick pressed a hand to his chest. "You have my deepest

apologies, Mrs. O'Neal, and I shall mend my ways. Emma, take tomorrow off."

"That I shall not, or my employer will begin to think I'm not indispensable. And then where will I be?"

We spent a homey evening together, enjoying the delicious meal Nanny had prepared with Katie's help. Though she, Katie, and I normally ate informally at the kitchen table, tonight we sat in the dining room, finally restored after a fire had damaged the room last summer. The calm, unhurried evening contrasted sharply with the frantic pace I had maintained these several days since Baldwin's murder, and reminded me to acknowledge my blessings and savor my good fortune.

It proved a much needed respite, though a short-lived one. Mrs. King sent a footman to Gull Manor in the morning, asking me to stop at Kingscote on my way into town.

Chapter 15

"Detective Whyte gave us permission to go through Baldwin's things and pack them up," Mrs. King explained as she led me into the library off the Stair Hall. "Mrs. Peake and Clarence have been carefully sifting through."

"Have you found the brooch Miss Riley claims he took from her?" I stopped short upon entering the library. Mrs. Peake stood near the hearth, a slip of paper in her hand.

"No," Mrs. King replied. "But we have something that might prove enlightening. Show her," she said to the house-keeper.

Mrs. Peake held out the paper to me. I skimmed it and glanced up in surprise. "A receipt for a brooch, from a jewelry store in town. It doesn't appear to have been very valuable, given what the jeweler paid for it." Or, had Baldwin been willing to part with it for a small sum? Perhaps only the jeweler could answer that question. I started to hand it back, but Mrs. King intercepted it.

"It was found among Baldwin's clothing," she informed me, "shoved into a pocket of a pair of trousers. I'm surprised Miss Riley didn't find it when she searched the room."

"She would have, if Mr. Merrin hadn't caught her before she had a chance." Mrs. Peake spoke so sternly I feared that, even if Miss Riley proved innocent of all misdeeds, she might be dismissed nonetheless. Would I be able to intercede on her behalf? "As it is, I'd been going through his possessions for well over an hour before I stumbled upon this."

"Did you find anything else of interest?" I asked her.

Mrs. Peake pursed her lips and traded a disapproving glance with her employer. "Seems he was quite a gambling man. Horses, dogs, even chickens, for heaven's sake. And boxing, of course." She gave an indignant shudder. When I thought she'd voice a self-righteous admonishment against gambling straight from a Protestant Sunday sermon, she surprised me. "To think, a man prospering, or trying to prosper, from the pain and suffering of others. Innocent animals, no less. And young men whose desperate circumstances lead them to put themselves at bodily risk." She again slid a glance to Mrs. King, then dropped her gaze. "I'm sorry, ma'am. I'm speaking out of turn. It's just that . . ."

"I happen to agree with you wholeheartedly, Louise." Mrs. King bestowed a benevolent smile on her housekeeper. "So you needn't apologize. However . . ." She turned back to me. "We wanted you to know about this, especially since this brooch only came to light because of your man's skillful snooping." She referred, of course, to Ethan, and I hid a smile at how she termed his efforts. "Louise and I intend to go down to this jewelry shop and inquire about the brooch. See if we can't buy it back. It could be evidence, after all. And if it proves not to be, I'm sure Olivia will wish to have it returned to her."

"It may not be as costly as we initially thought, but I'd still like to know what a girl in her position is doing with a brooch of any kind." The housekeeper assumed her disapproving air once again. "Where on earth would she ever wear it?"

"Olivia explained how she came by it, Louise." It was Mrs. King's turn to be disapproving, but not toward the housemaid. "Even the best of families can fall on hard times. We mustn't fault them for it or expect them to part with their heirlooms, valuable or otherwise."

I could have thrown my arms around her for her sense of fairness. But I saw something else in her countenance. Fear? Misgiving? Did thoughts of her own son falling on hard times someday, due to his irresponsibility, keep her awake at night? I didn't doubt it.

I hadn't forgotten the question Jesse had asked me to put to Mrs. King. "I understand you hired John Donavan, Olivia Riley, and Mr. Baldwin in New York. All three of them. Is that correct?"

The question seemed to surprise her. "Why, yes. I always hire a new staff when I arrive back in New York from our European travels. That way they can come up to Newport ahead of the rest of us and ready everything we'll need while we visit friends in the city and on Long Island."

"Did you find them separately?"

"I don't understand what you mean."

"Did you place ads for each position, and receive inquiries from each of them separately," I clarified, "or did one recommend the others?"

"Oh, I understand. Louise placed the ads and carried out the initial interviews." She turned to her housekeeper. "Louise, can you answer Miss Cross's question?"

"Hmm." Mrs. Peake frowned, thinking. "Miss Riley came on her own, but now that I think back, I do remember John Donavan mentioning he knew of a capable butler needing a position after the family he worked for relocated."

"Did this family provide a reference?"

"Of course they did." She stiffened indignantly. "I would not have considered sending him to interview with Mrs. King otherwise."

"No, I don't suppose you would," I said in an apologetic tone meant to appease her offended sensibilities. "But having a reference isn't the same as having an unblemished past. We've discovered that Baldwin and Donavan worked for the same family in Bristol before heading down to New York. Donavan admitted that Baldwin was blackmailing him over a carriage accident that occurred when both men worked for the family in Bristol."

"Donavan admitted . . ." Mrs. King looked mystified.

"Yes." I drew a breath. Mrs. King could remain ignorant of her coachman's actions no longer. "You see, the ruckus you heard outside last night was no drunkard from town who wandered onto your property. It was John Donavan. He'd been drinking and began ranting about the accident that killed his former employer's daughter."

"How horrible." Mrs. King's hands rose to her lips. Slowly, she lowered them back to her lap. "Why wasn't I told about this? Louise, did you know?"

"I . . . uh . . ."

"They kept silent at Detective Whyte's request," I said hurriedly. "No one meant to lie to you, Mrs. King. They were merely following orders."

"Well." She said it with a huff. "I suppose now I must hire a new coachman as well as a butler."

"Ma'am, perhaps you might hold off on that, for now."

"Why ever should I? You can't expect me to have Donavan back after his drunkenness, not to mention being responsible for someone's death."

I held out my hand in an appeal. "That death was deemed an accident, but Donavan has been living under the threat of never working again because of it. And as for his drunkenness, the guilt of that poor girl's death, which any man would naturally feel, drove him to it. But doesn't he have the right to exonerate himself?"

"Unless, of course, he murdered Baldwin to silence him about the past." Mrs. Peake spoke with deadly calm. "To end the blackmail."

Mrs. King announced her intention of going to the jeweler in town with the receipt found in Baldwin's pocket. I convinced her to let me go instead. She agreed only on the condition that Louise Peake accompany me.

Despite the housekeeper's often stern exterior, I found myself both respecting and liking her. I believed her to be more than dedicated to her employer, but rather a true friend, albeit a paid one. I therefore took no offense that our trip into town was conducted for the most part in silence. I'd left my horse and carriage at Kingscote, allowing us to walk the short distance into town on Bellevue Avenue. Along the way, Mrs. Peake gave me the impression that words, for her, served a purpose and were not to be wasted merely to fill a hush.

We found the jeweler, Charles Wilmont, Esquire, in a row of shops across from the Redwood Library. The gold lettering on the street window, and the glittering objects behind it, beckoned in the morning sunlight. I had been aware of the shop prior to this, but I had never gone inside. I'd had no reason to. Such a store, in its posh location, could sell nothing I could afford, nor would I have need of anything so costly as the wares to be found inside.

Indeed, the clerk's eager look, inspired as the bell above the door jangled to herald our entrance, faded as soon as his gaze traveled our lengths up and down and back again. "Good afternoon, ladies," he said correctly but without a shred of enthusiasm. "How may I help you?" The little sniff he gave impressed upon me his doubts that he could help us with anything.

Nonetheless, Mrs. Peake strode determinedly to the counter behind which he stood and thrust the receipt under his nose. "We believe a gentleman sold you a brooch recently. Here is the receipt. What can you tell us about the piece? Is it still here?"

"Hmm . . . let me see." He squinted down at the paper. While he did, I studied the trays of rings, bracelets, and necklaces in the glass case in front of him, all bearing a fortune's worth of diamonds, emeralds, rubies, and sapphires. "It says here it was a cameo . . . with pearls . . . hmm."

"Yes, yes. Is it here?" Mrs. Peake allowed her impatience to show.

"May I inquire why the gentleman himself didn't come to make the inquiry? Does he wish to buy it back? We are *not* a pawnbroker."

"The gentleman is deceased," I said bluntly, sending a wave of crimson to engulf his features. "Or hadn't you heard about the butler at Kingscote? Isaiah Baldwin? It's been in all the newspapers."

"Oh, dear me, yes. Yes, indeed. I hadn't realized . . ." Perplexed, the man scratched at his balding pate. His flush subsided.

"Well, now you know." Mrs. Peake allowed the clerk to take the receipt from her hand. He turned away behind him to another counter littered with tools of the jewelry trade and retrieved a pair of spectacles. He turned back to us and studied the receipt again.

"I believe this has already sold."

"Sold?" Mrs. Peake sounded outraged. "To whom?"

"Oh, I don't know if I should say."

"Why not?" I placed my hands on the counter and leaned toward him. If he found that slightly threatening, so be it.

"It isn't my place. I'm not the shop's owner, merely a clerk. I'll have to wait until I can speak with Mr. Wilmont."

"Have you a telephone here?" I asked him.

He nodded.

"Then speak with Mr. Wilmont." I smiled. "We'll wait." When he hesitated, clearly not liking the idea of telephoning his employer at home, I thought of a way that might persuade him. "Perhaps we shouldn't have bothered you. We'll bring the receipt to Detective Whyte at the police station and let him come and make inquiries. He won't be happy about it, as he's terribly busy trying to discover who murdered Isaiah Baldwin, and we believed we could take care of this one little errand for him. But if not—"

Behind his spectacles, the man's eyes flashed with alarm. I'd known good and well he would not want the police entering this establishment, nor would Charles Wilmont, Esquire relish that kind of publicity for his business. Perhaps a store on Thames Street or even Spring Street might enjoy the notoriety, but a jeweler on Bellevue who catered to the summering Four Hundred? Good heavens, neither Mrs. Astor nor Edith Wetmore, nor my aunt Alice Vanderbilt would ever again set foot in an establishment that bore the taint of scandal.

Now, women like my aunt Alva Belmont or Mamie Fish were another matter altogether, but this gentleman didn't need to know that.

"Perhaps I can take a look in our book," he said, and hurried through a curtain into a back room. When he returned, he held a second piece of paper in his hand. He handed it to me, along with the receipt. "Here. The item was sold to this lady. I'll probably get into a good deal of trouble because of this, but if you'll go and not come back . . ."

"Thank you, and we won't," I assured him. "And if Mr. Wilmont is angry, simply refer him to Detective Whyte."

Outside, I read what the clerk had scribbled on the scrap of paper he'd handed me. Grinning, I met Mrs. Peake's curious gaze. "Do you have time for another stop?"

We caught the uptown trolley and alighted at Rhode Island Avenue. A short walk brought us to the green clapboard house with white trim and a semicircular front porch. I had been here before, and the woman who opened the door to us showed little surprise at our appearance. "Ah, yes, I remember you." She opened the door wider and invited us in. "You're in luck. Mrs. Ross is in. Wait here, please. I'll just go up and see if she's receiving."

I was sorely tempted to follow at her heels, intent on barging in on Mrs. Ross whether she was receiving or not. Mrs. Peake seemed to feel the same urge, for she set a foot on the bottom step and hesitated before removing it and turning away.

"That woman," she murmured. "What I wouldn't like to say to her." Unlike during our quiet walk into town earlier, Mrs. Peake had made her sentiments quite clear on the trolley on the way here. She had borne witness to Eugenia Ross's harassment of the King family these many years and believed the woman to be unbalanced.

"Please don't," I said in response to her verbal musings. "We're here to retrieve Olivia's brooch. We don't want to antagonize Mrs. Ross if we can help it."

"Hmph. I can't understand what she would want with a piece of jewelry from the family of a housemaid."

"I have a hunch about that, but we'll have to wait and see."

Louise Peake flashed me a quizzical look. At the same time, the landlady started down the stairs toward us. "Mrs. Ross will see you. She's very curious as to why you've come."

If she added that last comment in hopes that we might enlighten her as well, I'm afraid we disappointed her. We thanked her and continued upstairs. Mrs. Ross awaited us at the open door to her rooms.

"Well, well. You're back." She frowned at my companion. "Louise Peake. Have you brought a message from Mrs. King? Is she ready to listen to reason?"

"Mrs. King has no notion that I'm here."

"How odd. Well, come in and have a seat, both of you. And tell me how I might help you."

Her amiable mood puzzled me, especially after our last encounter in this very parlor. I commented on how cheerful she appeared.

"Why, yes, thank you for noticing, Miss Cross. Oh, I'm sorry. Shall I ring my landlady for tea?"

"No, thank you," I said, even as Mrs. Peake wrinkled her nose at the very notion of accepting hospitality from her employer's nemesis.

"I suppose you're wondering why I'm in so pleased a mood today." When I nodded, she smiled broadly. "Word has just reached me that the date for the new hearing about my inheritance has been confirmed." She cast a triumphant look at Mrs. Peake. "Come September, all my troubles will be over."

"There have been hearings before, and your suit has always been denied," Mrs. Peake said bluntly. "What makes you think this one will turn out any different?"

"I'm ever the optimist, Mrs. Peake." She beamed at us in triumph, and I had my answer about why she had agreed to see us today: to gloat. "But do tell me, what has brought you here? I'm so very curious."

"We've just come from a jeweler in town." I met her brilliant smile with one of my own. "Charles Wilmont, Esquire."

"And that should mean what to me?" Despite her words,

her eyes sparked and her cheeks, already rouged, turned pinker.

"We were inquiring about an item. A brooch. It consists of a cameo surrounded by seed pearls. Apparently, you purchased it."

"Who told you that?"

"Is it true?" Mrs. Peake might as well have been challenging the other woman to a duel, for all the warmth in her voice.

Eugenia Ross hesitated, sizing the two of us up. Then she shrugged. "What difference does it make if you know? Yes, I purchased a brooch of that description. Why shouldn't I have?"

"Isaiah Baldwin had just sold the brooch to the jeweler, not that he had any right to do so," I said. "How did you know to go and buy it, and why would you?"

"If I said it was all merely a coincidence, I don't suppose you'd believe me." The idea amused her, and she let out a chuckle.

Mrs. Peake held her features utterly steady. "No, we would not."

Again, Mrs. Ross shrugged. "I suppose there's no reason I shouldn't tell you. I understood the brooch came from Kingscote. And since Kingscote should be mine, anything that originates there should be mine as well."

I gathered my brows together. "You must have been talking to Mr. Baldwin, then, for you to have known when and where he sold the item. Was he helping you with information about the family and house?"

"Perhaps. That matter is really none of your business."

"Perhaps it's the police's business," Mrs. Peake said in clear warning. "Perhaps we should refer the matter to them."

"Perhaps you should." Mrs. Ross seemed undaunted by

the prospect. "I've done nothing wrong. I merely purchased an item from a jewelry store. How they came by it is none of my concern."

My frown persisted. It wasn't one of perplexity, but of concentration. "You believed—that is, Baldwin led you to believe—that the brooch belonged to Mrs. King. Isn't that true?"

For the first time, her confidence slipped. "What do you mean, led me to believe?"

"Did you pay a great deal for it?" I asked rather than answered her question.

"No. A trifle, really. It was the sentimental value I wanted it for."

"Then I'd like to buy it back from you now."

Her gaze became stormy. "Tell me what you meant first."

"I believe Baldwin led you to believe he stole the brooch from Mrs. King, and as such, you believed you had a right to it. But he didn't. He took it from the housemaid. A young woman with no personal tie to the King family."

"The housemaid?" She pronounced the word with the utmost disdain. And shock. My hunch had been correct.

"Yes, Mrs. King's housemaid." It was Mrs. Peake's turn to grin. "I'm ashamed to say I didn't believe Miss Riley's story at first. I thought she might have stolen the brooch from Mrs. King. But no, the thief was Baldwin all along. I'm afraid you spent your good money on something with no meaning for Mrs. King."

Mrs. Ross jumped up from her seat. I braced, believing she would order us out of her parlor. Instead, she went into the bedroom, just as she had done when I'd asked her where she had been the night Isaiah Baldwin had been struck by the automobile. Instead of an opera ticket, she returned holding an item that filled the palm of her hand. She held it out to me.

"Is this your old brooch?"

Though I had never seen the piece before, it fit the description Miss Riley had given. I nodded. "How much do you want for it?"

"Only what I paid for it." Her mouth turned down at the corners. "I don't want to ever see it again."

She told me the amount, and I opened my drawstring bag. Mrs. Peake came to her feet, her own bag already open. "Let me, Miss Cross. I feel I owe Olivia recompense for the way I accused her." She dug out the small purse inside. She placed the correct amount in Mrs. Ross's hand.

That woman made a show of recounting the money before handing Mrs. Peake the brooch. "He was a cheat and a liar, that Isaiah Baldwin."

I couldn't contain my curiosity. "Why didn't he simply sell the brooch directly to you?"

"To vex me. I'd done him a favor or two, and he repaid me with disloyalty and deceit."

Mrs. Peake looked up from studying the brooch. "What kind of favors?"

"Nothing that concerns you."

Mrs. Peake's eyes narrowed. "His references, I'll wager. You probably forged them for him. Forgery is against the law, Mrs. Ross. Should I happen to bring those references to the police, they might wish to do a comparison with your handwriting. And then you could find yourself with an illegal link to a murdered man. The police would find that most interesting."

"You have your worthless brooch back. Take it and go."

"Yes, perhaps you're right." I touched Mrs. Peake's wrist, beckoning her to follow me to the door. On the threshold, I stopped and turned back to Mrs. Ross. "By the way, I paid a visit to the Opera House. Your torn ticket doesn't mean you entered the building at the start of the performance. You might have stolen in during the intermission. Or you might have left early. I'm afraid you don't have much of an alibi, unless you can produce someone who can vouch for your presence in the theater during the exact time frame in which Baldwin was struck. Good day to you, Mrs. Ross."

Mrs. Peake conjured her first genuine smile of the visit. "Yes. Good day, Mrs. Ross."

Chapter 16

Once we exited the trolley near the Newport Casino, I accompanied Mrs. Peake back to Kingscote to collect my horse and carriage. She had been noticeably chattier on the way back from Mrs. Ross's apartment. The confrontation, as well as recovering the brooch, seemed to have raised the housekeeper's spirits considerably.

They plunged minutes later, along with my own.

Kingscote's circular drive played host to several vehicles, including the ambulance wagon. Several uniformed policemen were scattered about the property. As Mrs. Peake and I hurried along the last dozen yards to the house, I spotted Jesse walking around the northwestern edge of the property toward the carriage house and stables.

With trepidation dragging at each step I took, I approached one of the blue-clad officers. "What's happened?"

He appeared about to brush me off when he recognized me. "Another murder, Miss Cross. One of the footmen."

"Oh no. Which one?" Mrs. Peake's shrill question made me jump. I hadn't realized she had followed me, much less so closely. Nor could I have imagined the high-pitched shriek coming from her lips. It made no difference to the officer. He waved the question away and hurried off.

"It was Clarence Dole." The somber voice came from behind us, and I pivoted to see Ethan looking grim and devoid of color.

"Clarence." Mrs. Peake went as white as the lace collar on her dress.

"Good heavens, Ethan." I grasped Mrs. Peake's arm when she let out a tremulous breath and appeared to wobble. "What happened?"

"I don't know." Ethan shook his head, his features tight. "The police haven't said much yet. But Clarence was found in the laundry yard."

"By whom?"

"Olivia. She's being questioned now."

A half dozen questions sprang to my mind, among them whether or not Olivia was a suspect, but I realized Ethan likely wouldn't have the answers. "Where is Mrs. King?"

"Upstairs, I believe." Ethan gestured up at the second floor. "In her room."

I led Mrs. Peake into the house and gently nudged her toward the staircase. "Come. Let's go up. Mrs. King will need you." Perhaps not as much as Mrs. Peake needed her, I thought.

"He was only nineteen." Her voice trembled and wavered. "That's too young to have done anyone any harm. Who would hurt him?"

"I wish I knew, Mrs. Peake."

As we reached the top of the stairs, Mrs. King came from down the corridor that led to her bedroom and crossed the gallery to us. "Oh, Louise. It's horrible. I feel as though Kingscote is cursed."

The two women embraced. Their arms around each other,

they disappeared back down the corridor. I had apparently been forgotten, but I didn't let it bother me. Assured they had each other, I turned to descend the staircase. I paused once to wonder where Gwendolen was. I also wondered about Philip. Was he still locked in his room? I quietly crossed the gallery to Philip's door and knocked softly. "Mr. King, are you there?"

"Who is that?" came his reply from the other side.

"It's Emma Cross."

"What the blazes is happening out there, Miss Cross? No one ever tells me anything. I'm stuck up here, locked away, and I could die, for all anyone cares."

Despite his petulant tone, I sympathized with his frustrations. And with his fears, as he must surely have been entertaining many. People dying at Kingscote had become an all-too-real occurrence, and I couldn't blame him for feeling trapped and vulnerable. "It's one of the footmen," I told him. "Clarence. It appears he's deceased, Mr. King."

"Clarence?" Philip King swore, just loud enough for me to hear. "What happened?"

I hesitated before saying, "He was murdered."

"Good God. Have they caught the killer?"

"I don't know anything yet, Mr. King. I'd only just arrived at the house to see all the commotion. Tell me, did you hear anything?" I tried to picture which part of the property his room overlooked. "Or perhaps see anything outside your windows?"

"I was asleep until I heard shouting coming from somewhere behind the house. Is that where they found him—outside, in the rear gardens?"

"Yes, I believe it was."

"What was Clarence doing outside at this time of day?"

"I can't answer that. Yet," I added. But if I discovered anything, would I return to inform young Philip? Could he be trusted? A sudden impulse sent my hand to the doorknob. I thought to try it, to see if his door was indeed locked. I remembered his being drunk recently during his confinement. For all anyone knew, Philip had a hidden key to his door and could let himself out anytime he wished. Had he killed Clarence?

I touched my fingertips to the knob. It moved slightly side to side as if loose, but it didn't turn.

"Miss Cross? Are you still there?"

"I am, but I'm going now to see what I can find out."

"Promise me you'll come back and tell me everything."

I again hesitated, then said, "That will be for the police to decide." I hurried away before he could plead with me.

Upon returning to the front of the house, I came upon Jesse. Two policemen came around the corner, carrying the cloth-covered body on a stretcher. The coroner followed them and directed them to the ambulance.

"Cause of death was drowning in a barrel of rainwater collected for the washing of clothes," Jesse told me succinctly, not bothering to soften his words. In the next instant, he looked contrite. "Sorry. I shouldn't have said it that way."

"Nonsense." I waved away his apology. The pair of us watched the men slide the stretcher into the back of the ambulance wagon. "Philip told me he heard shouting from the rear lawn. And Ethan told me Miss Riley found the body."

"That's right, and those were her screams Philip heard. She had gone out to collect bedding hanging on the lines. Clarence was bent over, his head submerged in the water. Must have been held down."

"Ethan said she was being questioned. Do you suspect her?"

"Hard to say." He let out a breath. "She's terribly shaken, believably so. It was difficult for her to give a statement."

"And she didn't see anyone leaving the vicinity of the laundry yard?"

He shot me an ironic look. "There are times I wish I could hire you on, you're that adept at thinking like a policeman. But no, she saw no one. And before you ask, no, there are no identifiable footprints. The ground all around the barrel is too muddy and churned up. It looks as though our culprit made an effort to kick up the mud and grass enough that we can't get a conclusive print."

"Not even size?"

He shrugged and shook his head. "And we've checked everyone's shoes for mud. What's especially odd is that there is no mud tracked across the lawn, either. As if the killer cleaned his shoes before making his getaway."

"And no one else saw anything at all? No one even saw Clarence go outside?"

"Not that anyone is admitting." He shook his head. "I don't know why I say it like that. The cook and her assistant were shopping in town. Mrs. Peake was out—"

"With me," I informed him. He looked puzzled, but continued with the whereabouts of each servant.

"Miss Riley says she was changing linens in the bedrooms, until she went outside herself. And Martin, the other footman, claims he was in the service room polishing silver. The groom, of course, was caring for the horses."

"You're certain?"

Jesse didn't hesitate. "The man has been with the Kings for years, like Mrs. Peake. They trust him completely. Besides, he has a solid alibi for the night Baldwin was struck with the motorcar. I firmly believe whoever killed the butler also killed this footman."

"What about Ethan?"

"He was in his pantry at the time, putting together a schedule for the next day's chores, so he can't vouch for the others. Surely if one of the servants witnessed something, they'd say so. I can't imagine any of them wanting to see a murderer go free."

"Not unless one of them *is* the murderer. Olivia Riley claims to have found Clarence already drowned. She could be lying. She could also have wiped off her shoes before she screamed." I didn't know where the accusations came from. I certainly didn't wish for the mother of a young child to be guilty.

"Yes, she could have," Jesse agreed. "But could she have overpowered a grown man?"

"Maids are stronger than they look. They have to be. Besides, do you know yet whether Clarence might have been struck on the head and rendered unconscious?" He had acknowledged my first point with a nod, and now shook his head at my question. We both fell to thinking. Another name hovered in my mind and prickled the back of my neck. "Are you certain Philip can't get out of his room?"

Jesse shrugged. "Not entirely, no. For all I know, there are secret passages from one room to another." He made a weary face. "Not that I believe that, mind you. Mrs. King assures me there is only one way out of Philip's room, and that's the door to the hallway. He can't get out unless he has a key we don't know about."

I spoke nearly those same words at the same time he did. We studied each other. "Or he is able to pick the lock," I added. "His room is closest to the back stairs. Could Philip have sneaked down those stairs, lured Clarence into the laundry yard, murdered him, and made his way back up without being seen?"

"Seeing as how the others were occupied or not in the house, it's possible. Not to mention if anyone could lure the footman anywhere, it would be a member of the family. Clarence wouldn't have dared to refuse him."

"When were you called?" I finally thought to ask.

"About a half hour ago."

"Then one person it couldn't be is Eugenia Ross," I mused aloud. "I've just been to see her. That's where Mrs. Peake and

I went. Among Baldwin's things, she and Clarence had found a receipt for Olivia's brooch, which he sold to a jeweler in town. Mrs. Ross purchased it thinking Baldwin stole it from Mrs. King. In a kind of twisted logic, she believed the piece to be rightfully hers. She was most unhappy when we informed her it wasn't Mrs. King's, but Olivia's. She even agreed to sell it back to us."

Jesse's countenance took on an eager look. "Do you have it?"

"Mrs. Peake does. She wishes to return it and apologize to Olivia for doubting her word about it."

"I'd like to get it from her and hang on to it for now, until matters are cleared up."

"Then you do suspect Olivia?"

"I don't *not* suspect her. Or Philip or the coachman."

I blinked in surprise. "John Donavan? Isn't he in jail?"

Jesse's mouth twisted with irritation. "Not anymore. Seems we didn't have enough evidence to hold him, and with the crowds that kept gathering outside the station, the chief feared there could be a riot. He ordered Donavan released a couple of hours ago. Says Philip is still our primary suspect, although Chief Rogers has gone back to calling it an accident."

"What?" Outrage coursed through me. "The autopsy ruled out an accident."

Jesse lifted his shoulders in another shrug. "I can't explain it. Maybe this"—he gestured at the ambulance—"will change his mind."

"It doesn't make any sense. It's as if . . ." I trailed off.

"Yes?"

"Well, it's as if someone is applying pressure to stop the investigation. Political or monetary pressure. Like when Brady stood accused."

In the summer of ninety-five, my half brother had been

accused of murder. No one had needed to convince me of his innocence, but not only did circumstances point to his being guilty, but my own relatives attempted to influence police procedures. Uncle Cornelius had feared one of his own sons might be accused instead, and had temporarily put pressure on the police to finish their investigation as quickly as possible. It might sound unforgivable, but I'd realized Cornelius Vanderbilt feared for his sons as dearly as I'd feared for my brother. I'd been willing to move heaven and earth to exonerate him, even to the point of suspecting my two Vanderbilt cousins, Neily and Reggie. Could I blame Uncle Cornelius for feeling the same?

But who would be using their power to influence this investigation? Surely not the family of a coachman or of a maid. My thoughts drifted to two suspects who might have the resources to sway the proceedings: Eugenia Ross and Francis Crane. Eugenia Ross had a solid alibi for Clarence's murder. But what about Francis?

"Does anyone know where John Donavan is now?" I asked Jesse.

"No. Once we release a man, it's his business where he goes. He's not anywhere on the property. That much we've determined. But that doesn't mean he wasn't here earlier." I'm sure it was the look on my face that prompted him to add, "Don't worry. We're already looking for him."

The coroner, finished with his inquiries, climbed up onto the driver's box of the ambulance with one of Jesse's uniformed men. The horses were set in motion. It was on my tongue to suggest Jesse also search out Francis Crane when another carriage passed the ambulance and swept along the wide arc of the driveway. I recognized the driver, as well as the two passengers beside him. Francis Crane guided his pair closer to the front door before coming to a stop and setting the brake.

"Dear heavens, what's happened now?" Gwendolen King swung down from the leather seat without waiting for Francis's assistance. Maude Wetmore slid out after her.

Her linen tennis dress fluttering around her ankles, Miss King ran over to Jesse and me. "Please don't tell me . . ." Her expression pleaded for news that would contradict the scene she had arrived home to. Then horror filled her eyes. "Not Mother or Philip or . . ."

"It's Clarence, your footman," I said as gently as I could. I placed a hand on her wrist. "I'm so sorry, Miss King. He's been murdered."

With a cry, she turned away and reached for Maude Wetmore. They caught each other up in an embrace, Miss King close to tears. Miss Wetmore, however, stared at Jesse and me over her friend's shoulder, her expression grim and speculative.

After several moments, Miss King straightened and dabbed the back of her hand at her damp cheeks. "Where is my mother?"

"She's upstairs in her room," I told her. "Mrs. Peake is with her. Your brother is still in his room. Safe," I added.

Nodding, the young woman appealed to her friend again, and together they hurried into the house.

"I have to finish up here, and then I'll speak with Mrs. King and her daughter. You'll stay for that?" I nodded, and Jesse patted my shoulder before walking away. Francis Crane took his place at my side.

"Again, Miss Cross? What in Sam Hill is happening here at Kingscote?"

"I wish I could tell you, Mr. Crane. I was in town with Mrs. Peake this afternoon on an errand for Mrs. King. We arrived to this chaos a little while ago." I indicated the policemen now congregating around their carriages.

"I heard you say it was one of the footmen?"

"Clarence, yes. The young man with the dark hair."

"This is terrible business. I only hope I can be of help to Mrs. King and Gwendolen."

I stole a glance at him. So it was Gwendolen now, not Miss King. Had she thawed toward his overtures? "I see you were with Miss King and Miss Wetmore. Playing tennis, by the way they were dressed. You too, Mr. Crane?" Only now did I take a moment to survey his attire. He wore a typical summer suit in a light beige color, his silk vest striped in brown, and a straw boater sat at an angle atop his light brown hair. His feet were not clad in rubber-soled tennis oxfords, but rather lace-up ankle boots.

I studied them for traces of mud; they were clean, obviously polished just that morning.

"No tennis for you today," I concluded.

"I merely watched," he confirmed with a smile. Would he have had time to clean and polish his boots after murdering Clarence and be at the Casino to watch Miss King and Miss Wetmore play their match? I didn't think so. "Has anyone told Philip yet?"

"I did."

"Poor Philip, locked away like a madman." He shook his head. "Perhaps this will finally exonerate him."

"It might. Except that somehow Philip managed to smuggle alcohol to his room. Remember? And no one admitted to bringing it to him." I paused to gauge his reaction to that. He made none whatsoever, not even the slightest tinge of guilty pink. He merely waited for me to complete my thought. "The detective has little choice but to suspect Mr. King has devised some way to sneak out of his room."

"The devil you say." Francis Crane pushed out a breath and shook his head. "Poor Philip," he said again. "He just can't seem to claw his way out of this mess."

"If he's innocent, Detective Whyte will exonerate him. If not, then he deserves the mess he's in, doesn't he?"

Mr. Crane regarded me with an ironic slant to his mouth

that might have been agreement, though I couldn't be certain. Then he nodded at me and set off into the house.

With no reason to remain, I lingered nonetheless. Two murders, both committed outside. Fog had obscured the night on which Baldwin had been hit by the automobile. Clarence had somehow been lured into the laundry yard, hidden from general view of the house and the rest of the grounds by tall hedges. This suggested neither murder had been spur of the moment, that the culprit had awaited the most advantageous circumstances at just the right moment.

Today's incident certainly ruled out Mrs. Ross, for she could not have traveled to Kingscote after Mrs. Peake and I left her and arrived here ahead of us by half an hour. Francis had an alibi, although not an unquestionable one, for he'd only been a couple of minutes away at the Casino. Where had John Donavan gone after being released from jail? Did he have family in town? Friends? Anyone who could vouch for him? Or had he returned to Kingscote, murdered Clarence, and then gotten away?

Clarence must have known something significant about Baldwin's death. Perhaps he had realized who murdered the butler, or had discovered a clue that could lead to identifying the killer. I wondered if Clarence had visited Donavan in jail. Perhaps he had, and confronted Donavan about what he knew, never expecting Donavan would be released. But then, why hadn't Clarence also shared his information with the police? Had it been another case of blackmail?

As I pondered these questions, I strode across the lawn and found myself near the weeping beech where the Hartley Steamer had pinned Baldwin. As I had done before, I tripped over one of the tree's sprawling roots hidden in the grass. My toes throbbed through my boot, but I kept walking, using my arm to sweep the trailing branches out of my way. The cool interior of the tree surrounded me, the moist air like kisses along my skin.

I made my way to the trunk at the center of the canopy. No traces showed where Baldwin had been nearly severed in two by the Hartley's front end. His body, it seemed, had protected the bark from the automobile's steel panel. But the ruts from the tires showed faintly in the dirt and fallen leaves. For no particular reason, I bent lower to inspect one of them. What conclusion could I hope to draw? I followed the ruts back to the outer edge of the branches, where a few pebbles from the gravel driveway had been dragged along by the car's tires. They glowed white in the shadows . . .

One glowed *too* brightly, and nestled unnaturally round in the dirt. Crouching down, I scooped it up into my palm. Upon pushing my way back out from beneath the tree, I studied the object in the sunlight.

It was no pebble, I immediately confirmed. I had found a pearl.

Jesse gathered the women—Mrs. King, her daughter, Miss Wetmore, and Mrs. Peake—in the south drawing room and showed them the pearl I had found. Miss King and her friend had changed from their tennis clothes into afternoon gowns of pastel muslin. Mr. Crane, after hesitating no doubt in hopes of receiving an invitation to stay and hear what Jesse had to say, took his leave.

While I looked on, the four passed the pearl from one to another, Miss King rising from the sofa to hand it to her mother where she sat in a damask armchair. They regarded Jesse with blank expressions. Ella King rolled the pearl from one palm to the other. "Are we supposed to recognize this, Detective?"

He stood in front of the fireplace, which was filled with a colorful assortment of hothouse flowers. "Have any of you broken a necklace recently? Or could it have fallen off a dress or other item of clothing?"

Gwendolen and Miss Wetmore exchanged a glance and

shook their heads no. Mrs. Peake did likewise. Mrs. King shrugged. "Not that any of us are aware of, apparently. Was this the only one you found?"

Jesse looked to me for a reply. I nodded. "I even got down on my hands and knees to search. I didn't find any others."

"I can't imagine where it came from," Miss King commented.

"Then perhaps I can." I went to Ella King and reached for the pearl. It was no small specimen, as pearls went, but nearly a quarter inch in diameter. The warm, golden tint and satin luster spoke of its fine quality. Such strands of pearls were no uncommon sight here in Newport, at least not in the summer. My own aunt Alice owned many pearl necklaces, some as long as my arm, secured by diamond-studded clasps.

But Aunt Alice would have no reason to have been at Kingscote recently. Nor Aunt Alva, nor any other society lady that I could think of except for Mrs. Wetmore, who'd had dinner here that night after the auto parade. Even if another woman *had* visited Kingscote, why would she have strayed off the driveway to the beech tree?

A society lady would not have. A pearl necklace, conjured by a memory, dangled in my mind's eye. The day of the parade. Mrs. Ross.

"I asked Detective Whyte to rule out all of you." I held the pearl up to the light. "Now, can any of you remember Mrs. Ross wearing a pearl necklace on any of the occasions you've seen her?"

Mrs. King eyed me shrewdly. "I'm assuming you can, Miss Cross."

"Yes. At the automobile parade. But my word alone isn't enough."

Gwendolen King leaned forward. "Then you're saying she was here the night Baldwin was struck? That possibly she and Baldwin struggled, and her necklace broke?"

"Yes, I'm saying it's possible. Although, she could not have returned today to attack Clarence. Mrs. Peake and I left her at her home *after* Olivia Riley discovered the body and the police had been telephoned."

"She might have hired someone to do her dirty work." With a disgusted look, Mrs. Peake folded her arms. "I wouldn't put it past her."

"Nor would I," Mrs. King readily agreed. "But Miss Cross is correct. Without some corroboration on whether or not Mrs. Ross owns such a pearl necklace, a single pearl will not incriminate her."

"That's correct," I said. "So all of you, please think hard. Can you remember Mrs. Ross wearing a pearl necklace at any time during your acquaintance with her?"

"Acquaintance." Miss King wrinkled her nose. "As if such a cordial term could be used to describe our experiences with that contemptible creature."

"Gwendolen," her mother gently chastised.

"I'm only speaking the truth, Mother." She gazed up at Jessie. "Shouldn't Philip be part of this conversation? He's as *acquainted* with Mrs. Ross as the rest of us." She said this last with blatant sarcasm. "We should bring him downstairs."

Jesse hesitated, drawing Mrs. King's attention to him. She studied him a moment before saying, "The detective isn't quite ready to exonerate your brother, Gwennie. He's afraid Philip might merely pretend to recognize this pearl as being from a necklace owned by Mrs. Ross. Isn't that right, Detective?"

"I'm afraid, ma'am, that your son's word on the matter won't carry much weight," he admitted with a doleful nod.

Gwendolen King surged to her feet. "Then perhaps it's time you left this house, Detective Whyte."

"Gwennie!" Her mother, too, rose to her feet.

From her place on the sofa, Maude Wetmore reached out a

hand to touch the back of her friend's arm. Just a gentle gesture, but one that caught Miss King's attention and brought a contrite look to her face. "I'm sorry. This is all so very upsetting."

"I understand, Miss King." Jesse offered her a deferential nod. "As soon as we're done here I'll go upstairs, show Mr. King the pearl, and see what he has to say. In the meantime, can any of you picture such a necklace on Mrs. Ross?"

They all made an effort to concentrate. Their winkled brows attested to that. But I saw, too, their frustration. Both Gwendolen and her mother had resumed their seats. Now Mrs. King tossed up her hands. "Pearls are so common, one barely notices them anymore."

I suppressed a sardonic chuckle at that, and forewent mentioning that for the vast majority of people, here in Newport and elsewhere, pearl necklaces, indeed necklaces of any kind, were neither common nor inconspicuous.

"That's very true, Mother," her daughter agreed. "And in the case of Mrs. Ross, I try not to look at her too closely. I'm merely anxious for her to go away. She has been a most unpleasant fixture in our lives these many years, since before Father died."

"What about the day she showed up on your doorstep, after Baldwin died?" I tried again to jog Mrs. King's memory. "When she informed you of the hearing set for September?"

She shook her head. "I don't remember her wearing any such necklace."

"Which could mean she wasn't," I pointed out. I turned to Jesse and spoke of Ethan under his assumed name. "Mr. Merrin opened the door to her. We should ask him as well."

He nodded, then appealed to Mrs. Peake. "Ma'am? Any recollections?"

"Only that she wasn't wearing pearls today. Was she, Miss Cross?"

"She was not." I thought back on my prior visit to Eugenia Ross. "Nor was she wearing the necklace the last time I called on her. But that, too, proves little. We saw her in her home. She might only wear that particular necklace when she's out." I gasped at a new thought. "The jeweler."

Jesse frowned in puzzlement. "Who?"

Mrs. Peake pointed a finger at me. "You're right, Miss Cross. She might have been wearing the necklace when she bought Olivia's brooch from the jeweler in town. *He* would certainly have noticed it." She turned to Jesse. "Charles Wilmont, Esquire, on Bellevue."

"I know the shop," he said. "I'll stop in on the way back to the station."

"Detective Whyte?"

We all turned our attention to the voice coming from the Stair Hall. A moment later a uniformed officer came into the parlor, though he ventured no farther than a couple of steps in, avoiding the area rug and looking apologetic for intruding. In one hand he held his cap, while in the other, an envelope, muddied and damp, its flap unsealed. "We found something new out in the laundry yard."

"I thought that area was combed when we first arrived," Jesse said brusquely enough that the policeman winced.

"It was, sir, but this was half hidden beneath the hedge behind the barrel."

Jesse held out his hand. "Give it here." Holding the soiled envelope in his palm, he peered into it, then reached in with his first and second fingers to slide an object out. I spied a thick, square piece of paper in an off-white color but yellowed with age, and, from its sojourn in the laundry yard, damp and stained. Red lettering blazed across what was visible of one side. Jesse studied the print. "It's an admission ticket to a boxing match."

"To the club in Middletown?" I spoke without much enthusiasm, doubting this item would yield any insights other than that the men of Kingscote enjoyed gambling on boxing matches. But Jesse shook his head.

"No. To a fight that took place nine years ago, in 1890. At the Delphi Athletic Club in Providence." He held the ticket out to me.

I could read the bold print announcing the fighters' names. A memory tumbled to the forefront of my thoughts. Grasping the ticket by its edges, I gasped. "The Midnight Hawk. Harry Ainsley called himself the Hawk. Are they the same?"

Chapter 17

"Nine years ago in Providence . . . It *could* be Harry. But who was this Bald Eagle he was scheduled to fight that night?" I continued to study the admission ticket. The aging paper offered quite a bit of information: the date, October seventeenth; the day of the week, a Tuesday; the time, half past eight o'clock in the evening; and the amount of admission, one dollar. A princely sum, especially all those years ago. I could only imagine the amounts of the wagers laid on the fight.

And yet, the most important information, which might have made so much difference, remained elusive. "Is this the very fight that incapacitated Harry Ainsley?" I shook my head in frustration. "And who dropped this in the laundry yard? Was it Clarence?"

"Who is Harry Ainsley?" I heard Mrs. King ask.

"Harry Ainsley was a boxer well on his way to becoming a champion, until a fight left him permanently addled nine years ago," Jesse explained to the Kingscote women. Then he turned to me. "Your first question should be easy to answer with an inquiry or two. As for your second question . . ." He trailed off and shrugged.

"Bald Eagle . . . Bald . . ." Shock dawned on Gwendolen King's features. "Why, isn't it obvious? Baldwin." Her mother and Miss Wetmore gasped. Miss King jumped up and came to my side, reaching for the ticket. I placed it in her palm. "Don't you think it's possible?"

"Our butler, a former boxer?" Mrs. King, too, came to her feet. She and Mrs. Peake traded astonished expressions. "Don't be absurd, Gwendolen."

"It's not absurd, ma'am," I said. "Your butler was fond of the sport. And he was quite good at predicting winners."

"But what could this mean?" Mrs. King addressed her question to the room in general. "The fight occurred nine years ago. What importance could it have on a man's life now?"

"Don't you see?" I held out my hands. "Whoever Harry Ainsley went up against in his last fight left Harry permanently incapacitated. If the opponent was Isaiah Baldwin, he may have been killed in revenge."

Jesse was nodding in agreement. "By a friend or a member of Harry Ainsley's family."

"But why now, after nine long years?" Mrs. Peake's mystification was reflected in the other women's faces.

"Opportunity," Jesse and I said at the same time. I let Jesse continue. "Somehow, fate finally brought together the players from that nine-year-old tragedy. Or so it would seem."

With two fingers, Miss Wetmore plucked the damp ticket from her friend's hand and held it up. "But if this is significant, if Clarence was killed because of it, why would his killer leave it behind?"

After a short silence, I said, "Perhaps he didn't. Perhaps he didn't know Clarence had it. Clarence might have confronted the killer with what he had guessed about the past, but kept his proof—the ticket—hidden. As his death became imminent, perhaps Clarence dropped the ticket in the mud . . . for someone to find."

"You call it proof." Gwendolen's voice became strained with frustration. "But all that ticket does is perhaps link Baldwin to this boxer, this Harry Ainsley. It doesn't tell us who or what part his killer might have played in what happened nine years ago."

"Not yet." Jesse went to Miss Wetmore and reclaimed the ticket. "But it's a start. It gives us a new direction to follow."

"Boxing has been part of the puzzle from the beginning," I said. Derrick and I had driven out to the boxing club in Middletown looking for information about Philip King's gambling habits. There we had learned that, besides Philip, Isaiah Baldwin had frequented the club. The manager, Mr. Tooley, had said Baldwin possessed a knack for picking winners. Now I understood why. It was because of Baldwin's prior experience in the ring.

Mrs. King folded her hands at her waist. "Then if boxing is the key, Mrs. Ross should be ruled out, shouldn't she?"

"Not necessarily," I countered. "She often visited the asylum where Harry Ainsley has been living. You see, it's the same facility where your husband's uncle, William King, was held the last few years of his life. Mrs. Ross might be well acquainted with Harry, might have taken up his cause. Or she might have some other connection to him and his family."

"Why, the woman is twisted enough to have decided Harry Ainsley is another of her long-lost relatives." Gwendolen scoffed. "To think, she approached us at the parade and stood right here on our very doorstep. A possible murderer." She cast a glance at the windows along the east side of the room. "Do you think she'll try to break in and murder us all in our sleep?"

"I'm fairly certain she won't do that. Mrs. Ross might be

calculating, might even be a killer, but she doesn't appear to do anything without a sound, logical reason," Jesse assured them all. "Still, I'll post a policeman here at night from now on. Keep the windows and doors locked."

Ella King nodded her thanks. She still didn't know that John Donavan had been released from jail. Jesse made no mention of it, and I concluded that he saw no reason to further worry the family, especially when he would be sending an officer to patrol the house at night. I would also advise Ethan to be extra vigilant in keeping track of who came and went during the day.

While I trekked into the servants' domain to speak with Ethan, Jesse went upstairs to speak with Philip, and we convened outside some twenty minutes later. Philip had no insights to offer. As he had told me earlier, he'd been asleep until Olivia Riley's cries woke him. As for pearl necklaces, he claimed never to notice such trifles.

After Jesse left Kingscote, I lingered outside on the driveway, studying the European beech and thinking. I had few doubts that Mrs. Ross had come here the night Baldwin had been struck. That perhaps she had argued with him. That somehow her pearl necklace had broken. Something, however, stopped me just shy of fully believing she pushed the Hartley Steamer into him.

What was it? What little detail continued to prod and nag at the corner of my mind? What could possibly rule out a woman who had every reason to wish ill on the King family, and who, by her own admission, had enlisted Baldwin's help in bringing the King family down. Or, at least, in helping her undermine their claim to William King's fortune.

I slowly walked around the sweep of the tree, then shouldered my way into the deep shade beneath its canopy. Dampness pervaded the air, and I felt the slight drop in the temperature, smelled the rich, earthy scents within, as if the interior of the foliage constituted a world unto itself. But nothing here spoke to my doubts concerning Mrs. Ross's guilt.

With a shrug, I stepped back into the sunlight and walked back to the driveway, my heels grinding against the gravel beneath them. A pearl. Bits of gravel. What else? Once more, I turned back and walked toward the tree . . .

And stumbled over the same half-hidden root that had tripped me at least twice before. I leaned down closer to inspect it, then crouched and ran my hands over its jagged bark. Here was no ripple in the grass, but a snaking, gnarled ridge, part of the tree's formidable root system that spread weblike from the trunk. It stood several inches up from the soil beneath the grass, and as I looked, I noticed the grass immediately to either side of it stood longer than the rest of the lawn. I concluded the gardeners could not push the lawn mowers over such a protrusion. No, here they must use hand clippers, and perhaps hadn't done so the last time they mowed.

Slowly, I pushed to standing. Could a woman summon the strength, even in a fit of temper, to push a vehicle over such a root? It would be difficult enough for a man, though I believed that with enough force—combined with enough willpower summoned by anger and loathing—he might accomplish the feat.

But that isn't to say Mrs. Ross couldn't have brought someone with her, a man willing to do her bidding.

On my way to the carriage house to retrieve Maestro and my buggy, I came upon Olivia Riley standing outside, a short distance from the house, beyond the laundry yard. She appeared to be staring at the clouds scuttling across the sky, or perhaps at nothing at all.

I thought about skirting her, leaving her to her thoughts.

She must be terribly shaken after what she'd been through. Was she also guilty? The thought filled my mind, unbidden. I exhaled and shook my head. Guilty or not, her future prospects, and those of her daughter, must have seemed dismal at best. I set my feet in her direction.

"Miss Riley, if you have a moment. Please."

She flinched, then quickly regained her composure, such as it was. Her eyes were red-rimmed, her cheeks mottled. "What can you possibly have to say to me? I found a body today, Miss Cross. The body of a nice young man who didn't deserve what happened to him." Her voice hitched and faltered. She swallowed. "Can I not be left alone?"

"I won't keep you long, I promise."

She cast a glance over her shoulder at the house before turning back with a resigned nod. When I hesitated, her attractive features hardened with anger. "This isn't only about today, is it? You followed me yesterday. I saw you in the trolley, and again on the wharf. Do you think I'm blind? Or just stupid?"

"I think you're neither, but if you saw me, why did you keep going?" I kept my tone even, without a hint of accusation. "Why didn't you confront me?"

"I had little choice."

"Because of your daughter."

She pivoted away, her black skirts swishing tersely about her ankles. "Blast you, Miss Cross. Leave my daughter out of this."

"I can't." I came up behind her and placed my hand on her shoulder. This conversation surely overstepped the bounds and interfered with Jesse's investigation. He might be angry when he learned of it, but I couldn't help myself. I'd known too many young women in Olivia's position. Many had knocked at Gull Manor's door asking for help and haven, for themselves and their illegitimate children. Olivia might be innocent of Baldwin's and Clarence's deaths, but with her daughter ill and her resources severely limited, how long before this housemaid would be driven to a desperate, illegal act?

"Yes, Miss Riley, I followed you." I saw no reason to mention anyone else if she didn't. "I did so because of the secretive nature of your errand, and, as you know, because I'm helping the police and Mrs. King discover who killed Baldwin."

She whirled back around to face me, her chin raised. "And you think I did it?"

I shook my head. "No, I don't. I never wished to distrust you. And that's not why I'm speaking to you now. I understand why you kept your daughter a secret from your employer. I don't believe Mrs. King would have held it against you, but many would have. I want you to know that if you need help, now or in the future, whether it's money or a doctor or food, or even a place to stay, you must come to me."

Her brows gathered, her lashes narrowing warily. "You're no society lady. You might not be as low as me, but neither are you from one of the grand families hereabouts."

So then, she didn't know of my background, or that my relatives owned three of Newport's most magnificent cottages. "I have resources," was all I said, certain that if I were to go to Aunt Alice for a loan, she would be only too happy to help. "I've assisted other women, plenty of them. You can ask other servants the next time you're in town or if you happen to attend one of their gatherings at Forty Steps. People know me and they'll tell you the truth about me."

Her guardedness eased slightly. "And in return? Nothing is ever free."

"There is nothing. Except to answer one question."

"Hmph." Her shoulders hunched as if she were preparing to fight me. "Did I push the motorcar into Mr. Baldwin? Is that your question?"

"No, Miss Riley. What I wish to know is whether Isaiah Baldwin is the father of your little girl, of Fiona."

Her mouth dropped open in what appeared to be genuine surprise. "Good grief, no. What gave you that idea?"

"Had you ever worked with him in the past?"

"No, never." Her lips gathered to form an O. "I see. You think he got me with child and then left me. Is that it? And I killed him out of vengeance?"

"It's been said he left his former position in Bristol after getting a maid in the family way. She, of course, was dismissed."

"It wasn't me." She laughed without a trace of humor. "Not that the same thing didn't happen to me. It just didn't happen with him. My last position, before Fiona was born, was with a family in Tiverton. And no, I wasn't dismissed. I left on my own before anyone knew what had happened."

"What did you do? Where did you go?"

"I moved in with my aunt. After I had Fiona, I went to New York and worked in the garment trade—that's right, not as a maid for a family. I only said that because I didn't want to have to answer questions about why I left domestic service. No, I worked at a sewing machine fourteen hours a day. If you think it's easier work than cleaning house, you're wrong, Miss Cross. Imagine all those hours sitting still until your legs go numb and your back aches so badly you can barely hold yourself up another minute. And your hands cramp from clutching the fabric and keeping it from bunching . . ." She shook her head. "I'd much rather scrub floors, beat rugs, and dust shelves any day. I was only too happy to sign on as Mrs. King's housemaid. And truly, Miss Cross, I couldn't ask for a better position. Fair pay, decent food, a bed I don't toss and turn in all night."

The anger and fear eased from her countenance. I studied her and reached a conclusion. "Then it was true what you and the other servants told my reporter from the *Messenger*, Jacob Stodges, about being happy working at Kingscote."

"It is. Oh, Isaiah Baldwin sometimes tried to make trouble, and his hands wandered my way a time or two. But I gave him what for and ignored his persnickety ways, for the most part. We all did. Why let a man like that ruin good employment for the rest of us? I only wish . . ." She sighed. "I only wish it would last. Come autumn, Mrs. King will close up the house, let us all go, and sail away to Europe. Even if she agreed to hire us all back when she returned in the spring, none of us can wait that long. We'll each need to find a new situation."

"Then who sent me that note?" I murmured, more to myself than to Miss Riley.

"What note?"

I shook my head. "Never mind, it doesn't matter." But it did. Someone had wished to incriminate one of Kingscote's servants. The individual probably hadn't cared who might be blamed. He—or she—had merely wished to deflect suspicion away from themselves. And I had allowed myself to be deceived.

Once again, I found myself gazing up at the stern façade of the Butler Hospital in Providence. Clarence's death, and the questions it raised, had sent Derrick and me back here, not to ask about William King this time, but with hopes of visiting Harry Ainsley. Derrick's memories of the fight that robbed Harry of his intellect were sketchy at best, but he had contacted a reporter at his family's newspaper to see what could be dug up about the fight at the Delphi Athletic Club nine years ago. He feared, however, that the man who had fought Harry that night, the Bald Eagle, had registered only under that name and had remained otherwise anonymous. Were the Bald Eagle and Isaiah Baldwin the same man?

On the way here on the train, we had discussed Clarence's death and the cryptic hint we believed he had left behind. "The question," Derrick had pointed out, "is how did Clarence come by that ticket. Did he find it among Baldwin's things while cleaning out the room? Or perhaps in the butler's pantry? Although, had that been the case, Ethan should have known about it."

"Or," I replied as the train jostled me against the back of the seat, "did Baldwin himself give Clarence the ticket for safekeeping? Perhaps he had known his life was in danger and didn't want it disappearing."

"If that's so, we can only assume the ticket is a direct link between Baldwin, Harry Ainsley, and the murderer."

We entered the hospital with hopes and doubts in equal measure. Would Harry Ainsley be able to tell us anything?

The man at the front desk, different from the one we'd met last time, inquired about our business with little apparent interest, until I mentioned Harry Ainsley's name. That produced a quirk of his eyebrow. He gave the desk telephone a crank and murmured into the handset. After hanging up he asked us to find seats in the waiting room. We were not detained there long, as only minutes later an orderly greeted us and bade us follow him.

He led us up to the building's second floor and down a scrupulously scrubbed corridor. From a window at the far end, bright, cheerful sunlight splashed the tiled floor and beige walls. Murmuring could be heard from the rooms on either side, their doors open. A man in a suit strode out from one, followed closely by a nurse. It was not the doctor we had spoken to last time, and I hoped we would not encounter Dr. Winston again. They passed us with brisk nods and kept going to the elevator. I couldn't help wondering what kind of errand they had set out upon. Something routine, or trouble with a patient?

The orderly escorted us past some of those open doors, whereupon I realized these were administrative offices, not patient quarters. He brought us to a large room near the end of the corridor, where he bade us again be seated. He took up position by the door, his feet braced wide, his arms crossed, and his gaze on us. No one else occupied the room.

I don't believe he meant to be rude or make us uncomfortable. I supposed he merely had the responsibility of seeing that we didn't go wandering off where visitors shouldn't be. Still, a sense of being scrutinized sent a chill across my shoulders. What would it be like to be watched all hours of the day, to have one's liberty curtailed, to wake, eat, bathe, and even walk in the sunlight, only when one was told to do so?

Derrick must have noticed my shiver, for his hand slid across to cover mine. The orderly made note of it with a little flick of his eyelids. Then he shifted his gaze away from us, toward the windows lining the outside wall. There were numerous chairs arranged in various groupings throughout the room, a piano in one corner, a card table, and a set of bookshelves filled with well-worn volumes, probably donations from local families. There was even a phonograph, with a gaily painted horn, sitting on top of an oak cabinet, which I assumed held the recorded discs.

"I wonder why we're waiting in such a large room?" I mused aloud, thinking only Derrick could hear me. I was wrong.

"Harry can become agitated meeting people in small surroundings," the orderly replied. "Makes him feel penned in. He does better in open spaces, but it isn't time for him to go outside, and we don't like to vary his routine too much. It's enough that he's being brought down here to see you two."

I detected disapproval and exchanged a glance with Derrick, who waggled an eyebrow. I shrugged off the orderly's censure, which after all showed he cared about the patient's well-being.

"I remember them," came a voice from the corridor. Harry Ainsley practically ran toward us, and Derrick and I came to our feet. Instinct urged me to back away from him, to seek cover and take Derrick with me. What if Harry became violent again, as when he'd tried to swing at Derrick?

My fears proved unnecessary. His attendant, the same man we'd met previously, caught Harry by the back of his arm and coaxed him to slow down, which he did. But his smile beamed as he approached us, and he took me aback by shaking both Derrick's hand and my own.

"Hello. Come all this way to see me?"

Did he know we'd come from Newport? The tolerant smiles on the two hospital workers' faces suggested this was merely something Harry asked anyone who came to visit him. I decided to play along.

"We did, Mr. Ainsley. How are you today?"

He gestured for us to resume our seats and chose one for himself, dragging it closer to ours before he sat and leaned toward us. "Been busy preparing for the big fight. Almost ready." He made a fist and bent his elbow to display the muscle beneath the sleeve of his robe.

"I can see that you are, Mr. Ainsley."

"What's your name?" He gestured at Derrick. "And yours. I remember your faces. Not your names."

We introduced ourselves, and Harry shook our hands again. Despite his predicament, which earned him my utmost compassion, his affability made me smile. "Coming to the fight?"

"Of course we are," Derrick assured him.

"And you'll root for me, not *him*?"

"We'd root for no other, Mr. Ainsley," I said. "But speaking of him, who is he? What is his name?"

Harry pulled back in his chair. "Don't want to talk about him."

"Oh, nor do I." I smiled to reassure him. "I'd only like to know who we're rooting *against*."

"He says I don't stand a chance."

"He would say that, you realize." Derrick leaned toward Harry and patted his knee. "You're the champion, after all, and he's desperately trying to gain some advantage over you."

"It won't work," I added.

"No . . . it won't work." Harry appeared to contemplate that, and his smile returned, although less certain than it had been.

"So then . . ." Derrick paused until Harry met his gaze. "Your opponent's name?"

"Eagle."

"Yes, but his real name," I prodded, then wished I hadn't when Harry's countenance fell and he hopped up from his chair. His attendant darted closer to him, all his attention riveted on his patient. Even the orderly had come to attention, ready to assist should it become necessary.

"It's all right, Harry, never mind," the attendant said. He placed his hands on Harry's shoulders and gave him a gentle, good-natured shake. "There's a good man. How about tapping on the piano keys a bit?"

Harry turned to view the instrument in the corner, and eagerly crossed the room to it. I expected nothing more than the pounding of keys, but a delicate, haunting melody reached my ears. As Harry began singing in a confident tenor, I recognized the song: "Red Is the Rose," a traditional Irish ballad that spoke of love and heartbreak. Despite the piano's dubious tuning, Harry played softly and sweetly, his fingers taking their time over the notes, and when he reached the chorus, his singing brought tears to sting my eyes.

The attendant noticed my emotional response. "I don't know where he learned to play," he said. "He came here knowing how, and that's a favorite song of his. Strange thing, he can do that, but doesn't fully understand where he is or what happened to him."

"The poor man," I murmured, my heart going out to him once more. Then I turned back to the attendant. "Tell us, does Harry ever have visitors? A woman, perhaps?"

"A woman?" The attendant laughed softly. "Miss, you're the only woman who's come to see Harry since I've worked here. But no, as for visitors of any sort, never. As I remember telling you last time." He raised an eyebrow to drive home the point.

I persisted nonetheless. "And you have no idea who his family was?"

He shrugged. "Maybe he came out of an orphanage." His expression changed, became quizzical. "Why all these questions about Harry?"

Derrick and I regarded each other. I nodded, and he said, "There was a murder in Newport recently. We believe Harry is somehow connected to the murderer."

"Harry? That's impossible. I told you last time, he's been here about three years now, and before that the McLean Asylum in Massachusetts."

"We know he's not directly involved," Derrick said, "but the man who was killed was named Isaiah Baldwin, and a ticket to a boxing match from nine years ago was found on the property where he died. The Black Hawk was named as one of the fighters. That was Harry, wasn't it? He was to come up against a man using the moniker Bald Eagle. We believe Isaiah Baldwin might have been this Bald Eagle, and might be the man who knocked the sense out of poor Harry nine years ago."

The attendant let out a low whistle. "You don't say."

"We do." I'd turned my attention back to Harry as he continued playing. Now I shifted my focus back to the attendant. "A second man was murdered yesterday, and it was because of him that the ticket was found. We think he guessed who the murderer was, and that the admission ticket was a clue into that person's identity."

Suddenly the piano went silent. Harry stood and retraced his steps. Stopping in front of us, he said, "The Eagle isn't gonna win. I'm the champion."

The attendant clapped Harry's shoulder. "You surely are, Harry. You know, Harry, it's almost time to go outside. Would you like that?" Harry nodded eagerly. "Then why don't you go look out the window and make sure it isn't raining."

Like a child, Harry scurried to the window. I regarded the attendant with a suspicious frown. "What was that about? One doesn't have to go to the window to see that it's a beautifully sunny day."

"I wanted Harry distracted for a moment. Because . . ." The man shuffled his feet and rubbed at the back of his neck. "I wasn't going to say anything, until you brought up those murders. That changes things a bit, doesn't it? Although, I don't see how Harry can have anything to do with any of that, mind you."

"Yes?" I held out my hand as if he could drop the answers into it.

Derrick took a more direct approach. "If there's something you have to tell us, out with it."

The attendant angled a look at Harry, who stood with his back to us as he surveyed the weather outside, and then slid another glance at the orderly beside the open door. He stepped closer to us, and said in a whisper, "Actually, Harry does have an occasional visitor. Just one, and just once a year. It's always in the spring. A young man. Rich sort, you know, well dressed, fancy boots, fine way of talking."

"And he came again this past spring?" I asked, wanting to be sure I understood him correctly.

The attendant nodded. "Spent about half an hour this last time. Nothing much happened. Harry stayed calm. Didn't seem to know the fellow. But this last time, when the young man left, he slipped me ten whole dollars and asked me not to mention that he was ever here, should anyone come asking."

"Didn't that strike you as strange, not to mention suspicious?" Derrick's voice carried an edge of anger.

The man shrugged. "Surely. But a whole sawbuck, and no harm came to Harry. He wasn't upset by the visit."

"What did this person look like?"

Another shrug. "I don't know. Young. Slender as young men are before they fill out. Dark hair."

A slender young man with dark hair, who hailed from the wealthy set. While that could describe an untold number of individuals, one in particular stood out in my mind, as it apparently did in Derrick's, too.

"What about his name?" Derrick made the query with such quiet force, it almost sounded like a threat. The attendant hesitated, undoubtedly thinking of those ten dollars he'd accepted to keep quiet. As Harry turned away from the window and started back toward us, Derrick murmured, "Do you wish to keep your position here?"

"King," the man said. "His name is Philip King."

Chapter 18

Once back in Newport, Derrick and I went directly to the police station and gave our full report to Jesse.

He scrubbed a hand across his face. "Why on earth would he go there? Is he trying to hammer the nails into his own coffin?"

"I suppose he might have met him the same way we did," I said, "accidently while inquiring after his uncle. And maybe he's gone back to visit Harry periodically out of pity. It might not have anything to do with Isaiah Baldwin."

Derrick made a dubious face. Jesse grumbled audibly and pushed out of his desk chair. "I suppose I'll have to go ask him, won't I? Not that I'll necessarily get anything approaching the truth out of him."

I stood up from my seat as well. "Do you want me to go with you?"

"No, I'll handle it, but I'll let you know what he says."

We all left the police station together, and Derrick accompanied me to Gull Manor, where Nanny insisted he stay to dinner. Before leaving the Butler Hospital earlier, we had asked Harry about Philip King, but he could tell us nothing. He'd become agitated and once more retreated to the piano. Now, the subject of Harry's musical talents arose around my kitchen table as we pondered how he could remember some things and not others.

"Music settles in one's soul," Nanny said with a sage nod. We all agreed.

"Odd, though, that he chose that song," Katie mused aloud as she set the pork roast at the center of the table, then turned back to the stove for the potatoes and cabbage. Patch, lying beneath the table, lifted his head from his paws and worked his nose at the tempting aromas.

"Why is that, Katie?" Derrick stood to help her with the heavy serving bowl. The window curtains stirred, catching the temperate breezes rolling in off the ocean.

As always when company addressed her directly, Katie blushed to the roots of her hair. Four years after coming to my household, she still wasn't comfortable with being treated like family. But she replied, " 'Red Is the Rose' is an Irish ballad, sir."

I tilted my head in puzzlement. "Why is that odd?"

"Ainsley's not an Irish name," she clarified. "It's Scottish."

I shrugged. "As far as I know, Harry was born in this country. He certainly sounds like an American. Likely he heard the song in a pub and took a fancy to it."

"I'm sure that's it, Miss Emma." Her look of perplexity lingering, Katie took her seat at the table and we all began helping ourselves to Nanny's simple but satisfying fare.

Derrick made sounds of appreciation, and said, "Getting back to Philip King. At the police station, Emma suggested he'd originally met Harry while visiting his uncle William."

"More than likely. What else could it be?" Nanny passed the bowl of cabbage and potatoes to Derrick, who accepted a second helping with a happy nod.

"But now that I think about it, I don't know that any of the Kings ever visited their uncle William," he said. "Especially the younger Kings."

"Another example of a patient being abandoned by his family?" I couldn't help murmuring. It still dismayed me that Harry Ainsley had been locked away and forgotten. And William King, too.

"I don't think it's a coincidence, Philip visiting Harry," Derrick observed. "Did he meet him accidentally, or did he learn of Harry from Baldwin because of their mutual interest in boxing? That's the question."

Before I could respond, a pounding on my front door echoed through the house. Patch, lurking about our feet hoping for falling crumbs, thumped against my knees as he jumped up. Katie stood to go, but some instinct or premonition, I wasn't sure which, sent me to my feet. "I'll go, Katie. You finish your supper."

Patch ran ahead of me. The pounding persisted, becoming even louder and more urgent. Patch barked in reply until I shushed him. At the same time, I heard footsteps behind me and felt the presence of the others at my back. Then a voice called out, "Miss Cross? Please, I need to see you."

I turned around and made eye contact with Derrick. "That sounds like Olivia Riley. Something must have happened at Kingscote." I hurried my steps until I reached the front door.

"Oh, Miss Cross," Olivia Riley said the moment I swung the door open. She wore her black maid's dress but had shed her pinafore and starched white cap. Her hair had fallen from its pins and her face was so flushed I could only surmise she had run practically all the way from Kingscote. "It's my daughter. It's Fiona. Another wire came from my aunt. It's an emergency. Fiona's taken a turn for the worse. Her fever's up, and there's no money for another visit from the doctor. You said . . ."

"Come in, Miss Riley." I reached out to grasp her shoulder and drew her across the threshold. From there I led her into the parlor. The others—Nanny, Katie, and Derrick—followed us in. Patch's nails clicked eagerly on the hardwood floor until he reached the area rug. I sat Miss Riley down on the sofa and settled in beside her. Patch took up position on the floor at her other side, gazing up at her with concern-filled eyes. To help calm her, I took her hand firmly in my own. "Yes, I told you to come to me for help, and help you shall have." I glanced first at the clock on my mantel, and then at Derrick. "It's not yet six o'clock. The Western Union office should still be open."

He nodded. "I'll go immediately and wire funds."

"There, you see?" Miss Riley had fallen to tears, and I leaned my face close to hers to gain her attention. "We'll wire the funds for the doctor. You need only tell us your aunt's name. Do you think she waited at the Western Union office for a reply?"

"I don't know. I suppose she must have. Or . . . what if she didn't? With Fiona ill, she might have asked a neighbor to send the telegram. I don't know what to do. You see . . . I haven't got the money."

"If your aunt isn't there, we'll request a message be brought to her residence," Derrick said. "The amount waiting for her will be indicated, so she can show it to the doctor. That should be enough to assure him of payment." He readied himself to leave while Miss Riley wrote down her aunt's name and the street she lived on. She folded the paper and handed it to Derrick, who slipped it into his coat pocket. "I'll be back as soon as I can."

While I continued to soothe Miss Riley, Katie ran back to the kitchen to make tea, and Nanny kept up a steady stream of conversation about how resilient children are and how quickly such fevers can come and go. She sounded cheerful and encouraging, but I knew that underneath that façade, she was worried about Miss Riley's child. True, some children proved impervious to fevers and recovered quickly, but many others died. And it seemed little Fiona had been suffering for some time now. How long could her little body hold out, especially if her nutrition hadn't been the best?

Slowly, Miss Riley rallied enough to stop the flow of her tears. Katie returned with tea for the three of us, and then excused herself to see to the supper dishes. Miss Riley sipped from her cup steadily, barely waiting for it to cool. She seemed to gain strength from it. "I'm so sorry to appear on your doorstep like this, Miss Cross," she said in a rush. "I didn't know what else to do. Wages aren't paid out for another fortnight and—"

"You did right in coming to me."

"I'll pay you back, I swear. Or, that nice Mr. . . . er . . ."

"Andrews. And don't worry about that just now. We'll figure it all out once your daughter is well." Silently, I prayed little Fiona would be well again, that Miss Riley wouldn't know the immeasurable grief of losing a child.

"Despite how she came into the world, she's everything to me, Miss Cross."

"Of course she is."

"If anything happens to her . . ."

"You mustn't think like that," Nanny gently admonished. I nodded in agreement but couldn't bring myself to offer false promises that perhaps couldn't be kept. For now, I merely wished to keep Miss Riley's spirits up.

"What if the office closes before Mr. Andrews gets there?"

I smiled. "Then he'll find the manager—go to his home, if need be—and ask him to reopen the office and send the wire."

"He'd do it, too," Nanny put in. "Our Mr. Andrews is a resourceful gentleman."

"You're all being so kind to me, and to my Fiona Rose. I can't thank you enough."

"There's no need to thank us," I said. "Hearing that Fiona has recovered will be thanks enough."

"Fiona Rose." Nanny drew out the names in an appreciative voice. "What a lovely and poetic name."

Miss Riley's lips curled in a shaky gesture approaching a smile. "Thank you. She's Fiona because I've always fancied the name, and Rose for my mother, who died not long after we came here from Ireland."

"I'm sorry." I patted her hand.

"And your father?" Nanny spoke softly. "Did he come to America with you?"

"My father was an American. My parents met in Ireland, while he was a seaman aboard a cargo ship. They fell in love and Da stayed, working the Dublin docks until I was about ten years old. Then they realized they'd never have more than a tiny flat there, would never be able to offer their family more. They had only me at the time—Mam had lost two others—when Da returned to America. He planned to work until he could send money for us. It took a couple of years, but the money came and Mam and I came over, with my aunt." Her voice trembled over the memories. "But Da . . . he died before we got here. And not long after, my mam died. Some said it was of a broken heart." She laughed bitterly. "It was from working herself so hard she became sick. Consumptive."

"Oh, I'm so sorry. You poor dear." Nanny rose to pour more tea into Miss Riley's cup. They continued to discuss Miss Riley's experiences after arriving in America, but I barely heard them. My mind tumbled over two facts I had just learned. First, that Miss Riley's father was an American; what's more he'd worked a very physical job, one that required great upper body strength. And secondly her mother's name had been Rose.

Harry Ainsley had sung "Red Is the Rose" . . .

Could it be more than coincidence? But I didn't believe in coincidence. Not in matters like this.

A chill of understanding went through me as several pieces of the puzzle fell into place. My own words came back to mock me: Maids are stronger than they look; they have to be. Yes, someone used to carrying rugs outside and beating them clean, who carried heavy trays through the house, who moved furniture to clean behind it, possessed greater than the average woman's strength. Enough strength, perhaps, to push an automobile into another person, possibly even over a tree root.

I hoped I was wrong. Prayed I was wrong. But I didn't believe I was.

"Nanny," I said, "would you excuse us?"

Nanny broke off from whatever she had been saying and frowned, clearly mystified.

"Please, Nanny. There's something Miss Riley and I need to discuss. And I'm sure Katie would appreciate your help in the kitchen." Her gaze bore into me as I tried to convey a silent message.

She nodded imperceptibly. Her frown didn't fade, but she eased herself up from her chair. "I'm sure she would. Excuse me, then."

I waited until I could no longer hear the heavy shuffling of her footsteps in the hallway. Then I turned back to Miss Riley. "Is Harry Ainsley your father?"

Miss Riley's lips parted but no sound came out. The room became so quiet I could hear crickets along with the distant sound of the ocean through the open windows. I braced for whatever she might do, quickly scanning the room for items I could use as weapons. The fire poker, the conch shell my cousin Neily brought me from a sailing trip around the Bahamas islands, the brass paperweight that kept our newspapers in a neat pile. And there was Patch, still sitting at Miss Riley's side. He seemed unperturbed, not at all on edge. I felt confident he would sense any ill intentions on Miss Riley's part and warn me.

After the moments stretched interminably, she said, "What are you going to do?"

I held her gaze another long moment, wondering that very same thing. Isaiah Baldwin had destroyed another man's life, and that of his daughter and granddaughter, who struggled all the more for having to make their own way in the world. Coupled with that, Isaiah Baldwin hadn't been a good man. He had preyed upon those beneath him, using his authority to make their lives difficult and to have his way with defenseless women.

But none of that justified murder.

I shook my head, caught in a wretchedness of indecision. "I don't know, Miss Riley, and that's the truth."

"How did you know?" she asked me so quietly it might have been the breeze rustling the trees outside.

"Your daughter's and mother's name, Rose. 'Red Is the Rose' is your father's favorite song. Did you know that? And no, he isn't dead. I know that because I saw Harry Ainsley only today."

She gasped as new tears gathered in her eyes. "You've seen my father? Is he . . . any better?"

"No, I wouldn't think so. Surely not well enough to leave the hospital. But obviously, in some way, he remembers his family. He remembers the love he felt for your mother."

"After the first couple of years, I couldn't bring myself to visit him again. It hurt too much. The man who had been my father no longer existed. Our family—the Ainsley family— no longer existed, and calling myself Olivia Ainsley brought me constant pain, so I began to use my mother's maiden name and tried to forget about what our family might have been." Her brow furrowed, and she stared down at her feet. "Poor Da. Mam never wanted him to fight. But he did it because he could make so much more money than working on the docks. He wanted to keep us in good style. A house. Plenty to eat . . . And look what happened." She shook her head, and when she spoke again, sobs clogged her throat—and my own. "He never knew she died. It happened only months after we arrived and discovered what had happened to him."

We both fell silent; she, as she waged a battle against the tears that fell freely now, and me, as I wrestled with what I should do. Logic told me the person sitting beside me had committed murder and must be apprehended, tried, and yes, convicted. Beyond that, I couldn't contemplate, for it was too horrible. I knew what happened to convicted murderers. Her being a woman wouldn't save her, not unless the judge and jury took pity on her because of her circumstances. Had she been an American born and raised, perhaps she would have been shown mercy. But opinions against the Irish, who had surged to our shores during the Great Famine and after, hadn't eased much in recent years. Her background would more than likely be held against her.

I couldn't bring myself to think it, much less speak of it. I had reached an impossible impasse, something I'd never experienced before—me, who believed in truth and taking responsibility for one's actions.

And then I remembered she hadn't only killed Isaiah Baldwin. There had been another, and she had put up quite an act about it afterward. "Why Clarence?" I whispered. "Why that honest young man? I realize he'd discovered the truth, but—" I broke off as her head swung up and her eyes blazed.

"I didn't. Not Clarence. I don't know who killed him, and I don't know why."

"I don't understand. He didn't come out to the laundry yard to confront you with that boxing match ticket?"

"What ticket, Miss Cross?" With her sleeve she wiped the tears off her cheeks. "It happened like I told the police. I went out to take sheets off the clothesline, and I found Clarence like . . . like that."

I came to my feet and started to pace. If Olivia Riley murdered Baldwin, what reason could someone else possibly have had to murder Clarence? The footman had had the boxing-match ticket in his possession—I was certain of it. Either Baldwin had left other hints, or he had told Clarence something that allowed the footman to discover the connection not only between Baldwin and Harry Ainsley, but between those two men and Miss Riley.

Or was she lying about everything? Everything, except that she had killed Baldwin.

I became aware of her watching me and ceased my pacing. "Miss Cross," she said with desperation in her voice, "I have a child who needs me. Who depends on me for her very survival. If I go to prison . . . or"—her voice dropped to a lifeless murmur—"the gallows, what will become of my Fiona Rose?"

Her words tore at my heart and filled me with agony. I knew what I wished could happen, but could I let a killer go free? She had committed the crime for a reason—a very specific one. Would she ever do it again? Would she someday find another reason to be rid of an inconvenient human being? Could I make the judgment and take such a risk with some unknown person's life? The answer might seem simple: no. And yet, a small person who *was* known to me, whose wan face would forever hover in my mind's eye, needed this woman.

For the first time in my life, I wished I could walk away and pretend I knew nothing. Pretend the truth didn't exist.

"I can't simply turn my back," I said before I'd even realized I'd answered my own questions. "You were going to let Philip King take the blame. He's innocent in what happened to your family. How could you allow his life to be taken from him?"

"I . . . They called it an accident. He wouldn't have gone to prison or the gallows. He'd have been let off and . . ." She fell silent, shamefaced and hiding her eyes behind her hands. "He's wealthy and the toffs are never held accountable. But me . . . I'll hang, won't I?"

"I don't know, Miss Riley. All I know is you can't keep lying and allow another person to suffer for your guilt."

Her hands fell away. Her eyes widened, the pupils large and black. Then she blinked and darted her gaze around the room. Was she looking for weapons, as I had done minutes ago? Which of us would arm herself first? Who would be the first to strike?

She would, because I would give her the benefit of the doubt until proven wrong.

But in the end, nothing needed to be proved. She tucked her chin low, into the stark white collar of her maid's uniform. "No, I can't. I don't suppose either of us can walk away from this. When I took the job at Kingscote, I had no idea I'd see that man. I discovered his identity quite by accident. By his own doing, actually. I overheard him boasting to the other manservants about what he'd done to some poor sot of a fighter years ago. He expressed no guilt about it, only smug arrogance. It didn't take me long to realize who he was talking about.

"And then, oh, Miss Cross, rage filled me. Rage for myself because yes, he'd made advances. And rage for my daughter and for Da, and my mam, too. Isaiah Baldwin as good as killed my father. He robbed him of his life, and because of it drove Mam to her death. I felt justified in doing the same to him. How many others has he destroyed? You talked about a maid he ruined. She can't have been the only one over the years." She shut her eyes and swallowed. "And yet, as soon as I'd acted, I realized I'd done wrong. I did regret it, Miss Cross. I still do. For my daughter's sake if nothing else, but I can't bring myself to mourn that man."

I folded my hands at my waist and stood motionless across from her. "Tell me what happened that night."

She exhaled a heavy breath. "He'd been at it again, putting his hands on me. And, somehow, he'd learned about Fiona. He must have gone through my things again, probably looking for more trinkets like my brooch. He threatened to tell Mrs. King about her. I should have let him, but I feared getting the sack. And he said if I didn't let him do what he wanted, Fiona would suffer." Her story turned my insides to ice and tied sickening knots in the pit of my stomach. Already, she had told me enough to rouse my loathing of the man. But there was more. And for the next several minutes she told me of it.

Then, she returned to the night in question. "That evening, I watched from my bedroom as he went outside to meet with some woman."

"Mrs. Ross?"

She shrugged. "I don't know. It was foggy, but they stood in the lamplight and I could just make them out. They kept their voices down, but I could see they were arguing. She slapped him, and he made to strike her back. He didn't, but he shoved her, and she stumbled to her knees."

As Miss Riley described these details, I surmised it was then that Mrs. Ross's pearl necklace broke.

"I made my way downstairs and outside," Miss Riley went on. "I'd decided that was the last time Isaiah Baldwin would hurt another person, especially a woman."

"What came next?"

"When I reached the lawn, they were still arguing. I don't even know what it was about. They stood near that big tree with the drooping branches, and their voices were so angry I thought they'd come to blows. I realized I shouldn't have come out alone, that I should have brought one of the footmen. I was about to go back for one of them when I heard Mrs. King's name mentioned. I wondered what this had to do with her.

"I hid behind the motorcar and waited to hear more, but when I leaned against it, it rolled. Just a tiny bit, because I stood up straight so it wouldn't keep going. Finally, the woman left, but Baldwin just stood there by the tree, watching her disappear into the fog. Even then, I had no plan to hurt him. Not until I heard him laugh. Oh, his mean, snide laughter. It went straight through me, like a pickax, and the next thing I knew, I was pushing the car. I gave it a good push to set it going, but almost immediately I regretted it, Miss Cross. Truly. I . . . I tried to stop it. I grabbed the rear panel, but I couldn't. It kept going. And at that point, I panicked and hurried back inside. I simply hoped Baldwin would see it coming and get out of the way . . ."

She fell silent, her eyes scrunched tight. Then, "If only I had been able to stop it. To stop *myself*. Because now . . ."

I regarded her from my stance above her. At long last, I said, "I don't believe you. I don't believe you never meant to kill him. That the thought didn't occur to you the moment you realized who he was."

Another long sigh left her. She shook her head, smiled grimly, and swallowed. "Yes, you're right, Miss Cross. You see, I'd grown up wanting to see him dead. I'd pictured it many times in my mind. Sometimes he died by my hand; other times I pictured some horrible accident taking his life. I wanted revenge, and that is the truth."

"You were also willing to let Philip King take the blame for something you did," I reminded her relentlessly.

She bowed her head. "I told you, I didn't think the law would deal harshly with him. He's . . . well, who he is, and I'm who I am. They would let him go, call it an accident. But me—I'd be made to suffer. *Will* be made to suffer." Yes, I couldn't deny that she spoke the truth, nor offer her false hope. In her position, might I have done the same? Another question I couldn't answer. "And now, because I couldn't let it go, my daughter will . . ."

"I'll see she's taken care of. She doesn't deserve to suffer." Miss Riley and I locked gazes with an intensity that all but drew a drop of blood from each of us, striking an unbreakable oath between us. Miss Riley stared hard at the floor, but I knew it wasn't my threadbare rug she saw. It was her daughter's face that filled her vision.

"That's it, then," she said with finality. "When your Mr. Andrews returns, will you come with me to the police station?"

"Of course I will." I went back to the sofa and resumed my seat beside her. I took her hand. "I'll even speak on your behalf, if it helps. Perhaps . . ." I trailed off as she shook her head.

"No, Miss Cross. There will be no second chances for me, I'm afraid. But if I can only know my daughter will be safe and cared for, that will be enough for me. My aunt would die for her, but she hasn't any money of her own."

"I'll see to it they have everything they need." It wasn't a hollow promise. I'd speak to all of my relatives if I had to. I thought of Louise, my uncle Frederick's wife. She loved children and they hadn't been able to have any of their own. I believed Louise would be more than willing to provide for an orphaned little girl.

Miss Riley drew a tremulous breath and let it out slowly. Her gaze now traveled the room, darting from one thing to another as if she were trying to memorize every line, though perhaps what she wished to remember was her sense of freedom, of liberty. Because soon enough—

A knocking on the front door, less urgent than when Miss Riley had arrived, sounded once again. Patch lurched to all four feet and let out a low bark. I frowned. It seemed much too soon for Derrick to be back from town. I went to answer the door, then wished I hadn't when I beheld who stood on the other side.

Chapter 19

John Donavan pushed his way into my foyer, thrusting me aside as he came over the threshold. When I let out a cry of protest and attempted to seize his arm, his other arm came up, a crowbar gripped in his hand. "Get out of my way, Miss Cross, or I'll crack your skull." He pointed the tool toward the back of the house. "And then I'll go smash the brains of those other two hens that live here."

My hands fell away and I lurched a step backward. At the same time, Patch came barreling into the hall. He showed no alarm; his tail wagged in his eagerness to see who had come to visit. Perhaps he believed Derrick had returned. Donavan scowled down at him and raised the crowbar.

"Patch, quiet," I commanded in alarm, fearing what Donavan would do to him. While his twitching nose and wagging tail told me his excitement hadn't abated, he backed away from the coachman and came to my side.

Donavan strode into the parlor. Miss Riley surged to her feet. "John? What are you doing here? And what is that for?" She pointed to the implement in his hand.

"I've come for you, Olivia. To take you away from here. I'm going to help you." He held his free hand out to her.

She didn't move. "How did you know I was here?"

He hesitated before admitting, "I followed you. Now let's go before it's too late."

She held her ground. "I don't understand."

"The police are looking for you, Mr. Donavan," I said to his back. "You'll never get off Aquidneck Island."

He half turned toward me and slapped the end of the crowbar against his other palm. Patch jumped, and I leaned to place a firm hand on the back of his neck. "I'll find a way."

I longed to send Patch to the kitchen, out of harm's way, but I knew he'd put up a fuss and refuse to budge. Better, then, to keep him beside me, where I could grab his collar to prevent him from doing something that would end in his being hurt. Nudging him to move along with me, I walked through the parlor doorway and circled John Donavan to stand beside Miss Riley. Patch sat directly in front of me, his rump resting on the tips of my boots. He was on the alert now, albeit he didn't quite know why. He watched John Donavan with wary interest.

My other foremost concern was whether Nanny or Katie might return to the parlor. True, Donavan knew they were in the house, but I considered them safer where they were in the kitchen. Better still, I wished they'd flee through the kitchen door and go for help.

"I've protected you so far, Olivia," Donavan was saying in a pleading voice. "You can trust me to go on protecting you."

Her pale, tearstained face turned whiter still. "What have you done?"

He didn't answer. In a flash of understanding, I supplied the answer for him. "He killed Clarence. For you, Miss Riley. He must have seen you push the Hartley Steamer into Baldwin—" I broke off, stunned by a single detail that suddenly burst, like lightning, across my brain. "Except that you couldn't have . . . you didn't." My mouth fell open as I continued to work it out.

"What? But I did. I just told you how I did it."

I grabbed her hand, almost jubilant. "There's a root in the grass that would have stopped the Hartley before it reached the tree. Unless you heaved hard enough to send the tires over it—"

She shook her head vigorously "I don't remember any such thing."

"Because you'd hurried inside. But he"—I pointed at John Donavan—"he was outside, and *he* pushed the Hartley when it stopped. Pushed it hard enough to send it over the root and into Baldwin with such force he died of the injuries."

Every last drop of color drained from Miss Riley's countenance. "Is this true, John?"

"I killed him for you, Olivia. For what he was trying to do to you."

"I never asked you to help me. And why Clarence?"

"He saw you hurrying back into the house. He'd gone looking for Baldwin when he didn't come back to serve in the dining room. And after everyone discovered what I'd . . . what happened to Baldwin, he assumed you did it, although he had no proof. And then he found that boxing-match ticket—from the fight Baldwin bragged about. Baldwin said the poor fool left behind a wife and daughter. Clarence was clever. Once he saw that ticket, he figured you were that man's daughter and that was why you killed him. He planned to go to the police. I couldn't let him do that to you. Or to us."

"I believed I killed Baldwin, too," she shouted at him. Then, quieter, "How could you let me believe that?"

"What does it matter? Baldwin is dead." Donavan held

out his hand as if he expected Miss Riley to take it. "That's what you wanted. I only did what you wanted."

"Dear Lord, no . . ." Miss Riley glared at him, loathing and sorrow warring across her features.

He once more held out his hand in supplication. "That's why I had to kill Clarence. After the police let me go, I went back to Kingscote to collect my things. Clarence saw me and told me that he found the ticket while they were clearing out Baldwin's room. He said I would be exonerated and you jailed in my place. He thought he was doing me a favor. But I couldn't let him turn you in. Who would believe in your innocence? But without him, you're safe, and so am I. No one need ever know what really happened." He shifted his attention to me. "Except you. Now, what do we do with you?"

"You're not to do anything with Miss Cross, John." Miss Riley spoke firmly, even forcefully. "Baldwin committed more sins than you know, but even he didn't deserve to be murdered. And Clarence was innocent. He certainly didn't deserve to die. How could you ever believe two deaths could help me?"

"But it will, Olivia. We'll go far from here and get married. You and me. Maybe we'll go as far as California. Just think of it."

Miss Riley shook her head at every word he spoke. "Never."

"But . . . I love you. Can you not see that? Haven't I proved it? Everything I did was for you."

"Vile, all of it. I could never love you. Even if you hadn't done these things, I never would have loved you." She raised a hand to gesture toward the front door. "Go. Get away if you can. I'm not going with you."

He didn't move to go. "I won't leave without you."

She walked past me, turning her face away from him and staring out the front window. "Then you'll be taken into custody along with me. After all, I did have a hand in Baldwin's death. If I hadn't started the motorcar rolling, if I hadn't gone outside that night, you wouldn't have done what you did. I realize that. I do bear some responsibility, and I won't hide from it. Miss Cross, I believe I saw a telephone beneath your staircase as I came in. You may as well summon the police."

She sounded so calm, so resigned, but the tips of her fingers trembled, while her breathing became labored and audible. I marveled at her courage, her calm acceptance of all that had happened, and what it could mean for her and her daughter's futures. The police and the courts could very well hold her partly responsible. They might charge her as an accomplice, and with only her word to attest to what happened that night, she could end up spending years in prison.

"I don't believe this." Mounting anger replaced the pleading in John Donavan's voice. "After everything I've done for you?"

Miss Riley made no reply.

"Look at me, you guttersnipe." He took a step toward her. Miss Riley flinched but maintained her resolve. Patch growled deep in his throat. I bent to place a hand on his collar while, with my other hand, I reached for the brass paperweight, the closest object within reach that could be used as a weapon. "Baldwin was right about you, Olivia," he said. "You aren't worth it. You never were." He spun toward me and raised the crowbar. "Put it down or you and your dog won't see another day."

I grabbed the hunk of brass anyway; he'd already hinted at killing me, so why go passively? My fingers closed around the cool metal. The weight of it filled my hand as I lifted it from the pile of newspapers. I watched in horror as the crowbar swung high over my head. My senses swam as Patch's fierce barking filled my ears. I braced for the agony of the blow, equally determined to strike a blow in return.

And then John Donavan's eyes rolled back in his head. His hand opened and the crowbar plummeted, landing with a sharp and heavy thwack on my shoulder—but not my head. The coachman's collapsing form revealed the figure of Miss Riley standing directly behind him, wielding the conch shell I had so recently considered using as a weapon, her fingers curled snugly inside it.

I barely had time to comprehend what happened when the front door burst open. Patch barked furiously as he jumped and darted around Donavan's prone form. Miss Riley had hardly moved, except to lower the conch shell to her side. Footsteps came at a run from the hallway: Derrick's and Nanny's and Katie's. They spoke all at once, a cacophony I could make no sense of.

Then Derrick's arms were around me. "What the blazes happened here? Emma, are you all right?"

"Emma? Emma, that man—" Nanny pointed down at Donavan. Her face became flushed with outrage as she scowled. "Good heavens, who is he?"

Katie said nothing but crouched beside John Donavan and placed her fingertips on the side of his neck, something I had taught her. "He's alive."

At that, Miss Riley let out a cry and sank to her knees. Derrick released me and I went to her, prying the conch shell from her hand. A crimson bead dripped from the twisted spire at one end. I set it aside and put my arm across her shoulders. "Can you stand?" I turned to Katie. "Please bring some water for Miss Riley and a rag and ice for . . . for him."

Katie came to her feet, then hesitated, her hands clutching at her apron. "Shouldn't I call the police, Miss Emma?"

Over Miss Riley's head, Derrick's gaze collided with mine. I shook my head slightly. He made no move, not even a change in his expression, but I knew he understood. Or, at least, he was willing to follow my lead. "Not yet, Katie," I said. "Please, the water and ice first. And more tea, I think. And then please telephone Dr. Kennison."

Derrick wasted no time. He followed Katie and returned holding a ball of twine. He tied Donavan's hands behind his back and then bound his ankles for good measure. With my help, we half dragged, half hauled him to the sofa and stretched him out on it. When Katie returned with a cloth-bound bundle of ice—delivered to me daily from The Breakers, my relatives' cottage—Nanny first dabbed at the cut on the back of his head and then placed the ice on the wound. He didn't stir, although his breathing seemed steady, and I hoped for Miss Riley's sake he recovered. I couldn't help thinking about Harry Ainsley's fate . . .

"I've done violence again." Miss Riley still sat on the floor, her hands gripped together. There were no tears now, only a piercing light in her eyes. "I'm sorry, Fiona," she whispered.

"In self-defense," I reminded her, though it didn't smooth the anxious lines from her face. "Actually, in *my* defense."

"What happened here while I was gone?" Derrick went to Miss Riley and offered his hand to help her up. She accepted it and rose shakily to her feet. He led her to one of the two armchairs facing the sofa and steadied her as she lowered herself into it. "How did he come to be here? That's John Donavan, isn't it?"

His second question needed no reply, but I answered the first. "He followed Miss Riley from Kingscote. He claims he's in love with her and thought he was doing her a favor by committing murder. Twice."

"Good God." Derrick rarely swore in my hearing, much less Nanny's, and that he did now proved how taken aback he was by this development. "He murdered two men . . . in the name of love?"

Miss Riley shook her head, clearly still blaming herself for the first, and possibly both, deaths. I went to her side, half blocking her from Derrick's view. "Yes," I said before she could speak. "You see, Miss Riley is . . . You might want to be seated for this." I gestured for Derrick to sit in the other armchair. Clearly baffled, he sat across the small oval table from Miss Riley, so that they were both facing me now. "Miss Riley is Harry Ainsley's daughter."

Before I could go on, Miss Riley jumped up. "I won't have you lie for me. Mr. Andrews, what Miss Cross says is true. I'm Harry Ainsley's daughter, and if not for me, for my actions that night, Isaiah Baldwin would still be alive. Donavan killed him, but he was finishing something I started. I wanted that man dead because of what he did to my father— to my entire family. I'm sorry for it, but I can't change it."

Derrick turned his bewildered face back to me. "Emma, is this true?"

I nodded. "There's much more to it. I believe Mrs. Ross sent that note to me, the one about things being amiss among Kingscote's servants and Isaiah Baldwin deserving what he got. She knew what he was like—an exceedingly bad man. That much I believe. And Nanny guessed the writer hadn't been formally educated, and I don't believe Mrs. Ross was, not in the traditional sense. She's clever and has managed to acquire the demeanor of a lady, but it's entirely possible she's had little classroom schooling, which was often the case in the rural South. But what's more, Miss Riley didn't set out to kill Baldwin. She saw him manhandling Mrs. Ross that night and went outside to see if she could help. She leaned against the motorcar to hear what the argument was about, and it started to roll." I quickly explained the rest, then came to a breathless silence.

He didn't speak for several long moments, but sat contemplating the unconscious man on the sofa. I gazed around me, half surprised to find Nanny still there. She, too, appeared to be deep in thought.

Finally, I broke the silence. "What are we going to do? Miss Riley didn't murder Baldwin, but she might be charged as an accomplice, mightn't she?"

"Yes, and once he wakes up and starts talking to the police, it'll be her word against his." Derrick propped an elbow on the arm of the chair and fisted his hand beneath his chin. "And Jesse's hands will be tied again, no matter which of them he believes."

"Derrick is right, Emma," Nanny said. "Jesse will be entirely sympathetic, but once the whole story comes out, he'll be forced to take Miss Riley's participation into account. And if he won't, Chief Rogers will. And we can't simply omit her part in what happened that night. You know you're not comfortable with out-and-out lying, especially to a good friend like Jesse." Nanny spoke the truth; how could I maintain a lie to my friend? But how could I turn Olivia Riley over to a prison cell, or possibly even the hangman's noose? In my mind's eye, little Fiona demanded the answer to that same question.

Miss Riley followed the discussion with anguish on her face, yet a glimmer of hope in her eyes. That glimmer tunneled its way through to my core. But she said nothing to plead her case or influence our decision.

"I'll be right back." Whirling away from three astonished faces, I darted out of the parlor and up the staircase. It took me only seconds to find what I had gone for. I took another moment to write several lines on a blank sheet of paper, and signed my name to it. Back downstairs, I paused in the parlor doorway. Was I truly going to do this? Would Derrick and Nanny stop me? Would Jesse, once he learned the truth, be forced to press charges against me?

Miss Riley might have intended to harm Isaiah Baldwin,

but she hadn't. She didn't deserve to suffer and neither did her daughter. At long last, would Harry Ainsley's family find some semblance of justice?

They would, if I had anything to say about it.

Vaguely, I heard Katie speaking into the telephone with Dr. Kennison, explaining the nature of the wound inflicted on John Donavan. I left her to it. Stepping into the room, I stood before Miss Riley, held out my fist, and uncurled my fingers. She gasped when she beheld what lay in my palm.

"What is this? I . . . I don't understand."

The diamond teardrop earrings my parents had given me years ago shimmered in the glow of the gas lamps Nanny had lighted while I was upstairs. With its sheltering shadows, night had fully set in. Miss Riley would need those shadows. "They're small and won't bring much," I explained, "but it will be enough for you to start somewhere new. If you leave now, no one will prevent you from boarding the train or the ferry. Go as far as you can before selling these earrings. I can give you the money for the ticket."

"Here." Derrick drew his purse from his inner coat pocket, counted out several bills, and held them out to Miss Riley.

Her eyes large, she shook her head adamantly. "No, I can't—"

"Take it," Nanny commanded in her softest, yet firmest, voice. "If Emma thinks this is right, then it's right."

"Thank you, Nanny." To Miss Riley, I said, "Take it for Fiona. And for Harry. Take it and go. In the meantime, we'll see to it that your daughter is cared for. Once you find a place to settle, write to me. You daren't contact your aunt, not at first, but I'll let her know where you are." I handed her the folded sheet of paper I'd brought with me from upstairs. "I've written you a letter of recommendation. And I'll see if I can get your brooch back from Detective Whyte. I'll bring it to your aunt." I pressed the diamonds into her free hand and closed her fingers around them. I gestured at John Donavan. "The police will have their murderer. Eventually, this will all die down and you needn't look over your shoulder anymore."

"I don't deserve any of this."

"Nor did you deserve what Baldwin did to your family." I smiled sadly. "Here is your second chance. Take it, Olivia."

I embraced her, and her arms went around me and squeezed. Then she released me and tucked the diamonds in a pocket in her dress, followed by the letter of recommendation and the bills Derrick handed her.

"Wait," I said, and quickly ran to the hall. I returned with a shawl and my straw boater hat. "Take these as well, so you don't appear as though you've just run off."

She put them on, transforming her maid's uniform into a simple black serge dress that any woman might wear. "Thank you, Miss Cross. My thanks to all of you. I don't know how I'll ever—"

"Go," I said, nudging her toward the front door. "Go before it's too late. Once the doctor arrives, we'll have no choice but to telephone the police." As if on cue, the man on the sofa let out a groan. "Donavan will probably tell them *you* rolled the Hartley Steamer into Isaiah Baldwin, and then they'll come looking for you, for questioning if nothing else."

"Will you lie for me?"

I shook my head. "I won't lie, but I won't necessarily offer up everything I know, either. Not all at once, at least. Now, please go."

I held the front door open, and Olivia Riley hurried off into the night.

As it happened, I didn't telephone Jesse that night; I didn't need to. He showed up at my door at the same time as the doctor to tell me to have a care, for he'd concluded that John

Donavan had murdered Clarence and was on the run, but, he believed, still on the island.

"That one detail about the lack of footprints kept nagging at me," he told us while Dr. Kennison attended to Donavan's head wound. "At first we simply believed our culprit had dried his feet on the grass and wiped off the mud, but then it struck me that he might have removed his shoes before he left the laundry yard. I decided to check the carriage house, and sure enough, I found traces of muddy water just inside the door to his rooms. He was careful not to leave a trail across the lawn, but I suspect once he'd retrieved what he wanted, he was in too much of a hurry to get away to bother cleaning the floor. He simply put on his shoes and fled."

"He'll have a lump the size of a crab apple and one zinger of a headache," Dr. Kennison pronounced after checking his patient over carefully, "but he'll be fine. Doesn't need stitches. The wound will heal on its own."

Jesse went to stand over his quarry. "John Donavan, you are under arrest for the murder of Clarence Dole, and if I can prove it, the murder of Isaiah Baldwin, too."

"I didn't kill Baldwin." Struggling against his bonds, Donavan slid his feet to the floor and slowly sat up. He let out a groan that did little to win my sympathy. "That little Irish witch did. Ask *her*." He indicated me with a thrust of his chin. "Blasted women."

"Emma?" Jesse folded his arms and lifted an eyebrow in question. "Is this true?"

I shrugged. "It's complicated, but you can be sure John Donavan murdered both men."

Jesse directed his gaze in a silent question at Derrick, who laid a hand against his chest with an air of innocence. "I wasn't here to witness what was said. I'd gone into town to wire funds for Miss Riley's aunt to be able to call a doctor for her daughter. Poor child's been sick, so we hear."

Jesse next turned to Nanny. "Mrs. O'Neal? What do you know?"

"Derrick's right, that poor child needs a doctor."

"I don't mean about that, Mrs. O'Neal."

"Oh . . . well, Katie and I were in the kitchen for most of the evening. Would you care for some tea?"

Jesse pivoted back toward me. "You and I are going to have a long talk tomorrow."

Derrick came to stand beside me in solidarity. The back of his hand touched mine. Whatever I faced, I knew he would face it with me. I nodded at Jesse, thinking tomorrow would give Miss Riley ample time to put many miles between herself and Newport. Would it be enough? Would Jesse press matters and issue an interstate search for her?

I had faith he would agree that Miss Riley didn't deserve to be treated like a criminal. Her momentary lapse in judgment had been simply that, and she had stopped herself just short of committing murder. She hadn't been at all complicit, either, for by the time Donavan had taken over pushing the Hartley, Miss Riley had fled the scene. Yes, she'd fled believing she *had* murdered Baldwin, and yes, it *had* been wrong of her to allow Philip King to take the blame—and perhaps for that she did deserve some form of punishment. But hadn't she already been punished, before the fact? Not to mention the weight of the guilt she would bear for the rest of her life.

But it hadn't merely been Miss Riley I'd helped to escape. It was her daughter as well, a third generation struggling to outrun the past. I prayed my diamonds and Derrick's money would help Fiona Rose escape a legacy she didn't deserve, the result of the actions of a dishonorable man she would never have to know. If any good could come of this, it would be in the person of Fiona Riley—Fiona Ainsley, really— when she grew up to be a healthy, happy young woman.

*   *   *

After an exhausted, dreamless sleep that night, the next afternoon saw me back at Kingscote. Mrs. King had sent an invitation and her carriage for me, driven by her trusted groom, Brian Farrell.

I arrived to find Derrick and Jesse already there. Mrs. King brought us into her beautiful dining room with its exotic blend of designs, where a luncheon had been laid out. Gwendolen and her brother, Philip, finally released from his room, awaited us there.

"Please, do sit," Mrs. King commanded in her genteel way. As we all found places around the table, she remained standing. She appeared to be waiting for something—or someone, as it turned out. Moments later Ethan strolled in, his butler's garb replaced by a summer suit of ivory seersucker. Mrs. King gestured for him to sit as well. Then she folded her hands at her waist. "I asked you all here today to thank you for what you did for my son and for this family. You put yourselves to considerable trouble and endangered yourselves, and for that you'll have our eternal gratitude."

"It's merely my job, ma'am." Jesse shifted in his seat, clearly uncomfortable with Mrs. King's praise.

She raised her chin a fraction as she peered down at him. "Perhaps, Detective. But I know you were under pressure to close the case and declare it an accident caused by my son. A lesser man would have done so."

"And let a killer go free? No, indeed." A blush crept across Jesse's face despite the gruffness of his tone.

Mrs. King only smiled at him, then turned her attention to another. "And you, Mr. . . . Merriman, I believe it is."

Ethan inclined his head.

"You disrupted your entire life to help us. And Miss Cross and Mr. Andrews, you both went to great lengths on our behalf. Miss Cross, I want you to know I will become your most generous contributor to St. Nicholas Orphanage in Providence."

"Thank you, Mrs. King. That's most appreciated." Dared I enlist her help for Fiona? Would she ask questions about the child's origins, or would she be willing to foster her from afar? I decided I would approach her, in time. I frowned and turned to Philip. "I do have one question for you, if I might."

Philip King raised his teacup to me as if in a toast. "Go right ahead, Miss Cross."

"How did you become acquainted with Harry Ainsley?"

"Harry Ainsley?" Mrs. King took her seat at the table and flicked her napkin to her lap. Her eyes widened as she turned to me. "The boxer you spoke of when that ticket was found in the laundry yard?"

Philip's gaze hadn't left me, as if he contemplated the wisdom of discussing the matter. Finally, and with a show of reluctance, he said, "Yes, the very same, Mother. After Baldwin maimed him in that fight, Harry ended up at Butler—with Uncle William. They were friends . . . of sorts."

Tight ridges formed above his mother's nose. "Uncle William? Philip, I don't understand. Were you—"

"Visiting Uncle William before he died? Yes, Mother, I did. Every spring when we returned from Europe."

"Why did you never say anything?"

Philip shrugged. "I don't know. I thought the whole matter would upset you. There were so many hard feelings between him and the family. But he was always happy to see me. He didn't blame me for his being there and . . . I could identify with him. Being the black sheep and all."

"Philip," his mother exclaimed, "you are not a black sheep."

"Aren't I, Mother? Haven't you, in all of this, doubted me just a little?"

"I . . ." She had no answer for him, a fact that brought her considerable discomfiture, if her tight expression gave any indication.

"Oh, come now, everyone." Gwendolen reached for a platter of roasted squab, and then the silver bowl of shallots and mushrooms in wine sauce and began the task of passing them around. "We're here to thank our friends, not make them uncomfortable. Philip has been exonerated and the danger is over. Let's all be grateful."

"Hear, hear," Philip agreed. A mischievous gleam entered his eyes. "But where is Francis, Gwennie? Aren't you grateful to him for helping you through such a trying time?"

"You're incorrigible." She made a gesture as if to slap his hand, though he sat across the table from her. "For your information, Francis *was* a help, and he's rather a dear, but I've had to be firm with him."

"What does that mean, darling?" her mother asked.

"It means there is no future for us, however much he might want it." Her cheeks pinked modestly. "He was always simply *showing up* places, uninvited. Like the other day—the day poor Clarence died—when he drove up in front of the Casino as Maude and I were leaving and insisted he drive us home, though we live such a short walk away."

I had just cut into my squab, but the morsel remained forgotten on the end of my fork. "Then Mr. Crane wasn't at the Casino that day watching you play tennis?"

"No. He actually seemed to be waiting outside for us."

"It's a good thing we didn't know that then," I said to Jesse and Derrick, "or poor Mr. Crane would have gone right back to the top of our list of suspects." Somewhat chagrined, I explained to the others, "You see, we did have reason to suspect Francis Crane. Mrs. Ross as well."

"A boy like Francis couldn't hurt a fly," Mrs. King said

dismissively. Apparently she had forgotten her own insinuations against him. "But Mrs. Ross on the other hand . . ." She shuddered. "I'm sure that woman isn't finished making trouble for us."

"I have a feeling she won't be plaguing us for much longer, Mother," Gwendolen said. "Eventually a judge is going to dismiss her claims once and for all and she'll disappear. Probably to find herself another financial victim."

"One can only hope," her brother put in in a murmur. Martin, Kingscote's remaining footman, entered the room to inquire if anything more was needed. To this, Philip said wryly, "Yes. A butler. Mr. Merriman, I don't suppose we could persuade you to stay on, at least until we've found yet another replacement?"

Ethan colored with embarrassment and laughed. "I don't suppose I've done the best job. I'm sorry, Mrs. King, but think I should return to the *Messenger*. It's where I belong."

Mrs. King sighed. "Butler, footman, coachman, and now my housemaid. What *has* become of Olivia?"

"Um . . ." I looked to Derrick for help. He shrugged.

Jesse came to the rescue. "It seems Miss Riley has a daughter who lives with an aunt, and the child is ill. She has gone home to care for her."

Thank you, I mouthed at him.

"Goodness, why didn't I know about this?" The woman appeared genuinely aggrieved by the news.

"She was afraid to come to you, ma'am," I said. "Most employers wouldn't approve of their housemaid having a child and . . ." I trailed off, realizing I'd wandered onto an indelicate subject, especially for the luncheon table.

"I would not have condemned her for it," Mrs. King declared with no uncertainty. "I do wish she had come to me for help. Miss Cross, if you hear from her—"

"Yes, ma'am, I'll convey the message." I darted a glance at Jesse, who watched me closely. "But I don't think it will be possible for her to return."

The following morning, I returned to the *Messenger* to discover an unhappy surprise: a resignation letter from Jacob Stodges. In it he explained his frustrations at being set aside, supplanted by Ethan and overshadowed by me. As I sank into my desk chair in front of the window overlooking Spring Street, several undeniable truths wended their way through me, and through my resolve to make a great success of my position as editor-in-chief.

I had *not* made a success of it. And I had not made a success of myself. This letter proved it. Jacob spoke truly. I *had* thrust him aside and ignored his professional needs in favor of my own. And my own simply did not include sitting here at this desk, running things, overseeing operations, and making decisions that affected the rest of the staff. My needs—my one need—was so much simpler.

When Derrick had first asked me to run his fledgling newspaper, I had jumped at the chance to prove myself in a capacity typically reserved for men. I'd wished to prove to myself, to him, and to the world, that I, a woman, could perform as well as any man. But I had overlooked one very vital point: reporting, for me, had never been about proving anything to anyone. It had been about the search for truth and the ability to convey those truths in a way that allowed readers to draw their own conclusions. The fact of my being a woman had only become significant when men refused to take me seriously, and refused to allow me to put my talents and enthusiasm to good use. I had wished only to report, not to prove anything other than that I had the ability to do the job.

I still wished to report. Somehow, reporting had gotten into my blood, became part of who I was, and now the greatest obstacle to my goals was not the men who stood in my way, but myself, because I'd come to see my goals as a competition.

They were not a competition. I need not compete at all, except with other reporters to see who could break the story first—who could unearth the most intimate details, analyze them, and present them in the clearest and most unbiased way. That was my passion and my calling. Not sitting at a desk and directing from behind the scenes.

Outside my window, a trolley rumbled by, raising clouds of dust behind it. Pedestrians ducked their heads and shielded their faces with their arms. As the swirls settled, the patrician features of a familiar face took shape. Derrick hurried across the street, sidestepping a vegetable cart and a pile of manure the street sweeper hadn't yet attended to. The bell jangled as he opened the door and stepped inside.

"Good morning," he said with an enthusiasm I didn't feel. How could I, when I had a disagreeable task before me? The light in his eyes didn't fade even though he lowered his voice when he spoke again. "I don't suppose you've had word from . . ."

"No, not yet. But I didn't expect to this soon. She'll contact me when she's ready, I'm sure."

"And Jesse hasn't pressed you for more details about what happened at Gull Manor that night?"

"We've talked, and he trusts me. He believes Miss Riley is innocent."

Derrick nodded and glanced around the small office. "It's quiet here this morning." Not entirely true, as we could hear the printing press rumbling from the rear of the building. "Has Ethan been in yet? I'll bet he's eager to get back to the typewriter."

"Ethan's at Mrs. King's equestrian outing and picnic, in the capacity of society columnist. He's very happy about it."

The event, spoken of that first night at Kingscote after the auto parade, had been put off, of course, during the investigation. Now, all the Kings could enjoy the day without apprehension, including Philip. *Especially* Philip, who no longer faced either murder charges or the ruin of his reputation for taking a man's life due to a drunken accident.

"What's that you've got there?"

Derrick pointed to the paper in my hand, and I realized I had held on to Jacob's letter the entire time I'd been contemplating my future. I handed it to him. "Jacob is leaving us."

He read the missive and frowned. Then he let out a *hmm.* "I'm sorry about this. But I've been thinking . . ."

When he hesitated, I came to my feet. Had he been having second thoughts about my running his newspaper? Did he see it from Jacob's perspective, that I was really no good at being in charge? After all, first I'd had to fire our office manager, Jimmy Hawkins, for attempting to sabotage our operations; and now my news reporter had quit. None of this spoke well of my abilities to keep order. No, and I decided to make this easy on Derrick.

I drew in a deep breath. "Derrick, I think it's time we both admitted—"

"Emma, you're fired."

I gasped in shock, but my startlement quickly abated and was replaced by a cascade of relief. Whatever happened now, wherever I went, I would go as a reporter and nothing else. "Thank goodness," I whispered.

He slapped Jacob's letter onto the desktop and reached for me, drawing me close for a moment. When he pulled away, holding me at arm's length, he smiled down at me. "You're a reporter, Emma. I truly saw that these past days. You're at your best when you're investigating. I asked you to do something that isn't in your nature, and I apologize for that."

"Don't. When you asked me to fill this position, I jumped

at the chance. I simply didn't realize what it would mean. And I'm afraid I've made a hash of it—"

"No, you haven't, not that at all. But . . . I *will* need to replace you."

I nodded, and had a thought that might rectify matters. "Perhaps Jacob."

"I don't think he's ready, not yet. I do have a couple of notions, though. But in the meantime . . ."

"Yes, of course I'll stay on until you can replace me." And then I would do what? Go where?

"Thank you," he said with a bob of his head, "I appreciate that. But there is still the matter of needing to replace my news reporter. I understand how poor Mrs. King is feeling, having to replace her house staff. Good people are so hard to find." He cocked his head at me and grinned. "I don't suppose you have any ideas as to who might like to fill the position of news reporter here at the *Messenger*?" His hand left my shoulder and cupped my chin, raising my face as he lowered his and kissed me.

I smiled all through that kiss, and the rest of the day, and that evening when I told Nanny and Katie that at long last, I was going to be what I'd always wished: a hard-news reporter, right here in Newport.

Author's Note

Kingscote, one of the oldest homes on Bellevue Avenue, is also one of its smallest, yet loveliest, gems. Having toured the house, I'd already developed a fondness for its remarkable blend of architecture and interior design styles, but writing this book has greatly increased my appreciation of the house and its history, along with that of the family who owned it. Having made his fortune in the China export business, William Henry King purchased Kingscote from its original owner, George Noble Jones, a Southerner who left Newport for good at the start of the Civil War. Soon after, William King retired and set about enjoying his wealth.

As I have it in the story, his relatives became so alarmed at his excessive lifestyle and penchant for globe-trotting that they had him declared insane. He was committed, first at the McLean Asylum in Massachusetts, and then the Butler Hospital in Providence, Rhode Island, where he eventually died. Meanwhile, Kingscote was taken over by William's nephew, David King Jr., and his wife, Ella Rives King. Had William King taken leave of his senses? Was his fate the result of genuine familial concern, or greed? Unfortunately, those are questions I cannot answer. However, I do believe Mrs. King and her children were blameless in these events.

Nor can I fully explain what drove Eugenia Webster Ross—a real-life figure—in her pursuit of William King and his fortune. Newspaper articles from the time document her relentless campaign to prove herself his heir. Did she misguidedly believe her assertions, or was she merely a con artist hoping for an easy buck? If the latter, she was to be disappointed, as there was nothing easy about her quest to gain the inheritance. She labored through the legal system for many years and in the end received nothing. The final court hearing was the one mentioned in this story, which took place in September of 1899. The judge dismissed the case, and I could find no further information about Mrs. Ross.

Mrs. Ella King, widowed in 1894, did eventually buy all shares of Kingscote from William's heirs and settled there happily for the rest of her life. As in the story, she loved Newport, loved horseback riding (a case of her medals hangs in the carriage house) and outdoor activities, and enjoyed an active social life with her family and a relatively small circle of close friends, preferring this to the ostentatious lifestyles of other members of the Four Hundred. She was active in community affairs and a committed philanthropist. Her daughter, likewise, was athletic and involved with her community, and adopted the more modern style of dress that emerged in the early twentieth century as women in general took on more expanded roles in society. She married Edward Maitland Armstrong, whose father, David Maitland Armstrong, was a member of the Hudson River School of artists. A number of his paintings hang in Kingscote today. Gwendolen was widowed in 1916 and spent most of the rest of her life at Kingscote.

Philip King, on the other hand, failed to rise to the level of hard work and entrepreneurship that brought such wealth to his father and uncles, and periodically indulged in drink. Mrs. King would despair of him as the years progressed. He married but had no children, and died in 1923 at the age of forty-four.

The servants in the story are all fictional, with the exception of Louise Peake, who served as Mrs. King's housekeeper and traveling companion. The other longtime employee was the coachman, but for the purposes of my plot, I switched his role with that of the groom. Both names I used for them are fictional.

The year 1899 did mark the first ever automobile parade in Newport, and it was much as I have described it, including the floral decorations and the obstacle course. Although I place it in July, it actually occurred in September. Mrs. Hermann Oelrichs, formally Theresa Fair, did win a sterling silver box of bonbons for coming in first place in the "best decorated vehicle" category.

Cars at this time were little more than horseless carriages. Most were steered with tillers, like in a boat, rather than steering wheels, and were powered in a variety of ways, including gasoline, electricity, kerosene, and steam power. There were no windows or doors, and if there was a roof, typically it was the folding kind made of canvas or leather, as often seen on smaller carriages. By the early years of the twentieth century, automobile races became a favorite pastime of the Four Hundred. Reckless driving became a problem on Aquidneck Island, with both pedestrians and livestock in danger of being hit.

Harry Ainsley is a fictional character. However, the sport of boxing had only recently progressed from bare fists to the use of boxing gloves. As mentioned, gloves made it harder to judge the force of blows while making it possible to hit much harder, and it soon became apparent that the rules needed to be changed to protect participants from dangerous head injuries.

The European beech tree in the story does stand beside Kingscote's driveway. Many of Bellevue Avenue's properties play host to these beautiful trees. In 1899 they would have been considerably smaller than the one described in the story, but it was my intention to make the tree recognizable to visitors today, to pay a kind of tribute to what has become a beloved part of Newport's greenery. What visitor, young or old, doesn't delight in walking through the curtain of trailing branches into the cool darkness inside, and feel a childlike sense of magic beneath those soaring, cathedral-like ceilings? Now over a hundred years old, many of the old European—or weeping—beeches have reached or are nearing the end of their lifespan, making it necessary to take them down. Each loss is a reason to grieve. It's hard to imagine Newport without them.

Once again, I've brought the Manuel Brothers Moving Company into the story. Although I've taken liberties with the timeline, the company existed, having been founded by my husband's great grandfather, Edwin, and his brother, Arthur. Besides transporting personal property, they also moved sets and costumes in and out of the Newport Opera House, as depicted in *Murder at Kingscote*. In the 1920s, as fortunes dwindled and the mansions began to be torn down, the Manuel Brothers diversified into demolition and reclamation, taking the mansions down and reclaiming woodwork and other materials that they then used in the construction of new homes, some of which can be seen today on the Point, just to the north of the Newport Bridge.

In the autumnal chill of Newport, Rhode Island, at the close of the nineteenth century, journalist Emma Cross discovers an instance of cold-blooded murder on the grounds of a mansion . . .

Following the death of her uncle, Cornelius Vanderbilt, in September 1899, a somber Emma is in no mood for one of Newport's extravagant parties. But to keep Vanderbilt's reckless son Neily out of trouble, she agrees to accompany him to an Elizabethan fete on the lavish grounds of Wakehurst, the Ochre Point "cottage" modeled after an English palace, owned by Anglophile James Van Alen.

Held in Wakehurst's English-style gardens, the festivities will include a swordplay demonstration, an archery competition, scenes from Shakespeare's plays, and even a joust. As Emma wanders the grounds distracted by grief, she overhears a fierce argument between a man and a woman behind a tall hedge. As the joust begins, she's drawn by the barking of Van Alen's dogs and finds a man on the ground, an arrow through his chest.

The victim is one of the Four Hundred's most influential members, Judge Clayton Schuyler. Could one of the countless criminals he'd imprisoned over the years have returned to seek revenge—or could one of his own family members have targeted him? With the help of her beau Derrick Andrews and Detective Jesse Whyte, Emma begins to learn the judge was not the straight arrow he appeared to be. As their investigation leads them in ever-widening circles, Emma will have to score a bull's-eye to stop the killer from taking another life . . .

Please turn the page for an exciting sneak peek of Alyssa Maxwell's next Gilded Newport mystery MURDER AT WAKEHURST coming soon wherever print and e-books are sold!

Chapter 1

September 14, 1899

The seemingly impossible had happened, and with so little fanfare it might almost have gone unnoticed. Except that overnight, the world had changed and would never be the same.

And now here I stood, on a hillside that commanded broad views of Staten Island and the entrance of New York Harbor, feeling as bereft as the fallen leaves that rustled across the ground in doleful whispers. A chill penetrated my wool carriage dress and jacket, but I neither hugged my arms around me nor tugged my collar higher. Instead, I allowed the cold and damp to seep into my bones, a physical reminder of the current state of my soul. Dominating the view before me, the granite stones of the Vanderbilt family mausoleum mirrored a cheerless sky—the clouds as gray as steel rails, their edges as black as coal-fed locomotives.

Cornelius Vanderbilt lay dead, "Uncle Cornelius," as I'd always called him, though we had in fact been cousins twice or thrice removed. How would this family ever go on without him?

Footsteps clattered as Aunt Alice, her grown children, and Uncle Cornelius's siblings and their families filed from the mausoleum. I turned away, unable to school my features to the stoic calm necessary for maintaining one's dignity. In fact, my facial muscles ached from the effort of holding them steady. Aunt Alice's eyes were red-rimmed, but not a tear had fallen since we had left the Fifth Avenue mansion that morning. Only Gladys, Cornelius and Alice's youngest child, had allowed her emotions their escape, but even she had wept quietly during the funeral and again here, during the interment.

"You all right, Em?" Brady Gale, my half brother, came up behind me and put an arm around my shoulders.

I shook my head and leaned against his shoulder, a few inches higher than my own. "No. Are you?"

"No." A gravelly sigh escaped him. The wind swept up leaves in a tiny whirlwind that hit a gravestone and scattered. "I know at first the old man only gave me a job because of you. That he probably would have rathered not."

"That's not true. Uncle Cornelius—"

"It's all right. I know what I was. And I know how I've changed, because of you and because of him."

Yes—and no. He had once drunk too much, caroused too much, fought too much. In the end, though, it hadn't been me or Uncle Cornelius or any one person who had inspired him to alter his ways. It had been life and the frightening turn it had taken; it had been Brady himself who, when faced with a choice, had chosen correctly.

He went on after a grim laugh. "He's always had the utmost faith in you, Em, and gradually, ever-so-slowly, he extended that faith to me. I'll never forget that." He broke off, swallowing hard and then clenching his teeth. His head bowed, his straight, sandy blond hair fell forward over his brow despite his attempts to tame it with Macassar oil. I looked away, allowing him his moment of grief.

From across the landscaped clearing in front of the mausoleum, I caught my cousin Neily's eye. He stood alone beside some trees, looking as forlorn as those gray branches against the grayer sky. He'd observed the funeral at St. Bartholomew's Church in the City from the back row, and I knew he was waiting now until everyone else vacated the area to pay his last respects to his father.

The father who had disinherited him only a few years earlier. I had wondered if he would even come today, and would not have thought him unjustified in staying home. Neily's mouth twitched as he returned my glance, and he gave me half a shrug before dropping his gaze to the ground. He'd come alone, his wife and young son having remained in Newport. Grace, Neily's wife, had been the reason for the family rift, and Aunt Alice made no secret of her belief that Neily had caused his father's early death. The first paralytic stroke had occurred the day Neily had announced his engagement to his parents. The final one, only days ago.

Like ashes scattering on a gust of wind, the black-clad assemblage broke apart to board the coaches for the short ride to the ferry that would take us back to Manhattan. Brady and I rode with my cousin Gertrude and her husband, Harry Whitney. He held her hand. She rested her cheek against his shoulder. Grief hovered in Gertrude's eyes and tightened the lines of her mouth, but like her mother, she buried the full extent of her grief beneath a veil of dignity. We spoke little. I planned to linger only briefly in the City to say my goodbyes. The train ride home to Rhode Island loomed ahead of me. It was sure to be a bleak journey.

Yet when we finally arrived at the Fifth Avenue mansion, Alfred, Cornelius's second son and primary heir, took me aside in the central hall while the others filed into the drawing room.

"You'll stay another night, won't you, Emmaline?"

I shook my head as I pulled my gloves from my hands. "I should be getting back. Besides, there are enough people here to console your mother. You don't need me."

"It isn't that—not *just* that—anyway." He offered me something approaching a smile. Younger than Neily, and younger than me for that matter, Alfred Vanderbilt was now the head of the family. He and Uncle William Vanderbilt would jointly hold the reins of the New York Central Railroad and dictate the company's major decisions. And yet, to me, he was still my little cousin Alfred.

I sensed in him a discomfort that bordered on embarrassment and couldn't fathom a reason for it. "Alfred, if something is wrong, please just come out with it. Nothing can be worse than today."

"It's nothing bad, actually. It's just so hard to speak of. So unreal and disquieting."

"Yes, I understand." I touched his wrist briefly. Alfred and I had never been as close as Neily and I, had never truly been confidants.

"It seems Father mentioned you in his will. Brady, too. Our lawyer said so. The reading is tomorrow morning and I think you should stay and hear it."

"Oh." I couldn't have been more dumbfounded. While it didn't surprise me that Uncle Cornelius might have left me a token gift, I wouldn't have thought it significant enough to warrant me staying to hear the reading. My thoughts immediately went to Neily, who had been existing outside the family circle for the past four years. "What about your brother?"

Alfred knew which of his two brothers I meant. He shook

his head. "I'll be surprised if Father left him anything at all. But don't worry, Emmaline, I won't let Neily suffer. I intend to—"

He broke off at the sound of his sister Gertrude's voice. "Alfred? Where are you? You're needed in the drawing room." She found us in the shadow of the Grand Staircase, a columned, circular structure carved from pure white Caen stone that dominated the Great Hall. She slipped her arm through her brother's. "Come. Mama is asking for you. You, too, Emmaline. You know how you're often able to calm her when the rest of us can't." She chuckled lightly, without mirth. "You and Gladys. Her favorites."

"I'm hardly that," I said, and fell into step beside them.

That next morning, the family and I gathered in the library, a large room so heavily gilded, carved, and filled with sumptuous textures I'd always found it difficult to concentrate amid such distraction. Today I barely saw the fortune's worth of treasures as we settled in. Brady and I sat together on one of the sofas, the furniture having been rearranged so that the seating all faced the rosewood and inlaid ivory desk. The man who occupied the desk chair, Uncle Cornelius's lawyer, stared silently back at us from within the pockets of sallow flesh that surrounded his eyes.

We were waiting . . .

"Sorry I'm late." Neily spoke in a murmur to no one in particular, and shrugged himself into a high-backed chair with a lion's head carved into the apex of the frame. Gertrude frowned and looked away. Alfred, Gladys, and youngest brother, Reggie, appeared relieved. Alice Vanderbilt gave no reaction, as if Neily didn't exist; as if no one, or perhaps merely a ghost, occupied that lion's head chair.

The lawyer cleared his throat and began. Names, figures, and properties touched my ears but made little impression. I could think only of Uncle Cornelius, of his life cut short so cruelly, and of how this family would continue without him. Then I heard my name spoken. "To Emmaline Cross, whom I consider my niece and has often been like a daughter to me, I leave the sum of $10,000, and an additional $10,000 in New York Central stock."

My mouth fell open. The blood rushed in my ears. The lawyer continued, but I remained fixed on what I'd heard, or *thought* I'd heard. Surely it must be a mistake. Oh, next to the Vanderbilt millions such a sum might seem trifling, but to me . . .

My heart pounded against my stays. What would I do with so much money? I couldn't begin to fathom it. I almost didn't wish to. One would think I would be overjoyed at such a boon. But thus far my life had had a routine, a method, an established order of the way things were done. Suddenly all of my meticulous arranging and scheduling and thrifty budgeting fell in jumbled heaps around me.

Before I could contemplate any further, for good or ill, the sound of Brady's name brought me tumbling headlong out of my thoughts. Uncle Cornelius left him a sum nearly as generous as mine. Brady smiled even as his eyes shone with moisture, and it made me gladder than I could express that Uncle Cornelius had embraced my half brother, who was related to me through our mother and not a Vanderbilt at all, as part of the family.

"To Cornelius Vanderbilt the third . . ."

Neily sat up straighter, while his siblings suddenly found the floor at their feet terribly interesting. His mother, on the other hand, continued staring straight ahead, as if once again her eldest living son did not exist.

". . . I leave the sum of one half of one million dollars . . ."

A vast sum, staggering from my point of view, and my first thought was thank goodness his father hadn't cut him off entirely. But one glance at Neily's tight-lipped expression, the ruddy color that flooded his face, dissuaded me of that conclusion.

To him, the amount could only be perceived as a slight. His siblings would each receive millions. Alfred received the bulk of the fortune—an astonishing seventy million, plus most of the shares in the New York Central Railroad along with countless other assets. Neily would receive none of that. He could live on what his father left him, certainly. Or so an ordinary individual might think. No, it wasn't so much the money, or the lack of it, but the sentiment behind Cornelius's bequest to his eldest son; the insult that now, in order to maintain the lifestyle he and Grace were accustomed to, they would have to continue living off her dowry, essentially making Neily a "kept" man. Despite his having attained a masters of engineering at Yale and proven himself to be a brilliant innovator, he could never earn the kind of money needed to run several homes and travel back and forth to Europe each season.

Uncle Cornelius had had the last word, a reprimand from the grave to which there could be no response.

That afternoon, I boarded the northbound train considerably wealthier than I had ever dreamed of being. From now on I would have significantly fewer financial worries as well as the ability to increase my charitable contributions. My altered circumstances made the trek north a bit less desolate, though I could not say I felt anything approaching cheerfulness. But the children of St. Nicholas Orphanage, to whom I regularly gave what I could, would certainly benefit from Uncle Cornelius's largesse. So would Nanny, my housekeeper, and Katie, my maid-of-all-work. Far from being mere servants in my household, they were family, kindred spirits, and beloved figures in my life. And from now on, they would no longer have to go without. None of us would. The house could be repaired when needed, fading furniture replaced, our larder kept full.

Despite what might be considered my good fortune, I spent the next few days enveloped in a deep sense of gloom. All the money in the world could not make up for so great a loss, neither to the country nor to myself. However much members of the Four Hundred might be criticized for their extravagant lifestyles and lack of empathy toward the lower classes, I knew my uncle Cornelius had not been such a man. Quite the contrary. If anything, he had been criticized by his own peers for his lack of vices. He'd shown no interest in yachting or horseracing, extravagant late-night parties, excessive spending—with the exceptions of his homes in New York and Newport, where no expense had been spared—or any of those overindulgences for which the Four Hundred were well known. It had even been a rare day that found him on the golf course or the tennis court. Rather, when not working diligently to expand the family business concerns, he, along with Alice, had dedicated himself to philanthropic projects to the benefit of many.

Each night, in my restless dreams as well as waking moments, I kept picturing him as I'd seen him last: serene, composed, his face surrounded by the satin lining of his coffin. His had been a well-favored countenance, some might even have said handsome, but there had been nothing there to suggest greatness, at least no more so than the average individual. Yet no one had ever doubted that greatness. How could such a formidable man, who could command a room with little more than a soft word—even in illness—be so suddenly and irrevocably gone?

Meanwhile, I went through the motions of daily life.

"You're not eating enough," Nanny pointed out to me on the third morning I'd been home. She gestured toward my plate of half-eaten toast and congealed eggs. "It won't help anyone for you to starve yourself. It won't bring your uncle back."

I glanced up from the newspaper I'd been pretending to read, the black print smudging my fingertips but failing to leave any impression on my brain. "I'm not starving myself. Don't be melodramatic."

Nanny shrugged, but a silvery eyebrow rose above her half-moon spectacles in that way she had of chastising me without speaking a word. For an instant she appeared to me years younger—the Nanny who had essentially raised me while my parents entertained their artist friends at our modest home on Easton's Point. It had been Nanny who had bandaged my skinned knees and elbows, taught me my letters before I'd gone to school, listened to my childish secrets, and coaxed me to finish whatever had been put on my plate each day. I had known Mary O'Neal all my life, and when I'd inherited my current home, Gull Manor, from my great aunt Sadie, I could think of no one else I'd rather have there with me as my housekeeper and my friend.

But she often knew me better than I knew myself, and at times I found that irritating. "Fine." I picked up my toast and took another bite. The bread tasted like dust, the blueberry jam like paste.

"Katie," Nanny called into the kitchen, "please bring Miss Emma another plate of eggs. She let the first ones go cold."

"Never mind, Katie," I countermanded. "Nanny, I'm fine. Just not hungry. I promise I'll eat a good lunch."

"Hmph."

The ringing of our telephone saved me from further debate, and I hurried out of the morning room and to the front of the house. There, however, I stopped in my tracks while the jangling continued, for in the alcove beneath my staircase lurked another reminder of Uncle Cornelius's kindness. When his summer cottage, The Breakers, had been built on

Bellevue Avenue, he'd had electricity and telephones installed. At the same time, he had insisting on installing one of those latter devices here at Gull Manor. I had protested. It had seemed so extravagant at the time, but he had adamantly insisted.

"You're all alone out there on Ocean Avenue, Emmaline," he'd said in that firm way of his. "You and that housekeeper of yours, two defenseless women living on the edge of the ocean far from town. Anything could happen. Do you think I'd ever forgive myself if a simple telephone call might have saved you?"

There had, of course, been no arguing with that.

I hurried the last few feet along the corridor and snatched the ear trumpet from its cradle. "Emma Cross here."

"Emma, it's Grace."

My heart lurched. Why would Neily's wife be calling me, especially first thing in the morning? I happened to know she rarely rose before ten o'clock. And like most members of the Four Hundred, New York's highest society, Grace Wilson Vanderbilt disdained using telephones, considering them intrusive and vulgar. Typically she had her social secretary, butler, or housekeeper make her telephone calls for her. "Grace, has something happened? Are you and Neily all right? Little Corneil? Where are you?"

"Emma, calm down. We're back in Newport, at Beaulieu. We arrived yesterday. And we're fine. I'm terribly sorry to worry you, but I've a favor to ask. An important one."

"Goodness, Grace. I'll admit you did give me a fright." I leaned against the wall while my racing heart gradually slowed. Under the circumstances, it didn't surprise me that Grace and Neily had left New York so soon after the funeral. "What can I do for you?"

"It's Neily." I heard a combination of distress and resignation in her voice.

"I thought you said nothing is wrong."

"Nothing is . . . yet. But there's a party at Wakehurst to-morrow night and Neily is insisting on going."

"Now, while he's in mourning?"

"That's what I said. No matter the situation between his parents and us, he just lost his father and has no business socializing. He's being so stubborn about it. He insists he lost his father years ago and has nothing therefore to mourn now. But you and I both know it's not as simple as that, or he wouldn't have gone to the funeral. I'm afraid he'll drink too much, something will set him off, and he'll end up doing or saying something regrettable."

"Oh, Grace, has he been drinking?" I knew all too well how some men resorted to alcohol in times of strife.

"No more than usual," Grace assured me, but went on to add, "not yet, anyway. But I'm afraid being out among people might encourage him to overindulge. He's not in a good state of mind. He's angry, and whether he wishes to admit it or not, he's also grieving."

Angry—yes. As for grieving . . . Grace was right in that however much Neily might deny it, he had lost a parent. He must not only be mourning his father's loss, but also regretting the lost opportunity to ever make amends.

"I'll talk to him, Grace. I'll try to make him see the folly of attending this party."

"Talk to him? No, that's not what I'm asking. He won't listen. His mind is made up."

"Then . . . what do you wish me to do?"

"Come with us, Emma. Please. At least if you're there, you can prevent him from doing something foolish. If he gets in a state and I try to restrain him, he'll consider it nagging. Coming from you, he'll see the sense in it."

"Grace, I don't know . . ." The mere thought of attending a function among the Four Hundred exhausted me. In fact, it seemed callous and selfish of James Van Alen to hold a party at Wakehurst at this, of all times. True, the event would have been planned weeks ago, and true again, the remaining members of the Four Hundred would be leaving Newport shortly in favor of their winter homes, so that a postponement wouldn't have been practical. Had it been me, however, I would have canceled and sent my regrets to the invitees, many of whom had prospered as a result of their acquaintance with Cornelius Vanderbilt.

"Emma, please. I'm frightened for Neily's sake."

"I do have to work the next morning, you realize."

"Pooh. You work for your beau, and he'll forgive you an hour's tardiness this one time. Please do this for me."

Her quiet pleas broke through my reservations, and I let out a sigh. "All right, I'll come."

"Thank you, Emma. I'll send over an outfit for you to wear. It's a Renaissance theme."

I very nearly groaned out loud. "A fancy dress ball?"

"No, not exactly. Van Alen's calling it an Elizabethan fete. You know how he is about all things English. The invitation came on parchment, handwritten in old-style script, in metered rhyme, no less. Would you like me to read it to you?"

"No, thank you," I quickly replied. I hoped I wouldn't feel pressured to dance, and perhaps I could keep an eye on Neily while remaining along the edges of the festivities. My heart certainly wouldn't be in it, but Neily and Grace were dear to me, and perhaps Neily would be persuaded to leave early. With that thought to bolster me, I said my goodbyes, hung up, and went about my day. But a sense of misgiving never quite left me.

Connect with U S

Visit us online at
KensingtonBooks.com
to read more from your favorite authors, see books
by series, view reading group guides, and more.

Join us on social media

for sneak peeks, chances to win books and prize packs,
and to share your thoughts with other readers.

facebook.com/kensingtonpublishing
twitter.com/kensingtonbooks

Tell us what you think!

To share your thoughts, submit a review,
or sign up for our eNewsletters, please visit:
KensingtonBooks.com/TellUs.